CONSPIRACY OF SILENCE

A RAVENWOOD MYSTERY

SABRINA FLYNN

www.sabrinaflynn.com

CONSPIRACY *of* SILENCE

by

SABRINA FLYNN

CONSPIRACY OF SILENCE is a work of fiction. Names, characters, places, and incidents are either the product of the author's overactive imagination or are chimerical delusions of a tired mind. Any resemblance to actual persons, living or dead, events, or locales is entirely due to the reader's wild imagination (that's you).

Published by Ink & Sea Publishing

www.sabrinaflynn.com

ISBN 978-1-955207-08-9

eBook ISBN 978-1-955207-09-6

Book 4 of Ravenwood Mysteries

Cover Design by Sabrina Flynn

ALSO BY SABRINA FLYNN

Ravenwood Mysteries

From the Ashes

A Bitter Draught

Record of Blood

Conspiracy of Silence

The Devil's Teeth

Uncharted Waters

Where Cowards Tread

Beyond the Pale

A Grim Telling

Spark of Chaos

Flame of Ruin

God of Ash

Untold Tales: Prequel

Bedlam

Windwalker

www.sabrinaflynn.com

to my two crazy imps

Weaving spiders, come not here.
—A Midsummer Night's Dream

1

THE STORM

Tuesday, April 17, 1900

"State your name for the court."

"Atticus James Riot."

"Do you solemnly swear that you will tell the truth, the whole truth, and nothing but the truth, so help you God?"

Riot stared down at a leather-bound bible. He could feel the embossing under his fingertips, and the trembling of the clerk's hand.

Death and life are in the power of a tongue. Killing words had put him here—in this hollow, wood-paneled court room. Only he hadn't counted on the price.

The court held its collective breath. He looked across to a pair of intent eyes, and gave his answer. "I do."

The clerk swept the bible away.

The prosecutor stood. Mr. Hill was a thin man with a neat little mustache, his eyes as intense as his starched collar. "Atticus James Riot," he repeated. "Is that your real name?"

Nathan Farnon hoisted himself out of his chair. "Objection. Irrelevant."

Judge Adams practically rolled his eyes. Gruff and direct, he wasn't one for theatrics. The defendant had had the audacity to plead not guilty. His day had already been ruined. He looked to Hill. "This had best lead somewhere."

Mr. Hill tilted his head.

"Proceed."

"To my knowledge." Riot's voice was deep and low, and yet it filled the court room.

"To your *knowledge*." In contrast, Hill's voice was clipped, as if each word were a bite. "You mean you aren't sure?"

"No."

The prosecutor waited for more; Riot gave him nothing.

"You're not sure if that's your real name or do you mean that your name is something different?"

"To my knowledge, that *is* my name."

"Was 'Riot' your mother's surname, or your father's?"

"I never asked."

"So Riot is not your birth name?"

"It's what I answer to."

Judge Adams shifted. "Mr. Riot, answer the question."

"I am, your honor," Riot said. "I believe Mr. Hill is trying to work his way around to announcing that my mother was a whore. Isn't that right? Because, if so, I think you could save the jury their time and patience, and simply ask me."

A wave of chuckles traveled around the gallery.

"*Was* your mother a whore?"

"Objection," Farnon huffed. "What possible relevance can that have on the present case?" Blond and balding, he wore a pince-nez that had a habit of falling off his nose.

Judge Adams raised his brows at the prosecutor.

"Mr. Riot's character has every bearing on this case."

"Proceed."

"My mother *was* a whore," Riot confirmed. "A Morton Street crib whore. She had a professional name, but I never learned her real name."

"I imagine you had a rough upbringing."

It wasn't a question, so Riot didn't answer.

"In fact, you're known as a gambler."

"In the past, yes."

"After your partner, Zephaniah Ravenwood, was murdered, you left San Francisco to travel. When did you return?"

"January second of this year on the SS *Australia*."

Hill plucked a paper from his desk, and held it up. "And only a month later you were fined for gambling and destruction of property. That's a *very* recent past, Mr. Riot."

"A woman was murdered. The case required me to ply my old trade to catch the killer. The murderer didn't much care to be caught."

"Yes, a Mrs. Rose Cottrill—a negro woman—was found dead." A few eyes narrowed in the audience. "Yet your supposed murderer was set free with nothing more than a gambling fine."

Again, Riot did not take the prosecutor's bait.

"And only weeks before that you were involved in another altercation aboard a sailing vessel, the *Pagan Lady*, which resulted in a death."

"Curtis Amsel fired at me. I returned the greeting. The coroner's report will show that I shot him in the shoulder."

"Resulting in his death."

"A firearm he had in his coat misfired. That's what killed him," Riot clarified.

"And only a few weeks after that you were involved in yet another altercation. You shot Virgil Cunningham."

"I pegged him in the hand. He was about to light a stick

of dynamite. Unfortunately, he was sitting on a mound of gunpowder."

The attorney smiled. "You seem to attract misfortune, Mr. Riot."

"I'm a detective. That's my lot."

"But you weren't always a detective. Your history of violence began long before you called yourself detective. At one time you were known as *The Undertaker's Friend*. Were you not?"

"I was," he confirmed.

"If I were to list your altercations, it would take up considerable time. All, I should add, were said to be in self-defense."

"As you say."

"Were you in a relationship with Abigail Parks?"

"On occasion," he answered easily.

"And did you go to a graveyard on March eighteenth intending to kill Jim Parks?"

"I did not."

"Yet you testified that Jim Parks killed not one, but three of your associates: Zephaniah Ravenwood, Abigail Parks, and your housekeeper, Mrs. Shaw."

"I also brought three policemen along to arrest him."

"And a revolver," Hill stated.

"As well as a walking stick. I'd have taken an umbrella, too, if it had been raining." His comment elicited a burst of laughter from the gallery. When silence settled on the court room, Riot continued, "I'd have been a fool to confront a man like Parks unarmed, and I'd be an idiot to invite three policemen along to witness a premeditated murder."

"Or you're simply a very calculating man, Mr. Riot. You have a reputation as a 'quick draw.'" Hill turned to the jury box. "I'd like to remind the members of the jury that Sgt.

Price and Deputy Inspector Coleman both testified that Jim Parks reached for his weapon, but Mr. Riot drew and fired before the man had even pulled his revolver from the holster."

He let that hang in the air, and then spread his fingers over the table. Long and fine, the attorney kept his nails as immaculate as his steely hair.

"By your own testimony, Mr. Riot, you've admitted to shooting two men, aiming for non-lethal areas. And yet you shot Jim Parks in the stomach. You are an expert gunman—again, by your own testimony."

"I had time to aim with the others. This was a quick draw, and my bullet didn't kill Jim Parks; he died by his own hand."

"Gut-shot is a painful way to die. Most men would be tempted to take their own life." Hill moved to the front of the table, and folded his hands behind his back. "It seems that your past is as wild as your fake name. And it begs the question, given your history of having carnal relations with married women, did you aid and abet the defendant's pseudocide?"

Atticus Riot looked across the well to the defendant's table. To the pair of gray eyes looking intently back. Her lips were taut, her face pale.

There was a plea in her eyes. *Please, no.*

"I did not meet the defendant until after she died."

"When did you discover the truth?"

"The fourth of January—the day after the body was identified."

"And yet you didn't inform my client."

"I did not."

"So you were a participant in the defendant's pseudocide."

"After the fact."

"Why?"

"To protect her."

"Or were the two of you a pair of lovers, scheming to collect her ransom payment."

"Objection." Farnon didn't bother standing.

"The prosecution will refrain from speculation," Judge Adams ordered.

Hill nodded, but the seeds of doubt had already been planted. "Why didn't you inform the authorities, Mr. Riot? Was it for love?"

"No, love came later. The defendant was in grave danger."

"So you say."

"*Sing Ping King Sur,*" Riot said slowly.

"I beg your pardon?"

He let the token he'd hid up his sleeve slip down into his palm, and as if by magic it appeared between his fingers. A red token. He held it up in front of the court.

"*This* is why I aided and abetted her ruse." And just like that, he marked them both for death.

2

KILLING WORDS

I am not gifted with reading people. They defy reason. As did this young man. —
Z.R. Journal Excerpt

Sunday, March 18, 1900

ATTICUS JAMES RIOT STARED DOWN AT THE RECENTLY deceased. By nature he was a calm fellow who took things as they came, but this—this had caught him by surprise.

A crimson stain blossomed over Jim Parks' clothing. His body twitched, refusing to release its hold on life and the bowie knife he had driven into his own heart.

'*Sing Ping King Sur,*' Parks had spat. '*Those words killed Ravenwood, and they'll do the same for you.*'

A death sentence from a dead man. If Riot had been the superstitious sort he might have been unnerved; instead, he was merely puzzled. But then Jim Parks had been prone to playing mind games—manipulation was his forté.

This might be his final game.

"What the blazes?" Deputy Inspector Coleman cursed.

Sgt. Price and a patrolman stepped out of a nearby mausoleum. The trio gathered around the gravesite and stared down at the corpse with a knife in its heart and a bullet in its gut.

Riot tucked his walking stick under an arm, and cracked his revolver open. He eyed Inspector Coleman. Silver-haired and courteous, the inspector's politeness was often mistaken for gullibility. "I sincerely hope you had a clear vantage point from your concealment."

"Yes, yes," Inspector Coleman said. "It was clear he was reaching for his revolver."

Riot removed the empty casing, replaced it with a fresh cartridge, and snapped his No. 3 closed. He holstered the weapon.

"I see your hand hasn't slowed in these last three years," Sgt. Price noted. "And left-handed, no less."

"Survival instincts," Riot said dryly. He could hardly have pulled the trigger with two broken fingers on his right hand, a parting gift from an angry hatchet man less than two weeks before. And that had been Jim Parks' mistake. He had seen a man in a fancy suit with two broken fingers. Easy prey, he had no doubt thought.

"But why the devil did he stab himself?"

The four men stood in a semi-circle around the body. Abigail Parks' gravestone completed the circle. Jim Parks had seen his wife as easy prey, too.

"You didn't hear our conversation?" Riot asked. But his seemingly casual question was everything opposite. He needed to know what these policemen had overheard.

"I heard him confess—to killing Zephaniah Ravenwood, Mrs. Shaw, and Abigail Parks," Sgt. Price said.

"As did I," Inspector Coleman confirmed, and turned to

his patrolman. "Summon the coroner, we'll need the dead wagon."

The policeman trotted off to find the nearest callbox.

"I couldn't make out anything after you shot him," the Inspector said. "It was garbled."

Riot slipped on a glove. "May I, Inspector?"

"You'd best let us search him." Coleman nodded to Sgt. Price, who knelt down and began rifling the man's pockets. "What did he say?"

"Parks told me I was a dead man for shooting him in cold blood," Riot said, watching every item that Price handed to his superior: a billfold, a folding knife, a pocket watch, and a slim cigarette case. "I told him that I'd only shot a slow man who fancied himself a gunfighter."

Inspector Coleman grunted.

"He asked me if I was going to finish the job, and I said no, that I'd let the law do that."

Sgt. Price opened the slim case, and a circle of red caught Riot's attention. It was a faro token.

"Was that all he said?" Coleman pressed.

Riot reached over and plucked the token from Sgt. Price's hand. He adjusted his spectacles and turned it over, studying the stamp: *The Palm.* Riot looked up at the Inspector, and lied straight to his face. "The rest was garbled nonsense."

"Does that token mean something to you?" Sgt. Price asked.

Riot wove the token over his fingers, and shook his head, before flipping it back to the sergeant. "I suppose the man liked his faro."

"Well, all the same, good work, Mr. Riot," the Inspector said. "We never did solve Mrs. Parks' or Ravenwood's murder."

Riot inclined his head.

"There'll be a coroner's inquest, of course. But it was clear self-defense. And your bullet didn't kill him. He did himself in."

"Unfortunately, you're not my jury, Inspector."

3

THE STORM

Tuesday, April 17, 1900

MURMURS TRAVELED AROUND THE COURT ROOM, THE SOUND rising with each passing second. Riot searched the crowd from his unobstructed vantage point on the witness stand. Without his revolver, he felt exposed.

Mr. Hill blinked once. The whispering rose to a fervor.

"Order!" Judge Adams slammed down his gavel. The echo swallowed the excitement. Alex Kingston pulled his attorney down by the arm, and the two consulted briefly.

Judge Adams looked to Riot. "None of us speak Chinese, Mr. Riot. What does *King Ping*...whatever the devil you said... mean?"

"*Sing Ping King Sur,*" Riot repeated. "It roughly translates into *Society of Peace and Prosperity.*"

"What does a Chinese tong have to do with this?" Judge Adams demanded.

"It's not a Chinese tong."

"Explain yourself."

"I intend to if given the chance."

Hill abruptly stood. "This matter has no bearing on the case."

"How do you know if you don't question the witness?" Judge Adams asked.

"A trivial red token is hardly an answer for the grief and heartache my client has suffered."

"Mr. Hill, do you mean to tell me that you don't intend to question Mr. Riot about *that* token?"

"I'd like a moment to confer with my client."

The judge consulted his watch. "Granted. Court will reconvene in fifteen minutes." He tapped his gavel on the block, stood and left the court room.

Conversation rose to a din. As soon as Riot stepped from the witness stand, Farnon pulled him to the side. "A word, Mr. Riot."

"Of course." Riot didn't look at the attorney; his gaze was on the audience. Watchful. Waiting. Tense.

"What is the meaning of that token? You didn't mention it during pretrial."

"Didn't I?"

"Don't play coy with me. What the devil is going on?"

"You'll learn soon enough."

"You're jeopardizing this trial."

"It was already in jeopardy."

Farnon made a frustrated noise. "This won't end well, Mr. Riot."

"I never thought it would," he murmured.

4

RING OF BLOOD

The men at the table turned in their chairs to regard me. But the Gambler spared only a glance. He betrayed nothing. I was instantly intrigued. —Z.R. *Journal Excerpt*

Sunday, March 18, 1900

TWO MEN STAGGERED AROUND A SAND PIT, HUNCHED AND squinting, their forearms raised. They were pinned in place by a ring of shouting men. *Round thirty.* Two brainless slabs of meat, who refused to stay down. Isobel Kingston had to admire their resolve, if not their clumsy methods.

A gentleman in front of her shifted, blocking her view of the fight. She nudged him aside with a flick of her fan.

"Sorry, Miss." The gentleman blushed, and ducked his head.

It wasn't the blood sport that captivated her, but rather the audience. The fevered hunger, the lust, and... the hope in the audience's eyes as two men beat each other senseless. She knew Riot fenced and boxed, and while it was clear that fencing had honed his physique (exceedingly well), she had trouble imagining him in a boxing ring surrounded by bloodthirsty men. That might have something to do with recent events—a giant highbinder had beaten him senseless. It was hardly a moment on which she cared to dwell.

The two prize-fighters stumbled towards each other. A big fellow called the Beast threw a wild swing. His opponent Jack 'Nimble' lived up to his name and ducked backwards, but lost balance and fell into the sand.

Isobel held her breath. Be it god or goddess, or the pantheon of all mythos, she prayed to them all that Nimble would stay down. He did not.

Cheers announced round thirty-one.

As the two men staggered around in the sand, she watched the crowd, searching for familiar faces. There were far too many for comfort. She recognized some as associates from her days as Alex Kingston's 'adoring society wife.' But then everyone in San Franciscan society tended to know each other. It was a small world of snobbery and smoldering feuds.

She glimpsed Parker Gray in the crowd, his head bent towards the Beast's manager. Square and chiseled, Gray wore a gun on his hip, and had a cigar in his hand. Contrary to appearances, the man wasn't dense, and she made sure to keep her hat tilted just so. Although he had seen her only in male clothing, she had no desire to test his powers of perception. Her arms were still sore from spending a day hog-tied in his cellar.

But his presence there meant nothing. Every gentleman within ten miles of San Francisco appeared to be present. She half-expected to see Lotario with some of his sporting friends. She glanced towards a raised platform where a group of men and women watched from a more civilized vantage point—away from the blood and sweat.

Frustrated that her despicable husband wasn't rubbing shoulders with the man who'd abducted her, she contented herself with looking for his associates on the platform. Her eyes narrowed on one particular gentleman. White-haired and round, he sat on a chair, much amused by the prize-fighters. Where had she seen him before?

The crowd erupted yet again. This time the Beast staggered back into the ring of men. The crowd pushed him into the fight, and he ran straight into another fist. The Beast dropped to his knees.

Isobel held her breath along with everyone else, but not for the same reasons. The Beast pushed himself back up. *Round thirty-two*. Shouts were thrown into the air, bets increased, and money changed hands.

Prize Fight of the Year! Mack McCormick had already had the typesetter prepare the heading for the article. His prediction was proving true. He stood beside her, scribbling in his notebook, blow by blow, all in gory detail. His notebook was nearing its end; she'd let him worry about that.

Isobel looked back to the gentleman on the platform, and like the sun piercing the fog it came to her. A pang stabbed her heart. He had been an associate of Curtis Amsel, her brother, whom she had killed.

The Beast collided with the ring of men, and the gentleman in front of her took a hasty step back. It knocked her thoughts from the regrettable past. Two men in front of her shoved the Beast back into the ring.

A right jab, a duck, and an unexpected left. Nimble's knuckles connected with the Beast's jaw. Blood and spit misted the crowd, and a single bloody tooth flew through the shower of pain. It hit her on the arm. The tooth fell along with its previous owner. He did not rise again.

Men roared, arms were thrown in victory, and the resulting surge of exultation and despair shook her bones.

At last, she thought.

"You're not gonna swoon on me, are you?" Mack yelled in her ear. Big and gruff, he emphasized his Scottish accent to near comical effect.

Isobel plucked the tooth from the ground, and studied it. Bloody tissue still clung to its shattered root. "Why do men always assume a woman will faint at the sight of blood?"

"It's the assault on your gentler sensibilities."

"Our 'gentler sensibilities' are assaulted monthly." Most women, she silently corrected. She was rarely plagued by that particular occurrence.

Mack blanched.

"Now that the show is over, who's our man?" she asked.

Mack drew her away from the makeshift ring. Men leered knowingly at her as she navigated the crowd, and yet another man leaned in close to whisper a proposition. At least this latest offer was imaginative.

Mack scowled at the gentleman in a cravat. Pleased that her disguise was giving off the correct impression, Isobel winked and slipped a fake calling card into the hopeful man's pocket.

"I don't know why you had to wear that get-up," Mack growled in her ear.

Isobel wore bright lip paint, shiny jewels, and silk trimmed with an obscene amount of lace. "I thought it fitting. Prostitution and boxing are practically one and the same. Both ruin one body for the pleasure of another."

"They are *not* the same."

"You're right. What *was* I thinking?" She fluttered her eyelashes. "Really, Mack, I simply thought you'd like it," she lied. High society gentlemen would hardly expect to find Alex Kingston's dead wife dressed as a prostitute.

"If I'd wanted a soiled dove, I woulda bought one. That's a lot less hassle."

"I'm hardly soiled. And I prefer 'adventuress'."

Mack grumbled. "*Our man* is that little fellow over there."

She followed the thumb he thrust to the right. The 'little fellow' was as slick as they came. He was looking pleased with himself as a line of despondent men tossed lost wagers into his bowler.

"What's his name?" Isobel asked.

"One second."

"*One Second*," Isobel mused. "I wonder where he got *that* nickname?"

Mack huffed at her. "You got the mind of an adventuress, that's for sure." He turned to a wiry boy, and dropped a coin into his hand. "Run this to the *Call* straight away. There'll be double that if we're the first on the press." The boy darted off as quickly as he'd appeared.

Mack turned back to her. "His name is Fredrick Ashworth."

"That's high-sounding."

"British." There was little love in that word. Clearly Mack McCormick was still smarting over the English invasion seven hundred years before. "According to my source he was talking with Andrew Ross the day he went missing."

Andrew Ross—the corpse she had shared a cellar with for a cold day. He'd been an associate of Parker Gray, and his life had ended with a hatchet in his skull. While Isobel and Riot had caught (and released) Ross's killer, questions remained, the foremost being: Why did Andrew Ross have calling cards in his pocket that didn't match his name? That unanswered question pricked her instincts. But this investigation was tediously slow. Lincoln Howe had been the name on the calling cards. They had no idea if the name was real or fictitious.

How did one go about investigating an unknown man whose very name would alert a group of criminals?

"But like I told you earlier, Andrew Ross was a regular at prize fights. What makes you want to talk with this fella?"

"Because I'd wager our man Fredrick wasn't seen talking to Andrew Ross at a prize fight." Isobel patted Mack's thick forearm, and nudged him towards Frederick Ashworth.

When they neared, she gave Frederick a lavish smile. "It appears you have an eye for flesh." The hat full of money was proof enough.

Frederick Ashworth used those eyes to appraise her from crown to toe, and back up again, before his gaze settled on her décolletage. It was amazing what a bodice and stuffing could do for her boyish physique. She had learned the trick from her twin brother.

Frederick offered her a smile as slick as his hair. "That I do. An eye for flesh, that is." His eyes found her own at last, and he took his time tucking away his winnings from the fight. He placed a bowler on his head, so he could remove it with a bow and kiss her hand. It was a noisy mess. Exactly as she had expected. Men were such predictable creatures. Almost all, she corrected—all save one.

Frederick introduced himself, and she gave him a pretty smile. "Violet Smith."

"My friends call me Freddy," he said, straightening. The nickname sent her heart racing. Her suspicion had been confirmed.

This time Frederick's eyes flickered to the side, and kept traveling upwards. Isobel cursed under her breath. She could *feel* Mack looming like a protective bear. And then he made things worse.

"I hear you were a friend of Andrew Ross," he growled. Blunt as ever. It was generally her place to be blunt, and she wondered if Riot felt the same flash of annoyance with her as she did with Mack.

Frederick's eyes rolled side to side, and he tensed. But before he could bolt, Isobel untangled her arm from Mack's and slipped it through the arm of her new gold mine. It was more the strength in her arm than her batting eyelashes that kept him in place. "Mack promised me some fun," she said with pouting lips. "But his eye is horrid for prize-fighters. Is Ross another one of your 'sure bets,' Mack?"

"Huh?"

She arched a brow at the Scotsman.

"Erm, no," he said slowly. It sounded like a question. "Ross died last week. Freddy here was his friend."

"I'm so sorry to hear," Isobel said to Frederick. "Is there anything I can do to lift your grief?"

Frederick looked from Isobel to Mack, and politely tried to retract his arm, but found it in an iron grip. If only he'd known of the callouses under her lacy gloves. "We weren't friends," he hastened. "I just saw him around once in a while."

"I heard you were the last to talk to him," Mack pressed.

"What of it?" Frederick's nervousness was noteworthy. Every instinct in her body was quivering like a hound on the hunt.

"I'm doing a story on his murder."

"Andrew was robbed in some back alley," Fredrick said. "What's there to say about it?"

"I think he mighta killed himself," Mack said. He paused

to show his teeth at Isobel. 'Aren't I clever', that smile said. She sighed.

"You know, *The Last Moments of a Pugilist's Life*, and all that. Makes for good press."

Frederick cocked his head. "We talked horses. And prize fights. Look, why don't you ask his best mate William Punt." Frederick thrust his finger towards a thin gentleman in a top hat.

Isobel glanced that way. There was something familiar about the man. His eyes met hers, and he tipped his hat. It was that gesture, and his ears that sparked memory. Ears were as unique as a fingerprint. The first and last time she had seen the man in the top hat, he'd been in a union suit and she'd had a gun to his back. He was one of Parker Gray's lackeys—a man from the brick building in Ocean Beach.

Had he recognized her? She had been wearing male clothing at the time. Both times—if he had been present in the cellar. She batted her eyelashes, and turned back to Frederick. Her heart was racing for an entirely different reason now.

Mack blew a breath past his mustache. "I'll talk to him. Come on, darling."

"You invited me for a day of entertainment, Mack. Not work." She ran her fingers along Frederick's arm. "I'd wager Mr. Ashworth knows how to show a girl around the city."

Frederick grinned. "That I do, Miss Smith."

She leaned close, pressing her breast against his arm to whisper in his ear. "He's as broke as a barfly, too."

Frederick laughed. "I'll buy you a drink, or five."

Mack stood in place, as dense as a statue.

"Oh, go on, Mack. You know where to find me."

"I do?"

She untangled herself from Frederick, and tucked one of her fake calling cards into Mack's coat pocket.

"Why are you going with him?" His whisper needed work.

"Freddy isn't here on business. No hard feelings." She stood on her tippy toes and kissed Mack's cheek, and in a low voice said urgently, "Take care with Punt. He's the dangerous sort we talked about."

The light went on in Mack's eyes. "Since we're acting…" Before she could stop him, he wrapped an arm around her waist, pulled her close, and kissed her full on the lips.

Isobel resisted the urge to bring up her knee. Instead, she slapped his chest with a laugh. It knocked him back a step. "Always the charmer, Mack. Win some cash, and look me up."

She slipped her arm through Frederick's, and he led her away, leaving Mack scowling at her back.

"WON'T YOUR LANDLADY MIND?" ISOBEL WHISPERED. HER words were slurred, and she stifled a giggle from behind her hand.

Frederick Ashworth tripped up the steps. He grabbed her wrist and pressed her against the wall. His breath nearly felled her.

"No one cares who I bring here." His lips were on her neck. Sloppy, clumsy, hungry—it reminded her of her despicable husband. Those same lips were traveling downwards. Isobel bit back a growl and shoved him, hard. Frederick hit the opposite wall with a thud. She covered the slip of control with a gasp.

"You tripped over your own feet, Freddy." She giggled,

and raced up the stairs before he could grab her again. Frederick gamely followed. As he fumbled at his door, she stood back, trying to get her breathing under control. During her months with Alex Kingston, she had shoved emotion and herself far to the side, and the person who emerged had terrified her. She could not live that sort of lie again. This was far too close to the woman she had played for months—the one Alex thought he had married.

"Damn door," he muttered. And turned to kiss her again. But she pressed a finger to his lips.

"I might not be a proper girl, but I do have standards. No hats and no hallways. Now hurry up and open that door."

He obliged, and under his leering eyes she tripped into his room. It wasn't a flophouse or cheap boarding room, but a pleasant little apartment much like her rooms at Sapphire House. A small parlor, water closet, a bedroom, but no kitchen. More importantly, it was empty.

Business first. "Name your pleasure, and I'll tell you my price."

Frederick leaned in and whispered his pleasure.

She rolled her eyes. "Every man wants that. Wouldn't you rather try something daring?"

"That's my middle name."

She tugged loose his tie, pushed him towards a chair, and as soon as the backs of his legs hit, she shoved him down. Off-balance and drunk, he sat down with a thud. Before he could get his bearings, Isobel wrenched his arms behind the chair and deftly tied his wrists with his own tie.

She blew on his ears and giggled as if it were a game. It was, to her at any rate. When she secured the final knot, sluggish alarm bells began to ring inside Frederick's whiskey-filled brain.

"Oy! What's this?" Frederick started straining against his bonds.

She grabbed his ear, and pulled.

"Ow!"

"*Stay*." All traces of drunken flirtatiousness vanished as she snapped her Tickler open with a click. Keeping well behind him, she let him see the razor-sharp blade. "You have two ears—you won't miss one, but you can keep both if you start talking."

"I'll holler for the—" She stuffed a dirty stocking in his mouth, and then ripped off her scarf to cinch it over his eyes.

Men never look at a whore's face—not really. But now he would certainly be paying attention. She yanked a rope off the curtains, and used it to secure his ankles. All the while he yelled through the stocking in his mouth. Isobel ignored his muffled pleas. She searched his pockets: a folding knife, roughly five hundred in cash, two ten-dollar gold pieces, some change, booking tickets, race track stubs, and a faro token. Red. No revolver.

Isobel held the faro token up to the light. *The Palm*. She had seen its like before in a dead man's coat. Riot had found one, too—in Lee Walker's home.

With quick efficiency, she searched his rooms, but turned up nothing more than numerous suits, expensive hats and shoes, and a collection of calling cards from a wide variety of working women. They put her own calling cards to shame.

"Now that you're cozy, we can get down to business." She kept the same voice she had used as Violet Smith— shrill and careless. "I'm going to remove your gag. I expect you to keep your voice low, or I'll be forced to take more permanent measures." Isobel pulled the stocking out of his mouth.

"What the bloody hell are you playing at, you bit—"

Isobel stuffed the stocking between his lips, silencing him. More would be required. With a sigh, she opened the front door, held it open a moment for a group of imaginary men to file in, then closed it. She walked over to the wash-basin and poured water from a pitcher. "We know who you are, Freddy," she said, watching him in the mirror. "My associates would like to know a few things about Andrew Ross and Lee Walker."

He stilled.

Isobel dragged a small table in front of him, and set it against his knees. He flinched. "The gentlemen in the room with us would like me to handle your questioning. You'll understand if I don't introduce them." She took out the bloody tooth from the prize fight and placed it dead center on the table. After checking the reflections in the mirror and windows, she positioned herself behind him, and removed his blindfold.

Frederick's eyes settled on the bloody tooth in front of his knees. He squirmed, and tried to twist around to get a look at her. She slapped his ear with the fan. "You don't want to see their faces. Trust me."

"What do you want?"

The question earned him a slap on the head. "This is not a two-way conversation, Mr. Ashworth. This is an inter-rogation. I've brought my tools, but torture is a messy busi-ness, and I'd rather not stain my gloves. So answer my questions and the only thing that will be wounded is your pride. Do you understand?"

"Yes."

She waited, letting that word hang in the air. When he was squirming, she struck. "Do you know Lee Walker?"

"Never heard of him."

She slapped her fan against his ear. Frederick jerked. "Wrong answer."

"I know him," he said.

"That's better." She let her pleasure shine through. "Why did you set him up to lose a wager at the race track?"

"All I did was tell him about the horse."

"After someone instructed you to help him lose."

Silence. Frederick's gaze settled on the tooth in front of him.

"Andrew Ross," she said the name abruptly.

Frederick licked his lips. It confirmed her suspicion.

"He wasn't killed in a robbery. He ran afoul of powerful men." It was a boldfaced lie. Andrew Ross was killed by a hatchet man in a completely unrelated incident. But she wanted him wondering if those same powerful men were in the room with her listening.

"What did Andrew Ross tell you to do?" she asked.

"Just like you said. He wanted me to steer Walker towards a bad bet. It wasn't difficult. I tipped him off with a few bankers, and then when he was oiled up, I set him up with a loser."

"What did you get out of it?"

"A cut of cash. A whole heap more than if I'd steered him towards a banker."

She toyed with the red token in her hand. "That would be a mighty tick against your reputation, Freddy. No betting man would trust your judgment after a sour bet that large. What else did you get out of the deal?"

"Money's not enough?" he shot back.

Isobel flicked her fan against his other ear, but he only shifted slightly. She was losing her advantage.

Isobel tossed the token on the table in front of him. "Tell me about that."

"It's a faro token."

"Andrew Ross carried the same one. So did Lee Walker."

"Maybe we all play faro?"

He was lying. There was too much coincidence surrounding that token. "I think you should tell me the whole story or I'll send a note informing Parker Gray that you've been talking."

"I haven't told you anything!" That threat had burrowed under his skin.

"Exactly," she purred in his ear. "But I already know enough to sign your death certificate. I'll pin enough on you that Gray will begin to have his doubts."

He laughed, nervously. "Nice bluff."

"I know Andrew Ross wasn't killed in an alley. I know you conned Lee Walker. I know Parker Gray has an interest in Vincent Claiborne. Why?"

"I don't know!"

"*Who* is Lincoln Howe?"

"I don't know," he hissed. "You know more than me. Look, Ross asked me to steer Lee Walker wrong. I told him no—that my reputation was at stake. But it was quick cash, and he flashed that token there. He said it would open all kinds of doors for me."

"Has it?"

Frederick nodded. "I'm in with a higher class of crowd. At *The Palm*—everywhere I go I have connections. Men with money use me as their bookie. Gray said I can cash the token in for a favor, too."

"What kind of favor?"

"I don't know precisely."

"How do you know where to show the token?"

"It's casual," he said. "I just keep it in my palm when I give a fellow my card. It doesn't mean a thing to someone who isn't savvy."

"Who will do you a favor?"

"I don't know. But this thing—this token—it's bigger than Parker Gray."

Those words stopped her dead. Her thoughts raced. They raced so far that she barely noticed Frederick was trying to work his way free. She let him struggle. Sailors never tied a shoddy knot. When perspiration broke on his brow, she slipped her closed fan under his chin, and raised it, speaking into his ear. "If I were you, Freddy, I'd take your cash and find somewhere to keep low for a while."

5

A LONG NIGHT

The Gambler had two coins and a pair of gold cufflinks left to his name. And a hat. It was new, and brushed to perfection. A flaw of ego in an otherwise flawless act. —Z.R. Journal Excerpt

THE *MORNING CALL* NEVER SLEPT. NIGHTS, EVEN ON A Sunday, were a chaotic dash fueled by coffee and cigarettes. But a deadline hardly kept a room full of men from noticing a whore. As Isobel walked through the bullpen, a sea of eyes followed her.

"How was whoring?" Mack asked when she stopped at his desk.

"Productive."

"Isn't it always? Did you find anything I can use?"

She shook her head. "Nothing you'd *want* to use, Mack. Trust me."

He smashed a cigarette into its tray. "This is a dead-end story."

"Did you talk with Ross's friend, William Punt?"

"I did. Same story I've been getting all over. Andrew Ross disappeared for a few days. The last anyone saw of

him was at the tracks or at *The Palm*. He left for home, and
that was that. Far as I can tell, that creepy fellow, Mr. Sims
in the morgue, is just spinning a story about the body being
moved."

"Whatever you make of it," she said. "What did you say
to Punt?"

Mack narrowed his eyes. "Now that's an odd question,
Charlie. Most would ask what *he* said. Is he involved with
whatever is going on?"

A fellow reporter stopped typing and cocked an ear
towards them in the noisy place. Isobel glared at the man,
and leaned in closer to Mack. "As I said, he's dangerous. I'd
rather not find you rotting in an alleyway."

"I could help you more if I knew what was going on."

"*I* don't know what's going on yet."

"I told Punt the same story as I told Freddy after you
threw me over for him."

"Did Punt buy it?"

"How the hell should I know? All I got out of him was
that Andrew Ross was a fine pugilist and he'd enjoyed spar-
ring with him. He seemed surprised when I told him the
body was moved."

"Mack, I told you not to let on anything that you know."

He lifted a shoulder. "How else am I going to justify
questioning? I asked if Ross might have run afoul of any
prize-fighters or creditors. He told me he didn't know. All
the same, I'm dropping this. It's not gettin' me anywhere."

Isobel nodded. It was for the best. But her lack of protest
raised his suspicions. "You *want* me to drop it. Don't you?"

"Now, yes." The key to this mystery was the red token;
she needed to find out more. Who, what, *why*? It was no
coincidence that Lee Walker, Freddy, and Andrew Ross all
carried one. She'd wager every penny in her purse that the

brick building run by Parker Gray was connected with *The Palm* saloon.

Mack sat back, and crossed his massive arms over his chest. He looked like a petulant child. "I can take care of myself."

"Bull-headedness won't stop a well-aimed bullet."

"I once knew a fellow who caught a bullet between his teeth." When the toothy grin he offered failed to elicit a chuckle, he checked his watch. "How 'bout we have a proper dinner?"

"I'm not hungry."

"You sure? I hear whoring works up quite an appetite."

"Did you happen to discover where Andrew Ross lived? And William Punt?"

"Dinner first."

"I can find out myself," she said.

"Oh, come on, Charlie. I took you to a prize fight. I don't even get a kiss?"

"You already stole a kiss."

"All part of the act."

"We're associates, Mack, not lovers."

"But you're interested. Why else did you practically beg me to take you to the prize fight?"

"For a story."

"Look, you don't need to work anymore. I'll look after you. It's plain as day you're a soiled dove in need of a caring man."

"Oh, am I?"

"'Course you are. Why else would a woman be a reporter?"

"Because we enjoy using our brains."

"You have brains?"

Isobel ground her teeth together. And then all at once,

Mack started laughing. He sounded like a braying donkey blowing a trumpet.

He wiped a tear from his eye. "If you're going to goad me, you'd best take it in return."

"Fair enough." She grinned. "You had me."

"I'd like to have more of you." He winked. But it was playful rather than leering, and she took it in good stride. Not that she doubted he'd turn down an invitation.

"Why'd you go off with that Brit?"

"I'm a soiled dove, remember. He was flush with cash."

He blew a breath past his mustache. "If that's all it takes," he muttered.

"Even though I found you a story, I'm too expensive for your pocket."

"I'll sell my gold tooth."

"Desperation is unbecoming, Mack. The addresses," she reminded.

Mack reached for a pen and paper, and scribbled the information down. But before she could get a glimpse of it, he took the slip of paper away. "Promise me you won't go alone."

"I won't." Charlotte Bonnie wouldn't go alone, but that didn't mean Isobel Kingston wouldn't.

"Bonnie!" The bellow came from the hallway that led to the editor's office. "Mr. Spreckles wants to see you."

Isobel arched a brow.

"You can bunk with me if you get the axe." Mack raised his brows twice.

"Remember, I'm too pricey."

Isobel walked towards the editor's office with more curiosity than dread. She could always find another job. During the two years she had roamed Europe without a chaperone, she'd never wanted for food.

Isobel made opportunities; she didn't wait for them to find her.

A blond-haired man with a walrus mustache sat behind a desk. The wood gleamed with polish, and a crystal ashtray held down a neat stack of papers. The man took in her finery in silence. Finally, his gaze settled on her eyes.

She thrust out a hand. "Charlotte Bonnie. We haven't met, sir."

"J.D. Spreckles." The editor shook her hand. Direct and strong, she made sure to return the gesture with equal strength. Newspapermen didn't appreciate a wilting flower. Editors wanted females they could send into a madhouse, or around the world—a woman game for stunt reporting. "I hear you cover the detective Atticus Riot."

"On occasion." Mostly mid-mornings, she thought. He covered her, too.

"Then you know him?"

"I do."

"I want you to get an interview. He's refused to talk with anyone."

Isobel cocked her head. "Has something happened?"

Spreckles regarded her severely. "How the devil don't you know?"

"Another story has me occupied."

"Well, this isn't a society soiree, Bonnie. I'd rather send one of my top reporters, but this detective is reticent."

Isobel bit back a retort, took a breath, and said it anyway. "If your 'top reporter' can't get the story, then perhaps you should reassess his position."

Spreckles raised his brows, and then broke into a low chuckle. "Maybe you're right."

But the minor victory felt hollow in her gut. She was

cold, and a dread caught in her throat. "What happened?" she asked.

Spreckles plucked a paper from the stack, and slid it towards her. "He shot and killed a man this morning. The inquest is tomorrow."

The ground dropped from beneath her feet.

WITH A TREMBLING HAND, ISOBEL SLID HER KEY INTO THE front door, and hurried into the foyer of Sapphire House. She needed to change into suitable clothing to search for Riot. A number of telephone calls had informed her that he wasn't in the city jail, but neither was he at Ravenwood Manor nor in his office.

A pit had opened in her belly. She felt hollow, like a drifting sort of apparition. Reason told her that Riot was alive and well, and the inquest only a formality, but love— that irrational, irritating state—made her drop her keys in the foyer.

A curly-haired woman scuttled out of her hole as Isobel bent to retrieve the keys. Mrs. Beeton walked right past Isobel, and applied her pristine rag to the door handle.

"Evening, Mrs. Beeton."

"Eight fifty-six," the landlady muttered. Narrow-sighted and single-minded, the woman didn't spare Isobel's silks and décolletage a single glance when she'd finished polishing the knob. Instead, her eyes sharpened on Isobel's costume jewelry. She admired it, and offered to polish the pieces.

Isobel extracted herself from the woman's beady eyes. "Perhaps later."

"They're fakes, you know," Mrs. Beeton huffed.

Offended by the notion, she turned to a grandfather clock to begin her ritual winding.

Isobel lifted her skirts, and bolted up the stairway. One of the many benefits of rooming at Sapphire House was a landlady who noticed only jewelry and time. Mrs. Beeton also believed that the room Isobel had rented was cursed (more than one occupant having died in it) and let it out for a fraction of the going rate. It fit nicely with Isobel's pocketbook.

As she inserted her key into the lock, her mind raced with possibilities. Had Riot murdered Jim Parks outright, or had it been in self-defense? She made a sound of frustration as her key scraped against brass. Where was he?

The door next to hers was wrenched open, and a tall, skeletal man with a mop of curly gray hair stepped into the hallway. His old-fashioned frock coat was patched in many places, and he had ink stains on his long fingers. His bushy brows drew together.

She nodded in greeting. "Mr. Crouch."

"I will not tolerate your noisy clients, *Miss* Bonnie."

"I beg your pardon?"

He gestured sporadically at her person.

Isobel glanced down. "Oh, yes, of course. Not to worry, I keep them gagged."

"Try not to stink up the place when you die," he snarled, and stalked over to the railing. "Mrs. Beeton!"

With more important things on her mind than what fresh offense the landlady had committed, Isobel stepped into her rooms and shut the door. She reached for the gas lamp, but froze. Moonlight streamed through a crack between curtains, illuminating a shadow. The intruder rose smoothly. She tensed, but a shift of light betrayed a hint of silver near the man's eyes.

All the worry and dread rushed from her bones. It left her unsteady. To buy herself time, she struck a match, and when she spoke her voice was light. "Just the man I wanted to see after a day of whoring."

The mantle caught in the lamp, and warmth flooded her room. Atticus Riot opened his mouth, but whatever he had been about to say died on his lips. He blinked at her dress.

At another time she might have laughed at his surprise. But not today. Relief drove her into his arms. His beard tickled her cheek, and she savored the scent of him: wool and silk, and a hint of sandalwood and myrrh.

"I thought I had the wrong room for a moment," he whispered in her ear.

Isobel pulled back to meet his eyes. They were warm and calm, and she felt as if she were falling. To steady herself, she glanced around her room. It was filled with wigs, racks of disguises, trunks, bladed instruments, and a narrow bed stuffed into the corner. "Unlikely," she said dryly. "Are you all right?" Even as the words left her lips, her fingers slipped beneath his coat, probing for wounds.

"I suppose you heard."

"Some of it. I was occupied elsewhere."

"Whoring?"

"I've certainly had my fill of men trying to kiss me today."

Riot brushed a thumb over her lips.

"You have gunpowder stains on your fingers," she noted absently.

"Can we talk about that later?" he murmured.

"You'll have to distract me."

"I thought you'd had your fill of men trying to kiss you."

"Not you." She removed his spectacles. "Never you," she breathed.

He was alive and well, and she needed to feel him.

Isobel ran her fingers over his beard, and he covered her hand with his own, turning it to bury his nose in her palm. Riot closed his eyes and breathed her in, then pulled her close and kissed her, gently at first.

Riot was all passion wrapped in control, a calm sea she loved to agitate. He opened his eyes. May I? Always a silent inquiry. She savored the moment before he gave into desire. It was irresistible.

When she ran her nails down his neck in answer, his control snapped. His lips came down on hers, and she threw herself into his advance. She ripped away his stiff collar, tore through his waistcoat and shirt, searching for the heat of his flesh. When she found it, she pressed her lips against his throat, and brushed her fingers over his ribs.

Riot groaned, every inch of the man trembling with intensity. He gripped her thigh, and pulled her firmly against his hips. It stole the breath from her lungs. And she lost herself to him.

"*CAFUNÉ*," SHE WHISPERED.

Riot stirred at the sound of her voice. "What does it mean?"

"There's no word for it in English. But it's this…" she ran her fingers through his hair. "…between lovers."

"I like that word."

They lay intertwined on the narrow bed. Half-undressed, her bodice was partially undone, enough to free her breasts. Her dress had disappeared on the floor, but she had somehow retained her silk stockings and garters. Other matters had been far more pressing.

Isobel held Riot in her arms. He was relaxed and limp, a warm weight that covered her like a cherished blanket. His head rested between her breasts, his body stretched along her own. She could feel him unwinding with every caress.

She traced the scar along his temple, trailed her fingers through his raven hair, and slipped her hand beneath his undershirt. His skin was damp from exertion. Needing to feel every inch of the man, she freed him of the last remnants of his clothing. His own fingers deftly worked at the hooks of her bodice, and she took a grateful breath. The rest of their clothing ended up on the floor. Riot shifted, reached an arm over the side of the bed, and came back with a blanket. He pulled it over them, and returned to her arms.

"My breasts have to be the flattest pillow you've ever laid on."

She felt him smile. "What they lack in volume, they make up with enthusiasm."

Isobel snorted, and flicked his ear. "Why don't you ever smoke?" she asked suddenly.

"I don't mind if you do." His breath tickled her skin.

She lifted a shoulder. "It takes all the fun out of it when no one minds."

He chuckled, a thing felt rather than heard.

"I like the flare of the match more than the taste," she admitted.

"Remind me to keep you well away from explosives."

Isobel sighed. "I've always dreamt of dynamiting a hole in a mountain...or anything, really."

He raised his head to look at her. Amusement danced in his eyes. "Some girls like flowers, others lace, but I reckon only one prefers dynamite."

"You can put that on your list of suitable gifts for me."

"Noted." He lay back down, and her fingers drifted over his neck and back, tracing the bullet and knife scars from a lifetime of threat.

"You never answered."

And he didn't, not immediately. He relaxed under her touch, and she thought he might have fallen asleep until his words warmed her breasts. "I never much cared for the taste of tobacco. Preference aside, the act of smoking is a 'tell'. It can reveal a great deal—the way the smoke seeps from a man's lips betrays his mood."

"I didn't think you played cards much anymore."

"I don't."

Silence wrapped around him. There was more. But Isobel let it be. Whatever that silence was, it wasn't comfortable.

Riot shifted onto his back, and folded an arm behind his head. He stared up at the ceiling. "There was a john," he began after a time, his voice soft, barely a whisper. "A regular of my mother's who used to strut in with a cheap cigar between his lips. He'd order me to hold it, then he'd disappear behind the curtain with my mother. And when he was done, he'd come strutting back out, pluck it straight from my fingers, and blow a cloud of smoke in my face."

A lump formed in Isobel's throat. There was nothing to say to that, so she pressed her lips over a round scar on his chest. "What happened to your mother?"

"She hanged herself." He took a breath.

"I'm sorry, Riot."

"It's long behind me, but thank you all the same. Death can be a merciful fellow. My mother didn't have much of a life." And neither did you, she thought.

"All the same, I'm glad she lived for a time, or I wouldn't

have you. It sounds as if I nearly lost you today." She looked down into his eyes.

He smiled. "Not even close."

"I should tell you," she said in a grave tone. "My editor sent me to interrogate you."

"I enjoy your interrogations."

"You might change your mind when I'm finished with you."

"I thought you *had* finished with me."

"Not even close." She trailed her fingers through the hair on his chest, over his ribs, and followed a line of dark hair ever downwards. "Talk, or else."

The edge of his lip raised. "I'll risk the 'or else'." Cock-sure, and eager for another round, he caressed her hip with his free hand.

At the last moment, she changed her course, and seized that hand. In one quick movement, she pinned it over his head, and straddled his hips. "Are you sure about that?"

His legs came up, and he caught her with his knees, pulling her backwards and to the side with a neat twist. Before he could gain a superior position, she rolled. And fell right off the bed.

The thud was loud, and Riot's laugh was sharp and sudden. He appeared over the side of the bed, grinning down at her. Both his chipped teeth were visible in the dim light.

"Oh, shut it." She tried to kick him, gently. But he grabbed her foot and held it fast. Before she could bring her other leg up, his beard tickled a tender spot on the side of her ankle. His lips came next, moving ever higher along her leg.

Riot was halfway off the bed when she decided her interrogation could wait until morning.

6

SECRETS

"I require your assistance."

The Gambler inclined his head politely. "I'm busy."

"At losing."

"Just so," he said. "I like to finish what I start."

"Time is of the essence."

"Then don't interrupt." —Z.R. Journal Excerpt

Monday, March 19, 1900

WILLIAM PUNT STOPPED ON A PORCH TO PULL ON HIS gloves. He surveyed the night like a king inspecting his domain. The street was dark save for a pool of lamplight in the night. Quiet. He breathed in the sharp air. Not the toxic pea soup of his childhood. No, the Pacific Ocean swept San Francisco clean every night. A wraithlike servant who left only cleanliness behind. It was refreshing. A new horizon. A new world born every night for his taking.

A hacking cough interrupted his peace. The sound drew William's eyes to a dark threshold across the street. A mound of rags and filth shifted. He sighed. Yet another vagrant.

William consulted his pocket watch, clicked it shut, and flicked his collar against the chill. Adjusting the umbrella on his arm, he walked across the street. The mound of rags huddled under a tattered coat. Its stench was horrid.

William nudged the vagrant with the tip of his umbrella. "You, there."

The mound grumbled, and raised a gin bottle as if to ward him off. His gloves were cut away at some of the knuckles, and were as filthy as his fingertips. The vagrant raised the bottle to his face, shifted a tattered scarf aside, and drank.

"I say, you can't sleep here."

The vagrant shook an empty bottle at him. "Gin'll move my arse," the vagrant snarled. The words were barely intelligible. One long slurred sentence that stretched for eternity.

"Or the police will," William shot back. But even as he said the words he was reaching into his pocket. He held up a silver dollar. A dark eye rolled in the vagrant's head. William moved the coin to the right, and then the left, watching the eye follow his offering like a moth to flame.

"Buy all the bottles you like with this, on one condition: find somewhere else to drink yourself to death."

The vagrant grunted, and reached for the coin. William snatched it away at the last second.

"Swear," he warned.

"I swear it on me mum's grave."

William gave a pleased smile, and dropped the coin on the ground. The vagrant scrambled for it. It amused William to see those questing fingers. William stood over the filthy thing, and watched while he gathered his sparse belongings. When the mound of rags was more or less on his feet, William walked away in disgust, and the vagrant shambled in his wake—towards a warren of buildings and one very dark secret.

7

MORNING AFTER

Hand after hand played. The Gambler's pile of gold accumulated with despairing ease. My patience had run out. So I accused him of cheating. —Z.R. Journal Excerpt

"*ALEX* IS YOUR ATTORNEY?" ISOBEL STARED AT RIOT IN THE mirror's glass.

"He insisted."

"Don't you find that odd?"

Riot considered her question while he threaded a cuff link through its button hole. His hair was damp and ruffled, and his shirt unbuttoned. A moment ago, she had wanted to drop what she was doing and run her fingers over his body all over again. But his revelation made a muscle in her jaw twitch. Any mention of Alex Kingston set her on edge, and the prospect of seeing her husband again nearly pushed her over it.

"I've been working myself into his good graces. I think his offer of assistance is proof that my efforts haven't been in vain."

Isobel made a frustrated sound as she worked at the hooks of her sports bodice. "Or he's planning on throwing you to the dogs."

"It's an inquest, not a murder trial."

"But it could easily *lead* to one." Her voice was far higher than was warranted, and she bit her words off abruptly. This wasn't about Alex. "Even if the jury agrees you killed Jim Parks in self-defense, the police can, and will, arrest you."

"Would it help any to know that this isn't my first inquest?"

"No."

He gave her a small smile, and turned to the buttons of his shirt. With two of the fingers on his right hand bandaged, it was clumsy work.

"Will you divulge Parks' final words during the inquest?" Again, silent consideration. Atticus Riot was not a man to be rushed. That trait could be both infuriating and deliciously pleasing.

"I don't think so. Not yet."

"So you believe Parks? That those words killed Ravenwood—that some secretive tong society did it?"

"I don't know, Bel."

"You told me Parks liked to play games with people—do you think he tossed that story out to play one final game with your mind?"

Riot flinched at the word. His mind was a damaged, unsteady thing at times. Partially due to the bullet that had carved a path along his skull, but mostly due to finding his partner's head on a table.

His fingers stilled. "Maybe so. Either way, Jim Parks had help. He didn't get himself out of prison early. I think we should keep things quiet until we discover more."

She growled softly. "Now we're both stuck with 'quiet' cases. You can't mention the name of a secret tong organization and I can't utter Lincoln Howe's name."

They locked eyes in the mirror.

"Do you think Parker Gray is working for *Sing Ping King Sur*?" she asked. "Big Queue *was* in Parker Gray's cellar." Big Queue was the highbinder who had beaten Riot to a pulp. Isobel had chopped off his queue during the fight, and she had little doubt he'd come to collect one day.

Riot forgot about his buttons for a moment. "All clues point in that direction. It's common for tongs to keep white attorneys, watchmen, and even police in their pockets. You don't have to be Chinese to join a tong, but I've never heard of this tong. On the other hand, Gray has connections with everyone who is in the business of supplying women. Besides, Big Queue works for *Hip Yee*," he reminded.

"Do you know that for sure? You, erm…"

"Assassinated their leaders and half their bodyguards?"

"I prefer the word *confronted*."

Riot sighed. "A few weeks ago you theorized that I was used as a pawn—manipulated into attacking the leaders of *Hip Yee*. Do you still feel that way?"

"Absolutely," she said. "Jim Parks' confession, if he's telling the truth, confirms it. Maybe *Sing Ping King Sur* is a rival tong that wanted *Hip Yee's* leader assassinated."

"That's a great deal of manipulating, Bel. And there's no honor in it. Wong Kau was right about that much—a hatchet man would have been crowing in the streets about killing Ravenwood."

She frowned. "Did the judge who released Jim Parks early tell you who paid him?"

"I may have bluffed on that point." Riot looked at her

reflection. With his deep brown eyes and ruffled hair, he resembled a sheepish boy.

"*May have?*" She arched a brow. "Why, Atticus, I'm shocked."

"One of my many sins, I'm afraid."

Her edges softened, and a smile played on her lips. "I like some sins more than others."

"I noticed that last night."

A blush heated her cheeks. She cleared her throat, and primly returned to dressing. "Was the judge murdered?" There was hope in her question—far too much for a normal woman.

"He succumbed to pneumonia a year after Parks was released. While an old man dying of pneumonia would be a perfect way to mask a murder, I can't imagine how one would go about arranging that method of death."

Isobel considered this problem. "It would require some knowledge of his habits and a fair amount of luck, but it *could* be done."

"I'll try not to get suspicious when you leave the window open at night."

"And be forced to find a new ship's cook?" She clucked her tongue. "Never."

After tucking his watch into its pocket, Riot moved behind her. His hands slid down her arms, and he bent slightly to place a kiss on the nape of her neck. She shivered at his touch. "Could I persuade you to stay away from the inquest?" he murmured against her skin.

Isobel narrowed her eyes, and reached for the buttons of her blouse. "I'll be in my 'dowdy working girl' guise in the middle of a murder of reporters. Alex won't see me."

Riot gave a slight nod. "For future reference: How many risks do you generally take in one day?"

"At *least* three."

Riot grunted.

She turned in his arms. "You're worried about me."

"Of course I am, Bel. I'm only flesh and bone, and I have the weak heart of a man in love." He lifted his left hand, and snapped his fingers. A red token appeared as if by magic. The flawless sleight of hand distracted her from his comment. "That was a risky move, confronting Fredrick Ashworth."

"But informative."

"Still."

Riot let that word hang in the space between them. It *had been* risky. She knew it. There was nothing to stop Fredrick from running straight to Parker Gray and spilling everything. But would they immediately connect a slap-happy prostitute to Ravenwood Agency? She thought not, and said as much. "There seems to be more going on than we know. That business with Jin and Mei was only an irritation to the men in that building."

"I reported their con man to Kingston," he reminded. "I'm sure our agency is included in a list of possibilities."

She plucked the token from his fingertips, and held it in her palm. A string of red connected the web. Four identical red tokens on four different men. Two of them dead. She had taken this one from a corpse in a basement—Andrew Ross. Riot had discovered a second token in Lee Walker's rooms. And now Jim Parks and Fredrick Ashworth. Three of the men were directly connected to the brick building, but how had Jim Parks fit into the web? It was too soon to connect the red tokens with his final words—*Sing Ping King Sur*.

Isobel sat on her dressing stool. "Whatever *this* is, it's not Alex."

"Disappointed?"

She flicked a blond wig in frustration. "I keep wanting Alex to be behind everything."

"Kingston is certainly on the other side of the coin. He's representing Vincent Claiborne, who was targeted by Parker Gray."

"Yes, but Gray rigged a fraudulent claim and runs a high-class brothel. Being on opposite sides of a man like that hardly makes Alex the villainous attorney that I wish him to be." She turned the token over in her hand. "Why did Gray and Ross go to all this trouble to stage an accident? And why target Vincent Claiborne? The liability damage could lead to a nice settlement, but it hardly seems worth the trouble."

"Maybe they're aiming for a quick pay out. A criminal organization's bank ledgers are often made up of small transactions. Large sums are hidden by purchasing property."

She studied the token—*The Palm*. A high-class saloon in the financial district, where every banker, lawyer, and tycoon lunched. It hardly seemed connected to a Chinese tong. "I wonder if I could infiltrate *The Palm*," she mused.

"You play the role of a young man well, but—"

"I knew there'd be a 'but'."

"A newcomer to that class of saloon would attract attention." He paused, studying her. "And I don't think we should go around flashing that token either."

Isobel looked at him, startled. He had read her mind. "I see you've considered it already."

"I did," he admitted. "That, and tying Parker Gray to a chair and beating him over the head with a fan."

"I'd pay to see that."

"We could charge admission for a new bawdy house act."

"Are you sure we can't tuck this in our palm and see where it leads us?"

"As a last resort." Riot held out his hand, and she reluctantly flipped it over to him.

"Has Tim discovered anything about Parker Gray?"

"The word at the racetracks is he was New York-born, and then moved from state to state making his way west before settling in California. He's an excellent pugilist, an expert shot, and a gambler."

"And he's seen my breasts. You two have so much in common."

Riot's face was impassive—that in itself was telling. "We do." A slight roughening of his voice. "Like me, he's made fortunes and lost them in a single day, only to make them again the next. Cash is fluid and easy for men like us."

"And that's where your similarities end. Family or mistress?"

"Not that Tim has discovered."

After putting the final touches on her guise, Riot helped her into a practical coat. "I'll keep tailing the patrons of the brick building," she said.

"Who's next?"

"William Punt. Don't worry, I'll keep my distance."

"Why would I worry?"

She fluttered her lashes. "You shouldn't. Surveillance is tedious work. I spend most my time trying not to fall asleep at the Falcon's Club. Ravenwood's journals have been a godsend."

"Any progress?"

"Some." She flipped through the latest journal, and handed him a slip of paper.

"He was definitely working on a case before he was murdered."

"Hmm," Riot said, as he read the deciphered notes. "You've made more progress than I have."

"He's fond of—*was* fond of patterns," she corrected. "He trades out different ciphers from sentence to sentence. That's why I've only managed a few lines here and there. I've been going through the entries looking for ciphers I've already unraveled. Some are simple substitution ciphers, but others are more complicated. Did he have a favorite book?"

"None that stands out. I'll look through his things and see if something strikes me. Have you eaten?"

She jerked her head towards a drawer. "There's day old biscuits in there. But don't worry, I'll claim that I interviewed you over a candlelit dinner at a French restaurant. My female readers will swoon."

"I suppose I'll get more practice catching fainting females." Riot picked up his hat. "As much as I'd like a candlelit dinner with you, I'm afraid a cafe will have to do this morning."

"Honestly, I don't think I could eat a bite."

"Tea for you then, and a full breakfast for me. It might be my last good meal for a while."

It was a poor joke. All at once she stepped into his arms. "I'd break you out of jail," she whispered fiercely.

"I know you would." He held her just as urgently.

Isobel took a steadying breath. "If we remain in this room any longer, I'll get distracted and you'll be arrested for ignoring a summons."

The edge of his lip quirked. "Tempting."

"My nights would be much colder." She brushed her fingers over his beard, and he gripped her hand, turning his face to kiss her palm.

"We can't have that," he murmured. Giving her hand a final squeeze, he opened the door for her.

Isobel stepped outside, looking right, then left. The hallway was clear. She motioned Riot out, but the moment she turned to put her key in the lock, the door next to hers flew open.

Mr. Crouch stuck his bony neck out. He opened his mouth to deliver a scathing rebuke, but the words died on his lips. The hallway nearly sparked between the two men. Crouch's eyes widened, and he bolted towards the stairs. Riot gave chase.

Isobel blinked. "Riot!" Her sharp hiss made his feet stutter. "*Why* are you chasing my neighbor?"

"Your neighbor is a notorious forger."

"Even less of a reason to chase the old fellow. That's the sort of neighbor I like." She hurried to the banister. "It's all right, Mr. Crouch. He'll behave."

"Like hell!" Crouch snarled, before slamming the front door.

Isobel sighed.

"You wouldn't think so highly of him if he forged documents to steal your fortune."

"Did he do that to you?"

"Not directly."

"Perhaps he's retired?"

A door opened from a story above, and a face peeked over the railing. "Is everything all right, Miss Bonnie?" It was Miss Merrily Taylor, a fellow resident, and a phone operator with a passion for mysteries and eavesdropping.

"Yes, Miss Merrily. Apparently Mr. Crouch has an even worse side of the bed to wake up on than we previously thought possible."

"Oh, dear. I told Mrs. Beeton not to polish his cufflinks."

"I'm sure he'll settle down," Isobel called back. "Have a

wonderful day." She looked at Riot. "Did you want to meet Miss Merrily to make sure she's not a cat burglar?"

"I'm already acquainted with you. I don't need to meet another."

8

INQUEST

*The Gambler had a quick hand. No one else had time to draw. I admire a steady
hand, and his was uncommonly so. —Z.R. Journal Excerpt*

"Now then, Mr. Riot, you stated that Jim Parks
reached for a revolver on his hip, you drew, and fired. Is that
correct?" Alex Kingston asked.

"It is."

Excited whispers traveled around the graveyard chapel.
It was full to bursting, with more oglers milling about
outside. Isobel stood in the back, on a chair that she had
wrestled away from an old man by throwing her 'feminine
frailty' in his face. As she had climbed atop for a better view
over taller heads, he had shot her a glare that lasted the
entire trial. She hardly noticed—her gaze was on Atticus
Riot. Only every time Alex Kingston stood to speak, her
stomach roiled and her knees shook, causing her chair to
chatter against the wood.

Alex turned slowly to take in the crowd. Her 'widowed'
husband struck an impressive figure in court. Tall, and as
solid as a bull, his voice carried to all corners, as loud as if

he were right beside her. He was the kind of man who could convince a crowd that the sky was green and the grass blue. Direct. Overpowering. Blunt. Jurors liked his style—a self-made man who spoke plain. In truth, he took what he wanted, and was as slick as a snake oil salesman.

"We've heard testimony from Sgt. Price and Inspector Coleman, both respected lawmen. Both testified under oath that they saw Jim Parks reach for his gun. And while Parks was shot in the stomach, he was still breathing and speaking, and had enough strength to unsheathe his knife and take his own life."

Alex paused to look at each of the six jurors in turn. A bent gravedigger, an undertaker who kept checking his pocket watch, and a fellow who seemed more concerned about the reporters than the trial. Then there were three crows, as Isobel thought of them. Dressed in dour black and eerily similar in appearance, they seemed better suited to sitting on a fence than a jury.

All in all, not a promising bunch. A hanging would be good business for the gravedigger and undertaker. And the dandy might push for a verdict of murder to get his name in the newspapers. The three crows looked the type to go along with the majority.

"The medical examiner testified that Jim Parks did not die from the bullet in his gut, but rather the knife he drove into his own heart. Now some of you may be wondering—did Jim Parks actually reach for his gun?" Alex gestured towards the lawmen. "We have the eyewitness accounts of not one, but *two* lawmen. And while all of us here in this court are law-abiding citizens, I, like yourselves, am a man of the world. We know enough to doubt anyone in a position of power. With good reason. So, gentlemen of the jury, I'd like to put a challenge to Mr. Riot. A challenge that will allow each of you to witness the duel, just as it happened, with your own eyes."

Voices rose in excitement at the prospect. Even the undertaker tucked away his pocket watch. Isobel glanced at Riot, who sat for all the world like a man sipping his morning tea. A segment of Ravenwood's journal floated to her mind: *I was first struck by the confidence of the young man. Affected or genuine? I would soon discover.*

Zephaniah Ravenwood had discovered that it was genuine. As had Isobel. Riot was as cool and calm as a man came. And the only reaction he gave to Alex's surprise proposal was a slight cock of his head. Atticus Riot was amused, while she felt like the chair had just been yanked from under her feet.

What was Alex playing at?

Coroner Weston cleared his throat. "What type of demonstration are you suggesting, Mr. Kingston?" The new coroner was a middle-aged man who appeared to have been fit at one time. His gut strained an expensive suit, and he tended to hunch his broad shoulders. He reminded her of a penguin.

"A mock duel. With your permission, I'd like to allow one of these fine gentlemen of the jury to draw against Mr. Riot. With unloaded revolvers, of course."

Excitement rose to a pitch, and the young dandy hopped to his feet with a wild *whoop!*

"Quiet down, now!" Coroner Weston banged the butt of his revolver on the table. "Are you sure about this, Mr. Turner?"

Mr. Turner grinned. "Sure as I'm standing here today."

With a glint in his icy eyes, Alex turned to the audience. Pure pleasure radiated from the man. It made Isobel sick. And then he stopped, his eyes narrowing on her.

Isobel quickly tilted her head, so he was staring at a hat brim. She let her knees slowly bend, making it appear natural, and sank back into the sea of reporters. The chair underneath her rattled on the planks. A hand touched her arm. She flinched, but stopped herself before striking.

"Are you all right, Miss Bonnie?" a fellow reporter from the Chronicle asked.

"I'm fine, thank you. It's only the excitement." Her voice wavered, breathless and unsteady.

"I'll say."

Clenching her teeth, she risked a glance towards the front of the chapel. Alex had turned his attention back to the case.

A patrolman unloaded two revolvers, his own and Riot's. By the order of the coroner, revolvers were handed out, and the juror and Riot faced off at ten feet. Turner wrapped a belt around his hips, and gave the gun a fancy twirl before dropping it into the holster. Someone in the crowd cheered. Bolstered, he drew a few times, each twirl more elaborate than the last.

Riot didn't glance at his opponent. Not trusting another man with his gun, he rechecked the chambers of his revolver. Satisfied, he slid his No. 3 into its holster. While Turner wore a holster on his hip, Riot preferred a shoulder holster, where it sat at his waist, stock facing out and angled slightly towards his left hand.

"I see you've handled a revolver before, Mr. Turner," Alex said.

"I'm a fair shot and a fast draw," Turner boasted. Another twirl drew more cheers.

"What luck," Alex said. "It appears, ladies…" His gaze swept over the crowd once again, focusing on the back of the room. Isobel made sure only her hat was showing. "…

and gentlemen, that we are to have an impromptu exhibition."

A number of bulbs flashed, choking the air with smoke. When it cleared, Alex turned to Inspector Coleman. "Is this the distance that was between Atticus Riot and Jim Parks while they were talking in the cemetery on the eighteenth of March?"

Coleman made a circuit of the two men. "It is," he confirmed.

Alex took a purposeful step back. "Mr. Riot, say your lines. I'll trust our volunteer has been paying enough attention to repeat Jim Parks' final words."

The audience laughed, and Turner smiled along with them. "I was, sir."

Alex nodded in approval. "I wish all my jurors were so attentive."

More laughter filled the chapel.

"At your leisure, Mr. Riot. Repeat the words you spoke to Jim Parks."

But Riot didn't speak right away. He let quiet settle, until every scuff and cleared throat echoed in the chapel.

"Who hired you?" Those three words sent a chill down Isobel's spine. Ten feet from death, and Riot stood cool and untroubled, his right hand resting on Ravenwood's walking stick.

Turner tucked back his coat, then held his hand just above the revolver stock.

Inspector Coleman cleared his throat. "That was not how Jim Parks was standing."

"Would you position Mr. Turner, Inspector? If he'll allow you?" Alex asked.

The Inspector obliged. And now Turner stood with his hands at his side, every muscle in his body ready to spring.

"I guess you'll never know," he said, and jerked for the revolver.

One moment Riot stood as casually as could be, and the next his revolver was out and pointed at the man. The hammer clicked when Turner's fingers clamped around his own stock.

The audience gasped, one person gave a wild *whoop*, and someone shouted, "Clear as day he went for his gun! What's all the fuss about?"

Other voices were quick to agree. Isobel looked for the owner of this first statement, but couldn't find him in the crush. It had sounded suspiciously like Tim, but the old leprechaun was shorter than she was, and a hundred times more conniving.

"I want another go," Turner said. "This isn't my revolver, and I'm not used to the weight of it."

"Of course," Alex said.

Riot slid his No. 3 into its holster, and the mock duel was repeated exactly as the first. The young dandy turned red.

"Thank you, Mr. Turner." Alex quickly stepped forward to shake the man's hand. "You've been invaluable. And you're a good sport as well. Not every man would have the guts to face an expert gunman." The compliment bolstered Turner's ego, which was precisely what Alex intended.

"And a fine demonstration of a road agent's spin," Riot added. "I've never been much good at twirling." Having seen the man spin cards on the tips of his fingers, Isobel knew he was lying through his teeth.

"I'd be happy to teach you some tricks."

"I'd be obliged."

"Gentlemen, this is not a social event," Coroner Weston growled. "Kindly sit."

Satisfied, Turner shook hands with Riot, and the two gentlemen retreated to their seats. Isobel blew out a breath.

When the court quieted down, Alex took center stage. "My client's skill has been demonstrated, the police have testified that the shooting was done in self-defense, and the medical examiner's report states that Jim Parks died of a puncture to his heart—by his own hand. That is all I have to say, Coroner Weston. I leave justice in the hands of these fine gentlemen."

Alex inclined his head to the coroner before taking his seat.

The coroner turned to the jury. "Gentlemen, while Jim Parks died from the blade he thrust into his own heart, we cannot discount the events leading up to that drastic action. It is your duty to decide today whether Atticus Riot acted in self-defense, or attempted to murder Jim Parks before he reached for his revolver. You may confer in the side room for as long as you need."

The men filed out, and conversation filled the chapel. The noise beat at Isobel's ears. Alex turned towards the audience, and she quickly bent her knees, deciding it was best to get off her chair. A few men left to smoke, greatly diminishing her cover. Had Alex seen her?

Leaning against the wall, backed into a corner, her heart fluttered. Isobel swallowed down an urge to bolt as voices pounded at her from every side. But she would not—could not—leave Riot to face the verdict alone.

Murder. That word sat in the hollow pit of her stomach. Isobel had studied law for two months, long enough for her to be afraid. Alex bent his head towards Riot's ear, and the latter gave a slight nod. Alex turned towards the door, reaching into his coat for his cigarette case.

Isobel edged into what was left of the crowd. When Alex

reached the very back, he paused at the door, and searched the sparse crowd. A mob of reporters ambushed him, all tossing questions and asking for a statement at once. But he towered over the lot.

Isobel could *feel* his eyes on her hat. Impulsively, she rested a hand on the nearest gentleman's arm, and sidled up close to make small talk.

"Er, Miss? I am… er, might I help you?"

"What do you think the verdict will be?" she asked.

"I don't much care for men going around shooting each other."

"But Jim Parks was a murderer."

"Murderers are slated for the noose, not a bullet."

"Hmm." She was only half-listening to the man. She watched Alex out of the corner of her eye. He was ingratiating himself with the reporters, his baritone carrying like a gong through the chapel. A minute later, he pushed his way through the ring of reporters, and she tensed to run. There was nowhere to go.

A banging on wood rescued her. "Take your seats," Coroner Weston ordered. Called to work, Alex abandoned his search and returned to his seat. As the audience settled, the jurors filed back into the chapel.

"Have you reached a verdict?" Coroner Weston asked.

With great ceremony, the gravedigger climbed to his feet, and cleared his throat. "We have."

Weston gestured impatiently.

"We, the jury…that is, all of us here, after much deliberation and consideration, have determined that the defendant acted in self-defense and Jim Parks died by his own hand."

Isobel took a deep breath, then let it out slowly. Voices slammed into her again. Reporters rushed forward for interviews, a few in the crowd surrendered cash to a lost wager, and the rest of the onlookers started to file out.

With her cover quickly dwindling, it took all her restraint not to bolt. Steeling herself, she walked at a decorous pace, the back of her neck prickling with the touch of eyes.

9

THE STORM

Tuesday, April 17, 1900

JUDGE ADAMS SCOWLED AT THE ATTORNEY, HIS EYEBROWS drawing together in one bristling line of white. "Have you had ample time to consult with your client, Mr. Hill?"

"I have, your honor."

"Proceed."

Hill stood. "You claim that you never met Mrs. Kingston prior to her pseudocide."

"I'm not claiming; I'm stating," Riot clarified. "I was as surprised to find her alive as you were."

"Have you had carnal relations with the defendant?"

Murmurs traveled through the audience. Riot glanced over Isobel's shoulder, to her mother and father and some of her brothers sitting in the gallery. Mrs. Amsel sat rigid, her cane planted in the aisle, her knuckles white. Mrs. Amsel was refusing to look at either Isobel or Lotario, yet she was present. Her steely gaze locked onto Riot, and he met it calmly.

"I object to that question on the basis of it being a private matter."

"Overruled, Mr. Riot."

"The fifth amendment claims otherwise," he returned.

Judge Adams leaned forward. "Answer the question, Mr. Riot. This is a court, not a church. I'm sure the prosecution will grant you immunity for the duration of the trial."

Alex Kingston leaned over to whisper in his attorney's ear. They consulted for a few hushed seconds. "The prosecution does indeed," Hill said.

Riot adjusted his spectacles. "It's a matter of principle, your honor. A gentleman would never divulge such information."

Adams grunted. "Then the gentleman will find himself in contempt of court."

Isobel leaned over and whispered in her attorney's ear. Thin, pale, and exhausted, she looked faded from her time in jail. The defense hoisted himself out of his chair. "My client has given the gentleman permission to answer the question."

A small smile played at the corners of Isobel's lips.

"I'll ask again, did you have carnal relations with *Mrs.* Kingston?"

The court room dropped away, and Riot matched her smile. "Not until three months after her supposed death," Riot stated. "Frequently, energetically, and thoroughly."

Throats cleared, and fans snapped open. Alex Kingston curled his fists.

"Thank you. I have no further questions."

Judge Adams frowned at Hill. "You don't intend to question the witness about that token?"

"The token is irrelevant, your honor."

Adams narrowed his eyes. "Mr. Riot."

"Yes, your honor."

"Kindly hand over the token."

Riot did as asked. When the bailiff had passed it to the judge, Adams began to study it under a magnifying glass. "Was the defense aware of this token, or of any reference to *Sing*... whatever the devil it is?"

Farnon adjusted his pince-nez. "I was not aware, your honor. I knew only that my client's life was in danger, that her brother tried to murder her, and her husband blackmailed and abused her."

"Objection!" Hill said.

Judge Adams looked from the token to Isobel. "Was the defendant aware of this token?"

Before her defense could consult, Isobel inclined her head.

Judge Adams puffed up his cheeks. He let out a slow breath, and looked to Riot in the witness stand. "You didn't mention *Sing Ping King Sur* during the pretrial." Judge Adams held the token up between his fingers. "This faro token wasn't submitted as evidence."

"No, your honor."

"You've been involved in enough court cases to know that I could charge you with obstruction of justice."

"I do, your honor, but I'll wager you'd have prisons full of attorneys if you made a practice of that."

The court laughed.

"I don't find you humorous, Mr. Riot."

"Neither will you find my reasons humorous, your honor."

"What *is* your reason? What is the significance of this token?"

"I intend to explain, if given the chance."

Judge Adams leaned back in his seat. "And why should I give you leeway?"

Riot met the judge's gaze. "I may never get another chance."

"Why is that?"

"Because someone will attempt to silence me. As well as the defendant. If you don't grant me leave today, I doubt either of us will be alive tomorrow."

10

THE VAGRANT

The beast is too powerful. Omnipresent.

    —Z.R. Journal Excerpt

Monday, March 19, 1900

SURVEILLANCE WORK WAS THE MOST TEDIOUS OF PASTIMES. But it was something—something to do, to distract, to occupy her restless mind. And just now, damned uncomfortable.

Isobel shivered in the dark. It was cold, yes. But she had started shaking after the inquest, and that chill hadn't left her bones.

A faint pool of light illuminated fine droplets drifting in the air. The fog seemed alive, the breath of San Francisco, rising and falling in the early morning hours. She shifted in the filthy doorway, and adjusted her tattered coat. One more vagrant huddling for warmth on the street. Unmoored and hiding from life, from her memories and her failures, Isobel had fled the inquest, the graveyard, and even Atticus Riot.

But unlike the other vagrants, she had her eye on a man. On a building, to be exact.

William Punt. He seemed a safer bet than Parker Gray. The latter was keen-eyed and dangerous, while William Punt had been easily overtaken in the brick building the night they had rescued Mei.

Isobel's near-nightly surveillance of the brick building on Ocean Beach had revealed an occasional patron to follow home. Slowly, while Riot was investigating Ravenwood's death, she had been building a list of men who frequented that building. The question she needed answered was, whether every one of those patrons possessed a red token.

Sadly, Alex Kingston had not turned up at the brick building. Yet.

The door to the house across the street opened. It was a quaint home, a single-stick sandwiched between a cigar shop and a barber. Light burst onto the street, and a man whistled his way down the steps. The man stopped to light a cigarette, his shoulders tilted at an angle. It wasn't William Punt. The Englishman carried an umbrella rather than slicker.

William Punt had disappeared inside the house, and had yet to reappear. Isobel might have suspected this was Punt's home, but it wasn't the address that Mack had given her, and there were an inordinate number of men coming and going. A classy boudoir, if she was any judge. And it just so happened she was. But why would Punt be here when he belonged to an elite gentleman's club? But then, she might as well ask why men went to cheap whores when they could afford better. Reason and thought were hardly involved.

She raised a bottle to her lips, and shifted again, as if searching for a better position, which was exactly what she was doing. The cobblestones were freezing, her backside was hurting, and her stomach ached from the stitch in her side that had tightened to a knot during the coroner's inquest.

The thought of Alex, along with the smell of gin, made her queasy. As much as she hated to admit it, Alex was an excellent attorney. He had spoken plainly, amiably, and had given the jurors a front page-worthy performance. Her husband had defended her lover with skill. The irony of the situation was not lost on her.

Alex could be charming when it suited him. He donned that guise as easily as she switched personas. He had certainly been charming to her last summer. As far as husbands went, blackmailing aside, he had not been deplorable. Gentle, no. But then, neither was she. A bully, yes. Demanding, certainly. But never an outright blackguard —not as bad as the stories she heard from other married women.

Isobel had tolerated his attentions in the bedroom, just like every other woman who married for money, and not love. Thankfully, he had been unimaginative and quick about the business.

Another society woman might have considered him a catch. But not Isobel. He had sabotaged her father, and blackmailed her when she'd confronted him about it. Thinking that she could uncover his secrets from the inside —as a blushing, simpering Trojan Horse—Isobel had walked willingly into his trap. Only it hadn't worked out the way she'd planned. Isobel had discovered just how human she was after all.

The cool logic and the emotional detachment she'd prided herself on had failed. She could lie through her teeth with the best of them, but could not maintain that intimate deception. Worse, she had no proof of Kingston's manipulation. He had won, forcing her into retreat. In a word, Alex

Kingston was her failure. And for a woman like her, that was hard to stomach.

Isobel hunkered down for an uncomfortable wait. An hour later, another man exited the house. An umbrella hung from his forearm, and his back was as straight as a British boarding school could whip it. There was her man.

After pausing to don his gloves, William Punt started down the street, but then stopped. He looked directly at her. It was too dark to see his expression.

Perhaps he was the charitable sort? Optimism hardly ever worked.

With brisk steps, Punt walked across the street. Isobel tensed, but if she ran her cover would be blown. She held her breath, hoping he'd pass her by, but no luck. His shoes halted directly in her line of sight, and he struck with his umbrella. A tip jabbed her ribs.

"You, there. I thought I told you to leave." Each word was emphasized by a thrust of his umbrella. She curled up into a ball, trying to protect vulnerable areas. No use.

Isobel grunted and swiped at the umbrella with her gin bottle. "I'll leave," she rasped.

"I won't pay you *this* time."

Hunched over, she used the doorway to help her upright. He hit her on the back once more, and she dropped to her knees. "If I see you again, I'll do far worse than summon the police."

Turning on his heel, he left, his shoes clicking on the boardwalk. Isobel clenched her jaw, and waited. With a groan, she picked herself up, and staggered. It wasn't an act. There would be new bruises to add to the faint yellow and black ones from two weeks before. Adjusting her rags, she limped forward, supporting herself on the wall until blood returned to her legs.

Apparently she hadn't been the first vagrant to huddle in that doorway. Why had it angered him so?

Keeping to the shadows, she stayed hunched, letting the gin bottle dangle from her fingertips. Punt strolled far ahead, nearly a block. He was headed towards Chinatown. She made sure to keep a safe distance. Limping along, she let him get farther ahead, and then he disappeared.

"Damn," she breathed. Isobel shot ahead, and stopped where she had lost sight of her quarry. Dim light from a seedy saloon leaked onto the planks. She peeked around the corner, down a narrow lane as black as pitch. She listened for faint footsteps. Nothing.

"Where did you go?" she muttered.

Isobel waited, letting her eyes adjust to the dark. When nothing moved, she reached into her pocket for her tickler. She eased the blade open, and kept it in hand as she shambled into the alley. Trash and rotting vegetables littered the narrow lane. A rat glanced up at her—too bold to be bothered with running.

Isobel stopped at the end of the lane, looking right, and then left. A single hack rolled through the fog, but it was headed towards her, not away. Had Punt sensed her pursuit and ducked into the saloon?

Isobel glanced back down the alleyway. A few doorways led off into the dark, but not many. She worked her way back through the alley, peering into each doorway. Most were filled with trash. She stopped at the last doorway, the one closest to the saloon. A grocer's entrance, she surmised. She tried the knob. It didn't budge.

He must have ducked into the saloon. With gin bottle in hand, Isobel shambled through the saloon doors. The interior was dark and moody.

It wasn't crowded, but all eyes traveled to her. There

were dives that opened their doors to everyone, and others that catered to a group of regulars. This did not feel like the welcoming kind.

The bartender confirmed her suspicion. "We don't want your kind."

She placed a nickel on the bar.

He recoiled. "Git out of here now. You smell like a donkey's ass."

Isobel snatched up her nickel. No matter, she had seen what she needed to. William Punt was not in the barroom, and it hardly looked like a place he would frequent. But where had he gone?

As she contemplated that question, she turned to leave and ran right into a large man. Pockmarks scarred his skin, and his nose was red and crooked.

"You should know better than to come in here," he rumbled.

Isobel tried to move around the big man, but he grabbed her shoulder. His fingers clamped down like a vice. Pain zipped down her arm, and propelled her into action. She swung her bottle. It shattered against the side of his face. Blood and glass, shouts, and scraping chairs filled the saloon. The big man reeled, and she twisted to the side, bolting towards the exit. A patron beat her to it, blocking the doorway.

Isobel didn't slow. She put her shoulder into her charge, and sent the man staggering backwards. She flew past, but a blow caught her lower back, dropping her to her knees. With a groan, she scrambled forward. Police whistles pierced the night and shouts flew at her back. She skidded over muck and cobblestone.

She glanced over her shoulder. A policeman was closing in fast, boots thudding on the planks. She turned into the alleyway and shot towards the opposite end, weaving between garbage cans and hopping over splintered crates, nearly slipping on rotting vegetables.

A figure appeared at the end, billy club in hand. "Stop! Police!"

Isobel turned on her heel, skidded, and raced to the middle of the alleyway. Both policemen slowed, approaching cautiously from either side. There was only one way to go. Up. She reached for a protruding brick.

A shadow shifted in a garbage strewn doorway. A pale face in the night, a sudden movement, and a hiss. She lost her grip and fell into muck as smoke filled the alleyway. Someone brushed past her. Swift footfalls echoed between buildings.

"Here he is!" a voice shouted. "Over here!"

Isobel sucked in a breath, and coughed. She scrambled to her feet, leapt for the brick and climbed. Her fingers had locked on a second handhold when a heavy weight knocked her from the side. She fell, arm blazing. A billy club hit her on the back, and more blows followed, one after another.

"Got 'im!"

The voice drove her into a frenzy. Her foot connected with a knee, her fist with a crotch, and then her feet left the ground as a policeman rammed her into a brick wall. The impact stunned her. Pain raced up her arms, and cold iron clamped around her wrists. And still she fought, until a fist knocked the wind from her lungs. Isobel went limp, fighting for air.

"You best stay still or we'll beat you there," a rough voice snarled in her ear. "Gah, he stinks. Your turn, Bill."

"Why do I have to search 'im?"

"Because you're the junior officer."

"Shit." Bill stepped up and roughly ran his hands over

her, searching for weapons. He stopped at her chest. "Uhm."
He squeezed again, just to make sure.

"How *dare* you assault me!" she gasped in her plummiest
tone.

"Oh, shit!" Bill jumped back. "I mean. Blast. Erm…"

"What the hell?"

"The vagrant's a woman."

"Impersonating a man."

"No," she corrected. "I'm with the *Morning Call*. You can
either release me now, and I'll forget about your assault on
my person, or I'll plaster your names all over the papers."

Bill reached for her handcuffs, but the other policeman
growled. "I don't care what you do. But what you're *doing* is
illegal. Take her in and book her."

11

A COLD TRAIL

I had wondered how a man like Mr. Jones Sr. came to own a lumber yard—property in San Francisco is as good as a gold mine. —Z.R. Journal Excerpt

Tuesday, March 20, 1900

ALL TRAILS LEAD SOMEWHERE, EVEN IF THAT SOMEWHERE IS a dead end. Atticus Riot found himself at such an end. Unwilling to risk the living with a reckless investigation, he decided to backtrack to the beginning—to Ravenwood's investigation.

From the outside, Mr. Abe Jones's home hadn't changed in three years, but the person who opened the door had. Instead of an elderly Chinese woman, a silk-clad gentleman with a pristine queue answered Riot's knock. He bowed in greeting, which Riot returned.

"Is Mr. Jones Sr. still in residence?"

"No, sir. He died nearly three years ago."

"I'm sorry to hear. Are you the resident now?"

The man shook his head. "I am the butler for Mrs. Jones. Charles Wong."

Riot presented his calling card. "Might I speak with her, Mr. Wong?"

The man showed him into a fine sitting room. The oriental decor had been replaced with a more modern style —curving metals, ornate filigree, colored glass. The butler left him to his thoughts.

From what Riot remembered, the elder Jones's wife had died. Had he remarried, or was this his son's wife? Given the modern decor, he'd place a wager on the latter.

A handsome, middle-aged woman marched towards the parlor with a swish of skirts. Blonde, pale, and blue-eyed, she possessed the kind of classical beauty that artists love. She stopped just inside the doorway, lips pressed into a thin line, her fine hands clenched until they were white. A chill radiated from her.

"Mrs. Jones, I'm afraid we haven't met. I'm Atticus—"

"Don't touch me," she bit out. He froze, his hand half-extended. "You're the man who murdered my husband."

Riot withdrew his hand. "I beg your pardon?"

"You don't even know." Her lip twisted. "You meddle, and then you wash your hands and move on to the next life to ruin. He was a good man. He had nothing to do with those murders. He was trying to help those Chinese girls." It took a moment for his mind to catch up to her accusations. Mr. Jones Jr. had run the lumber yard where his night watchman was abducting and killing Chinese slave girls. The Broken Blossom Murders.

"I never accused your husband of any involvement, Ma'am."

"Of course you did! His name was in the newspapers. He was so heartbroken, so distraught, that he—" She cut herself short and pressed a handkerchief to her nose. "He took his own life," she finished in a whisper.

"I am sorry to hear that."

She laughed—a bitter sound that was at odds with her angelic appearance. "Get out of my house. Take your meddling elsewhere!" Her hand snaked upwards. He reacted, catching her wrist before her open palm connected with his face.

He met her blazing eyes.

"Unhand me!"

"If I hadn't meddled, more girls would have been slaughtered." He released her hand.

"You should have informed him privately. He would have put a stop to it."

"Would he have, Mrs. Jones?"

"Get out of my house. Wong!"

The butler immediately appeared, and Riot gave him a nod as he slipped on his hat, and showed himself out.

12

AN INCH OF GOLD

Jones Jr. was a different matter. Raised in Canton. University educated. Moder-
ately religious. Why, I wondered, was a man such as he continuing the work of
his father in rescuing the odd slave girl? —Z.R. Journal Excerpt

RAILROAD MAPS COVERED THE OFFICE WALLS, AND THE DULL,
much abused furniture appeared better suited to a newspaper editor's office than to the Imperial Consul General of
the Chinese Empire.

Riot's eyes were drawn to a single decoration. Chinese
characters filled an unfurled banner hanging on the wall. He
worked through the translation: *One inch of time is equivalent to*
an inch of gold. With an inch of gold it is hard to buy an inch of time.
Should you lose your gold, somebody will find it. Should you lose your
time, nobody can find it.

Those words hit him right in the gut. He could not
regain lost time nor could he fix the past. If only it were as
simple as finding something that was lost. How many
enemies and widows had he made?

An adjoining door opened, and a trio of men exited.

Two of them wore skullcaps, long queues, silk blouses, and the third was dressed in a tailored suit.

Two of them bowed and left, and the third turned to Riot. He was in his early thirties, short-haired and sporting a bushy black mustache. There was a cheerfulness to his countenance.

"I'm here to speak with the Consul General," Riot said, producing his card.

The man scrutinized the card. "What has he done now?" He had a distinct British accent, the kind that universities produce.

"I beg your pardon?"

The man nodded at the card. "It says you are a detective. I assume he is being investigated for something?"

"Not to my knowledge."

The man gestured towards the open door. "Would you like some tea, Mr. Riot?"

"No, thank you." He walked into the office, which was similarly decorated, only a red-gold dragon banner hung on a wall instead of a proverb. Aside from a well-used desk and four chairs, the office was empty.

The man walked behind the desk, and smiled, a mischievous look in his eyes. He extended a hand. "Consul General Ho Yow."

Pleasantly surprised, Riot shook his hand. The consul's grip was strong, and heavily calloused. "Forgive me, Consul General, I knew your predecessor, and I was expecting someone…"

"Queue, skullcap, and silk robes? I only wear traditional attire when I'm standing in front of a photographer."

"I was going to say older. I hardly expected a harness-racing enthusiast."

Ho Yow paused. "How very Holmesian of you, Mr.

Riot. Since you did not immediately recognize me on sight, I must conclude you knew very little of me before coming here, and yet you have deduced this last by my...?" Ho paused, and then gave a satisfied smile. He held up his hands. They were as leathery as a mule driver.

Riot inclined his head. "Your musculature as well. I do apologize for failing to do my research."

"Nonsense. That gives me the advantage. I've heard of you, and I *have* done my research, but in the rare case, I find it best to form my own opinion. This is one of those occasions. Please, sit." Ho Yow gestured towards the chair opposite. "You are not the first man to assume I'm the secretary to the Consul." He smiled, amiably. "I have been expecting you to visit at some point. I've heard the rumors about you, and I'm greatly looking forward to discovering if they are true."

"Are those rumors good or bad?"

"From where I sit, all the rumors about *Din Gau*, the formidable detective, are good. We share a mutual enemy— the criminal tongs." Ho Yow poured himself some tea, and added a drop of milk and sugar. "You've certainly wasted little time in reestablishing your reputation in Chinatown."

"A habit of mine."

"Consul Chang warned me about you, Mr. Riot. He said that you are relentless and principled, and that makes you a dangerous man."

"Do you agree?"

"The criminal tongs are made up of relentless and principled men, too. We may not agree with their practices, but there is honor within their ranks—if a twisted kind of honor."

"*Know thyself, know thine enemy,*" Riot quoted Sun Tzu.

"*A thousand battles, a thousand victories,*" Ho Yow finished.

"When I studied law in England, I found little honor in the profession."

"Cambridge."

Ho Yow dipped his chin. "A guess?"

"No, your accent."

Ho Yow raised his brows. "As perceptive as the Great Detective."

"I'm afraid I don't hold a candle to Mr. Sherlock Holmes. He's brilliant. I'm more the Watson of Ravenwood Agency."

"And your partner was the Holmes?"

"Yes. Very much so."

"Still, you're more perceptive than Watson, I think."

"The good doctor is simply a humble man."

Ho Yow tilted his head slightly. "Yes, one could interpret the stories that way. Perhaps he is cunning, too."

"I wouldn't go that far."

"Still, the unexpected can be used to one's advantage. My background in law makes me a formidable consul. Politicians are not used to a British solicitor representing China." He smiled. "It was the student tradition of roof climbing that gave me a taste for adventure. Harness racing is equally exhilarating. But I doubt you came to hear about my university days, Mr. Riot. Unless you came to discuss horses, in which case I'll talk your ear off for hours. Fair warning."

The edge of Riot's lip quirked. "Noted." He studied the consul, letting silence hang in the air. How much should he tell this unknown man? Could he trust him? Sometimes, as the consul had insinuated, surprise was a detective's only card.

"How much do you know about *Sing Ping King Sur*?"

Ho Yow froze, his teacup poised in midair. He eyed Riot

over the brim. A moment later, Ho Yow abruptly set the cup in its saucer, stood, and closed his office door. "You certainly don't waste time."

"No one can find it," Riot replied, a subtle reference to the proverb hanging in the sitting room wall.

Ho Yow sat, and folded his hands. All trace of the cheerful young man vanished. The Imperial Consul General of the Chinese Empire sat across the desk from him now. "Where did you hear that name?"

"They were the last words of a man who drove a knife through his heart."

"Jim Parks."

Riot nodded.

"I read the newspaper articles. There was no mention of *Sing Ping King Sur* at the inquest."

Riot had been much amused by the article Isobel wrote detailing her interview with him. "Given your reaction, I think you know why I failed to mention that name."

"Do *you* know why?" Ho Yow asked. It was a profound question.

"I was told that the words killed my partner, Zephaniah Ravenwood. That those words would kill me, too. I assume it's a tong."

Ho Yow sat back in his chair and crossed his legs, his gaze traveling over a railroad map that stretched along a wall. He was deep in thought for a minute, and then returned his attention to his guest. "I know what happened three years ago, Mr. Riot. You did China a favor by executing the *Hip Yee* leaders. But it created a void of power. The tongs have been at war ever since. The violence has driven many residents to other parts of the state. It's much the same as when Little Pete was assassinated, only this is more brutal. There is no 'King of Chinatown' keeping the other tongs in check."

"And what of *Sing Ping King Sur*?"

"It is a whisper; a shadow. I do not think it exists. My detectives and informants have been unable to confirm its existence."

"But you don't deny it? You closed the door when I mentioned it."

"I understand the power of words. Whether truth or lies, words can incite a mob to murder innocent people."

"How did you first hear of *Sing Ping King Sur*?" Riot asked.

"A *boo how doy* working for *Bing On*. He was known as the *Butcher*. When *See Yup's* leader was found dead in a pool of blood, all eyes turned to him. But he did not take credit for the assassination. While he was heavy in his cups, he confided to a friend—one of my informants—that *Sing Ping King Sur* had carried out the assassination. My detectives found nothing. Only a phantom—a superstition as real as spirits and devils."

"Did anyone come forward?"

Ho Yow shook his head.

"That seems strange. *Boo how doy* are always eager to take credit for a kill."

"They are. Perhaps a devil killed the leader."

"I've met a few devils in my lifetime. They're gifted at keeping to the shadows."

"This devil was exceptional, then. I ask you, Mr. Riot, as a detective: How do you track a superstition?"

"It takes a relentless man."

"Do you believe Jim Parks? That a tong so mysterious, so shrouded in silence that no one can confirm its existence, killed your partner?"

"I intend to find out."

"Where my detectives have failed?"

"Perhaps it takes a devil to find one," Riot said.

Ho Yow looked him square in the eye. "And you are that devil?"

Riot didn't answer. Only waited.

"Remember, Mr. Riot, Americans have a habit of pinning things on the 'vile Chinese'. This would not be the first wild rumor to be spread by a white man. The word 'plague' is my current concern—*my* killing word. Yet another lie to spread hate and fear. I will not allow a repeat of Honolulu. Not in my quarter."

Honolulu's Chinatown had been incinerated only months before due to a plague outbreak. The resulting homeless were currently being housed in detention camps.

"Have the plague deaths been confirmed?" Riot asked.

"Doctor Kinyoun and a few city health officers say so, but the State Health Board have not confirmed the deaths as plague. And then there is this." Ho Yow opened a drawer, and tossed a sheet of paper onto the desk.

Riot read the note. '*The plague is a sham. I'll lift the quarantine for ten thousand in gold. Hang a red silk scarf from the second-story window of the consulate building when you're ready to pay. I'll contact you with further instructions.*'

"It was delivered by a carrier through a string of street urchins the day the quarantine barrier was put in place."

"Did you hang the scarf?"

"Of course," Ho Yow said. "I wanted to find out who made the offer. But I had no intention of paying. There was no further contact, and the quarantine was lifted a few days later. I have heard nothing more."

Riot put his nose to the parchment, took a deep breath,

and then reached into his pocket for his magnifying glass. He studied the paper closely.

Ho Yow raised his brows. "Let me guess. A man with a limp and a white terrier living on California Street wrote that?"

"I'm afraid I'm not that talented, Consul Ho. But this was written by a left-handed man who is educated. Although some say it's impossible to determine the sex from handwriting alone, I believe otherwise. He's confident, not desperate. This wasn't written by a man looking for an easy con. The paper is expensive, and it bears the same water-mark as the paper that's found in every room of the Palace Hotel—except that it has no hotel letterhead. This paper may have been taken from the man's personal office supply, or he may have purchased it from the boutique in the Palace. Based on the tobacco smell permeating the parch-ment and the lack of smell in your own office, I'd say it was written in a private office."

The consul leaned forward. "That is most impressive, Mr. Riot."

"A good guess."

Ho Yow huffed. "I will have my detectives follow up on that information. Perhaps we can trace this 'left-handed' man through the paper company. It's almost a shame that the quarantine was lifted. I was curious to see how he planned on transporting ten thousand dollars worth of gold without being discovered."

Riot considered the problem. "Discovery may not have been a concern."

"True. A white man conning the Chinese Consulate would have been heralded as a triumph, not a criminal act."

Riot frowned at the note. "There's another option. It

may have been intended as a warning—to sow doubt about Doctor Kinyoun's claim."

"In that case, it worked. Although I was already doubtful."

"A cry of plague goes both ways," Riot mused. "It may drive Chinese out of the Quarter, but there's also the possibility that it would shut down ports. White newspapers are calling it a sham as well."

"The ports would not be closed if the plague is contained to 'yellow people'. The Honolulu ports have already recovered from their plague. All it took was the torching of Chinatown. Then it was business as usual."

Riot had to agree with that sentiment. "Have you spoken with Dr. Kinyoun, and the officials who performed the post-mortems?"

"I have. Police Surgeon Wilson, a health officer by the name of O'Brien, and a bacteriologist, Wilfred Kellogg, are adamant that there have been five confirmed plague deaths. The guinea pigs, rats, and a monkey that Kinyoun injected with fluid from the dead have died as well. But is that really surprising? If you take fluid from a dead man and inject it into the living… it would most likely kill anything."

"I'm not a medical man, Consul," Riot admitted. "And I don't pretend to understand much about bacteriology, but Kinyoun and Kellogg are experts in their field."

"Experts, yes. But even white physicians view bacteriology as 'black magic'. The health officials are trying to pass a mandatory vaccination for Chinatown, with the Haffkine vaccine—a vaccine that causes sickness. But only for the Chinese." His words were clipped. An undercurrent of anger. "Tell me, Mr. Riot, if plague was brought to San Francisco on a steamer from Honolulu, how did this disease skip over eight blocks of the Barbary Coast to kill a lumber salesman in the Globe Hotel?"

"That'd be a question for a bacteriologist."

Ho Yow sat back. "I'm sure you can appreciate why I'm skeptical of 'expert' opinion."

"Would you like me to look into the matter?"

"Officially? No. I have my own detectives, but if you should hear anything, I would not turn down information."

"I'd appreciate it if you'd return the favor."

"For a man the tongs call *Din Gau*...? I would be a fool not to."

Riot stood to leave, and extended his hand, but then he stopped. His gaze fell on the magnificent dragon banner, with its shimmering scales and flashing eyes. "You frequent the horse tracks," he said, more to himself.

"As much as my duties allow." Ho Yow turned to admire his racing colors.

"Have you encountered a man by the name of Parker Gray or Andrew Ross?"

"I've met Andrew Ross, yes. He has an eye for winning horses that would rival Little Pete."

The innuendo was not lost on Riot. Little Pete had been infamous for rigging races and buying jockeys. He had made a fortune before his scam was uncovered.

"Ross is far more subtle, however."

"Was," Riot said.

Ho Yow raised his brows. "I see. I've been distracted by this plague business. What happened?"

"He was killed." Riot did not relate the entire story. That was not his aim.

"I can't say I'm sorry."

"Nor was I," Riot admitted. "Have you heard the name Lincoln Howe?"

Ho Yow frowned, his mustache accentuating the gesture. He rifled through a desk drawer, and laid out a telegram slip. "I have never met the man, but my people are being blamed for his disappearance. He is a health inspector. He came from Honolulu on the SS *Australia*, and went missing the first week of March."

And just like that, a piece fell into place. The mysterious Lincoln Howe had been found, or rather lost.

13

DROWNING

So absorbed in the infantile delight of destruction, Atticus ignored the recovered records. —Z.R. Journal Excerpt

Isobel paced in her holding cell, back and forth like a caged thing. One telephone call. Her choice had been obvious.

The other women in her cramped cell watched her. They kept their distance. It might have been the smell emanating from her person. The drab wool dress that a matron had forced her into had done nothing for the lingering scent of her vagrant guise.

"You sure that's a woman?" a prostitute called through the bars.

"Shut it, Mary," a matron snapped.

"Bloody crazy," Mary muttered.

Isobel felt as if she were mad. She could not breathe. Could not think in this small, cramped cell. It wasn't the first time she had seen the inside of a jail. But back then she'd always had her father's name to wave in front of the police.

Isobel walked back and forth on a worn little path, counting her steps. Her world ended at five steps.

"I think she's sick," another voice said. "Look at the girl's hair."

"She's right thin."

"Guard, we think this one's got the plague!"

Isobel ignored them. All her energy was focused on breathing, but her lungs had shrunk in size, and each breath came hard. She wanted to scream.

Five steps. She was drowning.

Isobel put her back to a corner, and slid down the cold stone, covering her head with her hands. No one came near her. The only sound in her self-made cocoon was the rush of blood in her ears. She was frozen in that corner. Trapped. For how long? Hours? Days?

Every regret, every foolish mistake and failure came crashing down on her like a wave. Her life seemed hopeless, and the irony of it was that she was already dead to the world.

"Charlotte Bonnie!" The call whipped her head up. A policeman stood at the bars of the holding cell. Isobel climbed to her feet and nearly fell. Needles pricked down her legs as she staggered towards the bars. The cell was empty. How long had she been there? "Your father is here for you."

Joy, dread, and puzzlement battled in the silence that followed.

"My father?" she breathed. Her father, Marcus Amsel—calm and warm, and always patient, he was the best father a daughter could ask for. And she was every father's nightmare. She didn't deserve him—not after all she had put him through.

A moment later, reason returned. In keeping with her

story to the police, she had telephoned Mack McCormick, only he hadn't been at the office. Had he received her message? But why would Mack pose as her father?

It wasn't Mack, and it wasn't her father. The man who claimed that title was neither tall and thin nor tall and solid. A wizened old man with a white beard rocked back and forth from toe to heel. He seemed ill-suited to a suit, and held his straw hat over his heart as if it would protect him from all the brass in the room.

Tim looked at her, blue eyes narrowing with anger. "I told you, gurl, this newspaper business isn't no profession for a woman!" he growled. "Whatcha do to her? Did you rough her up?" He shot an accusing eye at the police sergeant.

"My men were attacked," the sergeant said.

"By this beanpole of a gurl?"

Isobel clasped her hands in front of her, and let her head droop in remorse.

"She smashed a bottle over a patron's head."

"Now, I talked to your boy," Tim said. "He said there was *two* people in that alley. Sounds as if your boys went for the easier prey. And don't you worry, I'll see she's properly punished. I appreciate you dropping the charges, but goddammit, man. Your boys need to toughen up if they're claiming a wee thing like my darlin' Charlotte here got the better of 'em."

Tim continued to berate the sergeant, his patrolmen, and anyone else in range as he frog-marched Isobel towards the exit. But before he pushed her through the door, he yanked a frilly shawl free from his hat. "Put this on, quick now," Tim ordered. Without questioning him, she swept the shawl around her shoulders. He plopped his straw hat on her head, tilted it low, and fished his own cap out of his pocket.

Stark daylight blinded her. She blinked past the sun, disoriented and wishing she'd had sense enough to consult a clock. Voices battered her.

"Will you press charges, Miss Bonnie?"

"How serious are your injuries?"

"Wasn't that a risky stunt?"

"Foolish, more like!"

Reporters. A whole murder of them. The reason for hat and shawl became apparent. She made use of the accessories, making sure her face was obscured by the brim. A moment later, a flash bulb went off.

Tobias White hopped off a waiting hack, and opened the door for her. Eyes bright, he was trying to hold back a smile. He looked very official.

Isobel climbed inside the hack, and Tim followed on her heels. The door slammed shut, and the carriage lurched forward. As it rattled over cobblestones, she glanced out the window. What had seemed like a mob, was only five desperate reporters aching for a story and cash.

Tobias' face appeared in the window, and he folded his arms on the sill. "Where to?"

"My boat."

"Hold on, Tobias. You sure you don't want to head to the house for a hot bath?" Tim asked. "Pardon my French, but you smell like shit."

She stuck her head out the window. "The Folsom Street Pier, if you please, Grimm." Nearly a man, Grimm was as sober as his nickname. He gave a stoic nod.

"What if he don't please?" Tobias asked.

"Git back on the seat before you fall under the wheels," Tim ordered. Tobias made a face and disappeared, climbing alongside the hack.

Isobel sank back into the seat with a sigh. "How did you hear I was in a holding cell?"

Tim pulled out a newspaper from his coat. "Page four."

When she found the article, she let out a string of curses directed at Mack, her editor, and reporters in general.

"They are vultures, Miss Bel."

"I would have called you or Riot, but I didn't want my name tied to the agency anymore than it already is."

He blew out a breath, ruffling his beard. "I'd say that ship already sailed. But it's not as if I flashed around the agency's card. As much as I cackled when I got the news, A.J. would have had my neck if I'd let you fester in there."

"I'm touched," she said dryly. "It's fortunate you're an avid newspaper reader, seeing as I only made it on page four next to a hosiery and underwear advertisement."

"I have my ears everywhere, and I keep them to the ground. The police arrested fifty drunkards in the Barbary Coast last night and charged them all with vagrancy. A woman in the mix caught my attention. When I heard she was caught in a seedy alley near Chinatown after bashing a bottle over a man's head, I figured it was you."

"That's a fair guess." And if there was another woman running around San Francisco getting into trouble like that, she'd like to meet her. "Whatever fines you paid on my behalf, be sure to dock it from my pay."

"I got you off without a penny. I reckon the police had their hands full charging fifty drunkards. But even if I had to sell my soul, it'd have been a perk of the agency. All legal fees are covered by the agency if you run afoul of the law while on a case."

"You might want to rethink your policy where I'm concerned. I'm likely to bankrupt you."

Tim chuckled. "Between you and A.J., I have little

doubt. Good thing Zeph was a regular miser. That man was loath to part with a speck of gold dust."

"You appear to keep your gold close, too."

Tim flashed his gold teeth. "I'll part with it when I'm dead. I'll add you to my last will and testament. You can have my incisor."

"I'm honored."

"You look roughed up," he noted. "And sound worse."

It was true. She was exhausted. There was little life to her voice. To distract him from concern, she told him what had happened.

Tim whistled low.

"Do you know that saloon?" The sign had been so decrepit that she hadn't been able to read it in the dark.

"*The Drifter*," he answered straightaway. "It's not a place I'd waltz into. It's a known criminal den, and despite the name, no one that's not a recognized criminal is allowed to haunt it. The police don't even venture in there alone—they take four or five patrolmen to drag a man out."

She closed her eyes. "That would be why I was attacked so quickly. But why would William Punt go inside?"

"Are you sure he did? Every Irish hoodlum, cutthroat-for-hire, and thief holes up in there. I'd think he'd be picked apart in minutes."

"Punt's not precisely a saint, Tim. But you're right. I don't know if he went inside the saloon or not. I was being so cautious that I let him get too far ahead of me."

"Remind me to teach you a bit about tailing a suspect."

If any other man had said that, save Riot, she'd have snapped at him, but one look at Tim told her to accept his offer with gratitude.

"I'll put Monty on it. See what he can dig up."

"Riot thought it best if we play things safe. After last night, I'm inclined to agree. I don't want to spook them."

"It's not spookin' if a man rents a room from a boarding house and keeps an eye out a window."

"Monty will hate you."

Tim showed his teeth. "He already does."

"Was that you who yelled 'clear as day he reached for his gun' at the inquest yesterday?"

"It surely was." There was an impish glint in his blue eyes. "San Francisco is a mob, Miss Bel. Always remember that. One lone man can ignite a wildfire with a single word. It's always been that way, and I reckon it always will. It never hurts to stack the deck in your favor."

"I didn't get a chance to speak with Riot after the inquest. Will I find him on my boat?"

Tim shrugged. "Finding him is as time consuming as finding you, girl. I don't pretend to keep track unless I hear of a vagrant woman attacking coppers."

"You're a useful man, Tim."

"Some call me friend, too." He looked her over. "I know you get all prickly when someone tries to help you, but do you want me to light the stove for you, or fetch you some food?"

"I can manage."

"Well, good," he huffed. "I got better things to be doing."

On another day, she might have smiled. "I figured as much." Impulsively, she leaned over and kissed his cheek. "Thank you."

Tim turned brick red, and blustered his way through the rest of the trip.

14

REVELATIONS

I have observed that men take a certain satisfaction in physical exertion. Atticus,
sporadically brilliant as he may be, is no exception. —Z.R. Journal Excerpt

A CARRIAGE ROLLED TO A STOP AT THE END OF A NARROW lane. Atticus Riot alighted with an easy step. He set the tip of his walking stick on the cobblestones, and surveyed the row of stick houses. Cramped, gasping for air in the crush of buildings, Salmon Street was a quiet fringe on the edges of the Barbary Coast. It was also within easy walking distance of the city's worst alleyways.

"Wait here," he instructed the hackman. Riot walked up the steps and applied his stick to number forty-three. As he waited on the doorstep, he traced the silver knob of his walking stick—a restless habit that betrayed too much. His partner's murderer had been caught, and killed. So why did the thing feel half done?

He caught himself listening for his partner's goading voice. But there was no reply. Zephaniah Ravenwood had faded into memory. Jim Parks had murdered Ravenwood, but Riot had killed more than his fair share of men, too. A pang stabbed his heart. What kind of man was he? Hardly suitable association for a child.

Having second thoughts, Riot turned to leave, but the door opened. A lanky man with his arm in a sling stood in the doorway. His cheekbones were prominent, and his Adam's apple even more so. Two weeks before, with reporters present, he'd greeted Riot with an amiable smile. He was not so friendly now.

Lee Walker frowned in greeting.

"Mr. Walker." Riot inclined his head. "I was in the area, and I thought I'd call on Sarah."

"This isn't a good time."

"And why is that?"

"I don't think it's any of your business."

"The definition of a detective."

"Sarah is not your case anymore."

"She never was my case; she was an abandoned girl in a strange city. Now she's a friend. I take the happiness of my friends seriously."

"Sarah is doing just fine," Walker replied. "I still don't think you're proper company for my niece. I read about that shooting business in the newspapers. If you will excuse me. I'm a busy man."

The words echoed Riot's own thoughts, only now every protective instinct took over. Walker started to close the door, but Riot casually placed his stick in the way. "I'd wager a fair amount that I'm the *only* person who will help you when the men who set you up come calling."

Walker ground his teeth. "I'm on my way out."

"Then you won't mind if Sarah spends the day with me," Riot said reasonably.

Walker turned and called, "Sarah, you've a visitor. I'll be out for a bit."

Before waiting for his niece's reply, Walker grabbed his hat and coat, brushed past Riot, and moved quickly down the steps. Riot watched his brisk pace and darting eyes.

Something had changed.

Footsteps hurried down the stairway. Before he could remove his hat, Sarah Byrne threw her arms around him. "Mr. Riot!" Her dark hair was in one long braid cinched with a bow, and her freckled face beamed with joy.

"Hello, Miss Byrne." He gave her shoulder a fond squeeze, and looked her over. "How are you getting along?"

"Well enough. Won't you come in? I can make tea."

"I wondered if you'd like to lunch with me. Although, I suppose it's more of a late afternoon tea at this point. It's been a long day already, and I've not yet eaten."

"What were you doing?"

"I went to my gymnasium early this morning, and then I took a stroll through Chinatown."

Sarah sighed. "I wish I'd been with you. I've been here at the house all day."

"I'm afraid they don't allow ladies in my gymnasium."

"Are you a boxer?"

"That, and fencing."

"You sword fight, too? Could you teach me?"

"Not on an empty stomach."

She grinned. "Where will we be going?"

"Have you dined at the Cliff House?"

Her eyes widened. "That big house that looks like it's about ready to fall off the cliff?"

"You won't find a better view of the ocean."

Sarah Byrne was a girl of twelve closing in on womanhood, but at that moment her excitement made her seem half her age. "Let me get my things."

Riot waited on the doorstep while she raced through the

house. When she reappeared, she wore a simple hat and a warm coat, and carried a basket. He took it from her hand as she locked the door.

"Did you let Uncle Lee know I was going with you?"

"He knows you're with me," Riot said, and gave the basket a gentle shake. It rattled. "Sketching supplies?"

She turned, and raised her brows. "How'd you know?"

"Your fingertips are smudged with colored charcoal, and the ocean has been known to inspire more than one artist."

Color spread over her freckles. "I'm not an artist. I just like to draw."

Riot offered his arm. "You're a step ahead of some I've met."

"Do you know many?"

As they climbed into the hack, he told her about a color-blind artist who loved to use color—all of them at once. And another who destroyed every piece she completed. Sarah laughed, and when they were settled in the rattling carriage, she brought out her sketchbook to show off her work.

"Has your uncle looked into schools?" Riot asked as he flipped through the pages.

"Mr. Amsel took me around to the schools. I'll start next week. He also escorted me to a teahouse in the Palace Hotel. It was grand!"

"That was thoughtful of him." There more than one sketching of Lotario Amsel in her book, and he cringed to find one of Isobel. His reaction wasn't from the quality, but the striking likeness of her. "Sarah?"

"Yes?"

"I'm not being kind when I say that you're a talented artist. In fact, you're so talented, I must ask something of you."

"What is it?"

"Could I purchase this sketch from you?"

"No, you can't buy it, but you can certainly have it." She took the pad from him, and tore the page out of her book. "It's a gift—for all you've done for me."

Riot was loath to fold the sketch, but he did, careful not to crease Isobel's face. "Thank you." He tucked the sketch in his coat pocket. "It's probably best that you don't draw Miss Bonnie again."

"But her eyes are so interesting."

Captivating, he thought. *Fierce*. "It's for her safety."

"Did you help her like you helped me?"

The edge of his lip quirked. "Miss Bonnie helped me more than I helped her. But in a word, yes. Drawing her might be dangerous."

"I won't draw her again. Not until you tell me it's safe. Does it have to do with those men in that building on the beach?"

"Partly. There's plenty of other danger in this city, too."

"It seems that way. Mr. Amsel told me everywhere I was not to go."

"You'd be wise to listen to him," Riot said. "How are you finding your uncle's company?"

She avoided the question. "I didn't tell him a word of what happened with Jin and Tobias."

"That's entirely up to you." He kept his relief to himself. "And your uncle, is he treating you well?" he asked again.

"I can't complain."

"Most of us can't, but if you could, what would you say?"

She looked out the window. "I haven't seen much of him. He keeps to himself." And with those few words, Riot understood her forced cheerfulness. Sarah had desperately wanted a home. She had one—but it was proving to be a lonely existence.

"You'll be attending school soon. And I've wrapped up my current case. I'll have some extra time."

"Until the next one." He barely caught the words. Sarah looked over at him. "I read about your gun duel in the newspaper. That was horrible."

"It's a terrible thing," he agreed.

"Does it help?"

He cocked his head in question.

"Shooting the man who killed your partner?"

"It doesn't bring him back."

"I suppose not."

"Did you have many friends in Tennessee?" he asked.

Sarah pressed her lips together, and looked back to the city. "Don't matter if I did." She swiped a hand across her eyes.

"You have a few here—including me," he offered.

"And I'm glad for it, Mr. Riot. I don't keep secrets from my friends, but Uncle Lee made me swear I wouldn't say a word to you."

Instincts roused, Riot waited. In his experience, when an adult told a child to keep a secret it was never a good thing. "About what?"

"Uncle Lee took me to the Palace, too. He had business with some men there, but I wasn't allowed in the Gentleman's Grille Room, so I wandered around the place. I just acted like I belonged, and no one paid me any mind." Her soft southern drawl was smooth on the ears.

"That's the way it works most times," he said. "Who did your uncle meet?"

"A Mr. Kingston and a Mr. Claiborne. I didn't much care for either of them, but Uncle Lee was happy when he left. He told me the men paid him not to go to court. I don't much understand that."

Riot traced the engraving on his stick. "It is curious, isn't it?" he mused aloud.

"No, it's not curious!" Her sudden anger took him by surprise. Tears welled in her eyes. "Uncle Lee says that as soon as he settles his affairs we're moving to the country—to somewhere quiet."

Riot's throat tightened. He quickly reached in his pocket for a handkerchief. Sarah buried her face in the silk. He waited for her tears to dry. "You'll make a life for yourself wherever you settle, Sarah." But the words sounded hollow even to his own ears.

"Not much settlin' with all my movin' around."

"Things *will* settle eventually."

She looked at him, puffy eyes and nose. "Have they ever for you?"

"The thought never much appealed to me." It was a response born of habit, from a bachelor's life, but the words didn't quite ring true anymore.

———

THE CLIFF HOUSE IMPROVED SARAH'S MOOD, AND SHE seemed to forget about her distress while they strolled along the parapets. Fed, watered, and walked, they headed back to the city. As the hack rattled along streets, dodging streetcars and wagons, Sarah talked of her life in Tennessee, her Gramma, and what she remembered of her mother, which wasn't much at all. More like a dream.

Loath to return the girl to an empty home, Riot decided to check in with his office at Ravenwood Agency.

"Do you own this building?" Sarah asked, as they climbed the stairs.

"My agency lets an office here."

"Don't suppose you need an office girl?"

Riot smiled. "Are you offering?"

"'Course I am. I got to make my way somehow."

"School first, Sarah. Then University."

She looked at him like he'd sprouted wings. "Gramma seemed to have a different idea for my future. She always told me I was to find a respectable man, and marry."

"Do you want to marry?"

"Mr. Amsel is unattached, but I reckon I should finish school first."

"One step at a time," he agreed. "School is a fine idea. You can concern yourself with the rest when you get there." He opened the office door for her.

Tim, Matthew Smith, and Monty Johnson were deep in conversation when they entered. Tim took one look at Sarah, uncrossed his arms, and put on his 'crazy old man' act. "Did someone pin you with a daughter, A.J.?"

"I'd be a lucky man if that were so." He made introductions. Monty grunted his disapproval, while Matthew handed Riot a stack of telegrams.

"Would you give Sarah a tour?" he asked the young man. There wasn't much to the agency, but the ex-patrolman took the hint, and dutifully stepped up to the challenge.

Tim and Monty followed Riot into his office. He shut the door while Monty plopped in a chair behind the desk.

"I've discovered who Lincoln Howe is," Riot said.

Tim whistled. "How'd you manage that?"

"By accident."

"'Bout how you do everything, isn't it?" Monty asked. It

was an old joke, however, and Riot let it slide. He shared what he had learned.

"Doesn't sound as if Howe's disappearance garnered much attention," Tim said.

"It's not like we've been cooling our heels," Monty grumbled. "What with that society girl who went missing, that murdering sodomist, and all our side cases. We need more agents."

"It's not easy finding men with half a brain," Tim shot back. "I'm going to start hiring women."

"If you hire a woman Zeph will roll over in his grave. And I'll leave."

"You don't know what the hell Zeph would have done," Tim snapped.

"Gentlemen," Riot inserted. "I'd like to focus on our current issues instead of arguing over Ravenwood's misogyny."

"Monty's right," Tim grumbled. "If Howe went missing, we were too occupied to keep up with papers. I'll ask my man with the newspapers. See if he remembers running an article."

"And I'll question the quarantine station." It would also give Riot a chance to look into the plague matter for Consul Ho Yow. "Did you turn anything up about 'Freddy' Ashworth?"

Monty leaned back in his chair. "He's a nervous one. He's been keeping away from the tracks, frequents *The Palm* now, and has taken to prizefights. Getting above himself, and all that. He went off with some tart the other day after raking in a heap of cash."

"Freddy isn't entirely new to prizefights," Tim added. "He has his fingers in everything involving money."

"Well, something spooked him," Monty said.

Riot already knew what that something was. "What do you mean?"

"He disappeared into his rooms with that tart. She left, then he darted out of there with packed bags."

"Did you follow him?"

Monty scowled. "'Course I did." He crossed his big arms. "Am I going to get a bonus for it?"

"Depends on where he ended up."

"I trailed him to a quiet little town just north of Sacramento. He went into a house there. Turned out it's his sister's place."

"Tim will see to your bonus," Riot said. "But I don't want to lose track of him."

"I hired some nosy runts to wire me if Freddy leaves."

Riot nodded. If he didn't know the other half of the story, it could easily be excused as a visit to family. "Have either of you seen a token like this before?" He handed it to Tim, who flipped it to Monty.

"It's a Faro token from *The Palm*," Monty said.

"Like he don't know that," Tim said. Monty flicked the token at the old man, but Riot reached out and caught it midair before it hit.

"Do you know that for a fact, Monty?" Riot asked, genuinely curious.

"Well, it says so on the token."

"Have either of you ever played faro at *The Palm*?" Riot looked from Monty to Tim. Both shook their head.

"It's not really our type of place," Tim said.

"More for toffs like you."

"I haven't spent much time there, but I found that token on Jim Parks. Lee Walker had one too, as well as Andrew Ross and Freddy."

Monty frowned at the token. "So what does it mean?"

"I think it's an affiliation marker."

"For a tong?" Tim asked.

Monty breathed an oath. "I am sick of getting involved in their business."

"We're detectives; what the hell do you think we do? Pick flowers?" Tim shot back.

Monty's only answer was a grumble.

Riot looked to Tim. "Have you discovered anything more about Lee Walker?"

"Not much. Aside from the circus and fraudulent accidents, he appears to have gotten his second cousin with child. He took off when the family pressured him to make good and marry the girl."

"Her own fault," Monty said. "Girl shoulda kept her knees together."

Tim's beard twitched. "Wipe that smirk off your face and git out of his chair." Tim swatted Monty's head with a folded up newspaper. Monty jumped up, but while he was always keen to challenge Riot, he knew better than to cross Tim. The old man had a devious mind. He hadn't survived the Gold Rush by fighting fair.

Riot sat down, and as he began sorting through his stack of telegrams, Tim continued his report.

"There's not much on that brick house in Ocean Beach. Parker Gray is listed as the owner. I got in with a farrier who does occasional work there. The stable hand is deaf and dumb, just like you thought. Couldn't get a word out of him. I've been doing my best to tail Parker Gray. He mostly keeps to prize fights, the brick house, and his gymnasium at the Pavilion. But he did go to *The Palm* last week."

"It keeps coming back to that saloon," Riot murmured.

"Don't look at me to go in there. I'd stand out like a rotted tooth," Monty said.

"Nor Smith," Riot agreed. "He's too wet behind the ears."

"Do you know anyone we can send in?" Tim asked.

"I'll think on it." Lotario came instantly to mind, but Isobel's face was known to Gray. On the other hand, Lotario was a gifted actor and makeup artist. It took nerve to live a life of lies.

"What about your new favorite boy, Mr. Morgan? He can work there as a dishwasher. Far as I can tell the boy doesn't do a thing." Monty took out his tobacco, and started rolling a cigarette.

Again, Riot said nothing. Given Isobel's precarious situation, it was best to keep Monty in the dark about *Mr. Morgan's* abilities.

"The thing seems cut and dry, A.J.," Monty said. "Parker Gray conned Walker into taking a bad bet so they could cash in on a silver baron. Why are we still investigating this shit?"

Tim glanced at Riot. The question was in his own eyes as well.

"Because Jim Parks claimed he was paid by someone else to kill Ravenwood."

Monty grunted. "We suspected a tong killed him years ago, but you found out different. The Chinese aren't the issue. You killed Parks. It's done."

"Don't you want those people to answer for his death?"

"I blame the railroads and government for bringing Chinese scum into America in the first place—doesn't mean I'm going to shoot the president."

"Good to know." Riot paused, reading over the telegram in his hand. He looked up at both gentlemen. "Would you two excuse me?"

Monty stomped towards the door, and then stopped. "What the hell should I do now?"

"I'll have a job for you soon as I talk it over with A.J.," Tim said.

"You could talk it over with me."

"I could, but I won't." Tim waited until Monty left. "You should read page four." He tossed a newspaper down. "I took care of it."

Riot looked at him, puzzled. But he was distracted by the telegram. He picked up the receiver and requested 920 Sacramento. As he waited, he unfolded the newspaper and nearly dropped the receiver.

Woman Dressed As Vagrant Caught

Call reporter Charlotte Bonnie was arrested while on assignment for the paper. The lively young woman was disguised as a vagrant in order to investigate life on the street for the hopelessly destitute. Assaulted by a saloon patron, she was forced to defend herself by smashing a bottle on his head. Adding insult to injury, a trio of policemen roughed her up as she was fleeing her assailant. 'Bring me your poor and destitute' so says the good book. San Francisco, it seems, has other ideas.

"Hello? Hello, there?" a voice asked over the line.

"Here." Riot cleared his throat. "I apologize, Dolly."

"Is everything all right?"

He coughed, and set the newspaper aside. "I only just arrived in my office and received your missive about Jin."

"I'm sorry to bother you. What with your inquest only yesterday. I was relieved to read that there were no further charges placed."

"As was I," he said with feeling. "When did Jin disappear?"

"Yesterday. She's been in a mood. I'm surprised she's stayed this long. That girl is as fierce and bull-headed as they come. Mei is the only one who can get through to her, but not this time. Jin climbed out of a third-story window, and darted off. Another girl tried to follow, and...um, didn't fare as well."

"Is she all right?"

"The girl broke both her ankles when she fell."

Riot winced. "Sounds like you have your hands full."

"When don't I? As troublesome as she is, I am worried."

"Jin is likely holed up in Tobias' fort in my backyard. And if she isn't there, I believe I know where she is."

"I had hoped you would. She seemed taken with Mr. Morgan and his boat. Is he a reputable gentleman?"

"You don't have to worry about Mr. Morgan with the girl. He has my full trust."

"High praise, then."

"Though I can't speak for his reckless streak."

Donaldina laughed over the line—a crackle of amusement. "Well, I wouldn't speak for yours either, or mine, for that matter. Thank you, Atticus. Let me know the moment you find her, but please take your time in returning that girl."

"That bad?"

"One of my worst."

That was saying quite a bit. Donaldina Cameron was not one to exaggerate. But Jin was the last thing on his mind as he rang off. Riot picked up the newspaper again. "Tim!" he called.

15

NO REST FOR THE WEARY

While bent on destroying the tong headquarters, gambling dens, and brothels, Atticus has forgotten the ultimate goal—to discover the heart of this multi-headed beast. —Z.R. Journal Excerpt

ISOBEL DRAGGED HER FEET ALONG THE WHARF, SORELY regretting her choice to not eat breakfast with Riot the day before. The city jail hadn't provided any food. As she walked towards her boat, her mind reeled with possibilities. All of them grim.

Alex Kingston had seen her. There was no doubt. Would he connect the dots? Her husband was no fool.

To add salt to the wound, her assumed name was now plastered all over the newspapers. *Disguised as a vagrant.* If William Punt had half a brain, he'd put two and two together. The implications threatened to drown her. Her precarious world was spiraling out of control. Only now, she had others to worry about—a whole heap of people connected to her name.

Frustrated, she turned her mind to the night before. To facts, and the cool comfort of logic. Had Punt disappeared inside *The Drifter*? The side door seemed more likely. But who was that other man (or woman) in the alleyway? And the smoke. At first she'd thought it was a stick of dynamite or a firecracker. But there hadn't been a bang.

Seagulls circled overhead, screeching down at her. She could have sworn they were laughing. Exhausted, she ran her hands over her face, and picked up her pace. Her thoughts turned to a soft berth and a warm blanket.

Her feet were moving of their own accord when she reached the ladder to the *Pagan Lady's* berth. And stopped. The berth was empty. Only drifting rubbish rose and fell with the shifting water.

Her boat was gone.

The realization snapped her awake. She searched the jam of fishing boats, trawlers, and moored yachts, as if the *Lady* had simply decided to float away and call on her neighbors.

A tomcat hopped on a nearby pylon, and calmly began licking his paw. "Where is my boat?" she asked. Watson looked at her. He didn't even have the decency to look ashamed of himself.

"Let me guess, the boat thief bribed you with shrimp?" Surely Riot or Lotario wouldn't have taken her cutter?

Watson flicked his tail.

With a growl of frustration, Isobel raced towards the watchman's tower. She applied her fist to its door, the hinges shuddering under her barrage.

"Mr. Covel!"

A soft snore answered. She swore. The watchman was deep in his cups again—his perpetual state, and the reason the docking fees were so low.

Isobel dragged a rotting crate next to a storage shed, and used it to climb up onto the roof. A gust of wind snatched at her clothes, nearly knocking her off her flimsy perch. Belatedly, she realized she was still wearing the itchy dress from her night in jail. Hoping she wouldn't be committed for hysteria, she stood on the rickety shack and put a hand over her eyes to search the horizon. There. Over an expanse of choppy gray waves, her boat bobbed in the bay. It was adrift. The mainsail was fluttering dangerously, not even half raised. She narrowed her eyes. A small figure moved on deck.

Isobel climbed down, and made for the nearest rowboat. The oars were missing. This day, she thought, could get no worse. So why not? Not caring if anyone saw her, Isobel pulled the dress up and over her ears, tossed it on the wharf, and climbed down the last ladder in nothing but her bloomers.

A frisson of shock traveled through her body. She embraced the cold, let go of the ladder, and began swimming towards her ship. Garbage and clinging rats gave way to fresh sea and white-capped waves that pushed her from all sides. She only cared about her boat, and the miscreant who had dared steal it.

Aided by the current, she reached the *Lady*, gripped a dragging line, and hauled herself over the rail. Soaking wet and fuming, she hopped to her feet to confront the would-be thief.

A slip of a girl struggled with the mainsail, practically hanging from the halyards in an attempt to raise it. Sao Jin let out a scream of frustration.

"I should throw you overboard!" Isobel bellowed into the wind.

The girl turned. Physically she was around the age of ten, but mentally she was somewhere between a wildcat and a shark. A scar ran across her cheek, and another slashed across a jaw that was currently set in abject defiance. Her almond eyes blazed with fury. "Go ahead, *Faan Tung*! Sharks will devour my soul, and the next time you enter the water, I will eat you!"

"That's a mighty big plan for a girl who can't even hoist a sail. Were you planning on bobbing away?"

A string of Cantonese cuss words punctuated each tug on the halyard. "*Yiu!*" Jin let go of the line, and the gaff dropped with a thud. "I hate you, *Faan Tung*!"

"That's *Captain Faan Tung*, to you. You've tangled the lines." Isobel pointed to the top of the mast.

Jin turned red with fury.

"Why are you trying to steal my boat, and why aren't you at the mission?"

"*Sock nika tow!*" Jin snarled, and stomped below deck. Definitely a wildcat.

The padlock to the hatch had been unlocked. That girl and her lock picks. Sounds of fury beat from the cabin. Something shattered against the hull, and Isobel looked heavenward. Things had gotten worse.

A book flew through the open hatch, smacking against the tiller. "I hate this country! I hate the mission! I hate the girls!" A drawer of pots and utensils crashed on the cabin floor.

Isobel secured the mainsail, and checked the horizon. Assured that they weren't in imminent danger of running into something, she climbed into the wildcat's lair. A fork flew at her face.

Isobel ducked under the missile, and glared at the girl. Sao Jin had the decency to pause, a knife poised in her trembling hand. Instead of throwing it, she dropped it.

"What's gotten you in a rage?" Isobel asked. She tried to

keep her voice calm, but she was one step away from tying the girl to the bowsprit.

"*You!*" Jin growled, and went back to her carnage.

Isobel watched the girl rage back and forth across the saloon, wreaking havoc on her belongings. Anger turned to puzzlement. Jin was trying to provoke her on purpose. Why? She eyed the scars that crisscrossed the girl's face. The only attention Jin had ever known was cruelty. She wanted to be heard, to be noticed—she just didn't know how else to go about it.

Resigned to let the girl rage herself into exhaustion, Isobel quickly shed her bloomers, and pulled on a pair of trousers. A sweater followed, but as she reached for her peacoat Sao Jin screeched an unforgivable insult. "I hate this stupid boat!"

The echo rang in Isobel's ears. Calmly, she shrugged on her coat, and climbed the companionway ladder. She shut the hatch.

Footsteps marched up the ladder, and then angry knocking. "Let me out, *Faan Tung!*"

"Sorry, Jin. I'm worthless. I can't figure out how to open it!" Isobel called pleasantly back.

A loud kick shuddered on wood.

Isobel took a deep breath of sea and wind, and turned her gaze to the choppy gray horizon. She ran a hand over the *Pagan Lady's* cabin top. "I apologize for her rudeness."

As the wildcat raged below, Isobel scurried up the mast loops. She clung to the top, unwinding the tangled lines as the *Lady* swayed and rocked beneath her. The horizon heaved, but she paid it little mind. Even exhausted, it was second nature to her.

Satisfied, she climbed down, and moved forward to

unfurl the jib. Wind filled the voluminous sail, pushing the cutter farther into the chop.

The noise below stopped. Only the wind touched her ears now. Isobel unlocked the padlock, and opened the hatch. Sao Jin stomped on deck fuming. But whatever insult she was about to hurl died on her lips. The wind knocked her back a step, and her eyes widened.

Isobel cinched the tiller, and moved to the mainsail. She braced herself and pulled on the halyards, hoisting the sail. Her leg gave protest and she channeled the pain, heaving with every inch of her five-foot frame. "You can insult me, Jin." Heave and pull. "You can ruin my cabin, but you will *never* disrespect the *Lady*."

"Go to hell!" Jin spat.

Red sail filled the sky. Isobel dropped into the cockpit, tightening the mainsheet. The sail snapped taut, the *Lady* heeled sharply, and Jin scrambled to grab a railing as the deck tilted.

"I plan on taking you there!" Isobel yelled over the wind. "And I guarantee you will never say another ill word about my *Lady*." The cutter dipped, and the bowsprit crashed through a white-capped wave. Icy water drenched Jin, and all her fury washed away as she looked to the cold gray sea. The sea was in a mood, and so was Isobel.

16

AN AVERAGE MAN

My required use of a walking stick is an irritation more acute than the pain itself. With every limping step, I am reminded that my body—this shell—is deteriorating around my mind. —Z.R. Journal Excerpt

HULLS KNOCKED TOGETHER, AND THE WIND PICKED UP, bringing scents of rubbish and dead fish with an underlying seasoning of salt. Sarah wrinkled her nose at the water.

"The ocean is much prettier by Ocean Beach," she noted.

Riot didn't answer. His gaze was on the empty berth and its absent boat. He clutched his walking stick, swallowing down an irrational thought: Isobel had bolted. Her arrest was worrisome in more ways than one. *Beaten.* Although the newspapers were prone to exaggeration, that word stuck in his mind. He well knew how stubborn she could be. Isobel could have a knife in her gut and insist that she was fine.

San Francisco Bay was rough, and farther out a strong wind whipped up crests of white. This was no day for a casual sail on the bay. No, something had driven her out to sea.

"Doesn't look like much of a day for sailing," Sarah said, with a tremulous note in her voice.

"For the captain of this particular vessel it might be. It's *Mister* Morgan's boat."

"Oh." No more needed saying. Sarah knew more about Mr. Morgan and Charlotte Bonnie than was good for her. "Which boat is it?"

"The boat is gone." He consulted his watch.

"Did Jin go with he—him?" Sarah stumbled over the pronoun, but got it right in the end.

"That is an excellent question." Something caught his eye at the end of the wharf.

Riot hurried over to an orange lump atop a bed of wool. "Watson." There was an accusatory tone in his voice. As if it were the cat's fault that Isobel was missing.

The cat cracked an eye open, flicked his tail, and went back to sleep.

"Is that Mr. Morgan's cat?"

"Yes." Riot crouched, and scratched the cat between the ears. A purr rumbled from the big tom.

"I suppose that means Mr. Morgan is coming back?"

"I hope so." He tried to pick Watson up, but a low growl, a swipe of claws, and a warning hiss made Riot snatch away his hand. "Oh, come now, Watson. I just want a look at your bed."

Luminous eyes narrowed. Riot tried to get back in Watson's good graces with another head scratch, but was stopped short by a fresh rake of claws.

"He's not very friendly, is he?"

"You don't happen to have some food with you?"

"Actually…" Sarah opened her basket, and pulled out a freshly baked lemon square she had secreted away during lunch. She started to hand it over, and stopped. With a decisive click, she closed her basket, walked around the cat, grabbed the gray wool and yanked. Watson yowled with indignation as he was rolled to the side. Four sets of claws dug into wood. His hackles raised and he fluffed to double his size. Sarah ignored his low growl and handed the garment to Riot.

"Careful, Watson, she's not near as polite as I am." Riot's warning seemed to get through to the feline. Midway through a growl, it turned to a purr, and Watson began threading himself between Riot's legs, leaving orange hairs on his tailored trousers.

Sarah laughed. "I think he wants his bed back."

Riot shook out *his bed*.

"I'm surprised someone didn't at least make rags out of that. It's a waste to toss away good wool."

"It's a prison dress." Riot turned on his heel and stalked to the watchman's tower. The silver knob of his stick shuddered the wood. A snore stopped short, and footsteps stumbled to the door. It cracked opened, and a squinty eye peeked out. "What's this?" the watchman demanded.

Seeing the watchman's lack of attire, Riot stepped squarely in front of the door, blocking Sarah's view. "The *Pagan Lady*. Where is she?"

"I dunno." Mr. Covel started to exit his shack, saw Sarah, and quickly snatched a long coat. He stuffed himself into it and padded out on bare feet. "Well, looks like she's gone."

Sarah rolled her eyes.

"It does appear so, doesn't it? Do you happen to know where the captain of the vessel took her?"

"I don't rightly know." Mr. Covel picked at his teeth. "Capt'n Morgan is always comin' and goin'. He specified to me that he didn't want to be bothered. So I don't bother him. I told that other fellow what come by that he shouldn't bother him either. I'll tell you the same."

"What *other* fellow?"

Mr. Covel rubbed at a spot on his forehead. "Did you not hear the part about botherin'?"

Riot smiled. "I did, as a matter of fact. But my daughter and I chartered the *Pagan Lady* for the day. Captain Morgan was supposed to meet us here."

Mr. Covel glanced at Sarah, who looked as innocent as could be.

She folded her hands in front of her. "I really wanted to go sailing, Pa."

"There you have it," Riot said. "A disappointed young lady."

"'Ave you seen the weather today?"

It was trying to tear Riot's fedora from his head. He pulled down the brim, and smiled at the man. "You once told me that Captain Morgan could handle a cutter in any weather."

"I did?"

"Yes. The last time I chartered this boat."

"I suppose I did. But I'm sorry, I don't know where he mighta sailed off to in weather like this."

"This *other* man you mentioned? Did he sail away with Captain Morgan?"

"Oh, no. No, that fella come by this morning. The *Lady* was still in her berth. I can guarantee you that."

"What did this fellow look like?"

"Average."

"Average?"

"Sure, like any other fella." The watchman shrugged. "Brown hair, mustache, longish chops, square jaw, black suit.

We menfolk don't come in so many varieties. Not like the womenfolk."

"Was it a bespoke suit?"

"No, it didn't say nothin'. Why the hel—blazes would it?"

"Tailored. Was it well made?"

"I don't know."

"Did he leave a name?" Sarah asked.

"If he did, I don't recall it." Mr. Covel snapped his fingers. "Smith. His name was Smith."

The most common name in the United States, and the one generally adopted by anyone who didn't want his name known.

"Did he ask any questions?"

"He asked me if Captain Morgan was expected back. I said I don't know. Then he asked if the Captain ever entertained ladies aboard. And I says that yes, he has a sister—nothing at all improper there." Mr. Covel gave Sarah a pointed look.

"Did he leave a calling card so you might hand it off to Captain Morgan?"

"No, he just wandered away."

17

WILD CHANT

Jones Jr. was in fact rescuing slave girls from Chinatown. But only to ease his conscience. While not directly involved with the brutality, he certainly was profiting from it. —Z.R. Journal Excerpt

THE WORLD HOWLED, AND ISOBEL KINGSTON HOWLED RIGHT back at it. Sharp wind beat against her face, stinging her cheeks. She squinted through the sea spray, gauging her speed as the *Lady* sliced across the bay. The bowsprit dipped, and reared upwards, tossing seawater over the deck.

"You are *crazy!*" Sao Jin shouted. The rope that Isobel had tied around the girl's waist was the only thing keeping her in place. A roar of water silenced Jin's next insult, and she braced herself in the slanted cockpit like a cat over a sink.

The wind had caught the *Lady's* sails and wouldn't let go. Isobel tightened her grip on the tiller. Endless. Relentless. Merciless. All the power of man and beast amounted to a pinch of dust compared to the force of nature. It echoed her life. Isobel steered true.

Jin shivered, her teeth chattered, and fear widened her

eyes. "I am sorry I took your boat!" The wind snatched the words from the girl's lips, but Isobel caught the gist of her sentiment.

"Why are you sorry?" she hollered back. "Isn't this what you wanted? Can't you feel it? *This* is fury." Isobel showed her teeth at the girl—a wide grin full of life. "You want to rage, Jin? Here's where to do it! Add your weight to the rail, hold on, and join its fury."

Jin looked over her shoulder, up the heeled deck, to a rail that nearly touched the blue sky.

Isobel began chanting a wild song into the wind, a song of the Azores—her mother's people. "High are the waves, fierce, gleaming. High is the tempest roar! High the seabird screaming! High the Azore!" The ancient words rose and fell with the crashing sea.

Jin clenched her jaw, pulled herself up to sit on the side of the rail, balancing precariously on the edge with legs dangling over air. With the wind snatching at her braid and clothes, she screamed until she went hoarse.

As the sun dropped, so did the wind. And soon the *Lady* glided into a sheltered cove near a cliffside. Bone-weary and soaked, Isobel could no longer feel her fingers. The cold, and two nights without sleep and little food had taken their toll.

"We'll anchor here," she croaked. "Will you help me with the mainsail?"

"Yes, Captain."

Working silently, they furled the mainsail and tied it in place. Jin dropped the anchor when ordered to, and Isobel lashed the tiller, then took one last look at the shoreline. The sun had fallen, and the moon was glowing. A light breeze was rustling through the leaves of a nearby Eucalyptus grove. Isobel climbed below deck, and eyed the chaos in her cabin.

"I will clean this," Jin said to her back.

"Don't worry about it tonight. It's nothing a good storm wouldn't have done."

"That *was* a storm." Jin's teeth chattered so violently that her words were slurred.

Isobel chuckled, as she crouched in front of the Ship-mate stove. "No, that was just a bit of wind." Although her back was to the girl, she could feel her gawk. "There's a saying—if you can sail San Francisco Bay, you can sail anywhere." She glanced over her shoulder. "I grew up sailing these waters, and outside the Golden Gate, too. That wasn't a storm."

Jin picked up a pot, and placed it back on its hook. "Father used to carry me on his shoulders. He always bought me balloons from the toy merchant, and we would go to see the ocean. But mother never let me near the water." Her voice was faint, cracked from wind and emotion.

"The waves at Ocean Beach are treacherous." Isobel tried to keep her voice casual. She didn't want to press the girl. If she backed Jin into a corner, she'd bite. "How often did your parents take you there?"

Jin picked up a book, and held it in both hands, as if it held the answer. "It doesn't matter." She shoved the book back into the chest.

"Leave the mess until you get warm. A crew with pneumonia isn't much help. There's dry clothes under the berth bunk. Grab a fresh set for me, too."

Jin didn't argue. As the girl pulled out clothing, Isobel busied herself with lighting the fire. She scrubbed her hands on her trousers, and debated heating water, but in the end the only thing she wanted was sleep. And to eat. Besides, the ocean had practically washed her clean.

She glanced at the brass kettle, and saw Jin's reflection. The girl was folding a pile of clothes. She set the pile on Isobel's berth, and then pulled off her soaked jacket and tunic. Isobel's breath caught. All muscle and bone, the girl's thin back was puckered with angry scars—round burns and long lashes.

A muscle in Isobel's jaw twitched. She could not take the girl's past away, but she could give her warmth. The wood caught, and she closed the stove door.

Isobel peeled off her own damp clothes, hung them to dry, and turned to the galley. Out of the corner of her eye, she watched Jin working to clean the saloon. The girl was stubborn, and an efficient worker. Quick and thorough—so unlike any child Isobel had ever encountered. But then the scars crisscrossing the child's body were a stark reminder that efficiency had been beaten into her. Sao Jin had been *Mui Tsai*—a house slave. Too young for brothels, she had been sold to a cruel woman.

Isobel rummaged through the ship's stores. She sighed at the meager pickings. In the end, she gathered enough cheese, jerky, and apples for two. Sinking into her berth, she gulped down a jug of water, and applied herself to eating.

After awhile, Jin sat across from her, toying with a beaded bracelet, turning it over and over on her thin wrist. The string was frayed and stained, the beads blackened by time. Her gaze was far away.

"Eat, Jin. We still have to sail back in the morning."

The reminder seemed to snap the girl out of wherever she had been. Jin picked up the plate, and did as she was told, but it was more out of habit than want.

When the child had eaten every crumb, Isobel cleared

their plates and set them in the small galley sink. "Why did you leave the mission?"

Only the lap of waves and the gentle shift of rigging answered. Finally Jin spoke, her voice hoarse and low. "Mei is going back to China."

"I thought she was planning on taking you, too."

"I don't want to go."

"Why not?"

"This is my home. I'm American like you."

"You were born here?"

Jin nodded.

Only two years before, the Supreme Court had decided the fourteenth amendment did, in fact, apply to Chinese. Jin was right, she was American.

"If I go to China with Mei, I will be a slave."

"Mei cares for you. She won't make you a house slave."

"Her father will marry her off to a rich man. Even if I am treated like a daughter, I will be married off when I am older, too."

Isobel sighed. In China, Britain, Japan, and in most of the world, there weren't many choices for women. And those choices were shaved even further for a Chinese woman. California was Jin's best chance.

"Then stay at the mission."

"No." Jin tucked her legs on the berth, and curled against the pillow. She swam in the oversized sweater and long johns. "A doctor tried to poke me with a needle. I did not want the medicine."

Isobel frowned. "What did they try to give you?"

"Halfkeen."

"Haffkine," Isobel corrected. "It's a vaccine to help protect you from bubonic plague."

Jin crossed her arms. "I did not want it, so I climbed out the window."

"And tried to steal my boat. Where were you planning on sailing?"

"Away," Jin said quietly. "I am sorry, Captain. I will not do it again."

"Just don't insult her. All right?" Isobel ran her fingers over the sleek wood. "She's a special lady."

"It is only a boat."

"To you maybe, but not to me. This is *my* home."

Jin cocked her head and gently touched the hull.

"Will you go back to the mission if I have Riot talk with Miss Cameron?"

The girl's shoulders tensed. "I do not want to go back."

"Do you have any family?"

Jin gave a jerk of her head.

Isobel ran a hand through shaggy hair. It needed another cut, but she had been putting it off. Delaying the inevitable. With that thought, she decided to take the approach she was best suited for—a blunt one. "Miss Cameron told Riot that you came to the mission some years before. But a woman came with the police and took you away. She said she was your aunt. Was she?"

"No."

"Who was she?"

Jin shook her head. The girl's fingers went back to her bracelet, twisting the beaded string around and around. She wouldn't look at Isobel.

"What happened to your parents?"

Jin's nostrils flared. And her head snapped up. Her lips were a thin line, and her eyes blazed. "Why do you care? You have a home." She turned, hugged her knees to her chest, and curled into a tight ball. Her body shook with cold.

Isobel wished Riot were there. She was no good with distraught children, or distraught adults for that matter. She watched the girl's back, willing her to speak. But Jin remained tight-lipped. After awhile, Isobel pulled a spare blanket from storage and laid it over the girl. Bone-weary, she retreated to her own berth and fell onto it. For tonight at least, they were both free.

18

THE GIFT

A pattern emerged. Easily recognized once observed. —*Z.R. Journal Excerpt*

Wednesday, March 21, 1900

INFORMANTS WERE A DOUBLE-EDGED SWORD. IT MEANT RIOT could use Tim's contacts in the Coast Guard to inquire after a red-masted cutter, but it also meant someone else could find the *Pagan Lady*. That someone had known enough to ask after the cutter, and even more alarming was the inquiry about Captain Morgan's 'lady friends'.

Riot could think of a number of possibilities, some mundane and others not. Either way, all those theories pricked his instincts.

These instincts had sent him once again to the Folsom Street Pier. He sat against the cabin wall of a steam trawler shuffling his preferred deck. His movements weren't smooth. With his index and middle fingers bandaged, he found it hard going. But he managed. It helped distract him from the knot between his shoulders.

"So…we just sittin' here?" Tobias White asked at his

side. The boy drummed his heels against a crate in the universal tune of a bored child.

"I do not recall inviting you along, Tobias." The child had followed him from Ravenwood Manor. While his execution had not been skillful, Riot admired his determination.

Tobias artfully ignored his observation. "I thought we were gonna do something exciting."

"I am."

"What's that?"

"I'm thinking."

The boy looked to the fluttering cards. "Do you want to play Old Maid?"

"I don't recommend playing cards with me."

Tobias rolled his eyes, and hunched down into his coat.

Blue skies and a brisk breeze made for crisp air. Fishermen and crabbers tended to nets and traps on the dock, while junks and swift Feluccas with raked sails headed out to deeper waters. It was an excellent day for sailing. But Riot barely glanced at the waters. Leaning against the cabin wall, legs crossed, his gaze was fixed on the docks.

After awhile, Tobias' tongue became restless. "Is this your boat?"

"It is not."

The boy squirmed on the crate beside him. "You *stealin'* it?" The question was close to a stage whisper.

"Only using it to think."

"What if the owner catches us here?"

"Then we'll politely tip our hats and leave."

"Maybe that works for you. It don't work for me."

"Why's that?"

"I don't have a fancy suit."

"Would you keep a suit clean?"

Tobias thought about this for a time. "I'd do my best."

Riot looked down at Watson. The big Tomcat was using his leg as a rubbing post, and leaving white and orange hairs all over the dark fabric. "I rarely manage to keep my own suits clean. Would you like a job?"

"Yes, sir."

"Hunker down in the bow and watch for a gaff-rigged cutter with crimson sails."

"I *knew* we were waiting for Miss Bonnie."

"Captain Morgan," Riot corrected.

"Are you sweet on her?"

Riot glanced at the boy. "What do you think?"

Tobias White flashed his teeth. "I figured." Without another word, he bolted to the front of the boat, leaving Riot with his thoughts.

In under an hour, Tobias thudded back with a sighting. The *Lady* was on a direct course for her berth. Riot watched the wharf, but no one appeared to be interested in the cutter.

As the *Pagan Lady* drifted closer, the knot between his shoulder blades eased. Riot could see Isobel moving over the deck. The mainsail dropped, and she and a smaller figure began working to furl the sail. Just when he thought the boat would collide with the wharf, Isobel dropped into the cockpit and gripped the tiller. The cutter turned, and glided gently to a stop alongside the dock.

"Impressive, Captain," Riot called. Isobel was in her Captain Morgan guise: cap, peacoat and duckcloth trousers. As he had suspected, the runaway Sao Jin was with her.

"Ahoy, there," Isobel called.

"Before you drop anchor, I was hoping to charter your services."

The two sailors looked beaten around the edges, but

Isobel caught the underlying message. "Jin, climb up and hold the line for our guests."

"Yes, Captain."

At the honorific, without spite or anger, Riot raised his brows. The girl looked as though she had survived a squall. Given the wind yesterday and Isobel's haggard appearance, perhaps that wasn't far from the truth. Jin wrapped the line around a pylon, and held it fast.

"Come aboard," Isobel called. As if the invitation were for him alone, Watson trotted past Riot, and jumped from dock to boat.

Riot started to climb down the ladder, and Tobias stopped him with a hiss. "You sure it's safe?" The boy eyed the weathered boat dripping with ocean water.

"You don't have to accompany me, Tobias."

"I *can't* swim."

"Neither can I."

"Aren't you supposed to reassure me—you being an adult and everything?"

"I don't lie to reassure."

Tobias blew out a breath.

Jin started making chicken noises at the boy. Not to be outdone by a girl, Tobias quickly scrambled down. The moment his feet touched the bobbing deck, he threw himself into the cockpit, and clung to a line.

"Cast off, Jin." There was a tiredness to Isobel that made Riot want to take her straight back to his home and pour her a hot bath, but she was not a woman to be coddled. "Where to?" she asked.

"Hospital Cove."

Jin hopped back aboard, and Riot moved to help Isobel with the jib. As they worked, he kept his gaze on the docks.

"Trouble?" she asked under her breath.

"A man was asking after you yesterday while the *Lady* was still in her berth."

She muttered an oath. "I suppose you saw the newspaper?"

"I did. Tim filled me in on the rest." Their eyes touched, and he held her gaze; the weight of events sat between them.

"Did you wait for me all night?"

"That's awfully egotistical. Even for you, Bel."

She snorted.

When the jib had caught the wind, Isobel and Riot stepped into the cockpit. Tobias was trying to get Jin to give up the tiller, but the girl wouldn't budge.

"Tobias, leave her be. Keep a northeasterly course, Jin. We're heading to Angel Island."

"Yes, Captain."

Isobel looked at Tobias. "And you, young man—don't leave this cockpit."

"I'm not going anywhere."

"Good, because if you even *think* about it, I'll turn you into a rigging monkey and send you aloft."

The boy's gaze traveled upwards, then farther still to the top of the mast. He looked like he might be sick.

"Keep your eyes on the horizon. I don't want to mop up your breakfast."

Leaving the two on deck, Isobel climbed down the companionway. Her movements were stiff, and she held herself just so. Riot shut the hatch behind him.

She squared her shoulders. "What did this fellow look like?"

"Average."

"Average?"

"That's precisely what I asked Mr. Covel."

"He's not very helpful," she admitted.

"How badly did those policemen rough you up?" he asked.

"Just a few more bruises for my collection." Her eyes flickered to the side, a moment of hesitation. "It was more the cage that got to me. I don't much like the idea of going back there." For a moment, she stood utterly vulnerable, completely stripped. There was a plea in her eyes that he had seen in men who'd rather be shot than go to prison.

Something had shaken her. Something had changed.

"What happened in the alley? Tim said someone else was there."

She ran a hand through her hair. "I don't know. I keep going over the sequence of events. There was smoke, and then someone ran past me."

"Woodsmoke? Gunpowder? Chemical?"

She shook her head. "I'd say it was some kind of fire-cracker."

"Was there a sound?"

Color spread over her cheeks. "I was so focused on escaping that I'm not sure my ears were working."

Riot nodded. "Not uncommon. For a good many years, whenever I was in a gunfight noises fell away and my sight narrowed to a tunnel. I couldn't even hear the gunshots."

She cocked her head. "And now?"

He lifted a brow, a kind of shrug. "I've become accustomed to men trying to kill me." But he'd never get accustomed to Isobel being in danger. "Considering the events in the alleyway and the newspaper article, Parker Gray and his lot may have found you."

Isobel slumped on the berth bunk and rested her head in her hands. "Remember, Riot, I usually do at *least* three reckless things per day." Her voice was muffled by her hands.

Shaggy hair curled over the nape of her neck. He placed his fingers over that spot, and when she relaxed, he sat down beside her. "Do you mean to say that entering a notorious criminal den and picking a fight wasn't the *only* reckless thing you've done since I last saw you?" He tried to keep his voice light, but failed.

She glanced over at him. "Alex saw me at the inquest."

Another man might have asked, 'Are you sure?' But Riot knew better. He trusted her instincts as much as he trusted his own.

Her answer shed light on his concerns. That's what had changed—that was why she looked hunted. "And it spooked you," he observed.

"Something like that."

"Kingston knows about the *Pagan Lady* from the police report I filed after Curtis's death. So the 'average' man asking questions yesterday might have been one of Parker Gray's men or a detective working for Kingston."

She'd winced at her brother's name, and now quickly stood. "You need to keep as far away from me as you can—"

"We've been through this already, Bel."

"Yes, but it's only a matter of time before I'm cornered."

"Do you plan on leaving California?"

Isobel stopped in her pacing tracks. "I…" She hugged herself, looking lost, and then her mood shifted like the sea. "Damn you, Riot. Don't you have anything better to do? *One* man asks about me at the docks, and you spend all night lying in wait for me." But her anger sounded tired rather than genuine, an old armor she reached for in distress.

Unruffled, he shifted with her mood. "On the contrary, I had a pleasant visit with Tobias, and it gave me a chance to take in the fresh air."

"Fish gut-filled air," she growled.

"I didn't wait all night, Bel," he said gently. "I only went to the docks after I received word from the harbor patrol that the *Lady* was spotted sailing back to San Francisco."

She clenched her jaw. "You need to stop worrying about me. I tend to disappear for days on end."

"Approximately when should I start worrying?"

"Never."

He crossed his legs. "I would hope that if I disappeared, you'd come and rescue me sooner than that."

Isobel relented. "Three days."

"That's nine reckless things later. Your trail will grow cold, and you could very well be dead."

"You found me before."

"A near thing."

"You like a challenge. Why else would you love me?"

"How could I *not* love you?" he returned softly.

"You've had me every which way. You can turn off the charm now."

"I'm afraid it's chronic where you're concerned."

The comment softened her edges. "*Three* days," she stressed. "And then you can put on your deerstalker and come rescue me."

His eyes danced. "That is one hat I do not own."

Isobel studied him for a moment. "They're not very flattering," she agreed. "You know it's damn annoying when you don't yell back. It makes me feel a fool."

"You're between a rock and a hard place. Sometimes anger is a good thing. So is talking."

Isobel slumped, defeated. He wished for all the world that she had held on to that rage. "When I see him…Alex… I slip back into the role I played—the simpering society wife. I hate that. I hate him. I *hate* myself for failing."

Riot stood and took her hands. "Is the game over yet?"

She looked up into his eyes. "No, but the stakes don't involve just me anymore."

Riot drew her into an embrace, and buried his fingers in her hair. "We'll manage," he whispered. "At worst I'll return the offer that you made to me and break you out of jail."

He felt her smile against his neck. "You probably have more experience with jail breaks," she murmured.

"As a matter of fact, I do. But not nearly as much as Tim."

She pulled away. "Is there anything you haven't done?"

"I haven't married you."

"You're mad, Riot."

The edge of his lip quirked. "You can commit me after we're married. For future reference, I was rather taken with Bright Waters Asylum."

Isobel gave a bitter laugh. "I'm sure Alex will be happy to commit *me*." There was something in her voice, some urgent fear. That note gripped his heart. What precarious positions they were in. Yet another problem, another tangle, with no way out. He kissed her temple.

"You've solved another one of my cases," he murmured.

This piqued her interest. "Oh?"

"Jin. Miss Cameron asked me to find her."

Isobel glanced towards the hatch. Her gaze turned inward, as if she could see the *Lady's* course from inside the boat's belly. Satisfied that they weren't in imminent danger, she focused on him. "After Tim bailed me out, I came here wanting to sleep and found my boat gone."

"Jin stole the *Lady*, but didn't get far, so you shed your dress and swam to the boat," he finished the rest.

She nodded in confirmation.

"I'm surprised you didn't toss her overboard."

"The thought *did* cross my mind," she admitted.

"The two of you appear to have worked things out."

Isobel sat on the settee and surveyed her cabin. The lantern swung lightly on its rope, and a tin cup slid back and forth on the table. The saloon appeared to have been recently cleaned. "More or less, after she screamed herself hoarse. But I'm not sure if her newfound respect for me is sincere. She may be angling for something."

"You sound like you did your share of screaming as well."

"I like to holler at the wind. It's good for the soul."

"Did Jin tell you what upset her?"

"Mei is leaving for China in the next few months."

"She's made no secret of it."

"And then the mission tried to force Jin to take the Haffkine vaccine. It was the match that lit her keg. Between you and me, I would have climbed out of the window, too."

"Will she return to the mission?"

"I don't know, Riot. I haven't gotten that far with her yet."

"Miss Cameron suggested that I take my time in returning her. Jin is the worst girl she's ever had. That's saying something."

"Well, the child isn't my concern." As if to emphasize that sentiment, she scrubbed her hands along her thighs. "Why are we going to Angel Island?"

"I have a present for you."

"Oh?"

"Lincoln Howe."

Gray eyes lit with excitement. "By God, I love you, Riot."

19

HOSPITAL COVE

Lumber shipments. Mundane, yet carefully guarded. Another set of lists: Girls bought and sold, opium, gambling proceeds. Also mundane. —Z.R. *Journal Excerpt*

THE SEA HAD SPENT ITS FURY, THE FOG HAD ROLLED AWAY, and the sky celebrated with a burst of blue. The *Pagan Lady* glided from Raccoon Strait into the protected cove of Angel Island. A decommissioned warship, the USS *Omaha*, was moored in the cove. Her masts had been cropped and a large covered structure added to her deck. Isobel frowned at the wooden-screw sloop.

"Think of where she's been," she said softly, for his ears alone. "And now she's chained to the ocean floor."

Riot felt her shudder.

Detention barracks, a disinfection plant, laboratories, and barracks for staff huddled around Hospital Cove. Two small cottages stood higher up on a climbing hillside, nestled amid oak, madrone, and eucalyptus. With calm blue-green waters surrounded by trees swaying in the breeze, the cove might have been a perfect retreat—a vacation resort a mere ferry ride away. But a dilapidated wharf ruined the effect.

As they neared, Riot spotted a cluster of immigrants disembarking from a steamer. They were loaded down with all their worldly possessions, shivering in the cold, and being herded together by officers barking at them in a strange tongue.

Isobel dropped the mainsail, and guided the *Lady* towards a floating dock off to the side of the larger wharf. Jin hopped from boat to dock, and caught the moor lines.

A blue-uniformed health officer hurried down a ladder. "You can't anchor here. This is a quarantine station," he called.

Riot stepped from rail to dock. "I have business here."

"What's your business?"

"I'm here to see Dr. Kinyoun."

"I'm afraid he's busy."

Riot handed over his card. "I'm a patient man. I can wait."

The officer scrutinized his calling card. Thick paper and the embossed raven on the front always seemed to make an impression, or perhaps it was the grandiose name—Zephaniah Ravenwood was a name demanding respect. "You're not a reporter?" He eyed Riot's tailored suit, and then his hip, looking for a weapon. But Riot wore his revolver in a shoulder holster.

"Have you had trouble with reporters?" Riot asked.

"With the plague outbreak and the resulting backlash, yes. All kinds. Death threats even. You name it."

"Hence your assigned guard duty."

"That's right."

Riot turned to appreciate the view. "Dismal duty."

Despite his heavy wool coat, the younger man shivered. "It looks beautiful, but it's desolate."

Riot looked to the cluster of shivering immigrants. They would be soaked with disinfectant and left to wait in the cold. He bit his tongue, not mentioning that part, and put on an amiable face. "It's warm in the saloon if you'd like to come aboard."

"I'm afraid I can't, Mr. Riot."

"I didn't get your name, Officer."

"Cummings. Nicholas Cummings."

Riot shook his hand. "I'll wait here until you hand my card over to Dr. Kinyoun. He'll be eager to speak with me."

"Why is that?"

"I'm here about a missing officer of yours."

"Missing?"

"Lincoln Howe."

"I'm afraid I don't know him."

"That's why I need to speak with Dr. Kinyoun. As you said, death threats and backlash. A man's life is in danger." It was the truth.

"I feel like that every single day. I keep telling myself to head somewhere warmer before this weather kills me. It isn't the most pleasant post." Cummings gave a nervous chuckle. "Well, Dr. Kinyoun will be angrier if I turn away someone he'd like to see, so you might as well come along." He spoke more to himself than to Riot, as if he needed to reaffirm his decision.

"Thank you, Mr. Cummings. I'd like to bring my associate as well."

Without asking permission, Isobel climbed over the rail.

"Oh, right then. Can't hurt."

Watson crouched, tail flicking, preparing to jump. Isobel thrust a finger at the cat. "Watch those two."

As if it were his idea, Watson sat down and casually turned his head towards the children. He narrowed his eyes and flicked his tail.

Riot looked at the children. "Do not leave this boat." But their eager nods did nothing to reassure him. Before Riot could climb the ladder to the wharf, Isobel beat him to it, shooting upwards with all the speed of a rigging monkey.

He followed at a more decorous pace, and when he neared the top, she offered a hand. "Careful, sir." He gripped her hand, and let her pull him up onto the wharf. With her cap, thick coat, and hoarse voice, Isobel's male guise would convince all but the extremely observant.

As Cummings led them away from the wharf, he glanced longingly at the wooden structure with smoke billowing from its chimney. The road was thick with mud and it spattered Riot's trousers. At least, he thought, the mud will cover the cat hair. Cummings showed them into a sterile hallway. Their footsteps echoed in emptiness.

"Just this way."

Dr. Kinyoun's office was orderly and neat, its walls decorated with diplomas and awards. As they waited, Isobel studied the plaques. His achievements were taking up considerable space.

"Ravenwood mentioned a Dr. Kinyoun in his journals," she said.

"I seem to remember him critiquing one of the doctor's papers."

"He certainly appears qualified."

Riot chuckled.

"What?" Isobel asked.

"A remark Ravenwood once made. He called displays like this 'framed egos'."

Isobel smiled. "Did Ravenwood frame his egos?"

Riot shook his head. "He liked to frame particularly vehement letters written to him in response to his critiques on an expert's field of study."

"Isn't that nearly the same?"

"When I asked the same question, his reply was 'I never said there was anything wrong with an ego.'"

Isobel's eyes sharpened on him. That gaze seemed to go right through his flesh, down to his bones, and even into his thoughts. "Did Ravenwood just remind you of all that?"

"No. Only memories."

She nodded.

The door opened, and Joseph Kinyoun managed to scowl at both of them simultaneously. He quickly discounted Isobel, and focused on Riot. Portly and balding, he had a cleft chin and a jaw set in defiance. "I suppose you're here to 'debunk' my findings. It *is* bubonic plague. It's clear as day and I'll not say otherwise. I'm an expert in this field of study. I *know* plague when I see it."

Ego at its finest, Riot thought. Ravenwood was usually right. He didn't say anything. The man seemed happy to talk.

"I have all my findings here. All the records." One after another, Kinyoun slapped the reports down. "And I used carbon paper, so don't think about destroying these for your precious merchants and paid-off politicians."

Riot flipped through the files. "I'm afraid I wouldn't know what I'm looking for."

Kinyoun curled his fist. "So they don't even send a man who knows what he's looking at. That's what's wrong with San Francisco. They don't understand the danger. Ignorance is rampant. All they care about is their money. *Lives* are at stake, and they send me some idiot gun-for-hire who likely only knows his way around a barroom."

"I believe you corresponded with my partner, Zephaniah Ravenwood."

Dr. Kinyoun's forehead creased. "I remember Ravenwood."

Riot tapped his walking stick. "An opinionated man, to be sure."

Kinyoun grunted. "Intelligent. Misguided. Pompous."

"I worked with him for twenty years," Riot said.

"You poor man. Where is the old Scrooge?"

"He was murdered three years ago."

Dr. Kinyoun moved to straighten one of his framed diplomas. "I can't say I'm surprised and I'm not especially sorry, but it's always a shame to lose a man of science. Cummings said you're here about a missing officer?"

"Lincoln Howe. I'm told he went missing this month."

Kinyoun stared at him blankly. "*This* month? No, long before that. I was supposed to meet him back in January. In a correspondence, he told me he was arriving on the SS *Australia* from Honolulu, but he didn't keep our appointment. I made some inquiries, but the police didn't seem concerned."

"Is he an officer?

"A bacteriologist. He was assigned to the City Health Department in San Francisco. During the plague outbreak in Honolulu, I'd sent inquires hoping to acquire samples of the bacillus. When I heard Mr. Howe was coming to San Francisco, I made arrangements to meet him. The police insinuated that perhaps he was simply avoiding me."

"Do you happen to have a photograph of him?"

Kinyoun rolled his eyes. "Do you keep a photograph of every half-baked detective with a card?"

"It never hurts to ask."

"What University did he attend?" Isobel cut in.

"London University," Kinyoun bit back. "If both of you will excuse me. I have immigrants waiting for my inspection."

"One more question, Doctor."

Kinyoun wiped a handkerchief across his brow. "*Yes,* the plague is real."

Riot gave the man a self-deprecating smile. "I'm hardly the scientist that my partner was, but I'd like to see some of your work."

"If I showed every naysayer my work, I'd never get any done."

Riot folded his hands over his walking stick.

"I could always have a guard escort you off this island," Kinyoun added.

"You could do that. But you'd be perpetuating a plague of ignorance. I'd like to leave this isle with a pinch of enlightenment."

"I see you possess more charm than your late partner."

"That's why he kept me around, Doctor."

Impatiently, Kinyoun gestured at them to follow.

"Even *he* thinks you're charming," Isobel said under her breath as they were led out of the building. More roads of mud and cold, then Kinyoun ordered them to wipe their feet at a doorstep. Shoes cleaned, they walked down a lifeless corridor. He stopped at a door that had bold words painted on it: Keep Out.

The doctor looked to each of them in turn. "Don't touch *anything.*"

Kinyoun stepped inside. As Isobel passed the threshold, she ran her hand up and down the door jamb. Riot cleared his throat. He didn't dare meet her dancing eyes.

Kinyoun had gone straight for a microscope.

Riot was no scientist, but he had spent enough time with

Ravenwood to know what was what in a laboratory. Beakers, glass tubes, Bunsen burners, microscopes, and centrifuges. All the various apparatus of a fully functioning laboratory. A glass window looked into a smaller room, where a row of cages lined the walls, each with an animal awaiting its executioner.

Kinyoun opened a case, and selected a slide. "This was taken from the latest suspected plague death—a middle-aged laborer who collapsed in some twisted little alleyway: Oneida Place. Wilfred Kellogg performed the postmortem, and brought me the samples. I injected the lymph fluid into those animals yesterday. They are already showing symptoms of plague."

"The newspapers are claiming that the deaths are being caused by a venereal disease," Isobel said.

"The newspapers are run by businessmen who take payouts from merchants."

Kinyoun adjusted the microscope, switched off the overhead light, and stepped back. Riot removed his spectacles. A swarm of tiny organisms came into view. Clusters of gray bacilli were huddled under the lens. Short, rod-shaped, with rounded tips, they reminded Riot of safety pins.

"What am I looking at?" he asked. Isobel nudged his elbow, and he stepped back. As she skillfully adjusted the knobs of the microscope, he wondered when she had used one before.

"The plague bacillus. Causative agent of the bubonic plague, commonly known as the Black Death. Bacilli don't lie, Mr. Riot. The plague has arrived in America."

"How do you think the plague came to San Francisco?"

"From Honolulu, of course. We have steamers arriving every month. We are as thorough with our disinfecting practices as possible, but… obviously we failed."

A man with an ego, but an honest one. The Quarantine Station was the gateway, and Kinyoun was ultimately responsible for protecting the United States from infectious disease. Another man might have brushed this lapse under a rug, and hope it didn't spread. But he had been the first to sound the alarm.

Kinyoun switched on the light. "Doesn't it strike you as odd that the same man who owns the *Call*, one of my biggest critics, also owns the Oceanic Steamship Company? J.D. Spreckles is more concerned with his pocketbook. Confirmation of the plague would bring his steamers to a standstill. That's why San Francisco is so keen on discrediting me."

Isobel looked up from the microscope. She cocked her head, and then wandered over to the window of caged animals.

"Do not go in there, young man."

Isobel folded her hands behind her back in innocent compliance.

"Wouldn't passengers be infected as well?" Riot asked. "I arrived in January on the SS *Australia*."

"The incubation period varies," Kinyoun replied. "The first signs of illness could show themselves within the first day, or it could take as long as seven. The plague bacillus is hardy. It can survive in a corpse for days—animal or human —and even longer in soil. Yersin—the man who discovered the bacillus—found that rats are vectors of the bubonic plague. Paul-Louis Simond even suggests it's spread by fleas."

"What do you think?"

Kinyoun dismissed his question with a wave of a hand. "I'm conducting my own research on the subject. I don't trust anyone else's opinion."

Riot glanced towards the animals. "How do you account for the fact that the plague skipped six blocks—from the ports to Chinatown—to kill a laborer in the Globe Hotel?"

"Chinatown is overcrowded. Its basements are filthy."

"The Barbary Coast isn't precisely paradise."

Kinyoun looked towards the south wall, as if he could see San Francisco. "A rat could easily have skittered down a mooring line, swum across a harbor, climbed onto a wharf, and gone straight into the sewage outflow."

"And traveled six blocks?"

"They're rats. They go where there's food."

Isobel turned away from the cages. Her eyes were steely, glittering from across the room. "How did you infect the animals with the disease?"

Kinyoun smoothed his mustache. "During the post-mortem on the latest victim, Kellogg extracted fluid from the inflamed lymph nodes and placed it into a glass tube." He gestured to a rack of tubes. Slim, corked, and airtight. Pink, pulpy tissue floated in straw-colored fluid. "You simply pierce the cork with a needle, withdraw a sample, and inject it into a lab animal."

"That's a very simple process," Isobel noted.

A dark scowl came over his face. "If you are suggesting that Dr. Kellogg botched the collection process—"

"I am not," she said, interrupting his tirade. "Only noting that it sounds foolproof."

"Anyone can do it with minimal training," Kinyoun confirmed.

Isobel arched a brow towards Riot, and the penny dropped a moment later. His gaze traveled to the rats and guinea pigs—all of them injected with death.

20

MEETING OF MINDS

But together they were something entirely different. The lists were a map. A key to the shadowy lives of San Francisco's elite. —Z.R. Journal Excerpt

WATSON PERCHED ON A RAIL OF THE *PAGAN LADY*, SWISHING his tail in annoyance, as Isobel lowered the dinghy into the water. "Stay or come. It's your choice," Isobel told the cat. Rather than tie the *Lady* to the wharf, she had moored her in the harbor. One more step for any unwanted visitors to take.

"I will stay and watch the boat," Jin volunteered. The girl stood by the tiller, arms crossed, lips pressed together.

"And I'm not gettin' in that," Tobias said, pointing at the little dinghy.

With a quirk of his lips, Riot climbed over the rail and sat in the boat. "I'll hold it steady for you, Tobias. Besides, your mother will kill me if I leave you out here."

"No, she'll thank you for not drowning me."

Seeing that his favorite human was going ashore, Watson quickly hopped into the dinghy and took up his position as masthead. Isobel looked at the children. "Tobias, get in *now*, or I'll make you walk the plank."

Tobias' eyes widened, and he quickly scrambled over the rail. Riot reached up to help him over. Not trusting the bench, Tobias planted his rear on the bottom of the dinghy, and stretched his arms to grip the sides.

"I will not go back to the mission," Jin said. It wasn't defiant, but quiet, her fingers picking at the beaded bracelet. "I'd rather walk the plank."

Isobel believed her. "I'm not leaving you here."

"I'll clean. I'll scrub the deck. Whatever you need."

Isobel glanced at Riot, who answered her unuttered question. "Sarah's dining at the house tonight. Miss Lily will be laying a fine dinner. You're welcome to join us, Jin."

"And after?"

"As long as it's fine with Miss Lily you can stay at Ravenwood Manor for the night, but you'll have to speak with Miss Cameron tomorrow."

Jin tensed as if to run, but there was only the gray sea.

"Oh, get in, Jin," Tobias said. "Even if they send you back to the mission you'll just run away and hide out in my fort, anyhow."

This bit of reasoning decided the girl. She hopped overboard and Isobel passed down a rucksack full of Ravenwood's journals and her own notes. Someone had known enough to ask after Mr. Morgan and the *Pagan Lady*. She didn't want to leave anything of value aboard. Locks had a way of opening, especially with the company she was presently keeping.

Riot reached for the oars, but she shook her head. "Let me. It'll look suspicious otherwise." A captain would hardly allow his chartered client to row a dinghy ashore. He frowned at her, eyes full of concern.

Isobel leaned forward. "I intend to take a long soak in your bathtub tonight," she whispered. With that promise, he grudgingly surrendered the oars. She gritted her teeth, and put her back into it.

As she rowed, Riot kept an eye on the docks. A pair of sailors were arguing in Italian between feluccas, their voices carrying over the water, as did their broad gestures. A group of Chinese shrimpers sat on their boat repairing traps, and a yachtsman in a white sweater yelled at his crew as he fought with a sail. No one seemed to be taking an interest in the *Pagan Lady* or their dinghy.

Isobel drifted alongside a ladder, and Tobias scrambled up, followed by Jin. Watson yowled at Riot, who kindly picked the lazy cat up and carried him to the dock. Isobel tied off the boat, and followed.

As soon as she'd set foot on the dock, Mr. Covel came stomping towards them. With the sun ready to plummet into the sea, he was already well into his cups, but he maintained a relatively straight line.

"Cap'n Morgan." He tipped his cap, and then to them all, "Did you have a pleasant sail?"

She looked to her charter, and Riot answered, "That we did, sir. Morgan is a fine captain."

"Yes, yes." Mr. Covel stuck his thumbs in his waistcoat. "Erm, might I have a word?" The watchman jerked his head to the side, and Isobel followed. As the man leaned close to whisper, his breath nearly felled her. "A fella came looking for your sister. Yesterday and today."

"Did he leave a name?"

"No, no, just said he was a friend."

"Hardly sounds like a friend."

"Didn't look the sort, either. I didn't want to tell your charter there, but he looked a bad sort."

"How so?"

"Average, but he had a gun on his hip. I saw it when he turned."

"Most men have a gun on their hip in this city, Mr. Covel."

"True, true, but he had an air to 'im. Just like that fella there."

Isobel glanced at Riot, who was talking with the children. It was hardly a menacing scene, but still, there *was* something about Riot—the way his eyes watched and the way he stood. Completely at ease. Ready, calm, and altogether dangerous.

"What did you tell him?"

Mr. Covel turned redder than his nose. He stammered, and scuffed his foot against the dock. "What was I supposed to tell 'im but the truth? That the *Lady* was docked right here, and that 'er capt'n was a hard one to peg."

"You didn't think it odd that he didn't leave a card?"

"Like I was sayin', a dangerous sort. I'd keep myself scarce if I was you. Is your sister in some sort of trouble? Angry husband, maybe?"

"I think that might be it," she muttered.

"Looks like you got yourself into another fight."

"I'm always rarin' for one." She tipped her cap, and walked to the end of the wharf to hail a hack. Keeping in character as the junior member of Ravenwood Agency, she held the door open for Riot, Watson, and the children before climbing in herself. The cat stood on Riot's thigh to look out the window, its tail twitching as the carriage rolled forward.

Jin listened with narrowed eyes and Tobias with wide ones, as Isobel told Riot about her conversation with Mr. Covel. In her experience, keeping children in the dark was the quickest way to put them at risk. They'd ferret out the truth one way or another—and it was usually the dangerous way.

Riot said nothing, but Tobias had a whole heap to say. By the time the carriage rolled to a stop in front of Ravenwood Manor, the boy had convinced himself that a band of outlaws were after her buried treasure.

Without a word, Riot exited the hack. Alert and tense, he searched the quiet street. Isobel was unnerved as well. They had a number of enemies, and for all she knew there *might* be a band of outlaws after her.

Jin looked at the boy with disgust. "*Wun dan.*"

Tobias scrambled after. "What does that mean?"

"Cracked egg," Riot answered. He flipped the hackman his fare.

"What's so bad about a cracked egg? They taste good, don't they?"

When the hack had pulled away from the curb, Riot addressed the children. "Not a word about this." He stared at Tobias until the boy scuffed his feet, looking about to crawl out of his skin. Satisfied, Riot turned up the drive, Watson at his heel.

"I thought that was your cat," Tobias said to Isobel.

"I don't keep pets. He's his own man."

———

THE SCENT OF CANDLES MINGLED WITH HONEYSUCKLE, AND paper lanterns bobbed like fireflies in the conservatory. It was fogged with warm bodies. And warmer conversation.

"...there he was, no bigger than Tobias, cocky as could be, facing Wildeyed Hatfield with an old Colt Sidehammer that looked like it come from a gutter. So I says, 'A.J., how about a drink before you shoot this fella. It'll steady your hand.' Do you know what he says?"

All eyes looked to Tim. "He says, 'Don't think it matters. I can't see 'im anyway.'" Laughter erupted around the table, and Riot primly removed his spectacles to polish the lens. "So I says, 'A.J., Mr. Hatfield can see you just fine. As your second, I'd advise you to bow out of this duel.'

'No, sir,' he says, 'I just need to get closer.'

'That don't seem like such a good idea.'

'Hatfield accused me of pinching his billfold.'

'Well, did you?' I asked. And here he raises that stubborn chin of his and tells me straight to my face, 'Course I did. I can pinch any pocket in San Francisco.'

'That's mighty fine, A.J.. Let's celebrate that.' So I pretend to take a swig from my flask, and hand it over. He takes a mighty draught, screws on the cap, and looks at me. His eyes fly open, and a tick later he falls flat on his face." Tim cackled, and even Riot chuckled.

"So I says to Hatfield, 'I'll pay you what he stole, and we'll shake hands on it.' And Hatfield shakes his head. 'That boy is trouble. You best teach him a lesson or he'll not reach fifteen. But I'll take your offer. I wasn't going to shoot him anyhow. Just scare him. He stole twenty-five dollars.'

"I whistled low. That kind of cash hurt. *What the devil did he do with it?* I wondered, but it didn't matter, 'cause I didn't have twenty-five dollars. So I says to Hatfield, 'Give me two hours, and I'll have your money.' He was an honorable killer, so we shook on it, and I hoisted that son of a…gun over my shoulder, and marched straight to the nearest port. I looked over the ships, and recognized an old friend of mine. A captain he was, and sailing for Hong Kong. So I handed A.J. over to him, and told him to make sure the boy learnt some sense. And do you know the best thing of it?" Tim slapped the table. "I got fifty dollars for his head."

"And I've never forgiven you for it," Riot said when the laughter died.

"Did he learn any sense?" Miss Lily asked.

Tim cackled. "He learned to gamble and swear like a sailor."

She clucked her tongue. "Then I suppose it won't work for Tobias."

The boy's mouth fell open as he stared at his mother, betrayed.

"What did you do with the money, Mr. Riot?" Sarah asked.

Riot shifted. "I had used it to pay off a debt for a friend who was…" He cleared his throat. "…in service to another."

Jin narrowed her eyes. "You paid a whore's debt to a pimp," she said bluntly.

Maddie gasped, and covered her mouth with a hand. Isobel wasn't at all surprised. Young or old, Atticus Riot had a large and generous heart.

"That's an indelicate way to put it, but yes." He smiled.

"Why didn't you ask Mr. Tim to help you?" Tobias asked.

Riot considered the question. "It's not easy asking for help when you don't know what help looks like."

"Well, I for one am thrilled that Tim shanghaied you," Lotario Amsel said, patting the slight bulge that passed as his stomach. "Otherwise, I would not have been introduced to Miss Lily, her fine cooking, and her pleasant company."

"You make it sound like I'm three different people, Mr. Amsel."

"We all wear different masks. I'm honored you've graced me with your divine trinity. Dinner was superb." He plucked up Miss Lily's hand and kissed the air above her knuckles with a flourish. "You were trained in France, weren't you?"

Lily smiled, dimpling her cheeks. "A chef never shares her secrets, Mr. Amsel."

"Oh, come now. Call me Lotario. You've tantalized my senses all evening. We're far past that nonsense."

Tim snorted, a puff of pipe smoke billowing over his head. "Don't let that boy sweet talk you, Miss Lily. I'll wager he practices on himself in the mirror most evenings."

"It's practice made perfect." Miss Lily started to rise, reaching for the first plate, but Tim hopped to his feet.

"No, no. Sit. You treated us to a fine dinner. Me and the runts will get the dishes."

Grimm stood without complaint, but then he rarely said anything. Only looked to his younger brother.

"Mr. Riot promised he'd teach us tracking," Tobias argued.

"Oh, yes, please!" Sarah beamed, and put her hand over Riot's.

"When the dishes are done," Riot said.

Jin narrowed her eyes. Deciding that she wanted to learn this fascinating skill, she began clearing away dishes with a speed that left the adults struck. "Hurry, *Wun Dan*. And you, Sarah."

"*Wun Dan*?" Maddie asked as she stood to lend a hand.

"Cracked egg," Isobel explained.

"More like an annoying egg," Maddie muttered.

When the children had filed out with their dishes, Isobel leaned towards Riot. "Who did you help?" she whispered.

"A girl named Jesse."

Isobel arched a brow.

"Bak Siu Lui." *White Blossom*: a madam in Chinatown. Isobel wondered at their relationship, but Riot hadn't offered any additional information. That in itself was telling, and this latest detail more so.

"I read you were arrested, *Miss* Bonnie," Lotario said.

She looked at her twin, and sighed. He never missed a thing. And she doubted Miss Lily did either. There wasn't much use keeping up a ruse with their observant landlady. She glanced at Riot, and he lifted a brow. The cat was out of the bag, as the saying went. Why not entertain them?

Isobel gave the adults a summary of events, leaving out red tokens, mysterious tongs, and dangerous names. Her account of tying Freddy to a chair left Lotario in stitches. Conversation turned to the plague, and the *Call* and *Chronicle's* mockery of Doctor Kinyoun. No one wanted to believe the Health Department, especially merchants. Plague was bad for business.

A yawn cracked Isobel's jaw, and she stood. Riot quickly rose to his feet. It was an ingrained gesture, regardless of her attire. "You have a class to teach," she reminded.

"They'll come knocking if I don't go now," he agreed, brushing her fingertips. That brush felt like an electric jolt. She looked into his eyes a moment longer, and then turned away to thank Miss Lily for dinner. "If you'll excuse me, there is a bathtub with my name on it."

"I hope the children used up all the hot water on the dishes," Lotario drawled.

She flicked her twin's ear. "Good night, *Mr.* Amsel."

A grape hit her on the back as she walked out of the conservatory.

"BRING THE LANTERNS," RIOT INSTRUCTED. "SET THEM here, in a square. Now gather an armful each of those logs."

The children ran to the wood pile, each returning with a full armload. Tobias dropped two logs at Riot's feet, Sarah dropped four, and eight logs tumbled from Jin's arms. Maddie and Grimm added their own.

"Set the logs up in a line, here and here. Make a ladder out of them."

Tobias stared at Riot for a moment. Puzzlement plain in his eyes.

"It'll make sense when you do as you're told," Riot assured.

When the wooden ladder was laid out, he walked into the night, plucked an apple from its tree, and placed it in the first grid. Then he pressed his foot into the ground beside the apple, leaving a print. The children stared at the apple in wonderment.

"While walking on Mount Carmel, two Jews were taken prisoner and enslaved by a Persian. The Persian was wary, and so had his slaves walk in front of him," Riot began. He reached into his pocket and brought out a folded napkin. "As the Jews walked, one—"

"How come they didn't attack the Paris fellow?" Tobias asked. "There were two of them, and one of him."

Maddie glanced at her brother. "A *Persian*, not a Parisian."

Tobias waved his hand. "Did he have a gun?"

"Revolvers weren't invented yet."

"What?"

"This was a long time ago," Riot explained. "Biblical times."

"I thought we were gonna learn trackin'. What does Sunday school have to do with trackin'?" Tobias asked.

Jin growled low in her throat. "Shut up, *Wun Dan*, or Mr. Riot will be tracking your corpse to where I bury you."

Riot held up his hands for peace. "Observation is a tracker's first skill," he said gently. "That includes listening." He tapped his head. "Remembering, selecting, and analyzing." He gestured to the grid of logs. "And finally deduction. Be patient, Tobias. That's your first lesson."

Tobias blew out a breath.

"As the Jews walked, one said to the other, 'The camel that went before us four hours ago, is blind in one eye, is laden with two skin bottles, one containing wine and the other oil, and is driven by two men, one an Israelite and the other a Gentile.'"

"What's an Israelite and a Gentile?" Jin asked.

"One's a Jew and the Gentile isn't," Sarah replied.

Tobias narrowed his eyes at Riot. "How'd they know all that?"

"That's what the Persian asked," Riot said. "'You stiffnecked people', he cried. 'How do you know all this?' They replied, 'A camel as you know, usually grazes equally on both sides of the road. You can plainly see the grass here has been nibbled on only one side. The camel is surely blind in one eye.' The second Jew said, 'As for the kegs, all you need to do is examine the dregs left behind. The drops of wine on one side are sunk into the ground; whereas, the oil drops remain above it.' The Persian scoffed. 'And how do you know one is a Gentile and the other an Israelite?' The slaves smiled. 'Let us go, and we will answer.' The Persian's curiosity ate at him, because he didn't know the answer. Do any of you?"

The children shifted, looking one to another, and finally shook their heads in unison.

"The Persian agreed to let the slaves go free if they answered the question. The first Jew said, 'One of the drivers relieved nature at some distance from the road, the other, a Gentile who was indecent, relieved himself in the middle of the road.'"

Sarah wrinkled her nose.

"Did the Persian let them go?" Maddie asked.

"So the story goes."

Jin scoffed. "That would never happen."

"Is that 'cause slaves aren't clever enough?" Tobias shot back.

"No." That single word dripped venom. "The slave master would have been insulted by the slaves' intelligence. To make himself feel better, he would have beaten them until they passed out. Then he would have locked them in a small trunk for days with no food or water. Their wounds would swell, and their limbs would cramp, and they would beg for death. But every time they made a sound, the slave master would scream and kick the trunk." Jin's entire body was rigid, her jaw set, fists curled into white balls.

Grimm stared at the girl, his face a stony mask, but Tobias was oblivious to the deeper significance of her words. "There wasn't no mention of a trunk in the story."

Maddie was too stunned to correct his grammar.

"Would you *be quiet*!" Sarah hissed at Tobias.

Riot stepped beside Jin. He didn't touch her, only waited until she looked up at him. "That likely would have happened, but I think these slaves were clever enough to escape, no matter what they were put through. What do you think?" he asked gently.

Jin gave a stiff nod and turned away, her fingers toying with the frayed bracelet around her wrist. Now was not the time to press her. To take attention off the child, Riot returned to the lesson, hoping it would distract her. "Observation and deduction. Tracking is as simple, and as difficult as that. So we'll start with observation first."

"How'd the Persian know they were four hours ahead?" Sarah asked.

"That's what I intend to teach you." He gestured at the grid of logs. "This is an 'aging stand.' We can stand and observe all day, but unless we know what things look like when exposed to the elements, we can't make accurate deductions. I want you all to gather a variety of items: twigs, leaves, tin cans, clothing, shoes, flowers, paper—whatever strikes your fancy." He placed the napkin in the grid beside the apple. "Every day, I want each of you to visit the aging stand and take notes on any changes you observe. Have the twigs changed color? Did the paper start to fade? Understood?"

The children nodded.

"In a week, we'll put fresh items beside the old, and compare the two." He made a shooing gesture, and the children spread out on their mission. Riot sat on a low wall and watched with amusement as they ran back and forth, darting in and out of the house.

Sarah placed a final item in the grid, and sat beside him as he shuffled his cards. "Do you think I'll be able to learn all this?"

"I think you'll do just fine, Sarah. If you want to."

"I do." She hesitated. "Thank you, Mr. Riot. I'm not half as blue when I'm with you."

The deck stuttered in his hands. He bent to retrieve a card.

Jin moved a lantern closer to the grid, and began taking notes with a pencil and paper she had salvaged. The girl crouched, completely still, watching each item as if it might change before her eyes. Riot cocked his head. She reminded him of himself at that age.

"Where's Tobias?" Maddie asked.

"He was probably distracted by more food," Jin said.

As if on cue, the back door flew open and the boy jumped down the steps. He cradled something in his hands. Tobias scowled at everyone, hunched his shoulders, and turned his back so they couldn't see his bundle.

"What did you bring?" Maddie asked.

He made a face. "None of your business." Tobias set the bundle of brown paper inside one of the grids, and plucked at the edges. It opened, and he upended it onto the ground.

Maddie plugged her nose. And Jin slowly swiveled her head towards the boy, disgust plain on her face. Sarah stood up and leaned forward. "Is that—" she cut off.

Tobias crossed his arms. "That's what was in the story, wasn't it? Nature and all."

"I didn't know there was a dog in the house," Sarah said.

Jin sighed. "There is no dog."

"Tobias White! Is that *yours*?" Maddie asked, placing her hands on her hips.

"So what if it is?" Tobias defended.

The children fell to arguing, and Riot cut them short when he stood. He looked down at Tobias' offering. "I'd say you all have made an excellent start. Good thinking, Tobias." Halfway up to his rooms, Riot's lips cracked in a smile.

ISOBEL STUDIED THE CHESSBOARD. IT SAT BETWEEN Ravenwood's chair and Riot's—or had it become her own now? A half-played game from days ago remained, the pieces frozen in battle. But in her mind's eye the pieces were clues rather than players: names, dates, and tokens, with a string of red connecting them all. The chessboard looked like a giant red spiderweb. But where was the spider? Her gaze was drawn to a map on the wall, to Angel Island.

"We need to question the city health inspectors," she said to no one in particular.

Tim was perched on a windowsill, smoking his pipe. "Do you think Lincoln Howe fell into some bad business with this Parker Gray? Blackmail? Abduction? Murder?"

"It's too early to say," she said.

Riot was in his own chair, legs crossed, reading her notes on Ravenwood's journals. There were still a great deal more to decipher. She rubbed her temples. Not tonight. She couldn't tonight. Now that she was fed and watered, all she wanted was a soft bed.

She glanced at her partner. The firelight softened his features, and illuminated the spectacles over his eyes. She watched his fine fingers turning the pages, and wondered at his stillness. He was quiet. More so than usual.

A burst of laughter heralded an earthquake of boots, four children sounding like a herd. Sarah, Tobias, Jin, and another boarder's child were playing some game. As long as there were no knives, swords, or guns involved, Isobel didn't care what they did to the house. From a shuddering boom, she surmised it had to do with the banisters.

Riot flipped her notebook closed, and looked at the web of information scattered around his fireplace. For so few pages, the reading had taken him far too long.

"So what's the ol' miser have to say?" Tim asked.

Isobel took one look at Riot's stiff posture, and the Adam's apple moving in his throat, to know he was in no state to answer. So she answered for him. "Ravenwood was working on something to do with Jones Jr. He saw a connection with the lumber yard. Do you know anything about that, Tim?"

"I told you already, I don't know what Zeph did half the time. I'm not sure I wanted to know."

"We need to know now," Isobel said. If she stayed in that chair one more moment, she'd fall asleep. So she stood, and tapped Jim Parks' name. "We know that someone arranged for Jim Parks to leave prison two months early, in secret, to murder Ravenwood."

"Aye, that *Sing Ping King Sur*," Tim said.

Riot absently rubbed at his temple, tracing the scar beneath the wing of white hair. "We're not positive, but that's the working theory. That, or Jim Parks was toying with me."

"I dug up some information on the judge who released him early."

Both Isobel and Riot looked at the old man. He had a gleam in his eye. Tim always appreciated an audience, and he had their full attention. "His family is very well set up. They came into money three years ago." Tim rocked back and forth on his heels, looking immensely pleased with himself.

"That's more coincidence than I can stomach," Isobel said.

"I agree."

"Jim Parks was set to be released anyhow," Isobel said. "What judge wouldn't accept a bribe? What harm could there be in releasing a man a few months early?"

"Two murdered women and a murdered old man," Tim grumbled. "I'll see if I can't trace that money."

Riot nodded, reaching for a deck of cards. "Excellent." He pointed a card to a slip of paper with *Hip Yee* written on it. "Vengeful partner goes on a rampage. Kills most of a tong dealing in slavery, leaving a void that is quickly filled by…someone."

"It's brilliant," Isobel breathed.

Both men raised their brows.

She reached over to the chessboard, and idly traced the black queen's crown. "Well, it is if our theories are correct. If I were a secret organization, I'd operate from the shadows. Puppets, Riot. An army of ignorant puppets. Misdirection, chaos, and sacrifice. It's strategy at its finest. But it also requires a deep understanding of human nature."

"I'm relieved you did not turn to a life of crime," Riot said.

She flashed him a grin. "You'd have caught me."

Tim tugged on his beard. "Either get a room or focus, you two."

"You're *in* my room, Tim."

"Say the word and I'll leave. You can call me back in five minutes."

Isobel laughed.

Riot leveled a severe look on the old man. "Kindly refrain from being crude in front of a lady."

"She's wearing a man's clothing, boy. I'll treat her how she likes."

"Back to the matter at hand." Isobel plucked up the queen. "Three years later, we stumble over a runaway slave girl."

"Stumble isn't quite the word. You went looking for her," Riot corrected.

"And I uncovered a snake pit," she said. "But to be fair, you also found Sarah Byrne. I don't know how either of those encounters could have been staged. I'll chalk it up to our observant natures. So it's safe to assume we're not presently being manipulated for some unknown scheme."

"The curse of a detective: constant vigilance."

"Amen," Tim muttered.

Riot took up the narration. It was complex, and it needed sorting. "Andrew Ross, Lee Walker, Jim Parks, and Freddy all had these red tokens. And according to Jim Parks, if he can be believed, *Sing Ping King Sur* was behind Ravenwood's death. So he was implying that they hired him. That means the red token is a marker for whatever shadowy organization this is."

"Andrew Ross was killed while trying to recover Jin and Mei. Again, an accident. But it led me to Ross' corpse and the calling cards of Lincoln Howe."

"Who supposedly came over on the SS *Australia*, worked for the health department, and suspiciously disappeared the day Andrew Ross was murdered by the hatchet man."

"What a tangled web," Isobel muttered.

"It's a pile of shit," Tim grunted. "San Francisco's not a large city—not like New York or London. In this city, you can't take a step without finding a criminal's mess underfoot."

"I'll question the city health inspectors tomorrow," Riot offered. "Maybe they have a description of Lincoln Howe."

Tim scratched his beard. "Might be best to have it from another source, too. A quick telegram to Honolulu isn't possible. We'd have to send it by post. How about London University where he studied?"

"Ravenwood had a colleague in London. I'll send a telegram first thing."

"Is he reliable?" Isobel asked.

Riot flipped a card around with a flourish: the ace of spades. "I think you'll find him dependable."

Isobel arched a brow at the card, and placed her queen in the center of the board. "I find few men dependable. Whatever happened, I don't think Lincoln Howe willingly handed over his calling cards to Andrew Ross. We need to find him. He's our missing link."

"How do we do that?" Tim asked.

Riot caught the gleam in her eyes. "I thought you wanted a soft bed?" he murmured.

She sighed. "How do you know me so well?"

"I had in mind the same thing."

21

THE DRIFTER

This was proof. —Z.R. Journal Excerpt

As wide as she was tall and with a billyclub in hand, the landlady of this particular boardinghouse wasn't one to be crossed. Mrs. Kettle looked the young man in front of her up and down. Ragged, underfed, dark circles under his eyes. She'd seen it before. And the bruises. The man's palms were raw and his cheek swollen. She didn't ask. She never did. It wasn't her concern.

"I'd like a window, ma'am. I can't stand it with no windows," the young man muttered. His cap was pulled low, and he barely made eye contact. The young these days.

"That's extra," she said.

"And a room to myself."

Mrs. Kettle laughed. Her late husband had told her over and again that she sounded like a braying donkey. She had brayed the entire time she'd bashed in his cheating skull with her club. That was why she kept pigs in the basement. Useful animals, for all sorts of things.

"Livin' large, are ya?"

The young man dipped his head. Well, maybe he was only shy. She liked them shy.

"For a room with a window, it'll be twenty-five cents a night."

"Clean bedding, too, if you have it."

"Aren't you high-class." She sidled closer, and toyed with the young man's lapel. "Is there anything else you might fancy?"

The young man looked her in the eye, surprised. He had piercing eyes. The kind of grayish-silver eyes and cheek-bones that made her want to keep him. She'd give him her best room, and if he couldn't pay... Well, there were other ways a fine-looking man might earn his keep.

Mrs. Kettle scratched at the flea bites on her arm as she climbed the stairwell. She ignored the sagging planks and creaking stairs, and the mold climbing up the walls with her. She didn't mind it. Men still paid for rooms at her boarding-house, and she wasn't about to put a penny back into the rookery.

She opened the door. "Will this do?"

The young man stepped inside. He ignored the bed and small chest, and went straight for the window, twitching the curtain aside. His Levis hugged his backside. It was a lovely view.

"It'll do, ma'am."

A clink of coins dropped into her palm. She was almost disappointed.

CARDS FLUTTERED, A WHISPER OF WINGS IN THE DARK. ONLY a stream of silver light pierced the threadbare curtain. "Can you see anything?" Isobel whispered.

"I have the eyes of a cat," Riot replied.

"A half-blind one."

"My spectacles are firmly in place."

"That's good. It'll ensure you don't mistake the landlady for me."

"Doubtful," he said dryly.

"And here I thought it was only young women who were eyed up and down like slabs of meat for the taking."

Riot clucked his tongue. "It may come as a surprise to you, but women *do* have desires, the same as men."

"You *shock* me, Atticus."

The cards in his hand seemed to chuckle. "Someone has to."

"I don't think women are quite the same." Her gaze drifted to his lap.

"Different anatomy to be sure," he conceded. "Unlike men, the most sensitive sexual organ in a woman's body resides between her ears, not her legs."

Isobel's mind spun in all different directions. Her neck flushed with heat, and she found herself unable to formulate a response beyond straddling him and silencing him with her lips. Before thought gave way to action, she forced herself to focus. And that meant not looking at the man.

Keeping to the side, Isobel peeked through the dingy window. The street below was quiet, with saloon lights flickering in the fog. It wasn't thick tonight, but formed a hazy dream that made cobblestones shift. She squinted at a void between two buildings—the lane where she had been arrested. Impenetrable.

"Fire," she said.

Riot's cards shot from his hands, sending all fifty-two flying into the dark. She heard a muttered oath, and tried to hold back a laugh.

He cleared his throat. "What was that?"

"We could start a small, controlled fire in the alleyway." Keeping an eye on the saloon, she crouched to help pick up his cards.

"And draw every fire brigade in the city."

"Precisely."

"I don't think we'd be able to slip into the saloon with the fire brigade swarming the building." He had read her mind. As usual.

"We might be able to steal a coat and hat…"

"After we knock out a fireman?"

"That's a *splendid* idea."

Riot shifted. The light touched the wire of his silver spectacles. She could *feel* his eyes on her.

"You think it's a bad plan," she stated.

"I think it's a *complicated* plan. We're here to observe, not send some innocent fireman off to the receiving hospital."

"Monty has been watching the saloon for the past few days. He's seen nothing of interest."

"I thought you didn't put much stock in his observational skills?"

"I don't. I suspect he's been sleeping most of the time." She had intended to do more than observe tonight, but Riot had insisted on coming along. Small wonder, considering her last visit there.

"Patience, Bel."

Isobel made a frustrated sound. She wanted to *act*. Not conduct a study in patience. "I don't like where this trail is pointing. You had the same thought as me in Hospital Cove."

"I did," he agreed.

"It's no coincidence that Lincoln Howe's calling cards were in Andrew Ross' pocket."

"We need to gather as much information as possible. Otherwise the extent of this... conspiracy might never be uncovered."

"Then you do think it's a conspiracy?"

"I think Parker Gray and his lackeys are definitely up to more than simple scams. I just don't know what pieces belong to which puzzle."

Isobel blew out a breath. It was true. The whole mess was a web of clues. In the end, she deferred to his experience. Her rash action the other night certainly hadn't helped their investigation.

Isobel handed over the cards she'd collected, and he returned to his chair. Moonlight illuminated his hands. She watched him square the deck, and caress its edges. He was counting cards with a brush of his fingertips.

"You can sleep," he offered softly. "I'll wake you if anyone appears."

Isobel glanced at the narrow bed, and shuddered. Clean sheets or no, the red bites she'd seen trailing up the landlady's arm were enough to deter her.

"If Punt doesn't make an appearance, I'll have to continue my nightly surveillance of the brick building."

"I'll keep your side of the bed warm while you're gone."

Isobel crossed her arms. He had turned the tables on her subtle threat.

Riot tucked his cards away. Glancing at his hand, he carefully began unwinding the bandages protecting his broken fingers. "Given the newspaper article, I wouldn't advise the Falcon's Club for surveillance. Parker Gray knows you as Mr. Morgan, and now as Miss Bonnie."

She sighed. "It may have been one of Alex's trained dogs sniffing around the wharves," she reminded. Still, her options along Ocean Beach were limited, and she didn't much like the idea of spending a long night on the dunes. The bruising on her stomach from her first encounter with Parker Gray was only just beginning to fade.

"Have you considered moving the *Lady* to a different wharf?" he asked.

"Unless I move her to the East Bay, that only buys us time."

Riot didn't say a word.

Bristling at his silence, she found herself on the defensive. "I don't like having enemies I can't see. I'd rather draw them out."

"You mean you don't like waiting," he said calmly.

"There is that."

He flexed his right hand, and grimaced.

"How are they?" she asked softly.

"Stiff, mostly. I don't want to lose my range of motion."

"It hasn't been very long." She knelt and took his hand, gently probing his fingers. "At least they're not cracking when you move them anymore."

"Will you be accompanying me tomorrow?"

"I'm overdue at the *Call*. For the sake of appearances, I should write that article on *The Plight of the Vagrant*." She sighed. "Maybe we're overreacting—seeing more in the shadows than what's there."

"Not when someone was asking after you at the docks."

"Our 'average man' may have been a reporter," she mused. "I'll ask at the newspaper." Isobel studied his face in the moonlight. "You were quiet during dinner."

"Aren't I always?"

"This was a different sort of quiet."

Riot tucked the bandages into a pocket. "I was enjoying the conversation."

Isobel waited for more. He glanced down at their intertwined hands. Deep in thought, his thumb caressed her wrist in a gentle circle.

"Happiness," he finally whispered. "I'm not used to it, Bel. And it worries me."

"It's fragile."

"It's terrifying." He squeezed her hand. "But I intend to hold onto it."

"At the very least we'll put up a good fight." She bent forward and kissed his knuckles. "What do you think of Ravenwood's journals?"

"I think, even after twenty years, I barely knew the man."

"Do we ever really know someone?"

"I know you." His eyes held her own, and she felt the truth of his words in her bones.

A knot twisted in her chest. Isobel had never much cared for stories of doomed lovers. In her arrogance, she had always seen a simple way out—one where the lovers could have triumphed. She was not so confidant now.

Riot stared through the crack between curtains. "You're positive you didn't hear a sound before smoke filled the alleyway?"

Startled by the sudden shift in conversation, she slapped her maudlin thoughts to the side and focused on that night —to fear and chaos.

"There *was* a hiss," she said suddenly. "A steady hiss."

Riot considered her words. "Have you heard of Robert Yale?" he asked after a time.

Isobel shook her head. "A friend of yours?"

"A bit before my time. He was an inventor who modified fireworks. He came up with a way to create smoke. It's a common enough tool in theatrical productions."

"Why would a vagrant have a firecracker that creates smoke?"

"Distraction," he answered. "Why did you think him a vagrant?"

"It was more of an impression—a bundle of rags." Isobel narrowed her eyes at the alleyway. She wished she had a smoking firecracker. "We could try the side door with your lock picks."

"We could."

"But you won't."

"Have you been practicing?"

She took her hand away, and stood to lean against the wall. "Here and there. Not as much as I'd like. I've mostly been deciphering Ravenwood's journals, or trying to. Have you thought of any books he favored?"

"Favored is a strong word where he's concerned."

She crossed her arms, and waited.

Riot ticked off a list on his fingertips. "*Grey's Anatomy*, *On the Origin of the Species*, the *Old Testament*, *The Odyssey*, and *Frankenstein*. Or as he preferred, *The Modern Prometheus*."

"The *Old Testament*? Really?"

"Yes, he thought it a fine study of the futility of mankind."

Isobel chuckled. "He was a whimsical fellow."

Riot cocked his head. "I don't think I've ever heard 'Ravenwood' and 'whimsical' used in the same sentence."

"I'm being perfectly serious. I'm beginning to like the man."

"Careful, Bel. I'll think you mad and commit you to Bright Waters Asylum."

"We're not married," she reminded.

"Yet."

"Aren't you cocksure of yourself?"

"Only optimistic. It's a failing of mine."

"Hmm." She leveled her gaze at him. He didn't even have the decency to look ashamed of himself. "You were a puzzle to him."

Even in the dimness, she could see his surprise.

"I think that highly unlikely," he said.

"Didn't you read my notes?"

"I did."

"He wrote about you all the time. It's clear as day."

Riot stared at her, at a loss.

"I laughed myself breathless when I read his account of how you met."

Riot groaned, and she flashed a grin. Now he was uncomfortable. She rather liked it. "That man nearly got me killed."

"Sounds like you nearly shot him, then and there."

"I had a mind to." He thought back to that day. To a simpler time, when he'd been young and cocky, with no worries aside from where to place his next wager. "I *was* surprised to read that."

"Ravenwood loved you—in his own way."

"The way a biologist loves the frog he's about to dissect."

"That's a bit harsh."

"As much as a snake can love?" he tried again.

"You know, some people say that about me—that I'm cold-blooded, without a heart."

"You're definitely not cold."

"I managed to deceive one man already."

"I'd know it." His words were a deep kind of purr that made heat travel up her throat. He *would* know. As surely as he knew how many cards were in his desk with a caress of fingertips.

"Perhaps." She casually leaned against the wall; the

night air seeping through the window cooled her skin. The street below was quiet. Empty.

"That's odd," she murmured.

"What is?"

Isobel drew her brows together in thought. "We've been here half the night and there hasn't been a single patrolman. But they came readily enough the night I was arrested. I assumed they had been walking their regular beat."

Riot stood. "Let's try that door."

ISOBEL SCURRIED OVER ROOFTOPS. IT FELT GOOD TO MOVE, to *act*. She hopped over a gap between buildings, and dropped to a flat roof. She paused to glance over its edge. Riot strolled along a planked sidewalk. With rough cap, coat, and carrying his walking stick over a shoulder, he looked like any other hoodlum headed towards the delights of the Barbary Coast. He disappeared around a corner.

She followed. When rooftops gave out, she climbed down the nearest drain pipe, and came at the narrow lane from the shadows. The street was empty. Silent. Isobel slipped into the alleyway. Crouching in the garbage-strewn lane, she listened to rats gnawing on their meals.

A figure appeared at the far end. He walked straight into the darkness, but she wasn't concerned. Isobel would know that confident stride anywhere. Clothes most definitely did not make the man where Atticus Riot was concerned. Without a word, he stopped at the only door free of debris. Isobel kept watch as he inserted pick and wrench into the padlock.

A minute passed. Far too long for his skilled hands.

"It's rusted," he whispered.

She swore under her breath.

Riot tucked away his picks, and brought out a flash light. He flipped the switch, and a dim light filled the alleyway. He shined it over the padlock and along the edges of the door. The light made her uneasy. Riot ran a hand along the right edge. Something clicked, and the door swung open. The padlock had been a decoy.

With walking stick in hand, Riot stepped into the dark opening. Isobel quickly followed, but Riot caught the door before she closed it. He studied the interior. Satisfied they'd be able to exit, he closed it softly.

The light in his hand died, plunging them into darkness. She heard a soft oath, and a whack as he slapped the flash light against his palm.

Isobel quickly struck a match, lit the little candle she always carried, and placed it inside her folding lantern. "A sailor relies on the reliable," she whispered.

"Well, I've just mucked up my chances."

Isobel smiled as she held her lantern aloft. She had expected a storage room; instead, stone pushed at the edges of her light, and stairs plunged away into darkness. It was cramped and stifling. She sniffed the air. Wet mold, and a sharp reek of disinfectant.

Using her lantern to illuminate the path ahead, Riot led the way. The stairway quickly gave way to a long cellar. Brick lined the walls, and questionable beams strained under the ceiling.

They walked a circuit of the room. Sturdy shelves climbed the far wall, a long worktable sat in the center of the cellar, and electrical wires ran along the ceiling. A single bulb hung over the table.

Isobel followed the wires to a switch, and flicked it on. She blinked against the bright electric light. Riot moved to a low, reinforced door. A metal rung was attached to the wall beside it. He brushed his fingers over the metal, then lifted the bar barricading the door, and walked inside.

A cot, washbasin, an empty shelf, and a bucket. A brass grate high on a wall provided ventilation.

Isobel shivered, not from cold, but from the room. She quickly left to explore the larger area. The floor showed signs of recent sweeping. Perfectly round stains marred the worktable, as if someone had set down a mug filled with acid. She sniffed at the stains, and jerked back. A strong chemical odor stung her nostrils.

A gleam caught her eye. She walked to the spot, and crouched. The stone floor was cracked, and a thin glass tube had rolled into the crevice. "Riot?" she called softly.

He was at her side in an instant.

"Do you have one of your envelopes? And gloves?"

He produced both. Since the thin leather gloves fit him, he slipped them on and extracted the tube. She held out the envelope.

"A test tube," he noted before dropping it inside.

"I sincerely doubt someone was brewing beer to escape the liquor tax."

"Whatever was going on here, it appears William Punt has closed shop."

"All because of my blundering investigation."

A LETHAL CLUE

Slowly the puzzle takes shape. Little Pete's assassination created a void of power, and that void was filled by a beast of the shadows. A beast that prefers silent manipulation. —Z.R. Journal Excerpt

Thursday, March 22, 1900

"DR. KELLOGG?"

Three men looked up from a corpse. The youngest blinked. He had his hands in the abdominal cavity of a naked body that lay on a slab. A bowl provided temporary housing for the cadaver's entrails.

The young man brought out another loop of intestine that slipped its way into the bowl. "What can I do for you?" Dr. Kellogg wore sleeves and apron, all soaked with blood. "I'd shake hands, but...well, you understand, I'm sure."

"Don't let me interrupt."

"Don't faint on us."

"My name is Atticus Riot. I'm with Ravenwood Detective Agency."

"*The* Atticus Riot?" An older man half turned. His

mutton chops extended to form a mustache over his upper lip. Where Kellogg was covered in gore, this man was nearly pristine. A third man stood off to the side with pen and notebook in hand.

"As far as I know there's only one of me," Riot replied.

Mutton Chops gave him a guarded look. "Police Surgeon, F.P. Wilson. A colleague of mine performed the postmortem on Jim Parks."

"His report was thorough. I appreciate that. Is this another plague death?" Riot looked over the corpse. Male, Chinese, with an obscene incision splitting the body from shoulders to pubic bone. Flesh was splayed, revealing everything from the trachea down. Swollen lymph glands bulged on his thighs, and oozing sores dotted his skin.

"We'll know when we're through," Kellogg said. "It doesn't do to jump to conclusions. Bubonic plague shares many of the same symptoms as gonorrhea—on the surface, at any rate. But the dead speak for themselves. What can we do for you?"

"I'd hoped to speak with you about your missing health inspector—Lincoln Howe."

Kellogg looked to the third man.

He looked up from his notes. "A.P. O'Brien. City health officer." Prim and direct, he had a pince-nez on the tip of a pointed nose. "I spoke with the police about Mr. Howe's disappearance."

"You don't seem overly concerned."

"Neither were the police."

Kellogg dropped a lumpy mass of tissue onto a scale, and called out the weight. "Lincoln likely packed up, and took the first train out of town. I don't blame him. Nasty business."

"You think the plague outbreak scared him off?"

"That's exactly what I think. The man didn't have the stomach for any of this," said Wilson.

"And he wasn't very bright," Kellogg added. "He refused the Yersin antiserum. There's a risk of serum sickness, but there's far more risk with the plague."

"Did you know Lincoln Howe well?"

All three shook their heads. "He arrived in January from Honolulu," O'Brien said. "Highly recommended. As Wilfred mentioned, he wasn't the brightest, but he was always willing to go where others weren't."

"How so?" Riot asked.

"He was a rough sort. So I sent him into the seedier alleyways. Chinese residents were scared of him. They tended to make a quick exit."

"They hide whenever we're around," Kellogg said.

The Police Surgeon clucked his tongue. "It's been inconvenient."

Riot waited for an explanation. Kellogg took up the narration along with a scalpel. "The Chinese are hiding their dead. From what our interpreters tell us, it's bad luck for someone to die in a house. So the living haul the dead to the nearest coffin shop."

"Or residents stow the bodies somewhere so we can't perform a postmortem. They don't like what we do here, especially cremations," O'Brien said.

Kellogg's hand disappeared inside the abdominal cavity. "By the time the Health Department hears of a death, residents have managed to hide the body. I'm afraid there's been many more than what's been reported. And at this rate, the plague will spread."

"Did Lincoln Howe keep a room somewhere?"

"He gave an address. He was renting a room on Broadway, or so he claimed. But when I questioned the landlady, she said she rarely saw him. His room was empty," O'Brien said.

"Kept to himself." Kellogg offered.

"Can you provide a description?"

Kellogg lifted out another mass of tissue. From its texture, Riot thought it the liver, but it was massive. He placed it on the scale. After calling out the weight, he bent over the organ with scalpel in hand.

O'Brien adjusted his pince-nez. "Lincoln Howe was five-eleven, one hundred and eighty pounds. A mushroomed left ear, crooked nose, and scarred knuckles."

"It's a rare honor to speak with an observant witness."

"My line of work requires precision. I don't see how it's of help, though. There are a dozen boats and trains leaving east at any given time. Howe could be in New York by now."

"On the contrary, you've been exceptionally helpful." With that description, Riot knew exactly where the Health Department's Lincoln Howe was. "I take it he was assigned to the Globe Hotel?"

Kellogg looked up, startled. "How could you possibly know that?"

"Observation," Riot answered. "I wonder if one of you gentleman could tell me what this is." He held up his envelope. "There's a test tube inside."

O'Brien set aside his pen and note pad, and took the envelope.

"Careful. I'm not sure what's inside. If anything."

O'Brien took out the tube and held it to a light. "It's definitely been used. There's a filmy layer inside, but the cork is intact. The microscopist can analyze it after he's done with the stomach contents of this one." He patted the knee of the corpse.

"I suspect it will prove urgent."

Wilson frowned. "Why is that?"

"Instinct."

The police surgeon's brows shot up. "Notes can wait, O'Brien. Mr. Riot has a reputation that only an idiot would ignore."

Without a word, O'Brien walked into an adjacent room. Riot followed. It was a cramped, windowless room with a pale man hunched at a worktable. A small electric light illuminated the object of his study.

"We need this analyzed straight away."

"I'm not finished with the stomach contents."

"It's urgent, Philip," O'Brien said.

Philip gave a sigh, straightened with a crack of his back, and flicked on a switch. Electric light burst into the room from an overhead bulb. Philip snatched the tube from O'Brien, plucked the cork free, and put his nose to the opening. He sniffed. "Musty and sweet," he murmured. "The little buggers are making themselves at home in here." There was affection in his voice.

Philip tipped the tube towards a slide. A drop touched glass, and he covered it with a thinner piece of glass. The drop spread to the corners. He flicked off the switch, plunging Riot into darkness.

"A lively little bunch of bacilli," Philip murmured. "I'll need two hours for fixation and dyeing with aniline, and then I'll perform a Gram test."

Riot spent the next two hours watching three men mutilate a corpse. Always humbling, as Ravenwood would say.

The adjacent door opened, and Philip poked his squinty eyes into the light. "Where'd you get this?"

"I found it."

"*Where?*" Philip hissed.

"What did you find?" O'Brien asked.

"Plague bacilli."

23

FIVE STORIES

Each small piece, seemingly unconnected, is moved into place. A link in a chain
of henchmen, each knowing nothing of the next, leaving a trail of ignorance. —
Z.R. Journal Excerpt

RICKETY STAIRS SAGGED UNDER RIOT'S FEET, AND HIS
shoulders brushed mold growing on rotting walls. He turned
sideways, taking care where he stepped. His guide's back
was nearly lost in the underground warren.

Ma Gee skipped over a puddle. "Watch yourself." His
voice was muffled by a handkerchief pressed over his nose.

Riot dipped his head to avoid the sagging ceiling as he
followed suit. The Consul General's detective hurried down
the murky passage. To the basement. Ma Gee stopped in
front of a boarded-up doorway. The hallway smelled of
sewage and rotting eggs—sulfur. A result of the health officers' fumigation efforts.

"Wong Chut King was found in this room." The lumber
yard salesman was the first purported plague death on
March seventh. He had been scraping by in the *Globe Hotel*
—it was the worst rookery in Chinatown and known as *Five*

Stories. Riot had seen all five stories, and he could confirm the rookery lived up to its reputation.

"It was not plague," Ma Gee said. "It was gonorrhea." In Cantonese the word roughly translated to 'poisonous mango-shaped death'.

Riot eyed the boarded-up doorway. Dim gaslight illuminated a painted 'X' across its center. "Who carried him to the undertakers on Clay Street?" *Sau pan po*, the coffin shop, translated to *long-life boards*. Riot had always found the translation whimsical.

"The caretaker. It's bad luck to have a tenant die inside a home—even Five Stories."

The basement hallway was covered in mold. There were cracks in the brick, and ominous ooze leaked from pipes. Riot resisted the urge to scratch his arms. Whoever this caretaker was, he wasn't much of one.

"I'll take you to the caretaker." Eager to be gone from the basement, Ma Gee turned to leave, but Riot gave a slight shake of his head. He moved farther into the dim, and stopped at the next doorway. A thin curtain hung over the opening. Riot used his stick to nudge the curtain aside.

A single candle burned on a mound of wax. Two bunk beds, three-tiered high, were crammed inside. Flophouses like the Globe Hotel housed bachelors and laborers who usually slept in eight hour shifts, two to a bunk. But today there were only four men instead of the usual twelve. With the tong war and quarantine scare, residents were fleeing Chinatown. The population was at an all-time low.

The men sat on a bottom bunk playing *pai gow*, the colored tiles arranged on a makeshift table. When they caught sight of Riot, the men jumped to their feet in the narrow space.

"I'm looking into a matter for Consul General Ho Yow.

About the man who died next door." Surprise widened their eyes. Few expected a white man in a tailored suit to speak Cantonese. Despite their living conditions their clothes and hair were immaculate, and the floor showed marks of a broom having recently passed over it.

The men glanced at each other. And a fifth stirred on a top bunk. Although young, his back was horribly bent. Riot doubted he could straighten.

Their gazes traveled over Riot's shoulder, to Ma Gee, who stood in the hallway. "We don't know anything about him."

"Do you think it was plague?" Riot asked.

"*No*," they said at once.

"That's what I aim to prove—that his death wasn't what the health officials are claiming." Half-truths were the most convincing. His words put them at ease.

The hunched man swung his legs over the edge of the bunk, the top of his head brushing the ceiling. "Chut King was sick with gonorrhea. He was spending all his money on green mansions."

Perhaps, but it certainly didn't account for the four other deaths. "Did you know him?"

The men consulted each other with a glance. A man with horribly pox-scarred cheeks spoke. "We worked at the same lumber yard."

"What were his symptoms?"

"He was curled in his bunk. He wouldn't come to work, so I fetched a doctor. But he came down with a fever and began vomiting," the pockmarked man said. "His tongue was white, and he developed the poisonous mango and didn't wake up. I helped the landlord take him to the under-takers. There was nothing else to do for him."

"Did anyone visit Chut King before he fell ill? A health officer perhaps?"

The men shook their heads, and Riot moved to the next room. Conversations went much the same, until he came to the final doorway. It was a loose term. The bricks had been removed, or perhaps fallen, and a crude wooden board had been placed over the opening. Riot rapped his walking stick on the board.

No one answered.

"So polite, *Din Gau*." Ma Gee looked amused as he stepped forward and slid the board to the side. They recoiled at the smell. Fuzzy mold covered the walls and leaky pipes. From the smell, Riot gathered those pipes led to the sewers.

"Worse than rats," Ma Gee muttered, smoothing his sleeves.

Riot took out his flash light. The electric light barely pierced the small room. It was empty save for a lump on a bottom bunk. A slight rise and fall in the blanket told Riot that the lump was alive.

He moved into the room. "Hello?" he asked in Cantonese. When a more forceful attempt elicited no movement, he lifted the blanket aside with the tip of his stick. The lump came alive. An old man sprang to a crouching position on the bunk, a knife flashing in his hand.

Riot deftly parried the weak attempt with his stick. The blade fell, and Riot snatched it up, turning it around to offer it back to the man. "We've come to ask after your neighbor."

Stunned, the old man blinked. After a moment's hesitation he accepted his knife, and tucked it away in his voluminous tunic. He said something that Riot didn't understand. A different dialect, from one of the surrounding providences of Canton.

Ma Gee spoke in yet another dialect. It was a question. And the man nodded and replied. The detective looked relieved. They had found a common language.

"He says that he knows nothing about the man who died."

Riot studied the crouched old man. It was more difficult to get a feel for someone when he couldn't understand their language. But still, there were 'tells': small flutters of a lash, purposeful eye contact, a ready answer. This old man was too quick to reply.

"Ask him if we are the first men who've come by asking after Chut King."

Riot waited for the exchange. At first the old man shook his head. But Ma Gee sensed there was more, and pressed him. "Health officers did come here," Ma Gee translated.

"Did the health officers come before the quarantine?"

Ma Gee tilted his head, but he asked the question.

The old man looked at Riot, and nodded. He held up a single finger. A flurry of words flew back and forth as the two men conversed. Riot had the sense that Ma Gee was reassuring him, convincing him to trust them. Riot caught General Consul Ho Yow's name and *Din Gau* in the conversation, but little else.

"He's worried about his safety," Ma Gee finally said.

Riot reached into his waistcoat pocket and pulled out a five dollar gold piece. "This is enough to buy you a train ticket to anywhere in California, plus room and board when you get there." And just like that, gold loosened the old man's tongue.

MA GEE AND RIOT TOOK A DEEP BREATH OF FRESHER AIR. Burning sulfur, roasting pork, and incense were a welcome relief after the interior of the Globe Hotel.

Men in wide hats and voluminous tunics walked down Dupont Street. Riot tucked back his coat. Just in case. He had enemies in Chinatown. "If I might make a suggestion?"

The detective glanced at him.

"Follow the old man and make sure he's safe."

Ma Gee stuck a cigarette between his lips. "Why? So he'll be fit to testify in court against a white man?"

There was that. "You never know," Riot said simply. "At the very least he was willing to speak with us. And he's observant."

Ma Gee struck a match. He took a drag, savoring the tobacco as he considered Riot's words. "I'll question the other residents. Do you know who this health officer is?"

"Yes."

"Who?"

"I want to gather more facts first. We'll interview residents in the other plague death locations."

"Purported," Ma Gee said, blowing a line of smoke into the air.

Riot didn't answer.

"I think it's best if I go alone."

"Why's that?" Riot asked.

Ma Gee gestured with his cigarette at men walking by. "Your name is on the Dead Wall."

Riot looked down the street towards the opening of a dead-end lane plastered with *chun hungs*—tong-sanctioned assassinations.

"It's been there before."

"You will attract attention if you come with me."

Two white men strolled by, bowlers cocked at an angle, but Ma Gee was right. A Chinese detective asking questions for the Consul General was expected, but a white man with a price on his head? That would hardly put residents at ease.

"You're right. I'll question the undertaker while you handle the residents. But we need to tread carefully," Riot warned. "Not a word until we report to the Consul General."

Ma Gee nodded. "When, *Din Gau*?"

"How long do you need to question the other residents?"

"Two days."

"Send me a missive." Riot touched the brim of his hat, then headed for Sacramento Street.

Children played in doorways, and a father strolled with his silk-clad daughter on his shoulders. Riot saw him stop to buy her a balloon from a Jewish merchant. It might have been just another quiet day in the Quarter, except that odors of incense, roasting pork, and fish were fighting with sulfur fumes.

He turned up Washington, onto Waverly Place, and sidestepped a man selling peanuts. Out of the corner of his eye, he noticed a white man suddenly stop to study a hawker's tea offerings. Riot kept a steady pace, the beat of his walking stick clicking with his heels. He cut across the street, in front of a carriage bursting with tourists who were gawking at the Quarter. The white man began walking again.

It was the way he walked that warned Riot. It wasn't a leisurely stroll through exotic streets or the purposeful gait of a man on a mission. This man walked with both purpose *and* leisure. It was forced.

Riot stepped into Wing Sang coffin shop on the corner of Clay and Waverly Place. Scents of fresh pine, varnish,

and death permeated the shop. The steady sound of a
hammer tapping nails brought a rush of memory back. Riot
stopped, gripping his walking stick for support.

Three years before, as he lay dying on a filthy cot, he
had listened to that very sound.

The undertaker stopped, and looked up. It wasn't
everyday that a white man walked into his shop. He was a
small, bent man who tapped on nails with expert precision.
"I don't speak English," he said in Cantonese.

Riot swallowed. Words stuck in his throat. *Would he ever be
free of these memories?* He focused on the feel of cold metal in
his palm and the floorboards beneath his feet, until he felt
grounded again.

"Atticus Riot." At the introduction, the undertaker's eyes
widened. Too rattled by the sound of tapping nails, Riot had
forgotten his reputation. But it was too late to take back the
introduction. "I'm investigating a matter for General Consul
Ho Yow—" The undertaker started shaking his head, clearly
dismayed that 'no sabe' hadn't cut it. "I have a few questions
about a man who was brought to your shop on the seventh
of March."

"I don't know anything about him."

Riot smiled. "I didn't tell you his name yet."

"I don't know."

"His name was Wong Chut King. Health officers took
him from your shop after he died."

"It was gonorrhea," the undertaker insisted.

"I'm trying to prove that very thing for the Consul
General, but I need your help."

The undertaker took one look at Riot, put down his
hammer, and quickly shuffled backwards, bowing until he
disappeared behind a curtain.

Riot slapped an open palm against the knob of his stick.

One mistake and he had lost his chance. A simple introduction had invoked fear and death. Not justice.

Hoping to salvage the situation, he walked through the
curtain, and froze. A line of cots stretched across the room.
An old woman lay on the top of the nearest. Pale and
marbled, she had been dead a few days, and awaited her
journey home. Then there were the not quite dead, festering
with infection and sickness. A young woman was missing
half her jaw, ravaged by syphilis, clinging to life yet begging
to die.

Riot sucked in a sharp breath of foul air. The stench
knocked him back a step. Pain laced his temple and beat at
his skull as the room spun. He saw the room as if looking
down from above, but it wasn't this coffin shop. It was
another. His own blood-soaked body was being carried by a
mound of rags.

The world snapped back into place, and Riot fled the
coffin shop. There wasn't enough air in the world to fill his
lungs. He walked in a daze, without seeing, setting a brisk
pace that bordered on a run.

By the time he came back to himself, he was nearing
Golden Gate Park. Exhausted, he stopped to pry his fingers
from the knob of his walking stick. Riot stared at his palm.
The engraving was etched into his skin. He took a breath,
and massaged feeling back into his fingers. As he stood
there, trying to regain his senses, he spotted a man rounding
the corner—the same who had been following him in
Chinatown. Only now the man was perspiring. When he
spied Riot's glance, his feet stuttered, and he quickly ducked
into a barber shop.

Clenching his jaw, Riot slapped the point of his stick
against the boardwalk. If there was one thing he hated

worse than being shadowed, it was being shadowed by an amateur.

Riot entered the barber shop. The Shadow was sitting in a chair, preparing for a shave, only his skin was awfully smooth.

Riot sat in a chair, and ran a hand over his beard. "A trim, if you please," he said to the barber.

The Shadow shifted in his seat. Brown hair, long side-burns, and a mustache. There was nothing spectacular about him, except that he wasn't in the least bit threatening. Not sitting in a chair with his throat about to be exposed.

The barber nodded to Riot. "You're next, sir."

"That suits me just fine."

The barber nodded, and draped an apron over his customer with a flourish. He worked a lever, and the chair tilted back. The Shadow's throat was vulnerable, and his eyes rolled to the side.

Riot crossed his legs and regarded the man. "You look as though you were only shaved this morning."

The barber applied lather. "I like to be fresh," the Shadow said with a chuckle.

"Hardly fresh with the way you're perspiring. Didn't I see you in Chinatown?"

"Maybe so. I was just there."

"That's quite a walk."

A skilled razor zipped over the Shadow's cheeks.

"I'd like to know who hired you," Riot said.

"What?"

"Who hired you to follow me."

The barber paused, razor poised. He raised inquiring brows that were hairless. Why are barbers always bald? Riot mused silently.

"By all means, sir. Keep at it," Riot said to the barber.

But the Shadow would have none of it. He ripped off his apron, and made to stand. "I don't know what you're—"

Riot slapped his walking stick to the side, hitting the Shadow square across the chest. It knocked him back into the chair, and Riot stood, pinning the man with the tip of his stick. "Who hired you?"

A movement off to the side warned him. Without taking his eyes off the Shadow, he drew his revolver and pointed it at the barber. "Do not involve yourself in this, sir."

Riot stared down at the Shadow. When the barber raised his hands, Riot inclined his head. In one smooth motion he uncocked his revolver, and holstered it.

The Shadow had his lips pressed tightly together. At least he had some professional principles. Riot patted him down. A Shopkeeper and a billfold were in his pockets. Riot ignored the revolver and rifled through the man's billfold. No red token. But a calling card for a Mr. Bill Wyatt, Private Investigator.

"Mr. Wyatt, I'll ask you again. Politely. Who hired you to follow me?"

"Summon the police," Mr. Wyatt said.

The barber didn't make a move.

"He's a wise fellow, Mr. Wyatt. You, however, are not." Riot pulled out a stack of cards from Wyatt's billfold. A single one caught his eye. Alex Kingston.

"If I ever catch you following me again, I'll take it as a threat. Do you understand?"

"Yes, Mr. Riot."

"And keep away from the *Pagan Lady*, or I'll take it personal."

Mr. Wyatt's forehead creased. Only a fraction. It was

enough. He had no idea what the *Pagan Lady* was. With a curse, Riot flicked the card at the man's face, and walked out of the barbershop.

24

ALL IS LOST

It was safer to meet at my manor, in the conservatory. Informants came and went

without notice. —Z.R. Journal Excerpt

"You left me in jail, Mack!" Isobel Kingston had the big Scotsman cornered. Bells, rings, and the chatter of type-writers drifted from the corral.

"I dinna leave you there. I dinna get your message."

Isobel pinned the man to the wall with her gaze.

Mack McCormick deflated. "Until later."

"The message boy said he gave it to you straightaway." A nickel had loosened the messenger's tongue.

Mack muttered under his breath. "I was on my way to bail you out, but the editor told me to wait—to give you more material for your story."

Isobel ground her teeth together. "Except someone else stole my story out from under me."

"It was bound to get out," he said.

"I hope he managed to make his rent for the month."

"I hear she only got a dollar for it."

"She?"

Mack clamped his lips together.

"It was one of the Sob Sisters, wasn't it?"

"I'm not saying a word."

"You already have." She jabbed a finger into his gut. "*Talk.*"

"Or what? You'll box my ears?"

Mack McCormick was over six feet tall and solid as a bull. Even so, every bull had a weak spot. Her fist wasn't far from his, but she reeled herself in. Dropping a fellow reporter to the ground wasn't quite called for. Yet. Besides, he might be her only ally—as much as any reporter could be.

"I would have bailed you out, Charlie," he rumbled, and then flashed a grin. "After making a deal that I get a cut of your story."

"At least you're honest. Which one of my 'sisters' left me in there to rot?"

Mack crossed his arms. "Does it matter? You still have your vagrant story. This way it's been primed, and readers are waiting to hear more. The public love a damsel in distress. Besides, it's not like the *Call* was the only one to catch wind of your arrest. We were just the first to get it on the press. There's always a mob of reporters loitering around the station, waiting for a story."

"You're right." She took a step back. He couldn't know of course. That there was an excellent chance that Parker Gray and his lot had been alerted. And now, thanks to the unknown snitch, Parker Gray could easily discover her *nom de plume.*

Isobel rubbed her forehead.

"You might as well go and write an exclusive, Charlie."

Mack nodded to a reporter walking by, waiting until he was
out of earshot. "What were you really doing out there at
night?"

She smiled. "Just like I said."

"Do you ever tell the truth?"

"Always."

Isobel ignored further questions, and left him in the
corridor looking disgruntled. But the story she really wanted
to tell wasn't ready yet. She and Riot suspected Parker Gray
and his associates were dealing in far more than flesh for
sale.

Isobel walked through the crowded corral, aware of eyes
on her.

"Nice work, Bonnie," a reporter called out.

"Whatcha do to get that exclusive with Atticus Riot?"

She had forgotten all about the inquest. "Took a bath.
Try it sometime, Willy." Open stares turned to laughter in
her wake.

The Sob Sister's office was full. Sara Rogers, her hair in
a severe bun; an older, worn woman by the name of Rose;
and a woman a few years older than herself, Jo Kelly. And,
of course, the indomitable Cara Sharpe. The other women
were always on their best behavior when Sharpe was
present.

"I'm nearly through here," said Miss Rogers. Her
working space was as tidy as one came. Everything was laid
at right angles and spaced with deliberation. There was not
a crease in a paper. She gathered her papers up, and
knocked them against the desk with a sharp slap.

"How did jail treat you?" Jo Kelly asked. She was
dressed in the latest fashion, her walking dress was tailored,
and her copper hair curled to perfection. She covered
society affairs, and dressed the part, even in the office.

"About the same as I remember."

The women in the room paused, and looked at her. Isobel flashed a grin. But Jo Kelly wasn't shocked at all. The look of satisfaction on her face made Isobel's skin crawl.

Sara Rogers stood, her papers in hand. "Let's hope the almighty desk editor gives me good pay for this." She didn't look hopeful.

"I'll beseech the gods of ink and pen," Isobel said, taking over her desk. A round of *Amens* were muttered into the air. After Sara Rogers had marched out, Isobel turned to the others. "Who wrote the article about me being locked up in jail?"

"I did," Rose said. "My boy at the jailhouse relayed it to me. I needed rent." The older woman was haggard and thin. Isobel could hardly come up with an ulterior motive for her bit of reporting. "I figured it would help your story rather than hurt it. I wasn't planning on sniping it out from under you."

"You should have interviewed her in the jailhouse," Cara Sharpe said, without looking up from her desk. "You published half a story."

Rose wilted. "I got it on the press before the other newspapers."

"If someone had thought to bail me out when I called, I might have had an *entire* story to publish," Isobel said.

Cara Sharpe regarded her. "Spreckles thought otherwise."

"Perhaps there's a bigger story brewing." Jo Kelly smiled. Before Isobel could ask about the comment, Jo stood, gathered her things, and left.

Squaring her shoulders, Isobel turned to her typewriter. As her fingers flew over the keys, her mind raced ahead. Sorting facts. Sifting details. Moving pieces around her mental chessboard. As far as games went, things looked grim.

"Look, Bonnie," Cara interrupted her thoughts.

She looked up from her typewriter to find the office empty, and a fully typed article in her reel.

"You have steel in your spine, but you need to be careful. Stunt reporting has to be authorized, or the paper won't back you when you land into trouble. And even if your story *is* authorized by the editor, sometimes they throw you to the dogs anyway."

Isobel lifted a shoulder. "I seized an opportunity."

"A man came looking for you the other day," Cara said.

"I figured as much."

"Average fellow. I didn't like the look of him."

"If he was average, then what struck you?"

"There are men, and there are killers. Whatever story you're working on, leave it alone."

An average killer. Isobel had always imagined that she'd receive her quieting dose of lead from a man with an eyepatch, or one wearing turquoise boots. But average? How tedious.

It didn't matter now. Time had run out, and danger stood at her doorstep. She casually took out her cigarette case. The red token that she had taken from Andrew Ross was tucked neatly in the case. Isobel offered a cigarette to Cara, tilting the case so the token was visible. As Cara took a cigarette, her eyes lingered on that token.

"You seem to have an inkling of what I'm digging at," Isobel said.

"What you're digging is your own grave." Cara's fingers trembled as she struck a match.

Isobel leaned towards the woman. "Tell me what you know."

Cara shook her head. "I know enough to keep my mouth shut."

"You're a reporter."

"I'm a reporter who's still alive," Cara said. "There are a handful of men in this city who can't be bought. Most of them are dead, or have been brushed aside. There are stories that *no* newspaper will touch. Do you understand?"

"That I'm on my own? Yes."

Cara nodded.

"That's exactly why I didn't want my name in a newspaper."

"You should have thought about that before you pulled that stunt. I hope it was worth it."

"You said *some* of those men are dead. Who do you know that can't be bought?"

"Fremont Older, but he doesn't *own* the *Bulletin*, so he can only go so far. Money turns San Francisco's gears. It's a well-oiled graft machine, as he's fond of saying."

"Anyone else?"

"The *Examiner*. But Hearst is a wild card. He has his own agendas."

Isobel turned back around, and stared out the window. A shadowy organization of powerful men with money to bribe judges, jury, and police. Even if she and Riot were able to gather solid evidence, the conspiracy, whatever it was, might not even reach the courts. A pretty little problem.

"Bonnie!" a voice snapped her around. A skinny boy bolted into the room. He was built like a reed and had the voice of a ringmaster. "The editor wants to see you."

"*Joey*," Cara said. "That is no way to speak to a lady. How many times have I told you to behave like a gentleman?"

Joey ducked his head. "Yes, ma'am. Sorry, ma'am. Sorry,
Miss Bonnie."

When Joey had stumbled out, Cara said, "Good luck,
Bonnie. You'll either be promoted or fired."

"There's no gamble without risk." The comment made
the older woman flinch.

Isobel marched across the corral, article in hand. She
wasn't about to surrender her exclusive to the desk editor
until she discovered if she was about to be fired. She could
always take her skills to another newspaper.

Isobel knocked on the editor's door.

"Come."

Determined, Isobel marched into the office. Scent came
first. Familiar, cloying cigar smoke, sharp aftershave, and
copious amounts of pomade. Sight came next, as her gaze
jerked to the side, to a bull of a man towering over her. Alex
Kingston. Isobel turned to run, but her blackmailing
husband stepped in front of the doorway.

All her resolve bled into the ground.

"Mr. Kingston. *Mrs.* Kingston." Spreckles inclined his
head. "My office is at your disposal. Take as long as you
need."

The editor slipped out, Alex slammed the door, and
grabbed her by the throat. "I *knew* it was you at that
inquest." His voice shook her bones.

He pushed her against the wall. Frames clattered to the
ground. She didn't flinch. She hung helpless in his iron grip,
her toes just brushing the floor.

"I *thought* you were a ghost," he hissed in her ear.

"Clearly I'm not." Her voice was threadbare.

"No." His face twisted. "What you are is a conniving
bitch!" The back of her head hit the wall.

"Men abducted me, Alex." She sounded desperate to her

own ears. Confronted with him, she felt herself slipping back into the role she had assumed: a timid, sweet-natured socialite. It made her sick. "I thought it was you—"

"Why the devil would I abduct my own wife?"

"I thought you were tired of me and wanted me dead."

"You're lying." His lip curled. "It was another man, wasn't it?"

"Those men tried to kill me—"

"Shut up!" The back of his left hand slapped her face. A sharp, lingering sting that awakened her rage.

"You blackmailed me into marrying you, Alex!"

"I *loved* you."

"You were destroying my father."

"That was business, but you were pleasure." His thumb caressed her cheek, over the burn of his strike. Bile rose in her throat.

"You can't bully someone into loving you," she growled.

"I don't give a damn if you love me." His eyes turned to ice, and that hand tightened until air came scarce. Spots danced in the corner of her vision. She had to focus on breathing. "It's that damn detective I sent after you. Atticus Riot. You've both been playing me this entire time. You're after *my money!*" His left hand came up a second time, whipping her head to the side. She tasted blood.

Isobel reacted. She reached up, gripped the fingers clenching her neck, and wrenched two of them backwards. A snap, a roar, and Alex Kingston released her.

Moving to the middle of the office, Isobel wiped the blood from her lip. "I want a divorce, Alex."

Clutching his broken fingers, he straightened. Now he was wounded, and as furious as ever. "You committed fraud," he panted.

"No." The word gave him pause. Gone was the society

wife. There was only steel in her eyes and voice. "I escaped a belligerent husband." All at once, she dropped back into her role, and batted her eyes at him. "I can play the victim, dear husband. Who do you think the jury will believe?"

He chuckled. It made her skin crawl. "I buy jurors, *dear* wife. Judges, too. And police." He took a step forward. "You have no choice but to come back to me."

"So that's it? You want me to come back to you?" She laughed.

There was a pleased look in his eye that cut her amusement short. "You *will* come back. Your mistaken death can easily be excused. The newspapers will publish any story I feed them."

She cocked her head. "I don't think so."

"You may not now. But think longer on it, my sweet. I'll ruin your father and mother. And I'll ruin you. The only work you'll be able to find will be in the cribs and cow-yards. And if you think you can run to Atticus Riot… think again. There are plenty in this city who'd like to see him dead."

"No," she whispered, taking a step back towards the desk. Alex took a step forward. "Men tried to kill me. I thought it was you, but it turned out it was my brother Curtis."

"Why should I believe a word you say?"

"Because I'm backed into a corner." She knocked on the desk.

"You think I give a damn about the truth?"

"I thought Curtis was working for you."

Alex grunted. "You're delusional. I would never have done business with that sniveling brother of yours." It was true. She knew it. There was hate in his voice. And that puzzled her. Her mind raced.

"After you're used up from whoring, I think an asylum will suit you. You'll still be my wife, after all."

"You're not the lead dog in the pack, are you? You're more a lapdog for the Pacific-Union Club. The railway has enemies."

"You think you're *clever*? You think you can *threaten me*?"

She cocked her head. Why had he thought it a threat? "I can help you, Alex," she ventured.

"The only help I want from you is my husbandly due. And if you think I'll treat you like a lady this time around, you'll be sorely mistaken." With every word, he neared. He lunged, reaching for her hair, and she let him have it. The wig came off, and he stuttered in surprise. The moment cost him dearly. Isobel grabbed him by the lapels, yanked him forward, and twisted to the side. His groin hit the corner of the desk.

Alex Kingston bent over double, puffing out his cheeks.

"How careless of you," she said, opening her cigarette case. "Your first mistake was to think me a lady. And here is your second." She slapped the red token on the desk, under his eyes. "I know far more than you think. I know this plague will hit the Big Four in the same place that the desk just hit you."

Eyes blazing, he straightened, ignoring the token. She had hoped to see fear in his eyes, but there was only fury.

Alex wrenched the door open. "Spreckles! I want this woman fired immediately."

"Of course, Mr. Kingston."

Alex turned back to her. "Bring your things home tonight. Otherwise, I'll make good on my threats."

Without another word, he limped out.

Isobel blew out a breath, and picked up her wig. Gathering her dignity, she ignored the closest exit, and walked through the corral. Bruises, bloody lip, and a wig in hand. All eyes bore witness. She wondered if anyone would dare testify against Alex Kingston.

Isobel was as good as ruined.

25

SHATTERED

The signal was simple: a bit of silk tied around the grocer's delivery. And for me:

two lights left on in my conservatory. —Z.R. Journal Excerpt

ATTICUS RIOT STOPPED UNDER A LAMP POST. HE COCKED HIS head, listening. Muted voices drifted from a waterfront saloon, but there was no patter of footsteps. No one was following him in the fog. He stood for a few more breaths before walking onto the wharf.

The surf lapped at pilings under his feet. A few lanterns bobbed in the murk, but most of the boats were only dark shapes in the water. Secured, scrubbed, and moored for the night, their crews were spending earnings in saloons and bagnios.

A swift shadow moved from behind a storage shed. Riot reached for his revolver, but stopped. The shadow gave a plaintive meow.

"Did you follow me from home?"

Watson wrapped around his legs. His meow sounded suspiciously like an affirmative answer. Riot had been tailed after all. By an expert.

The cat bumped his leg, nudging him towards what Riot feared might be the end of the dock. When Watson was sure he had Riot's attention, he darted away.

Light was useless in this murk; it only scattered the beam. As a child he had become accustomed to trusting his keener senses more than his myopic eyes. He was at home in fog. He strode along the dock, using his walking stick to search for the edge. He found Watson waiting patiently by a ladder.

He and Isobel had planned to meet at Ravenwood Manor after her visit to the *Call*. But the sun had dropped and dinner had passed, and she hadn't appeared. The Shadow had unnerved him. After he'd checked at Sapphire House, he decided to head to the *Pagan Lady*. He only hoped the boat was moored in the same place.

He climbed onto a trawler, and untied its dinghy. After Watson hopped into the stolen boat, he picked up the oars, and trusted to his sense of direction. The bay was cold and still, and water lapped at the hull. He glanced over his shoulder. A dark shape loomed in the fog.

Riot pulled alongside the formless shape. Wood bumped wood, and he ran his hand along the hull. The *Lady's* curves were as familiar to him as her captain's.

"Ahoy there." His voice bounced over the water and was crushed by fog.

Watson leapt aboard. After securing the dinghy, Riot followed. "Ahoy?" he called again.

A cat answered.

The padlock was missing from the hatch. He drew his No. 3, and opened it. Watson darted into darkness. The cat called from the cabin's depths.

The cabin smelled of salt and emptiness. It was dreadfully cold. Riot paused at the lantern, and struck a match.

Soft light flooded the saloon. A lump lay on the berth, and a bare foot stuck from beneath a blanket. The dainty foot and thin ankle made his breath go still. It looked lifeless.

Riot hurried forward. "Bel?"

"Go away," she croaked.

"Are you ill?" He nudged down the blanket, and placed a hand on her forehead. It was cold rather than hot. She jerked away from his touch, and pulled the blanket firmly over her head.

"Go away," she growled again. But it sounded more like a plea.

Riot considered the lump, glanced at the pile of clothing on the floor, and then looked to the galley. "Have you eaten anything today?"

No answer. Watson threaded his bulky body between Riot's legs, his purr filling the saloon. "Well, I haven't either."

Hanging up his coat, Riot unbuckled his holster, rolled up his sleeves, and set to work. After lighting a fire in the potbellied stove, he turned to the galley.

His movements were pure instinct, born from months spent at sea with an old cook from Canton. As a young man between hay and grass, Riot had worked alongside him. The old man's voice came to his ears from the past. At first, it seemed senseless babble. But slowly a rhythm emerged; the rhythm turned to tones; the tones slowly gave way to understanding, until the boy who had been Riot began to answer in the cook's own Cantonese tongue.

A feline inquiry interrupted his memories. "I'm sure she'll be all right." He set down a bowl of water. The feline looked insulted. "I'm afraid I don't have shrimp today, Watson."

The cat's eyes narrowed. He swiveled on his paws, and returned to his mistress, curling atop the lump.

While rice was cooking on the stovetop, Riot carried a cup of steaming tea to the table. He added a plate of apples, cheese, and crackers. It was not the most tempting meal, but the ship's stores were low. Food was always an afterthought for Isobel, as if she forgot her brilliant mind was attached to a body. Riot nudged her foot aside and sat, then pulled it back onto his lap.

"I'm in no mood." Her bite was muffled by the blanket.

"Your foot is cold."

He expected her to toss the blanket aside, and give him hell. But she didn't stir. She didn't even reply, and that was the most worrying of all.

Riot ate in silence, and then reached for a book. As the cabin warmed, he read, his left hand rubbing the cold foot on his lap. Slowly, it warmed under his touch.

After a time, he heard a sigh. "Just go, Riot. It will pass," she murmured. "That's what I keep telling myself, anyway."

Ordinarily, he would not ignore a request from a lady. But this was different. *She* was different. He recalled the words of her murderous brother Curtis. *Bursts of energy and wild ideas, followed by foul moods and long stretches of solitude.* As vile as that particular brother had turned out to be, perhaps there was truth to his words. Lotario had hinted at the same. A 'brown study' worthy of the Great Detective.

"*I am tired of myself tonight. I should like to be somebody else,*" he quoted from the book in his hand. The words rang true. For both of them. He could not shake the memory of being carried into a coffin shop and left for dead. Why had the vagrant in that alleyway helped him three years before? Why had he gone to all the trouble of carrying him to an undertaker?

"I've tried that. It doesn't work."

The words knocked him back to the present. "It never does," he whispered.

Isobel nudged the blanket down. "Are you all right?"

"I'm splendid. That's why I keep a painting of myself in a locked room."

"What does it look like today?" she asked.

He glanced at her. A single eye stared at him from the blanket.

Riot pulled his tie free, removed his collar, and tossed them on the table. "Shaken. Exhausted. Worried."

The eye narrowed. "What happened?"

"A memory," he said softly. "Of someone carrying me into a coffin shop." He shook his head in frustration. "It spooked me enough that I left the shop before properly questioning the undertaker."

Isobel shifted, reaching for his hand. Her touch eased his worry.

"I'll return with you tomorrow. We can question him then."

"I'm afraid that ship has sailed. I made the mistake of introducing myself. I suppose I should add 'fool' to the painting."

"Promise me you won't add 'fury' to your list?"

He cocked his head in question. Isobel dragged herself upright, keeping her foot in place. The breath caught in his throat, then came fury—the cold, dangerous kind. It flicked his heart to racing. Swollen and bruised cheek, a split lip, and angry bruising around her throat. She had cut her hair again, butchered it, more like, and dyed it a severe black. But it was her eyes that struck him most. Dull and gray, all the life had left them. She looked defeated.

Swallowing down his reaction, he kept his voice light.

"You entered a prizefight, lost, and had a blind barber cut your hair?"

Not even a smile.

"I was going to sail away." The words were pained, her eyes shimmered. "I couldn't do it." He handed over her tea, and she accepted it, warming her hands on the cup. "You should just leave now."

Contrary to her words, she hadn't taken her foot away, so he listened to her body.

Isobel took a shaky breath. "I thought we'd have our fun, and you'd get tired of me and move on."

His fingers stilled. "What happened, Bel?"

"I'm trouble, Riot. Pure trouble. What if I'm with child? With Alex's child?"

"*Are* you with child?" he asked softly.

She lifted a shoulder. "I honestly don't know. Years ago, a doctor in Europe told me it was unlikely that I would ever have children, but Dr. Wise hinted at the possibility when he examined me."

Riot took a breath. "I've already considered the possibility. You *were* married for two months."

Isobel set aside her tea. "Of course you have." She ran her hands through her butchered hair, and dug her nails into her scalp, holding her head there. "You'd be saddled with another man's child."

"I've yet to meet an infant who could make me turn coward and run." She tucked her feet in and scooted to the end of the berth. There was a time and place for humor. This wasn't it. "As a bastard myself, it's never much mattered to me. A child is still a child."

She swallowed. "Yes, I know. I heard you with the children the other night. You're wonderful with them. It's plain you care for them. What do you possibly see for our future?

Do you expect children from me? I'm no mother to be tied to a home. So before the heartache, before whatever comes between us… You should leave now."

Riot considered her in silence, and came to one conclusion: Isobel was terrified. "Through any storm that comes our way," he said softly. The words she had uttered to him two weeks ago. "I'm not abandoning ship."

"I don't see a horizon."

Her hopelessness stabbed his heart. He brushed a cat hair from his trousers, and kept his voice casual. "You know, I never thought I'd make it to forty. I had never even seen a horizon until I met you."

"But you *deserve* more—not a barren woman or another man's child."

Riot looked into her eyes. "The *only* thing I want is to wake up beside you every morning."

Isobel hugged herself, clutching her elbows.

"I have the distinct feeling you're trying to drive me away. I'll leave if you insist, but it won't be willingly. Child or no, I'm not going anywhere."

It was on the tip of her tongue to send him away. But she didn't speak the word. She couldn't order him to leave. "I'm only trying to save you," she whispered.

"Did someone threaten to kill me again?"

"Something like that."

He waited for more, but when none came, he made his own deductions. The bruises, the split lip, her despair. "Alex confronted you today."

Isobel took a deep breath—the gasp of a drowning woman. "At the *Call*. In the editor's office. He swore to ruin me, and my family, and to have you killed if I didn't go back to him tonight. I was fired on the spot."

A muscle in his jaw twitched.

"You *cannot* storm into his home with guns blazing."

Riot tore his gaze from his holstered revolver hanging on a hook. "I admit, that was my first thought." To ease her fears, he unbuttoned his waistcoat, tossed it across the way, and slipped his shoes off. "Better?"

Two tears slipped down her cheeks. Isobel tried to keep them at bay, but the moment he reached across the space, she lost her thread of control. Isobel buried herself in his arms as emotion shook her body. As quickly as the storm came, it passed, leaving her quiet and still.

Riot handed her a handkerchief.

"I broke two of his fingers and ran his testicles into a desk," she said between nose blowing.

Riot pressed his lips to her temple. "I'd wager on you in any fight."

She pulled back to meet his eyes. "It was reckless. I lost any advantage I had by showing my true self."

"You may have shaken him."

"A wounded bull is a fearsome thing."

"It's wounded. That's what counts."

"Unfortunately, that's not the only reckless thing I did."

The edge of Riot's lip twitched. "I'm hardly surprised." Before she could explain, he held up a hand. "Eat first, then tell me. And after, I have news of my own."

To his relief, she ate a bowl of rice, most of the cheese and apples, and settled back with her tea. As her fingers traced the contours of the chipped teacup, she told him everything that had happened.

"How curious," he mused when she fell silent.

"I thought so too," she admitted. "I had hoped to see fear in his eyes when I laid that token down, but he barely glanced at it."

"It *was* a risk."

"A thoughtless one."

"Aren't they all?"

"Mine, perhaps. You seem to be more of a calculating risk taker."

Riot flashed his chipped teeth. "Your instincts are incomparable, but your judgment is sorely lacking."

"Ravenwood wrote that about you."

"And he reminded me of it often enough." He nodded towards the book he had been reading: The Portrait of Dorian Gray. "*Experience is merely the name men gave to their mistakes.*"

"Then I'm full to bursting with experience. And I'm only twenty-one."

"We learned something though. It's doubtful that Kingston knows the token's significance."

"*We* don't precisely know what it means."

"We have an idea."

She stared into the dregs of her teacup. "When I saw him at the inquest… I felt sick. I saw *my* failure. I couldn't do it, Riot. When I was pretending to be someone else—his delicate society wife—I couldn't continue the ruse a moment longer. Other women pretend to love men all the time, but this… It felt wrong."

"That's not a bad thing, Bel."

"The *one* time I develop a conscience." She gave a bitter laugh. Another tear slipped free, and she scrubbed at her cheeks with her palm. "I didn't know who I was when I was with him. I was unraveling. And now the pieces don't fit. Maybe he wasn't the cause of my father's misfortune. Maybe it was Curtis all along."

"Only a few hours ago, he threatened to ruin you and your family. I'd say that's fairly incriminating."

"It doesn't do us a lick of good. The editor didn't even

ask why I was being fired. There was no hesitation. Alex controls the newspapers, and I have no reason to doubt his other words. He has judges and the police in his pocket."

Riot's gaze was drawn to his revolver. A noose around his neck would be a small price to pay for Isobel's safety. But it was easy to die for someone; it was much more difficult to live for them.

"I can't see a way out of this."

"We'll manage," he said softly.

"How?" she demanded.

Riot removed his spectacles to polish the lens. "We'll run away and join a circus."

Isobel closed her eyes. A smile tugged at her lips, and she started to laugh. More tears leaked from her eyes, but it was more release than despair. Riot set aside his spectacles, and took her in his arms. They stretched along the settee, and he tugged a blanket over their bodies.

"I don't think you have a future as a barber," he whispered into her hair.

"It's horrid," she agreed. "Ari is going to kill me. I'm surprised the sight of it wasn't enough to drive you away."

"You could take a razor to it, and I'd still be here."

"Yes, well, it helps that you're half-blind without your spectacles."

He smiled, and kissed her ear. "I've always enjoyed a more tactile approach."

Isobel turned in his arms, and stroked his beard. "Before you distract me, what news do you have?"

With every word that left his lips, Isobel sat up straighter with alarm. "What did the old man say?" she asked at last.

"The old man recognized the health officer. It was Andrew Ross—who ran with the most hated policeman in

Chinatown. The old man said Ross was lurking around the Globe Hotel, checking for sleeping laborers. Bullying them, if they made a fuss."

Her eyes narrowed. "We have to find William Punt."

"Yes."

26

THE STORM

Tuesday, April 17, 1900

Murmurs traveled around the court. Reporters scratched furiously, and a few darted out to send messengers running to editors.

The defense stared at the witness. "Mr. Riot. You're claiming that the bubonic plague was manufactured by Parker Gray, Andrew Ross, and William Punt?"

"Yes." Riot let his answer sink in. The murmurs grew to anger.

"The plague is a sham!" a gentleman in the audience shouted.

"It's a yellow problem!" another voice argued.

"Science never lies!"

The audience began arguing the heated topic.

Judge Adams slammed his gavel down. "Order! Quiet down or I'll clear the room."

Silence. No one wanted to leave. On the outside, Riot was as calm as could be, but inwardly was another matter—they *needed* an audience.

Adams fixed Riot with a scowl, and leaned forward, his chair creaking in protest. "Do you have proof?"

"Ma Gee questioned the residents about each reported plague death. Andrew Ross was present at every location— the Globe Hotel, a lodging house on the corner of Sacramento and Dupont, and finally Oneida Place. Police Surgeon Wilson can confirm the presence of plague in the test tube we discovered."

Judge Adams shifted his weight on the bench. "Did you report this to the police?"

"We did. To Deputy Inspector Coleman and Sergeant Price, who reported it to the Chief of Police."

"And was an investigation conducted?" Judge Adams asked.

"No."

Judge Adams' whiskers twitched. "Why the devil not?"

Riot glanced at the judge. "I think you know the answer to that, your honor."

"I want *your* answer."

"The reasons will become apparent. If I may continue?"

Judge Adams consulted his watch. "After lunch. You may step down, Mr. Riot."

Riot did as ordered, returning to his seat. He tried to catch Isobel's gaze, but she stared ahead. Dark circles ringed her eyes, and her cheekbones had sharpened over the past three weeks. From the tilt of her shoulders, he suspected if she looked at him, she'd break down. When he was seated, Judge Adams tapped his gavel on the block. "We'll reconvene in an hour. Defense, Prosecution—in my office. Now."

Riot watched as the bailiff escorted Isobel out of the court room, until a shadow loomed over him, blocking his view. Riot stood and met the cool blue gaze of Alex Kingston. A flimsy partition separated the two men.

What are you playing at?" Kingston said under his breath.

"We gave you a chance."

"We could have settled this out of court."

"And yet we're here," Riot stated.

"None of this will save her."

Riot glanced towards the jury who were filing out. "I'm well aware of your jury-rigging."

Alex Kingston smiled down at him. "That bitch humiliated me. I'll return the favor when she's in prison," he said for Riot's ears alone.

Riot didn't reply, didn't rise to the bait, only waited. This went on long enough for the reporters to fall silent. A puff of photography smoke gave Kingston an excuse to back away. He stalked out of the court room.

As lawless as times had been, Riot would have given a great deal to settle things the old-fashioned way—with a duel at sundown. Keeping a tight restraint on his self-control, he took a calming breath.

A thin barrier was keeping the reporters at bay, but that didn't stop them from yelling questions his way. "Is Mrs. Kingston a prostitute?"

He ignored their questions. But Jin did not. The girl tensed to lunge at the latest outrage. Riot grabbed her shoulder and spun her around. "No," he said simply.

"I heard what he said. I am going to kill that man," Jin bit out.

Riot did not doubt her resolve or her willingness. He'd even wager on her ability to carry out that threat. "Breathe, Jin," he whispered. "In and out. This isn't a place for a fight."

"They're only words," Lotario said at his side. Although from the look on his face, Riot surmised that Lotario was only trying to calm the girl. "How do you think the trial is going?"

Riot surveyed the court. "I'm still on the witness stand."

"Surely the jurors will see she was in danger."

"I wouldn't be surprised if the jury is fixed."

The young man made a strangled sound. "Then the judge will overrule their verdict."

"Doubtful."

Lotario gripped his arm. Desperation lay in his hand. Riot met his eyes. Gray like his twin, the same high cheeks and sharp nose. Those eyes glistened. "Bel *can't* go to prison. It will destroy her."

"I know," he whispered.

"There's twelve men on that jury—at *least* half will have secrets they'd rather keep hidden. We'll blackmail the jury."

"And become Kingston?"

"It's Bel we're talking about."

"Bel and I considered that approach. We decided against it."

"I'm glad you consulted me." Lotario let go of his arm. "She'll get two to six years for fraud."

"Bel assured me she could endure it."

"And you believed her?"

"No."

A severe woman interrupted their conversation. Lotario instantly transformed, tucking his emotion behind an indolent mask. "Hello, Mother," he drawled.

Mrs. Amsel ignored her wayward son, and looked to Riot. She had greeted him at the beginning of the trial with a sharp slap on each cheek. He had accepted her gesture without a word. The other Amsel brothers, Emmett, Aubert, and Vicilia, had given Riot apologetic glances. And then there was Mr. Amsel—grief had taken its toll on Isobel's father. He now needed the arm of his eldest son. Weeks before, when Isobel was brought into the court room, he had wept with joy. But joy had turned to grief when Judge Adams declared Isobel a 'flight risk' and denied bail.

"I only have two cheeks, Mrs. Amsel," he said.

Mrs. Amsel raised her hands, and paused. Slowly, she reached forward and took his head in her hands. She planted a kiss on each cheek. "Thank you for helping my daughter," she said.

"Lotario helped, too."

Her gaze slid to her son, and back to Riot.

Lotario rolled his eyes. "Don't even try. I'm dead to her."

"*No*," Mrs. Amsel snapped. "You are *lazy*."

Lotario smirked. "My clients think otherwise, Mother." He winked.

Mrs. Amsel gripped her cane, turned, and walked away.

"Do you really need to throw it in her face?" Riot asked.

"She's my mother. I can do what I like. She's always been disgusted with me."

Riot consulted his pocket watch. "That look on your mother's face wasn't disgust, it was pain. How would you feel if Bel were a prostitute?"

Lotario flinched, and Riot left him with those words. He had someone to meet.

27

WEAVING SPIDERS

We are close. —Z.R. Journal Excerpt

Friday, March 23, 1900

A BLACK SPIDER FLOATED IN THE CORNER, EIGHT LEGS dancing in mid-air. Sarah Byrne nudged a lamp an inch to the right and tilted her mirror. Perfect. She could see the crimson hourglass glistening on the bulbous black body.

Sarah knew that shape. The spider was deadly. She sketched in the mark of death on her drawing pad, but her pencil didn't do it justice. When she was finished with the sketch, she'd fill in the hourglass-shape with some red charcoal, or maybe even paint.

Startled, Sarah looked up from her drawing pad to check on the spider. She didn't like to take her eyes off it for too long. What if it crawled away? Leaning in closer, she watched the spindly legs reaching and weaving in chaotic order.

What masterpiece would the widow weave?

As a little girl, Sarah had sat and watched her gramma

knitting. The widow's movements reminded her of the swift click of sticks and her grandmother's gentle rocking. Her gramma would barely glance at her work, and Sarah wondered if, like her gramma, the spider even needed to see those invisible threads. Did the widow instinctively know the shape of her web?

Although Sarah's own efforts had been doomed to disaster, she had been mesmerized by her grandmother. The spider was the same. She glanced back at her drawing. The web wasn't finished, she realized. Moving quickly, she sketched in lines, as if she might discover the pattern before the web was complete. But that glistening black body, those needle-like legs, and that mark on its belly made her shiver.

How long before those weaving needles touched her?

A door opened downstairs, and Sarah jumped out of her skin. With her heart in her throat, she reached over to turn down the oil lamp. Footsteps creaked in the entryway. She snapped her book closed, tucked a pencil behind her ear, and hurried to her bedroom door.

It was likely her uncle coming home. He was away on business more often than not, and at the wise old age of twelve, she was far too old for a mammy. Still, Sarah yearned for company and missed her friends at Ravenwood Manor.

Picking up her oil lamp, she walked downstairs. It was late—pitch outside with a hidden moon. "Uncle Lee?" Her voice sounded hollow in the empty house. She waited for his greeting, but none came. Standing on her toes, she turned up the gas to the hallway light. Light flooded the stairway, but no one was standing in the entryway. The front door was closed.

Maybe she had imagined the noise?

"Uncle Lee, is that you?"

"No, but I'm a friend." A man stepped into view at the bottom of the stairway.

Sarah clutched the sketchbook to her chest.

He smiled. "Where is the old fellow?"

It took a moment for her to translate the words. The stranger had a high-sounding accent. "Uncle Lee's here somewhere," she lied. "Who are you?" It was rude. But then she was too scared to be polite.

"William Punt." He smiled again. "Why don't you run along and fetch your uncle."

He'd caught her in her own lie. "My uncle must have just stepped out. He'll be back any moment." She watched William Punt for a reaction, but this bit of news didn't seem to bother him.

"I'll just wait in the parlor. Might I have a cup of tea?"

Good manners kicked caution soundly to the side. She found herself nodding despite every bone in her body telling her to race out the front door. Mr. Punt stepped into the parlor, and she let out a breath of relief. There *was* something familiar about the man. Maybe he was one of Uncle Lee's friends.

Sarah walked slowly down the stairway, one step at a time, looking over the banister, preparing for an ambush. The man looked like a gentleman in his fine suit. And it wasn't as if she knew all of her uncle's friends. In fact, she hadn't met a single one yet. Surely, her uncle wouldn't give a key to just anyone. But Sarah also knew from her time with Tobias and Jin that a person didn't always need a key.

Would a burglar sit in a parlor and wait for the owner to return? The answer bolstered her.

A sinuous line of smoke drifted into the hallway. A cigar. Its smell clogged her nose. Gramma would have kicked the man out for such an offense, but Sarah didn't know the rules of her uncle's home. He was hardly ever there.

On her way to the kitchen, she glanced through the open doorway. There were *two* men in the parlor. She could barely make out the second man in the dimly lit room. He sat in an armchair, smoking. Sarah's feet stuttered.

William Punt flashed his smile again. "Do you need help with the tray?" He had an accent that sounded like Mr. Riot, but his eyes were looking down on her from a mighty tall place. Politeness as fake as a false front building.

"No, sir," she answered. "I was wondering if your friend would like tea, too."

Mr. Punt glanced at the cigar man, who hadn't spared her so much as a glance. He was too occupied with his cigar.

"I think not. Tea for two will do. You and me."

Sarah hurried to the kitchen, and set the kettle. While waiting for the water to boil, she glanced down the hallway to the telephone. She could ring Mr. Riot, but the men would hear. And what would she say—that her uncle's friends had come to visit?

She hadn't traveled halfway across the United States to be skittish now.

When the tray was arranged, she added some muffins that she had baked for her uncle. They had gone cold.

Squaring her shoulders, Sarah carried the tray towards the parlor, determined that she would be a good hostess, every bit as gracious as her gramma.

The tray barely rattled as she entered. She smiled at the two men. "I didn't get your friend's name."

"Gray. Parker Gray," the man said. "Bill, why don't you help her with that tray."

William Punt hopped forward to take it from her hands. It was a good thing he had, because Sarah froze. Her fingers went numb. She *knew* that voice—had heard it the night she'd followed Jin to the brick house.

Tell him to hitch up the wagon, she's too lively for a horse. Parker Gray had said those words to a man named Bill.

Sarah's heart leapt in her throat. She could feel Gray's eyes on her as he puffed away on his cigar. She swallowed, and focused on the cups, not daring to look at him.

"Thank you." Her voice came out like a squeak. Sarah reached for the teapot, poured a cup for Mr. Punt and herself, one for Mr. Gray to be polite, and one in the name of hope—a fourth cup for her uncle.

"Have a seat, Sarah." Mr. Punt gestured towards the settee. She didn't recall mentioning her name. And she certainly didn't want to sit. Sarah wanted to bolt from the room to telephone Mr. Riot, but something warned her not to. A wild dog had cornered her once, and while every bone in her body had screamed at her to run, she had stood her ground. Running only sparked viciousness.

So Sarah sat, and to her dismay, Mr. Punt sat beside her. "Your uncle's told us a great deal about you," he said. "Imagine that—you traveling across the country all on your own."

Gray blew a great, slow cloud of smoke from his lips. He had a careless way about him—his bowler was cocked at an angle and he sat with his ankle on his knee, as if he owned the house. The man looked bored.

It was hard not to stare at him.

"And then you ran straight into Atticus Riot." Mr. Punt whistled low.

"Yes, it was fortunate," she said.

Mr. Punt crossed his legs, and sipped his tea for a contemplative moment. "What's the old fellow like?"

"My uncle?"

"Atticus James Riot—detective of infamy." Mr. Punt said Riot's name with a clipped voice, as if biting off each word.

"He's famous?"

"Not the good sort of famous. I'm afraid he's a very dangerous fellow."

"He is?"

Mr. Punt nodded. "And he's been making things difficult for your uncle."

Sarah took a sip of her tea to hide her surprise. She had gotten that same feeling. It was clear her uncle didn't care for Mr. Riot, but what could he possibly have done to make things difficult for her uncle?

"Uncle Lee doesn't tell me a thing of his affairs," she said.

"Understandable. But your uncle should have warned you about Atticus Riot. Did you know he's a *gambler?*"

Sarah's eyes widened. Gamblers were legends— dangerous sorts who were right up there with whores and thieves in Gramma's book.

"And a killer," Mr. Punt whispered.

Sarah forced herself to blink—to feign shock rather than outrage. How could he accuse Mr. Riot of such a thing? Mr. Punt gave her a slight nod that seemed to say 'Consider yourself warned.'

"I'll keep that in mind, sir. Thank you."

"Not at all. I don't know if he's the type to harm a girl, but then you're practically a woman." Mr. Punt looked her over. A little too long. He set his tea on its saucer, and slid his arm along the back of the settee. His arm seemed impossibly long.

Sarah leaned forward, picking up the butter knife and a muffin. Any excuse to get away from that arm. As she sawed her muffin in half, she glared at the silver utensil, wishing it were sharper. Her fingers were trembling.

"I'll just ring my uncle." She started to rise, but the cigar man gave a quick shake of his head, and Mr. Punt's hand clamped down on her shoulder. He pushed her back down with a casual sort of touch.

"No need for that, Sarah. Let me butter that muffin for you." Mr. Punt took the knife from her fingers, and Sarah tensed to run, but Mr. Gray's eyes pinned her in place.

The front door opened, and Sarah nearly fainted with relief. Before she could hop to her feet, Mr. Punt thrust the plate and muffin back into her hand, and sat back, returning his arm to the settee.

Her uncle whistled as he shed his hat and coat, and then the tune cut off. Smoke was thick in the parlor, and it was sure to have traveled to the entryway. Lee Walker suddenly appeared in the doorway. Thin and wiry, he looked pale under the light. His gaze darted from her to the man beside her, then over to a glowing circle of ember before finally settling on the eyes of Parker Gray.

"We were just getting acquainted with your niece," Mr. Gray said.

"She's a lovely thing," Mr. Punt said, letting his long arm drape over her shoulder.

Sarah tried to shift away from him, but she was pressed against the armrest.

"Sarah, come here," her uncle ordered. His voice was hoarse. She moved quickly to obey, but Mr. Punt's arm tightened around her.

"Why don't you sit down and join us, Lee. We'd like to catch up on business," Gray said.

"I don't discuss business with Sarah present."

"Of course." Parker Gray gestured at Mr. Punt with his

cigar. As soon as he released his hold, she bolted for her uncle.

"They said they were friends of yours," she whispered.

Lee Walker glanced towards the corner of the parlor, at Parker Gray, and he put a smile on his face. "They are friends. No harm done. Run along to bed now."

He gently pushed her out of the parlor, and shut the door in her face. Sarah walked up the stairs, and then remembered her sketchbook in the hallway. Taking care to avoid the creaks and groans of the house, she sneaked downstairs to retrieve her book. But that closed door beckoned. She thought of Tobias and Jin, wishing they were there. It was much easier to be foolish with friends.

Careful not to let her shadow fall over the crack under the door, she moved closer, and pressed an ear to the wall.

"That wasn't our deal," said Gray.

"I did just like you told me—you said all my debts would be cleared."

"You didn't follow our instructions."

"I staged that accident. It's done," Walker bit out. He sounded desperate. "Kingston settled with me out of court. I gave Fields his cut of the settlement."

"The deal was for you to fall down that hatch, take Claiborne to court, and *then* give Fields his cut of a settlement. Not for you to take a payout."

"What does it matter? We wouldn't have won a dime in court. Atticus Riot dug up dirt on me, and told Kingston about the incident in Chicago. If we had gone to court, it would've all come out, and I'd be in prison for fraud."

"That wasn't our deal," Gray repeated.

"I got your money!"

Sarah jerked her head away from the wall. Her uncle's shout would have carried clear to her attic room.

"You broke our deal." The words were a whisper—the kind that made Sarah shiver. "You can make it right by giving Kingston back his money and telling him you've changed your mind."

"With my past I'll get ten years in San Quentin."

"That's not my concern," Gray said. "Trust me, a jail cell is preferable to backing out on a deal with me. If you do as I say you'll be alive and pain free. Do we have an agreement?"

"I can't."

"Fair enough," Gray purred. "I'll take the money you owe us from the racetracks."

"You said my debt would be cancelled if I did this."

Gray clucked his tongue. "If you followed the plan to completion."

"I don't have enough money."

"That's unfortunate. I suppose you'll have to sell this house."

"I don't own it." Walker sounded like he might be sick.

"That's a shame. A real shame. Fortunately, there are other ways of extracting payment out of a man's flesh. Or his kin's. Your charming niece will help you settle your debt."

Silence hung in the room. Sarah held her breath, listening with all her might.

"I'll get the money, and give it back. I'll do whatever you say."

"I like a man who is willing to change his mind, but we'll need collateral, of course."

Sarah didn't like the tone of his voice, or the stark silence from her uncle. Fear zipped down her spine, and jolted her feet to action. She raced up the stairway, clutching her drawing pad.

"No, you can't!" Uncle Lee's voice yelped from below. The door downstairs opened, and Sarah bolted up the next flight of stairs. She slipped into her attic room, shut the door, turned the key, and waited.

Someone was walking up the stairs.

Heart fluttering, she cast around for somewhere to hide. A knock spun her around.

"Oh, Sarah dear." William Punt's voice came through the flimsy barrier. "Your uncle was wondering if you could make us more tea."

Sarah froze. These were the men from the brick building. They had tried to kill Jin.

Sarah dragged a stool over to her dresser and climbed on top. The knocking at her door became more demanding. Her knees shook on her precarious perch. She stood on the tips of her toes, and pushed at the skylight. But the edges were too far away. She was too short to reach them.

The door shuddered, she began to slip, and the dresser started to tip. She leapt for an edge of the skylight as her dresser toppled. Her feet dangled in midair.

Clenching her teeth, Sarah tried to pull herself up through the skylight, but she had never been good at tree climbing. She couldn't hold on. Her fingers started slipping. The door crashed open, and Sarah looked upwards, through the open skylight to the night sky and cold air, thinking it would be her last glimpse of freedom. Determined, she gathered herself for a final heave, but her situation turned hopeless—a man with almond-shaped eyes appeared overhead. There was no escaping now.

28

A WATERY GRAVE

One right does not soothe a multitude of wrongs. The scales of justice were far
from balanced. —Z.R. Journal Excerpt

THE SEA WAS BLACK AS NIGHT AND SMOOTH AS GLASS. NOT A
ripple stirred in the dark. Isobel drifted, going nowhere. Her
sail hung limp, her boat was dead in the water.

She looked heavenward, searching for stars to anchor
herself, only to discover that the stars were missing. Pinpricks
of red gleamed down at her, all connected by gossamer
strands. The strands grew closer—a spider web was falling
from the sky.

She was the fly.

Isobel reached for an oar, and braced herself, preparing
to flee. Her oar dipped in the water. But it wasn't the sea. It
was thick and black. Oil. Undaunted, she began to paddle.
Every stroke was tedious. Her arms ached and her back
strained. Slowly, her boat inched forward.

Her oar snagged on something. She cursed, yanked it
out, and peered overboard. A pale oval shape was floating
below the surface. She stared, mesmerized, unable to move

—unable to look away. A face broke through the dim—a dead man, eyes picked clean by the sea, lips black, face marbled and bloated. It was Curtis, the brother she had killed. His lips parted in speech. *We move in the same circles.*

Isobel tightened her grip on the oar, clenched her jaw, and swung at the talking dead man. Again and again, full of rage. After all, he had put her there.

ISOBEL GROWLED, BORDERING ON A SCREAM. SHE FOUGHT and thrashed until a heavy weight crushed her.

"You're dreaming, Bel," a voice said. It was calm and warm. She opened her eyes. A face that was very much alive with worry stared back. Blood leaked from Riot's bottom lip.

His chest was pressing against her thundering heart. Isobel wanted to wipe the blood away, but her wrists were pinned to the settee. She swallowed down bile.

"I'm fine."

He released her wrists.

"I hit you," she rasped.

Surprised, he touched his lips, fingertips coming back red. "I've never yet managed to dodge a punch in my sleep, but I intend to keep practicing."

Isobel closed her eyes. "Curtis. I was dreaming of Curtis."

The weight pressing down on her shifted, but didn't leave entirely. Riot slid to the side, his arms still around her. There was peace in that heartbeat—more so than she had ever imagined possible.

A slight vibration in the hull caught Isobel's attention. Untangling herself from Riot, she threw open a porthole shutter. Still dark, but lightening, murky fog swam outside.

Water lapped at the hull, and the boat rose and fell like a breath.

"What is it?" he asked.

On the opposite settee, Watson snapped his eyes open. The cat stood, hackles raised. She smelled—

Isobel grabbed Riot's arms, and heaved him to the side. They tumbled off the settee, over the table, and a moment later thunder struck. A crash, splintering wood, and a groan that shook her bones. The cutter heeled sharply to starboard. Isobel slammed into the opposite hull, a teacup crunching under her body as the lantern swung wildly. Then glass shattered, snuffing the light.

Shouts of alarms, bells, and an angry cat confused the darkness. The *Lady* seemed to sigh, and with a groan she rolled on her belly, towards the gaping hole in her side. Frigid water rushed into the cabin, steam hissing from the pot-bellied stove. Somewhere, Riot was shouting.

"No!" A roar of water silenced her despair. Isobel fought her way free of blankets and clothing, and scrambled towards the hatch. Pain laced across her bare feet. The companionway ladder sat on its side. She threw herself at the hatch. It didn't budge.

Riot found her in confusion. He gripped her arms, and she could feel terror in his bones. He hadn't yet learned to swim.

"Try your hand at the hatch." In contrast, her voice was calm—that of a captain. Riot moved to obey, as she fought her way through water and wreckage. With every crack and groan of the *Lady*, she felt her heart splintering right along with her boat.

Isobel waded into the forward cabin, and tried the hatch. "Damn." She picked up a spare anchor and started hammering, the water rising with every blow.

"I can't open it, Bel!"

"Come here."

When Riot appeared, she thrust the anchor into his hands. "Keep trying," she shouted in his ear. "I'm going to see how large the breach is."

His hand clamped around her arm, and she squeezed it in return. He knew what she planned to do. Communicating more in that touch than words could convey, Isobel left him, dragging herself through the water into the saloon.

A plaintive cry gave her pause. Watson clung to the wood. She unlatched a porthole on the ceiling, and pushed the feline through. At least Watson would survive.

Peeling off her chemise, she breathed deeply, calming herself. She took in one last lungful and dove under the icy water. Blind, moving by touch, she pulled herself down to the breach in the hull, and probed the jagged wound. It stoked fury. Someone had injured her *Lady*.

She stuck an arm through the breach, and then her head, kicking furiously. It was tight. Wooden shards dug into her skin, as the water fought her. She slapped a hand on the outside of the hull. Isobel emptied her lungs. That final inch made the difference. As she pulled herself through the breach, pain slashed down her back. She slipped through the opening.

Lines and broken timber clogged the water. Empty and lightheaded from lack of air, she forced herself to relax, to take her time navigating the tangle. Her throat spasmed, aching to breathe. She swallowed, and her head broke the surface.

Isobel gulped in air.

A trawler loomed overhead. Its crew were shining lanterns at the sinking boat, but they weren't moving to help.

The *Lady* was on her side, her mast level with the water,

slowly sinking. Under cover of fog, Isobel swam towards Riot's banging, and stood on the rail. With numb fingers, she explored the hatch. A bar had been wedged against the wood. She gave the bar a sharp, upwards jab. It fell into the water, and the hatch flew open.

Water surged. Isobel thrust her arm inside. A hand clamped onto her own, and she pulled, fighting the rush of water.

She squeezed Riot's hand. *Wait a moment,* she thought. When water had filled the space, she pulled him through, and he fought his way to the surface.

Beams of light touched their heads, but moved on. "Someone wedged the hatches closed. I'm not keen on signaling for help," she said in his ear. She felt him nod in agreement. They were in no state to raid the trawler and demand answers.

Riot had a death grip on a line. Without a word, Isobel pulled herself along the capsized boat. Working quickly, she untied a small barrel she used to collect rain, and pushed it back towards Riot. The whites of his eyes were luminous in the fog. And for a moment, she feared he wouldn't budge. But with her gentle reassurance, he released the line, and grabbed for the barrel. Together, they swam from her ruined home.

WITH EVERY KICK, WITH EVERY BEAM OF LANTERN LIGHT reflecting off a broken hull, Isobel's heart broke a little more.

Her *Lady*.

Isobel was not a sentimental person. But this hurt.

She and Riot kicked to a far wharf, and dragged themselves onto a floating dock. Riot peeled off his wet shirt, wrung it out, and draped it over her bare shoulders. She hadn't even escaped with the shirt on her back, let alone her trousers.

The wet shirt made her colder. Teeth chattering, she looked towards the scattered lights. Her *Lady*. An ache stabbed her heart.

A hand clamped around her arm. The combined shivering of two made her shake even more. She glanced at her partner. Riot's beard glistened in the dark. He had retained his spectacles, an undershirt, and trousers.

"Your pocket watch was aboard," she chattered. It had been Ravenwood's, along with the walking stick, to say nothing of Riot's revolver and his lock picks.

"I have the only thing that matters."

"Your spectacles?"

"You know me so well." He reached for the wharf ladder.

Isobel gripped the ladder, and paused. Had Watson managed to swim to safety? Her gaze was drawn to the lights—to the wreckage. With a growl, she climbed.

Alex would pay for this.

Riot padded over the planks on silent feet. He seemed to have a destination in mind, but she was too numb to inquire, so she simply followed. A sea of masts bobbed in the shrouded harbor and the watchman's shack was only a dim outline. It was the early hours between night and dawn, edging towards sunrise. San Francisco was stirring. And all she wore was a wet shirt.

Riot led the way through narrow streets and lanes. Lights began blinking on in boarding house windows. A lone hay wagon trundled past, and Riot ushered her down an alleyway. It was clean and empty. He stopped at an unmarked door, and knocked.

A dark face poked out of a second-story window, and Riot took a step back. "Mr. Cottrill, you once offered your help. I've come to accept it."

The face disappeared without a word.

Cottrill. That name was familiar. Of course, she thought. The proprietor of the *Fragrant Rose*—the tobacconist whose wife had been murdered.

The door opened, and Silas Cottrill ushered them inside. He glanced at her, did a double take, and quickly averted his eyes.

"Thank you, Mr. Cottrill. We're in need of warmth and clothing."

"I have both." The man's voice was soft. Everything about the place was polished, from his bald head to his brushed slippers, the banister, even the oak steps. The living area was as tidy. Rich aromas of herbs and spices warmed her throat and senses.

Riot touched her back. "You're injured," he said under his breath. She glanced over her shoulder in surprise.

"I can't feel a thing," she chattered.

In short order, she was pushed towards a bathroom. Riot followed, closed the door, and turned on the taps. She peeled off her shirt and looked at her reflection in the mirror. A long red line slashed her flesh. "I barely squeezed through the breach," she explained. With every word, her chattering teeth nipped at her tongue. The result was a sort of drunken slur.

Riot set aside his steamed spectacles, picked up a cloth, and wiped away the blood. "I don't think it needs stitching."

"More of a scrape," she agreed.

Riot was pale, his lips tinted blue, fingers trembling with

cold. Not caring what Mr. Cottrill thought of the two of them in his bathroom, she slipped off his braces, pulled off his undershirt, and unbuttoned his trousers. He didn't argue. Only shivered his way into the steaming tub.

Isobel hissed when the heat touched her skin. Retreating, she gathered herself for another try. This time, she eased in slowly, and leaned against Riot. His arms encircled her, more for shared heat than affection.

"I'm going to kill Alex," she said after the tub filled.

"We're not sure he orchestrated this."

"There were bars across the hatches."

"The detective who followed me earlier didn't seem to know anything about the *Pagan Lady*."

He was right. As usual. In her fury, she had simply assumed it was Alex who'd arranged the 'accident'. But there was another possibility. That 'average' man who'd been lurking around the docks could very well belong to Parker Gray. They were caught between two powerful factions, and she felt crushed.

Isobel clenched her teeth together to stop from shivering, but it only seemed to drive the cold deeper down in her bones. Riot tightened his arms, and she lay her head against his shoulder. He made a fine pillow. "I dreamed of Curtis just before that trawler rammed us. I was dead in the water, and a web was falling from the sky. Curtis spoke to me." Her words didn't do the nightmare justice.

Riot waited, his hands slowly caressing her arms. The dream had dredged up memories best left buried.

"Men in shadows," she murmured.

"I beg your pardon?"

"Curtis said something to me that night." Realization hit. "I never told you his exact words, did I?"

"You were in shock."

She thought back to that night—to the horror of realizing that her own flesh and blood had betrayed her, and had meant to kill her. "Curtis said, 'I'm an Engineer, in more ways than one. Exactly like Kingston, but not near as clumsy. We are not so petty and narrow-sighted as that. There are powerful men in the shadows—men who can accomplish anything.'"

Isobel shivered anew.

"I've been assuming Curtis was working with Kingston, or moving in the same circle, but prizefighters move in a circle, too. And they're not friends." Her thoughts raced, and ended on the tongs. "What if there are *two* sets of men in the shadows—like warring tongs—only these are white men with considerable power and money."

"*Engineers* manipulating San Francisco from the shadows."

She nodded. "Curtis wanted me out of the way. I thought he was after my inheritance, but what if there was more." She sat up, and turned to look at Riot. "I assumed Alex was working *with* Curtis, but their actions were contrary to each other."

"Kingston didn't react to the token," he reminded.

"No, he didn't, but this…*Sing Ping King Sur* is secretive. Perhaps they haven't revealed themselves yet. Maybe Curtis feared something else when I married Alex—that he was angling towards something."

"Kingston works for the Southern Pacific Railways." A group of rich investors who nearly controlled California along with the rest of America. But they had not been altogether successful in San Francisco.

"It makes sense, doesn't it? That the Southern Pacific would have enemies. But as powerful as they are, those enemies might not want themselves known yet."

"Do you think Curtis was working with *Sing Ping King Sur*?" Riot asked.

She raised her brows. "What better way to hide than behind the mask of a secretive Chinese tong. I doubt the Southern Pacific would look twice at a tong."

"So who's behind it?"

That was the question. Who was the spider that sat in the middle of the web—the mastermind? It wasn't Parker Gray. It was clear he was a middleman.

"I haven't thought of my brother...of that night. I didn't want to," she murmured. Cold and drained, she hugged herself. "I'm full of bluster sometimes."

He cupped her face in his hands. "You're full of courage, Bel. But that doesn't erase bad memories. It only means you eventually need to turn around and face your demons."

"Like you?"

He gave her a rueful smile. "It took me three years, and a great deal of help from you. I'm not sure I've faced them all."

"We can scratch off nearly drowning in a shipwreck."

"I nearly drowned last month."

She snorted, and stood, water trailing down her body. "You weren't even close, Riot."

His gaze traveled upwards.

Isobel glanced down at him. "It appears you've warmed up."

"Considerably."

With a small smile, she stepped over the rim, and threw a towel at him. Riot paused, eyeing her injuries. After he dried himself, he wrapped the towel around his waist, and left, returning shortly with disinfectant, plaster, and a pile of clothing.

Isobel sat through Riot's doctoring as he gently teased

splinters from her back. As the sting of disinfectant receded, he covered the cut in plaster.

"I didn't much fancy a watery grave," he said after a time. "Thank you, Bel." His lips touched the nape of her neck. It made her shiver all over again. "I'm sorry about your *Lady*."

She met his gaze in the mirror. There were no words. Isobel grabbed a chemise that had likely belonged to Mr. Cottrill's deceased wife, and dropped it over her head. "I think it high time we go on the offensive."

"Agreed."

Feeling renewed, and brimming with determination, she dressed and left the bathroom.

Mr. Cottrill was waiting. "I have a spare bedroom if you need, Miss, erm…"

"It's probably best you don't know my name. And you've been so kind that I'd rather not give a false one." She gripped his hand. "Thank you."

"It's no trouble."

Riot polished his spectacles on a handkerchief. "Do you happen to have a spare revolver? I'll return it as soon as I'm able." On the surface, he was calm, but Isobel felt rather than observed an undercurrent of tension. If the *Pagan Lady* had been targeted, what of Ravenwood Manor?

With a revolver settled in Riot's coat pocket, they stepped out into the silver light of a new day. San Francisco was awake, her streets bustling with the early morning rush of men and women hurrying about their business.

They hopped on the rails of a crowded cable car, and as they were pulled up California, she kept a covert eye on their fellow travelers. Were they being followed, even now?

They disembarked, and walked the few blocks to Ravenwood Manor. Riot's brisk pace finished warming her bones, and as they neared, he let out a long breath—the sprawling home sat on its hill as arrogantly as they had left it.

They walked up the side lane to find Jin and Tobias checking their aging stand. Tobias charged them. "Are you just now getting home, Mr. Riot? Anything happen? You look a bit rough."

Jin stood silently, watching.

"All quiet here?" Riot asked, looking to Jin.

"Not with these two rascals," a voice came from the carriage house. Tim walked out with a pitchfork in hand. When he caught sight of them, he stopped, bushy brows shooting upwards. "Long night?"

"We could use some breakfast," Riot answered.

Drawn by currents of warmth, Isobel stumbled through the grocer's door. She stopped, and sighed with relief. An orange cat warmed himself in front of the stove.

"Watson," she breathed. He flicked his tail.

"He was cold and miserable when he arrived," Lily said. She pulled a tray of scones from the wood-burning oven, and turned to greet the new arrivals. She took one look at Isobel and Riot, and ordered them to sit.

Isobel didn't argue. Hot coffee and oatmeal appeared. They ate in silence. A plate of eggs and bacon later, Isobel surfaced. Riot was telling Tim, and therefore the entire family, what had happened. Grimm stared at the tabletop, listening, while his mother betrayed her concern by refilling their coffee every few sips. When the story was finished, Tobias darted out of the kitchen without a word.

Jin looked to Isobel, eyes burning and fists clenched in knots.

"Whatever tongue lashing you're about to deliver, I'm not in the mood," Isobel warned.

The girl clamped her lips together and looked away.

"I certainly wouldn't mind if Mr. Payne and Mr. Meekins returned," Lily said. "They might be rough around the edges, but they're fine gentlemen. I'd feel much safer."

Tim grunted in agreement. "You read my mind. I'll send a message and get the pair here within the hour."

"I'd appreciate that, Mr. Tim. Let them know I have a maintenance man coming from the gas company, though. I'd hate for them to rough him up."

Tim glanced at the ancient stove in the kitchen. "I was wondering why you were using that old thing. You need me to fix something?"

"That's why I have someone from the gas company coming. You're busy enough as it is with all this," Lily said. Tim loved to tinker. Unfortunately, his efforts weren't always successful. Whenever gas and electricity were involved, Lily tried to steer the old man clear of it.

"What about your boat?" Tim asked Isobel.

"Whoever tried to kill us knew we were aboard. They're probably lingering around the wharf to watch the police fish out our bodies."

"They'll know us on sight," Riot said. "To say nothing of the police. I'd rather keep you away from their scrutiny."

Isobel stared into her coffee mug in thought. Her position was precarious. Her "death" had its complications. But she doubted this afterlife of hers would last much longer.

When she remained silent, Riot looked to Tim. "Send Smith and Monty to take care of it. Have them keep an eye out for anyone suspicious. And see if there's something left to salvage."

Isobel frowned. A small hand stole over hers. "We will fix her, Captain." The soft voice made Isobel blink. As fast as the touch came, Jin snatched her hand away, color rising in her cheeks, as she fidgeted with the frayed bracelet around her wrist.

Isobel reached over, and squeezed the girl's hand. "Most everything can be mended," she agreed.

Riot pushed back his chair, and stood. "Thank you kindly, Miss Lily."

"What next, A.J.?" Tim asked.

"I have a number of calls to make." Riot replied. His voice was hard, and his eyes dark. Isobel was glad he was on her side. But man plans and God laughs. Racing footsteps signaled Tobias' return. The kitchen door flew open with such a force that it slammed against the wall. Lily gathered herself up to reprimand her son, but he cut her short with a rush of panicked words.

"I checked the newspaper to see if the shipwreck was in there, and...it's Sarah, I'm sure of it!" The boy thrust the *Morning Call* at Riot. He shook it open, and Isobel rushed to his side. She sucked in a breath, and Riot sat down, hard.

29

HUSK

Even now, as Atticus sleeps in his chair, I sign my death warrant. A small price to ensure his safety. I only hope he does not react foolishly. —Z.R. Journal Excerpt

SAN FRANCISCANS LOVE A GOOD FIRE. MUCH TO THE gathered crowd's delight number forty-three Salmon Street had gone up in flames. The windows bled char, and its innards were splattered all over the cobblestones.

The honor of 'first water' had belonged to Truck Co. No 2. Its steam engine sat in the narrow street amid remnants of broken champagne bottles that had fueled the firefighters' efforts. It was a wonder the fire hadn't spread to neighboring houses.

Atticus Riot pushed past the last line of gawkers, and went straight for the gaping doorway. He made it up the first step before a fireman caught his arm.

"You can't go in there."

"A girl lives inside. Sarah Byrne. Where is she?" His voice was hoarse, his body rigid, waiting to receive a blow that he couldn't hope to withstand.

"Is she a relation of yours?"

"Of a sort."

The firefighter glanced at his crew—a swarm of brawny, red-shirted men with leather helmets. A steady rhythm of axes and splintering wood echoed in the narrow lane.

"Capt'n Gabe!"

A fireman standing near the steam engine trotted over. He had a long mustache, soft jaw, and compassionate eyes.

"This gentleman knows the occupants."

Those eyes turned sympathetic. "I'm sorry to report there was a death."

"*A death*?" he croaked.

Isobel gripped Riot's shoulder.

"An adult male was inside."

"What about a girl?"

Captain Gabe glanced at the burnt-out singlestick. "We're still clearing out wreckage."

Riot made to slip past, but a firefighter with an axe appeared in the doorway. "It's not safe in here."

Riot relaxed, and warning bells went off in Isobel's head. She knew that stance.

"Please," Isobel cut in. "We're detectives." She produced a card. "This is Atticus Riot, he was helping the girl. We need to know if she was inside." The last thing they needed was to pick a fight with an entire fire brigade.

"I knew her uncle. I can identify his body," Riot added.

The fire captain smoothed his mustache, and studied the card. "I've read about you, and that girl you rescued. Gabriel Woods."

Riot shook hands. "I'd be obliged if you would escort us inside."

"It's not safe," the captain repeated the warning.

"I *need* to know if Sarah is in there."

"My men are taking care of it."

"Do you know what started the fire?" Isobel asked. It was an odd feeling, having their roles reversed. Although usually calm on the surface, passion ran through Riot's bones. He was all heart, and that heart had taken over. Isobel well knew what he was capable of.

Gabriel considered the question, glanced at the card again, and jerked his head at the axeman. "Come with me."

Water dripped from every surface, and sinuous lines of smoke hissed from charred wood. Isobel pressed a handkerchief to her nose as they picked their way through the wreckage. Riot stopped in the hallway, and looked upwards. She followed his gaze. A patch of gray sky shone through a hole in the second floor, the attic, and finally the roof. Ash drifted in the silver light.

Riot tore his gaze from Sarah's attic room. He looked down at the wreckage, and nudged a pile of debris with his foot.

"The fire was caused by a gas explosion from the stove," Gabriel said.

Riot picked up the remains of a sketchbook. Half of it was burnt, the other soaked. He peeled the papers apart. A sketched eye stared from one page. He peeled back another piece, and the page crumbled in his hands.

"I'd like to see what you make of it. This way."

The fire captain turned towards the kitchen, but Riot had other plans. Without warning, he flew up the stairway. Gabriel cursed, and quickly followed. Wood cracked and soot rained down on Isobel's head. She cringed, and followed at a cautious pace, catching up to the men at the attic door. Bare black bones of wood were exposed.

"Mr. Riot, I can't have you up here. You can see it won't

hold. The more stomping about we do, the more chance it'll all come down."

"This was her room."

Gabriel wiped his face with a handkerchief. "We haven't found her body." The sentence was clipped. The word 'yet' wanted saying.

A muscle in Riot's jaw flexed. She knew what he was thinking. There was a possibility that fire had rendered Sarah's bones to ash. But if no trace of her was discovered, the question would remain: where was Sarah Byrne?

ISOBEL AND RIOT STOOD OVER A CHARRED CORPSE. NOT much remained of Lee Walker, but he smelled like roasted pork.

The corpse was curled in a fetal position. His head had taken the brunt of the abuse. Skull shattered, the covering of flesh had been stripped away by fire, leaving a greasy sheen to the bone. His chest and thighs were also burned down to the bone. Isobel suspected the bits of black char by his shriveled hands were his fingers.

"We found him under the cabinet."

The cabinet was a charred husk surrounded by broken pottery. Isobel glanced at the worst area of the kitchen—the stove. While Riot was bent over examining the corpse, she picked her way through debris and stopped in front of a blasted area. Isobel frowned, and turned. An explosion. The table, chairs, and windows had been blown outwards. She hurried to the scorched wall where the cabinet had stood.

"Do you recall how the cabinet was positioned?" she asked.

Riot had his magnifying glass aimed at the corpse's skull. "Against the wall," he answered without looking up.

"And yet it fell forward, into the center of the room? Why wasn't it blown towards the hallway like everything else?"

Gabriel looked pleased. "You're a sharp lad. Suspicious, isn't it?"

Riot tucked away his magnifying glass. "This appears to be Lee Walker. I hope you're planning on requesting a postmortem?"

"I am."

Riot nodded. "What do you make of his skull?"

"The blast must have sent him flying and he knocked his head. Or maybe the smoke got to him and he fell." Gabriel scratched the back of his neck in thought. His gaze swept over the kitchen, envisioning the burst pattern. "Maybe the blast didn't move the cabinet, but it caught on fire. As it burned, it might have fallen on the corpse. Fire burns the tissue from a skull quickly. When bones get brittle, they shatter. It's like poking at logs in a fire. They break apart and burn brighter."

"But that doesn't explain why the cabinet fell *forward*," Isobel said.

"No, it doesn't," Gabriel agreed.

"It doesn't what?" a voice asked.

Isobel pressed her lips together. She knew that voice. A moment later, Inspector Geary strolled in, crushing everything underfoot. Thick brows, heavy jowls, and a neck resting on an expansive chest. He looked like a gargoyle. And he walked like one.

"If it isn't Atticus Riot." Geary planted himself over the corpse, and Riot stepped back, tucking away his magnifying glass. But his gaze wasn't on the Inspector, it was on the man who followed. The newly appointed coroner had a hunched posture, reminding Isobel of a penguin in an expensive suit.

"Coroner Weston," Riot greeted.

"I see we have an audience. Who let them in?"

Gabriel cleared his throat. "I did, sir."

Weston glanced towards the stove. "Why?"

"To identify the body. They're detectives—"

"But not police."

"No, but I wanted a second opinion."

"Why is that?"

"The cabinet, sir. I think it fell before the explosion."

Weston looked at the cabinet, and made a notation in his notebook. He took his time writing, and when he was done, he looked at Riot for the first time. "Weren't you recently tried for murder at one of my inquests?"

"Self-defense," Riot answered.

Gabriel glanced at Riot, and shifted.

"You were fortunate, Mr. Riot. Very fortunate that I agreed with the jury's verdict." The threat was clear. Isobel could well imagine the series of telegrams that Alex Kingston had dispatched last night.

"I should think the Fire Captain's opinion would be of more interest in this current situation."

"Gawd." Inspector Geary spat. "Are you always a smart-mouthed little prick, Riot?"

"I'm afraid so. Idiocy isn't in my nature."

Weston ignored the two men. He walked around the wreckage, taking notes.

"I'm requesting a postmortem, Coroner," Gabriel said.

"Noted." He scratched a pen across a death certificate. "Do we know the name of the deceased?"

"Mr. Riot identified him as Lee Walker," Gabriel answered.

Isobel had a habit of reading over shoulders. "*Accidental death?*" she blurted out.

Weston half turned, and arched a brow. She shut her mouth immediately, and resisted the urge to pull her cap lower. Had Alex already told every official in San Francisco that his dead wife was alive and masquerading as a man?

"Look here, I don't like the look of this," Gabriel said, distracting the coroner.

"I'm afraid I disagree with your opinion. My office is swamped. I don't need more investigations into something that is clearly an unfortunate accident. Inspector Geary, bring the dead wagon."

The gargoyle snickered, and stomped outside to summon his men.

"There, uhm…" Gabriel cleared his throat. "There may be a girl in here. We're still looking. It's the deceased's niece."

"She's not here?"

"We're still searching the rubble. Sometimes fire can…" Gabriel gave an apologetic glance to Riot. "…reduce a body to teeth."

Coroner Weston straightened. "Perhaps she tired of her uncle, pushed the cabinet over on him while he ate, and set the stove on fire to cover up a murder?" His voice was mocking, but his eyes were not. The penguin had fangs. And he showed his teeth to Riot. "Leave well enough alone, Mr. Riot. You can never be sure which way a jury will lean." He signed the death certificate with a flourish.

"Captain, I don't tolerate civilians mucking around a body. Get them out of here."

Gabriel chewed on the inside of his cheeks. A rambunctious nature gleamed in the firefighter's eyes, but he nodded. "This way."

Fresh, foggy air cleared her head. Gabriel stopped by his

steam engine, and took off his hat. "I'll have my men comb every inch of that house, Mr. Riot. If that girl of yours was unfortunate enough to be inside, we'll recover her. But if she was in there, I think we would have found something by now. I read the newspapers, and I'll be honest, that uncle didn't sound like much of one. Maybe they quarreled, and she ran away. Any idea where she might have gone?"

"I have a few ideas." His voice was opposite of reassuring. It sounded like a cocking hammer to her ears.

———

TIM LEANED AGAINST A HACK, PUFFING ON HIS PIPE, AND Grimm stood by, soothing the horse. When Tim caught sight of Riot and Isobel, he perked up. "Sarah?"

"They haven't found her inside yet."

Isobel glanced at Riot. His eyes were as hard as his voice. Cool, calm, and dangerous. "Lee Walker is dead," she added. "We don't think the fire was an accident."

"Hum," Tim said around his pipe stem. "Easy enough to arrange a gas leak and a stove explosion." With every word, a puff of smoke left his lips. "Was it Kingston or Gray?"

Riot looked back towards the congested lane. "Sarah told me her uncle cut a deal with Kingston to settle out of court. Both parties seemed happy with the arrangement. But the third party, Parker Gray, may not have been happy about it."

"Has news of the settlement reached the papers?" Isobel hadn't had time to read of late.

Tim scratched his bald pate "Not that I saw."

It was Grimm who answered with a shake of his head. The young man read everything he could get his hands on.

"You said Sarah wasn't supposed to know about the deal." Isobel said.

Riot nodded. "Her uncle wasn't supposed to tell her."

"And now Lee Walker is dead. If our theory about two rival organizations is correct, this could be bad for my *dear* husband."

"It could," Riot agreed.

Isobel tugged on her cap. "If Sarah weren't missing, I'd be content to sit back and let Parker Gray have his way with Alex."

"So where *is* Sarah?" This question came from Grimm. All eyes looked to him in surprise. Grimm hadn't spoken for six years. He'd broken that silence the week before, but hadn't said a word since.

"We don't know." Riot opened the hack door, and dragged a locked box from under the seat. Tim liked to keep a small arsenal at hand. Riot took out a belt and holster, and wrapped it around his waist. He picked up a Colt Peacemaker and meticulously began to load the chambers.

His favored No. 3 was at the bottom of the bay, but he had extra—a double-action Colt Lightning was nestled in his spare shoulder holster and a concealed Shopkeeper was strapped to his ankle.

"So now you're going to burst into the brick building and shoot the lot of them?" Isobel asked.

"If need be."

Isobel sidled up to him, and lowered her voice. "You tried that before, and nearly died. Your partner *did* die. As your current partner, I don't much care for that plan."

"I didn't just 'shoot the lot of them.'" Isobel's brows shot up, and he relented. "That came later. I tried to do things properly, and that's what got Ravenwood killed."

"So guns blazing this time? We don't even know if Sarah is in the brick building."

"I'll wager Parker Gray knows where she is."

"And he can kill her the moment he catches sight of us."

Riot snapped the loading gate closed.

Isobel touched his arm. "Do you know why Ari doesn't like guns?" she asked softly.

"Because they aren't for anything but killing?"

"No, because when a man has a gun in his hand, he can't think of any other option. So put the gun down and *talk* with me."

"I am talking, Bel. But you and I come from different times. Men like Parker Gray and Alex Kingston can't be stopped in courts. I won't let them hurt Sarah, and I don't intend to let them harm my current partner."

"I can take care of myself. Same as you. And, well, if I don't, you can slap an 'I told you so' on my headstone."

A half smile cracked his grim mask. "Right alongside the 'we managed'?" He holstered his revolver—a smooth, no nonsense maneuver.

"What? No twirling gun?"

"I'm a gunfighter, not a gunslinger. A gun is for killing, not flashing."

The memory of squeezing the trigger in Curtis' pocket hit her. "No," she breathed, feeling lightheaded. "There's nothing flashy about them."

Riot leaned in closer. "Here's a question for you, Bel. Are you willing to gamble a girl's life on your choice?"

Isobel held his eyes. And she felt responsibility settle on her shoulders—that heavy, stifling weight that he had lived with every single day of his professional career. It was crippling.

She squared her shoulders. "I'm *not* willing to risk her life by rushing in blind."

"What do you have in mind?"

That was the question. Their enemies had every advantage. She and Riot were flies caught in a web, waiting for the widow's whim.

Isobel looked to the crowd, to the husk of charred brick, to the brave men in their war-like helmets who'd been fighting the blaze. "*In the midst of chaos, there is also opportunity*," she quoted *The Art of War* under her breath. And then she had it, a pleased smile spreading over her lips.

"We bring in another spider."

30

THE SPIDER

I hope he will forgive me. For what I have done, and for what I am about to do.

—Z.R. Journal Excerpt

Saturday, March 24, 1900

SHADOWS MOVED LIKE WRAITHS AROUND A THREE-STORY brick building. Guards. Armed men had replaced gentlemen seeking carnal pleasures. While light leaked from between curtains, it deepened the foggy night rather than illuminating it.

San Francisco's silver mistress served Isobel's purposes nicely.

Beyond, a cluster of fairy lights floated in the murk, where the *Falcons Bicycle Club* were hosting a banquet. Laughter traveled over the dunes. Some thirty people were crammed around a giant outdoor table. The impromptu celebration had been joined by the *Fuzzy Bunch*, a group of long-haired Bohemians who were always game for fun.

"Lotario certainly delivered," Riot said in her ear.

"You paid for the champagne."

"And the fireworks."

"He's convinced you're courting him."

"I'm certainly courting his favor. I'll need his blessing when you accept my marriage proposal."

Isobel glanced sideways at her companion. "You are an optimistic fellow."

"That is no way to propose to a woman, boy," a gruff voice said. Tim glared over her head at Riot.

"Do you mind, old man?"

"Yes, I do. Do it proper or I'll shanghai you all over again."

"That is precisely why I do not drink anything you hand me."

Tim muttered and returned his gaze on the gentleman's club. "You sure about this, Miss Bel?"

"Of course not." She glanced towards the floating lights. "But from what I've heard, the *Falcons'* festivities shouldn't raise suspicion."

Tim grunted. "You sound like you're trying to convince yourself."

A firework burst in the night, flowering into a bloom of red. Cheers rang from the Falcons' clubhouse, and a burst of blue followed. That was her signal. Isobel placed a hand on Riot's bearded cheek, and turned his face towards hers. She kissed him for a good five seconds. Leaving him dazed, she hoisted her rucksack and darted down the dune carrying a saddle blanket under her arm.

The guards seemed hypnotized by the fireworks, and they drifted towards the display. Away from Isobel. She crouched at a corner post of the wrought iron fence. Another explosion of light and a hundred crackling pops burst over the brick building. And then another. This one thundering over the building's roof.

A guard hurried inside. Isobel tossed the saddle blanket over the top of the fence, covering its spikes. She climbed up and over, and pulled the blanket off in one smooth motion. Safely down, she dropped the blanket and kicked sand over it.

Firecrackers lit the fog with a crackling rainbow of colors. Bicyclists sped past the building, sparklers tied to their wheels and handlebars, aiming others into the air. And at each other.

Isobel raced over the sand, grabbed the drainage pipe, and climbed up with all the speed of a rigging monkey. For a girl who had spent her life at sea, the drain pipe was no more than a staircase compared to a mast in a storm.

The fog parted, and the moon shone for a second. She pulled herself onto the roof, and moved towards the first chimney. A firework burst overhead, illuminating her. She dropped to her belly with a curse, but the guards below were busy shouting at the bicyclists.

Opening her rucksack, she selected two cylinders. Striking a match, she lit fuses, and tossed them both down the nearest chimney. With a wild grin, she hurried to the next chimney, repeating the process. Smoke billowed out of the stacks, and windows were thrown open. When every pipe was choking out smoke, she uncorked a bottle of paraffin and upended her rucksack. Tucking smoke bombs in her coat pockets, she poured a line of paraffin to the roof's edge. Isobel lit a match. "For my *Lady*." She touched the flame to the oil.

If only it were dynamite. As a trail of fire snaked towards the pile of explosives, Isobel disappeared over the edge and began to scurry down the drainpipe. An explosion of fireworks rocked the roof. Broken brick rained down, and she pressed against the side of the building. When the smoke finally cleared, she slid down the pipe. Her feet hit the sand and she darted towards the carriage house.

Men ran for the pump, shouting in confusion. A panicked bell rang in the night as flames licked at the fog. Isobel lit her remaining smoke bombs and rolled them into the carriage house. Then as casual as could be, she strolled out the front gate and joined the *Falcons*, *Fuzzy Bunch*, and all the residents of Carville who had come to watch the bastion of wealth burn.

"If only it was a real fire," Lotario whispered at her side.

"At least you have your champagne and fireworks."

Lotario smiled, and passed her a bottle. "To mischief."

"To chaos."

"If they've harmed Sarah…" his voice cracked.

She slipped an arm around her twin's waist. But her gaze was elsewhere, roaming over the crowd of spectators. A lone man caught her attention. Lean and tall, he was fleeing the brick building. She recognized that gait.

"Hold this." She thrust the bottle at Lotario, and turned to one of the Falcon's members. Margaret was grinning from ear to ear.

"Can I borrow that." It was more demand than question.

Margaret tightened her grip on the handlebars. "You can borrow his. I'm going with you."

Isobel groaned. Without asking, she liberated a bicycle from a gentleman and peddled after William Punt.

Tim whistled low. "That woman of yours is trouble."

Atticus Riot watched the flames rising into the night. "I know." He traded bowler for leather fire helmet, and patted

Tim on the back. "Keep an eye on her." His old friend had his one good eye glued to a sight, and his Winchester rifle aimed at the building.

"Whose gonna keep an eye on you?" Tim asked, without looking up.

Riot flashed his teeth, hoisted an axe, and walked towards the road to meet his ride.

Three white horses galloped down Ocean Boulevard pulling a steam engine. A wagon of red shirts followed, champagne bottles and axes in hand. In the commotion, Riot joined the rush of redshirts from Chemical Engine No. 8.

Captain Kelly, a friend of Captain Gabriel Wood's, pretended not to notice the newcomer. "You know what to do, boys!"

The firefighters took a swig from their bottles, then pulled wet handkerchiefs over their faces. Ladders were hoisted, hoses aimed at the fire, and a rush of boots slammed into the building. Axes were raised, wood splintered, and they barged into the smoke-filled house.

"Out! Everyone out!" the Captain bellowed.

Parker Gray stood his ground in the foyer. "We can handle this ourselves."

"Tell it to the mayor." Captain Kelly shoved passed him, and his men raced up the staircase. Others branched out, smashing furniture, vases, and anything that looked expensive.

Riot tightened his grip on the axe. Parker Gray stood defenseless as firefighters rushed past. Though sorely tempted, Riot swallowed down his anger and shouldered past the man, bumping him to the side. Five men moved towards the back of the building, veering off in different directions. Riot slipped off to the side, down a stairwell, and unbarred the basement door. Taking the bar with him, he thumbed on his light, and stepped inside.

Cobwebs covered the brick, and a lingering scent of mold permeated the cold. This was where Parker Gray had dragged Isobel to torture her. He shined his light into the corners, to see if Sarah might be hiding in a shadow. She wasn't there. Clenching his jaw, he tossed the bar down, turned on his heel and stalked out into the smoke-filled hallway.

A revolver barked, and Riot was showered with splintered wood. Pain dug into his cheek and Riot threw his axe. It spun wildly towards his attacker. With his left hand, he drew. Before the axe reached the end of the hallway, he squeezed the trigger—twice. The attacker dropped his revolver as blood blossomed on his shoulder. But the man didn't fall. He bent to pick up his weapon. Riot rushed forward, snatched up his axe and drove the butt of it into the man's stomach.

The man dropped to his knees. As he fell, Parker Gray rounded the corner. Riot lunged. But his axe was too poorly balanced for the maneuver. A gunshot burst into the hallway, and the axe shaft shuddered in his hands. The impact of the bullet traveled up his arms until he was numb. He lost his grip on the axe, but didn't hesitate. Riot stepped inside Gray's reach, locked Gray's arm under his own, and jerked. A bone snapped. Gray's revolver clattered to the ground.

Riot was blinded by gun smoke, and a neat left hook caught him off guard. His head slammed against the wall. A fist to his kidney, and another. Riot lifted his foot, and brought it down on Gray's knee.

The man buckled.

Riot stepped back, and locked his arms around Parker Gray's neck. Fists pummeled his thigh and knee. Riot squeezed. One jerk would silence Gray for good. Riot gritted his teeth, and held on tight. Slowly, Gray lost his strength, and finally slumped. Releasing the choke hold, Riot drove a fist into Gray's face. It knocked the man out cold.

A round of cheers was raised in the hallway. Riot blinked past blood to see a sea of fuzzy red. He swiped a hand across his eyes. No spectacles.

"Damn it," he muttered. Feeling a revolver underfoot, he crouched to pick it up while squinting at the floor for a sheen of silver.

Boots marched forward. Riot was patted on the back. "Nice bit a'work." This was followed by the distinct crunch of glass as the firefighters filed past.

With a sigh, Riot straightened. And as each face came into his circle of vision, he nodded his thanks. "What do we do with him?" a voice asked. It belonged to Monty.

Riot squinted at his agent, an indistinct outline of red. "Did you find Sarah?"

A round blob of flesh on a pair of shoulders moved from side to side. "She's not here. But I found this." Monty stepped forward, and his edges sharpened. He held Raven-wood's walking stick—the one Riot abandoned on the *Pagan Lady*. "It's the only thing me and Matt didn't find aboard the boat."

Monty handed it over. Riot's knuckles whitened as he looked down at Parker Gray. "Is William Punt here?"

"Maybe Tim's rounded him up." Monty kicked his boot against Gray. "Whatcha want to do with this sack of meat?"

"Arrest him, of course."

Monty grunted. "And the butler that's just standing in the sitting room—him too?"

"Watch Gray." Riot walked briskly down the hallway,

dodging blurry red shirts, and receiving pats on the back. Along with supplying the *Falcons Club*, he had also bought the fire station enough champagne to last them a year.

A blurry slash of black stood in the sitting room. Riot cautiously moved towards it, until Mr. Jon swam into view. He stood silent, clad in elegant silks, his hands clasped behind his back.

"Where is Sarah?" Riot asked in Cantonese.

"We do not have her, *Din Gau*."

"Who does?"

"I do not know."

"Does Punt?"

"Not that I am aware."

Riot took a step forward. "Don't you know everything that goes on here?"

Mr. Jon raised his brows. "I see many things. I don't *know*."

"Where did you last see Mr. Punt?"

"Here."

Riot tapped the knob of his stick. Why had they taken the walking stick from the *Pagan Lady*? As a trophy?

"Last night a boat was rammed. I was on it."

"Too bad."

Riot tossed up the stick, and caught it in the middle. Mr. Jon flinched, and Riot leaned forward, the silver knob between their chins. "My walking stick was aboard, and now I find it here. I know you will take whatever information you have to the hangman's noose, so I won't bother asking you how this turned up here."

"Salvage."

"You can tell that to the police."

"I intend to."

Riot paused. There was an inflection in his voice—a

knowing. Mr. Jon was not intimidated by threats of police. And why would he be? If *Sing Ping King Sur* could bribe a judge to release Jim Parks early, who else might they have in their pocket?

Riot took out a red token and held it in front of Mr. Jon's eyes. "I know what this is. Tell the old fat man who was sitting in that chair the other night, that if Sarah Byrne is not returned to me by morning, I will bring hell down on every one of you."

"We do not have her."

"You set fire to her uncle's home."

Mr. Jon frowned. "When?"

"Last night."

"I'm only a butler. I don't know everything Parker Gray does. A chain's link only knows what it is connected to."

"Then you won't mind if I take Parker Gray to the police?"

"You may do *whatever* you wish, *Din Gau*."

THOSE FINAL WORDS WHISPERED IN RIOT'S MIND. *WHATEVER I wish*. Mr. Jon seemed to be washing his hands of Parker Gray. Odd for a butler.

The rowboat rose and fell with a swell, and the sea misted his face. It burned. Riot didn't much care to know what he looked like. The right side of his face was swollen, and he took care with how he moved. But all of that was of secondary concern. Parker Gray groaned, and lifted his head. Then he froze. He was a fish on a line—hooked, caught, and trapped.

"This good?" Monty asked.

Riot squinted at the night. "Good enough." Without

spectacles, he had no idea how far they were from shore. He tried not to think about it.

Monty secured the oars, as the rowboat bobbed on a black sea.

Parker Gray lay on the bottom of the rowboat, his hands tied in front, his feet bound. It was comfortable compared to how he had kept Isobel for a day.

Riot dabbed at the blood leaking from his nose and washed it away in the water. "When I was younger, one of the sailors I sailed with was attacked by a great white shark. It's not something you forget." He reached behind him and picked up a bucket, removing the lid. A rank smell assaulted his senses. Riot tapped the bucket. "He was fishing. Hooked a big one, and was pulled right overboard into a sea of chum."

Riot dumped the bucket of chum overboard. Fish guts plopped into the water, and Parker Gray's eyes flew open.

"The thing of it was…the shark didn't eat him. It only *sampled* him, and left." He traced a curve from his upper rib, to his belly button, and down to his hip. "You'd think a man would die instantly, but not this fellow. He howled for a good minute."

Riot reached for the next bucket. Another mass of fish heads and guts splattered into the water. "Did you know great whites breed twenty miles from here?"

"You'll regret this," Gray spat.

"I see you do." Riot let his words hang in the silence, until it settled between Gray's ears. "Where is Sarah?" he asked.

"Go to hell."

Without ceremony, Riot grabbed the ropes around Gray's legs, and yanked him towards the edge of the rowboat. Monty moved to the other side, acting as a counterweight.

"Hawaiians believe that some of the dead transform into sharks. An *aumakua*. I wonder how many dead bodies you've tossed in this ocean? What shark is waiting for you, Gray?"

"You're bluffing."

Riot grabbed Gray by the arms and yanked him off the bottom of the boat. "I never bluff." He shoved him overboard.

Gray yelped, and desperately turned, catching his armpits on the boat's rim. Cold water sucked the air from his lungs. He gasped. His legs, bound with rope, kicked ineffectively, splashing in the sea.

"Where is Sarah?" Riot asked again.

"I don't know!" It was pure panic. Freezing water and sharks were a potent combination.

Monty picked up another bucket, and upended it over Gray's head. "Whoops."

Gray fought for air. "We don't have her!"

"You killed Lee Walker."

Gray tried to shimmy back aboard, his eyes rolling to the side, searching the black water. "Walker backed out of our deal."

"And what did you do with Sarah?"

"She ran. We thought *you* had her."

Riot searched his face. Open terror. No lies.

"And Lincoln Howe?"

Parker Gray pressed his lips together, but there was a tremble in his mask. Riot grabbed his arms and lifted, shoving him backwards. A splash bounced off the water.

Gray came up spluttering. "I can't swim!"

"You didn't seem overly concerned that I couldn't swim when you rammed the *Pagan Lady*."

"I'll tell you whatever you want!" Gray's head went under. He came up coughing. Riot tossed him a cork vest. He grabbed onto it and clung, gasping for air.

"Where is Lincoln Howe?"

"Haul me back in the boat!"

"You best talk fast, Gray. I saw a fin. And the thing of it is, after that first bite I'll pull you out of the water. So don't imagine I intend to make death easy for you." Imagination is a curious thing. Shadows become leviathans, and a ripple of a wave becomes a hunter.

"Andrew Ross was handling Howe. Bill took over after Ross was murdered by that hatchet man."

"On whose orders?"

Gray clung to his cork vest, head swiveling from side to side. He jerked, as if something had brushed his legs. "The Engineer."

"The old man who was giving you orders the night I visited?"

Gray nodded.

"Name?"

"I don't know."

"Where did William Punt move his plague operation?"

Gray's eyes widened.

"I know more than you think. And I'll know if you lie. I'll only ask once more: where did he move his operation?"

"I don't know!"

"What *do* you know?"

"I was supposed to have Lee Walker stage an accident on one of Vincent Claiborne's properties. It didn't matter which one. I was told that it needed to go to court. I don't know why. We don't ask questions."

"Whose 'we'?" Riot showed his teeth.

Gray clamped his lips together.

"Do you know why sailors never learn to swim?" Riot asked. "Because they'd rather drown than be picked apart by sharks."

"There aren't any sharks here."

"Not *yet*." Riot searched the darkness. It was a blur. "But they're attracted to splashing."

Gray stilled.

"You haven't told me anything I don't already know. If you won't talk, then I'll say my goodbyes. Don't worry, if the sharks don't come, the cold will kill you." Riot touched the brim of his hat. "Enjoy the night, Gray. The stars are brilliant out here."

Monty smirked, and reached for the oars. The rowboat slid away from Parker Gray.

"Riot!" Gray shouted. "You can't leave me out here! I swear, I don't know where the girl is! She escaped through the skylight and vanished!" His cries bounced over the water, becoming more desperate. "Claiborne was being set up for something. I don't know what it was!"

His shouts faded, and Monty chuckled. "You're a cold-hearted bastard, A.J." His admiration was plain. Then a line attached to the cork vest went taut. Monty grunted at the added weight as Gray was tugged in their wake.

"I'm afraid I'm not as cold-hearted as you'd like."

31

MARK OF DEATH

I have made a deal with the devil. —Z.R. Journal Excerpt

ISOBEL KINGSTON ROLLED TO A STOP, AND PUT HER FOOT down for balance. She listened for a number of seconds. Slowly, she edged forward, peeking around a corner. William Punt had hopped aboard the Park and Ocean line, disembarked at Market, and taken a brisk walk to Second Street. She had nearly lost him twice. The fog had been both savior and villain, serving as cover—for both of them.

And now her quarry was slowing, a hunted man finally reaching safety. William Punt glanced over his shoulder. Isobel froze. Sudden movement attracts the eye, where a still shadow does not. She remained still.

Heavy breathing approached from behind her. Isobel thrust her hand backwards, signaling for her companion to stop. Breaks squeaked, and she hissed. But she didn't take her eyes from Punt. From the panting sounds, she imagined her twin hunched over the handlebars.

"Did we lose him *again*?" Margaret whispered. A seasoned bicyclist, she wasn't even winded.

Isobel didn't answer. She watched Punt turn a corner, counted to thirty, and zipped across the street. The process was repeated twice, until they came to an empty street.

The trio stared in dismay.

"How could you lose him again?" Lotario murmured.

Isobel glanced at her twin, and he arched a cheeky brow in reply.

A light flicked on in an upper-story window. "Do you think that's him?" Margaret asked.

A door was squashed between a haberdashery and a pharmacy. "There's only one way to find out." Isobel leaned her bicycle against a wall.

"Did you bring a revolver?" Margaret asked Lotario.

Lotario sniffed. "I'm hardly Watson."

"I did," Isobel said.

"Good ol' Watson," Lotario drawled.

"Guard the bicycles, Holmes. Stay here, both of you."

Before her friends could protest, she trotted across the street. The thought of putting Margaret and Lotario in harm's way made her sick. She hoped they would take her order to heart, but she couldn't waste time making sure. Sarah might be inside that home.

A veil of silver muted edges, creating a dreamlike atmosphere that swam with gaslights. So close to Market, the buildings here were ornate and gaudy, which made for easy climbing.

Isobel slipped behind a column, braced herself against a nearby wall, and shimmied her way upwards. When she ran out of wall, she reached around an overhang, and found a ledge. With a foot braced on the wall, she stretched and gripped the ledge with both hands. A silent swing, and she pulled herself upwards. The rest was simple, and she came to balance on a jutting ledge just under a windowsill. Few residents ever locked upper-story windows. As she had hoped the window was cracked open, and she peeked through a gap in the curtains.

William Punt rushed from room to room, collecting belongings and tossing them into a suitcase. He was packing some clothes, but mostly jewelry and cash. A fire was roaring in the hearth. Not the deep burn of charcoal or wood, but a hungry flame that curled a mound of papers black.

He was jumping ship. But where was Sarah?

Isobel tightened her grip on the ledge and squeezed her eyes shut, as the sickening answer washed over her. Gray and Punt had already killed the girl.

A carriage rattled over cobblestones. Isobel pressed herself against the stone front. The carriage rolled to a stop, and the door opened. She watched as a figure wearing a bowler exited. He walked underneath her perch, and a few seconds later, the door below opened.

The hackman clucked his horse forward, and the carriage disappeared into the fog. Isobel squinted through the curtain gap. She could hear footsteps climbing stairs. William Punt rushed to his overcoat, and drew a revolver from its pocket. It was a brazen little gold-plated gun. He aimed it at the exit.

A man appeared in the doorway, and William took a step back.

"Leaving?" the man asked. The stranger hadn't even blinked. Few men could keep their cool when faced with the business end of a revolver. He had mustache and side burns, and there was nothing at all remarkable about him. Brown hair poked from under his hat brim, and his dull eyes and whiskers were no different than those of a thousand men in San Francisco.

"It's you." William lowered his weapon. "Everything is completely buggered."

"What happened?" the stranger asked.

William gave a sharp laugh. "What happened? Atticus Riot and his cross-dressing bitch happened. They've meddled, and thwarted us at every step."

The stranger crossed his arms, and leaned casually against the doorway. It put William at ease. He stuffed his revolver back into his pocket.

"*Thwarted*," the stranger said. He had a bland, monotone voice. "Now there's a fancy British word, but was *thwarted* reason enough to kill them?"

William growled, and clicked his suitcase shut. "We *tried*, but they escaped. We rammed their boat and boarded, but it was empty. They knew about Lee Walker, the basement, and I suspect they took the girl. Someone is playing informant."

Or someone, namely me, is overly curious, Isobel thought.

"What happened to Lee Walker?"

"Parker decided to abandon the plan."

"So you killed him?" the Stranger asked.

"Accidental fire." William said it proudly, as if he were a child expecting a treat. "You'll tell the Engineer? There was nothing we could do to salvage the operation. But the seeds have been planted—the plague *is* seeping into Chinatown."

"I'm sure he'll understand. Secrecy trumps all else."

"Yes, of course." William ran a relieved hand through his hair.

"And where is Parker Gray?"

"I don't know. There was a fire at the Ocean Club. It turned out to be Riot's doing. I saw him with the firefighters. Parker went after him, and there were gunshots. I thought it best to leave, so I could make a report."

Isobel's heart lurched.

The stranger dipped his chin. "Understandable. Did the girl, Sarah Byrne, see you at her uncle's home?"

"Yes."

"Where is she?"

"She disappeared. As I said, we think Riot took her. We're sure of it. But we retrieved his walking stick from the boat wreckage."

The stranger glanced around the sitting room. "Where is it?"

William deflated. "At the club."

"I gathered information about Charlotte Bonnie so you could retrieve that stick—not try to kill Atticus Riot."

"They *needed* killing."

"I told you, Atticus Riot is off limits."

"He's meddling in our affairs!"

"You were ordered to keep away from him, and yet you provoked him."

"We didn't do a thing."

The stranger cocked his head. "I'd say abducting his woman was an act of aggression."

"We didn't know!"

The man reached into his pocket, and brought out a cigarette. With slow, careful movements, he struck a match, and lit the cigarette. When smoke caressed the air in front of his face, he looked back to William, as if remembering he was still there. "It's your job to know."

"A mistake that won't happen again."

"I'm afraid it's already happened again."

William took a step backwards towards the window.

"Atticus Riot believes *you* have Sarah Byrne. He gave Mr. Jon a message. I warned you, and yet you poked the rabid dog, Bill."

"Gray and I will make things right."

The stranger blew out a thin line of smoke. He reached into his inner pocket again, and laid something on a side table. "From the Engineer."

William raised his hands. "Let me speak with him. We can salvage this. We'll start over—I have ideas."

"You brought attention to us."

"It was Riot and his bitch!" William hissed.

"You know what to do. What is required of you."

William went rigid.

"Where's that stiff British upper lip I've heard so much about?"

He squared his shoulders. "I'd rather be alone."

"I question your resolve." A gunshot rocked the window pane. Blood splattered the glass in front of her. Isobel jerked, lost her footing, and slipped. Fingers latched onto the ledge, as her boots scuffed stone.

Footsteps approached the window, and she went still, dangling by her fingertips. The curtains twitched to the side, and then the footsteps moved away. The door below her opened, and all thoughts of confronting the man ran to the farthest corner of her mind. So quick. One moment he was standing there as calm as could be, and the next—

She swallowed down panic, and held her breath. Smoke tickled her nostrils. Every fiber of her body shook, waiting for the inevitable gunshot that would drop her to the earth.

The stranger breathed in the night air. Casual, unhurried, enjoying his smoke. A frantic sound interrupted him. Someone was beating a lamppost. Isobel didn't dare move, not even to glance to the side. Her fingers were cramped, on the verge of slipping.

The man's footsteps faded down the street, and Isobel

pulled herself up to safety. Arms trembling, she gripped the windowsill and searched the street. He was gone.

Shaken, she forced herself to look through the curtain gap. William Punt lay on the carpet. Blood seeped from a hole in his forehead, and a pool had spread underneath him. Open eyes stared at the ceiling. The suitcase was gone.

Curiosity overrode all sense. Unthinking, Isobel wrenched open the window and slipped inside. She didn't look at William Punt—didn't trust herself to. Instead, she focused on avoiding his blood and hurried over to the side table. A single disc of white lay on its top. Drops of blood polluted its pristine surface.

A sharp whistle slapped sense into her. Isobel whipped a handkerchief from her pocket to snatch up the token. She poked her head into the other rooms. All empty.

She bolted towards the window to peek outside. Two policemen were headed towards the house. Isobel ducked back inside, and took a moment to curse her stupidity. With a gun in her pocket and a man bleeding into the carpet, there was only one place she'd be headed. The gallows.

Lotario and Margaret rushed from a side street, waving their hands in panic. Isobel watched as they pointed down the street in the direction of the actual killer.

The first policeman took off in that direction, but to her dismay, the second ran towards William Punt's house. He went straight up the stairway, and Isobel slipped out the window, easing it closed.

There'd be more police on the way. Without wasting time, she hung from the ledge, and dropped. Her ankle buckled, and pain shot up her leg. She rolled onto hands and knees, and tried to rise, but her right foot wasn't cooperating. She fell back down.

A hand grabbed her arm and pulled her to her feet.

Before she could fall, a man smelling of pipe smoke ducked under her arm to support her weight.

"*Keep an eye on her*, he says," Tim mumbled, hoisting a Winchester in his other hand.

Isobel wobbled with relief. Together, they made a quick beat down the street.

"Gawd dammit, that was dumb," he spat when they were clear of danger.

Margaret poked her head from around a building. "Who are you talking to?"

"All of you!" Tim growled.

Lotario rushed over. "Were you shot?"

"No. I hurt my foot," she bit out.

Lotario fired off a string of questions. "Was Sarah in there? Who was that man in the window? Where's Punt?"

Tim hissed them to silence. "Bring the bicycles."

They did as ordered, Lotario laboring as he tried to push two bicycles, his own and Isobel's. When they were out of earshot, Tim stopped, and managed to simultaneously glare at all three of them. "*Never* summon the police until you're sure your friend didn't do the shooting."

"I thought that man was going to shoot her. He looked dangerous," Lotario defended.

"You think? I had a rifle trained on him."

"*We* didn't know that," Margaret shot back. "Why didn't you shoot him?"

"I'd like to make it to eighty without a noose around my neck. 'He looked dangerous' doesn't justify killing a man, especially in court these days."

"She was about to fall," Margaret added sullenly.

Tim ignored the observation. "And *you*, Miss Bel—"

"I'm grateful for your assistance."

He grumbled.

"That man shot William Punt in cold blood. There was no warning." Her voice shook, and Tim tightened his hold on her. Even without her throbbing ankle, she doubted she'd be able to stand without his aid.

"I figured something happened when you nearly fell."

"How did you find us?" Isobel asked.

"I saw you go after Punt. He struck me as the yellow-bellied type, so I figured he'd head home first."

Ahead, a horse stood calmly in the middle of the street. Tim whistled the same warning that he had given Isobel through the window. The horse trotted over to him. The mare was as old as Tim, and nipped Isobel as he helped her climb into the saddle.

Tim eyed the bicycle that Lotario was wheeling along with his own. "A.J. is going to owe me for this," he grumbled. Tim slung his Winchester over a shoulder, gripped the handlebars, and flashed his gold teeth. "Did you know I used to do trick riding on the ol' penny-farthings?"

After tonight, she'd never doubt Tim's wild claims again.

32

DEFEAT

The proof is at hand. —Z.R. Journal Excerpt

SECRECY WAS IMPOSSIBLE IN A HOME OF ALERT EARS. THE moment Tim lit a lantern in the barn, Jin sat up from where she had been sleeping. Hay stuck out from her hair, and she narrowed her eyes. "Why are you limping?"

"I'm a *faan tung*," Isobel answered. A rice bucket. She felt as worthless as its meaning.

"That's *Captain Faan Tung*," Jin corrected.

"Not tonight."

The girl cocked her head, but remained silent. It was just as well. The tornado pounding down the stairway would have drowned a scream. Tobias darted into the barn. "Did you find her? Did you find Sarah?" the boy demanded.

Isobel shook her head.

"Leave her be, boy," Tim said.

Mr. Payne poked his head in the barn to mumble something.

"Might be," Tim answered.

Another indecipherable reply.

Tim nodded. "Will do."

Mr. Payne disappeared back into the fog.

"I need to find Riot," she said.

Lotario frowned. "You are not going back out there."

"You're dead on your feet," Margaret agreed.

"Tobias and Jin, make sure these three get inside. If they put up a fight, holler your heads off." Tim took the reins from her. "I'll get A.J."

Isobel opened her mouth to protest.

"Whatcha gonna do, *limp* after someone?"

She shut her mouth with a click.

Tim clucked, and his mare followed him back out into the early morning.

Confronted with stinging reason, she submitted to Lotario's lead. Her thoughts spun. Where was Sarah? The answer sickened her. As long as Riot wasn't back, there was hope, but it was a fragile thing.

As always, when she limped into the kitchen, she was greeted by warmth. Miss Lily stood in dressing gown and cap. She looked from one twin to the other, a thoughtful look in her eyes. They wore nearly identical clothing.

Lotario took off his cap, and his golden hair tumbled free. "This should help."

Jin narrowed her eyes at him.

"I had it figured out," Lily said. "Mr. Morgan will be the one who is battered. You're as bad as Tobias."

"And he's in need of ice," Lotario added.

"Hmm." Lily turned to the ice box.

Margaret ushered Isobel to a chair. Grimm walked into the kitchen, took in the crowd, and hoisted his suspenders over his shoulders while heading for the stove.

Lotario bent over her laces. "Do you think it's broken?"

Isobel hardly heard his words. Her thoughts were else-where, examining the past three months from every angle.

At Tobias' urging, Margaret told them what happened. The kitchen filled with conversation, speculation, and wild ideas that made more sense than the truth. Words flowed over Isobel's head. Ice took the sting out of her ankle, but it was a distant feeling. Her head swam—facts tumbling inside, clattering against one another.

Isobel snapped back to the present. The family sat around the big table, and Isobel's leg was propped on a chair with a bag of ice on her ankle.

"Jin," she said suddenly. At the sound of her name, the girl sat up straight.

Carefully, Isobel removed the handkerchief from her pocket, set it on the table, and unfolded it. Blood had dried on the white token. "What does red symbolize in your culture?"

"I am *American*," Jin growled.

Isobel rubbed her temple.

Tobias sighed. "Just answer the question."

The girl relented. "It means good fortune."

"And white?"

"It is death. The color of mourning."

I question your resolve. The shot echoed, and blood and brains misted the window. Isobel shuddered. A hand gripped her own. "You need rest." It was Lotario; concern filled his every word. As sensitive as he was to her moods, she may as well have just screamed.

She opened her eyes. "Not yet." Isobel pushed herself out of the chair. "I need your help, Jin."

The girl hopped to her feet, and rushed to her side to act as a support. Isobel blinked down at the girl. "Erm, no. Thank you, though." She patted the girl's shoulder awkwardly, and drew her away from the rest. "The Master... The blond fellow you saw at the brothel. Did he look anything like Lotario?"

Jin glanced his way. "A little."

Isobel straightened. "Ari, do your impression of Curtis." As children, the twins had mimicked all of their older siblings, driving them to rage.

Lotario gaped at her. "Even *I* don't mock the dead." There wasn't a hint of grief in his voice, but respect was ingrained.

"Please."

Lotario turned away. He ripped off his tie, retied it into a crude bowtie, then pulled his blond hair back. With a shift of shoulders, he turned back around. Lotario was transformed. His eyes were cheerful, and he gave Jin a friendly smile. "By God, you've grown. I told you to eat that broccoli, didn't I? Have you got hair on your chest yet?" It was pitch perfect, and he shrugged, not with his shoulders, but with his eyebrows and hands.

Jin glanced at Isobel. "This is not him."

"Do his other personality," Isobel ordered.

Lotario rolled back his shoulders, and snapped his head from side to side, loosening up. He cleared his throat. Eyes became hard, creases lined his lips and forehead, and he seemed larger, looming over Jin. "You two are miscreants. You're going to give mother a heart attack, and don't think you can run to father for sympathy. This is the *final* straw."

Jin took a step back.

"Walk," Isobel ordered.

Lotario turned, and walked through the doorway.

Jin inhaled sharply. "*Fahn Quai*." White Devil.

Isobel had her answer. She sat down before her legs gave

way. Half aware of a number of eyes on her, she cleared her throat, and looked at her surroundings for the first time.

Candles flickered on the table, and Grimm was crouched in front of the second stove, an older one, stoking the wood in its chamber.

"Why aren't you using the gas stove and lamps?"

"It's nothing to concern yourself with, Mr. Morgan. I'll have it sorted out tomorrow."

"Miss Lily, I need to know. Yesterday, when Riot and I were here, you thought it was a maintenance issue and you had someone coming by."

Grimm closed the door with extreme care. His mother sighed. "A man from the Gas Light Company *did* come by, but it wasn't a mechanical issue. The Gas Light Company shut off our line. They claimed I didn't settle the bill."

There was no doubt in Isobel's mind that Lily *had* settled the bill. The landlady managed this house with an expert hand. This had Alex's stink all over it. With yet another blow delivered, Isobel placed her elbows on the table, and dropped her head into her hands.

"You're not supposed to have your elbows on the table," Tobias said.

His mother swatted his head with a rag. "Go to bed."

For the first time in her life, Isobel listened to that command.

Defeated, exposed, standing at the gallows, sleep seemed the only option left to her. But it eluded her when she finally dragged herself to Riot's room. She sat in Ravenwood's chair, staring at the wall of information. It ran together. Her vision blurred. Sarah was lost.

The door opened, and Isobel stirred. Her hand had left an imprint on her cheek. In the early morning light, she watched Riot shed his hat and coat. The tilt of his shoulders told everything. He had not found Sarah.

As he walked towards the bathroom, he touched her shoulder, and she reached for his hand. He answered her silent question with a shake of his head. "Gray has no idea where she is."

"Where is he now?"

"I took him to the police department. They slapped him with a pimping fine and sent him on his way."

"But..." she stuttered to a stop. "Without an investigation? Without a trial?"

"Inspector Coleman argued it with Chief Esola. But I'm not surprised. It's no secret that Mayor Phelan forced the old police chief into retirement to make way for Esola."

That scandal had hit newspapers in January. Isobel remembered a blurb published in the *Call*: '*We predict that the man elected will be Lawrence's Esola—and then may the Lord have mercy on everybody in that great city who is innocent.*'

"Mayor Phelan is a strong supporter of Chinese exclusion." And Chinatown was sitting on prime real estate. The elite considered Chinatown a blight, even as they profited from it.

Riot nodded. "But mayors are never elected without help. He's likely a puppet, too—the same as his police chief."

How could there be justice when the city ran on graft? San Francisco was a warring snake pit of greed. Even with honest men in power, what witnesses did they have? Only a Chinese girl, a missing white girl, and a dead woman.

His gaze fell to her ankle.

"I suppose Tim told you what happened?"

Riot gave a slight nod. "I think it was the same man who was lurking in front of our house two weeks ago." He hadn't seemed to notice his choice of words, and that made it all the more touching.

Isobel shuddered, and pushed the 'average' killer to the side—he'd find them or not. There were more important things to worry about—Sarah.

"We'll question the neighbors. We'll find her." The other possibility—the logical conclusion—stuck in her throat. That Sarah hadn't escaped, that her bones were somewhere in the charred house.

Exhaustion and grief lined Riot's face. One eye was swollen, and his cheek bruised. She wondered what injuries his beard concealed. Riot walked stiffly towards the bathroom. When she heard running water, she pushed herself out of the chair, and hobbled to the doorway.

Isobel sucked in a breath. Shirtless, he bent over the sink, scrubbing his face. Mottled bruising covered the muscles of his lower back. She limped forward and placed a hand over the bruises.

Riot straightened, and turned. Water dripped from his hair, over his face, and down his chest. His skin was cold to the touch. She reached for a washcloth, and dabbed at a cut on his cheek.

"The man who shot Punt... he's quick. Faster than you, even."

"There's always someone quicker," Riot murmured.

"The white token was a death sentence. I think William Punt was supposed to take his own life. One moment they were standing there, and the next..." A gun's bark. Blood on the window pane. His fingers curled around her wrist, and he took her hand in both of his, pressing his lips to her knuckles.

Isobel swallowed. "I think Alex might have her."

"Why? How? There's no reason. It makes no sense."

"What else makes sense?"

"That Sarah died in the fire." His voice cracked.

She squeezed his hand. "Until we find her bones, I won't stop looking."

"Nor I, Bel."

Isobel searched his eyes, then let her forehead fall against his chest. "I'll visit Alex tomorrow—today," she corrected. Riot's arms came around her. He didn't protest. Didn't say a word, but his arms stayed wrapped around her long after they'd both succumbed to exhaustion.

33

ACE OF SPADES

A FIRM KNOCK JERKED HER AWAKE. AND HER BEDMATE. Atticus Riot sat bolt upright, revolver cocked and ready in his hand. Isobel didn't dare move. He was not a man to startle. Another knock, and her ankle throbbed, clearing away the wool in her head. Memory of the previous day snapped her into focus.

Riot reached for his spare spectacles that had a crack in the lens. Hair askew, gun pointed towards the floor, and clad only in long underwear, he opened the door.

Miss Lily stood outside. She kept her eyes on his face. Recalling his state of undress, he stepped partly behind the door.

"This was in the grocer's delivery basket, and a messenger came with a telegram."

She handed both off. "And Mr. Riot?"

He waited.

"The water has been disconnected, too."

A crude oath slipped from Isobel's lips. Lily pretended not notice—both the cuss word and Isobel's presence in the big bed. "Mr. Tim went off to see what he could do."

"I doubt there is anything to be done, Miss Lily. We're the victims of a cruel and powerful man."

Lily's brows drew together. "Who?"

"*My* husband," Isobel growled. "I intend to kill him."

"It's complicated," Riot explained to Lily's surprise.

"I disagree, Mr. Riot, there's nothing complex about cruelty." Her eyes were distant, voice fragile. "You'll let me know if I can help?"

"Keep the children close."

She dipped her head.

"Thank you." He closed the door, and ripped open the envelope. Isobel ignored her throbbing ankle as she limped across the room to read over his shoulder.

She is alive. And safe.
Take the Chinatown tour this afternoon.
Follow the blue ribbon.

A shudder traveled from Riot's hands to his feet. Isobel steered him towards the bed, where his legs gave out, and he sat down. She took the paper from his shaking hand, and turned it over. No name. Why had she expected a name? It was written on cheap paper. The handwriting was neat and square. It smelled of broccoli and garlic. If ever there were a vegetable to overpower every other scent, it was broccoli or garlic. Dumb luck or purposeful?

"It could be a trap," she said. Although, broccoli-scented paper hardly screamed trap.

Riot didn't answer. The bait was irresistible, and Sarah's unknown fate was already inflicting far more pain than any trap that might be waiting.

She sat down next to him. "None of this makes sense."

Riot adjusted his spectacles, and set aside his revolver.

He looked to the wall of information. "Perhaps we're not the only ones fighting shadows," he said after a time.

"I don't dare hope." Isobel reached for the forgotten Western Union telegram. She realized what she had done after she ripped it open. "I do apologize, Riot. I've just opened your missive."

She handed it over.

"Take all the liberties you like with me."

"Hmm." She gave him a smile that only he was privy to, and turned her eyes on the telegram.

One hundred and fifty-two centimetres. Ten stone. Brown hair. Mole on right thumb. Scarlet fever scarring across cheeks from childhood. Tilts head to right when speaking. Glad you are back. -H

"Does your colleague know Lincoln Howe?"

"Doubtful."

"How could he possibly know that Lincoln Howe tilts his face to the right while speaking?" Isobel asked.

"He has his methods."

That, or Riot's colleague had a very high opinion of himself, she thought. Isobel glanced at the clock. "No water, no gas. Shall we visit the morgue and your optometrist before our tour?"

"You've read my mind, Bel."

34

THE STORM

THE SCRATCH OF PENS GRATED ON RIOT'S EARS. EVERY newspaper in the city was represented, poised to hit the evening edition when the court closed session for the day. But would it work?

Riot caught Isobel's eye, and she stared back, lips pressed together. She'd been in jail twenty-one days already. He tried not to think of the years that would separate them.

"Are you saying Sarah Byrne is alive?" Farnon asked.

"Yes."

Every sentence he uttered produced a ripple from the audience. Lunch had either subdued Judge Adams' enthusiastic gavel, or he had given up trying to silence the crowd. During this afternoon session, he'd reserved his cries of Order! for only truly loud outbursts.

"A death certificate was issued for Sarah Byrne. Another faked death, Mr. Riot?" Judge Adams inquired.

"Mrs. Kingston and I only discovered Sarah's whereabouts after it was signed. Considering the circumstances, we thought it best to keep the child hidden."

Judge Adams grunted. He did not voice an objection.

The prosecution stood. "Your honor, circumstances aside, Mr. Riot has admitted to abduction, trespassing, and vandalism."

"Let us not forget that the prosecution has granted Mr. Riot immunity for the duration of this trial," Farnon said.

"The stenographer will make a note of that," Judge Adams said. He waited until the note was made, and then asked, "What happened to Sarah Byrne?"

"When William Punt came for her, she had climbed through the skylight. She was frightened, rightly so, and hid in a basement." Riot had left out a good many things in his narration, including the note in the grocer's basket.

"And where is she now?"

"Until she's summoned to testify against Parker Gray, her location will remain a mystery."

Farnon nodded his approval. "With men like Gray roaming our streets, a wise precaution. Were you able to discover the whereabouts of Lincoln Howe?"

"Yes."

"Where?"

"Mrs. Kingston and I visited the city morgue. We relayed the telegram description to the assistant, Mr. Sims. He remembered an unidentified body with a mole on the right thumb. The man appeared to be a robbery victim. His face had been bashed in, his features unrecognizable. Without identification, he was buried nameless at Odd Fellows Cemetery. As it turned out, he had shared the morgue with his murderer for a time—Andrew Ross. Police Surgeon Wilson and Dr. Kellogg had the body exhumed and performed a postmortem. The body showed signs of further abuse—including marks indicative of shackles around his ankles.

"We then checked the SS *Australia* passenger list, and confirmed that Lincoln Howe arrived on that steamer. According to Doctor Kinyoun, he was carrying plague samples from Honolulu. I believe Lincoln Howe climbed into a hack straight off the steamer, and was taken to a basement near *The Drifter*, where he was kept in the cell and forced to…harvest the plague. Meanwhile, health officers can confirm that a man of Andrew Ross' description worked as a health inspector under the name of Lincoln Howe. When Andrew Ross and William Punt learned the harvesting technique, they disposed of Howe."

"And what of the murder of William Punt? Did you identify the gunman?"

"Not yet."

35

SLUM TOURS

I leave pain. I leave turmoil. I leave a son.

   —Z.R. *(last known journal entry)*

Sunday, March 25, 1900

BOWLER HATS MIXED WITH FLOWERY ONES, AS WELL-BRED women clung to the arms of their gentlemen, clogging the passageway. Isobel held onto Riot's arm to help her walk, and used Ravenwood's walking stick for additional support.

"We go to tong underground. Criminal slavers of noble women. Forcing them to life of shame," the guide announced. His accent was thick, and it echoed off the brick. Fay Chie let his gaze sweep over the women. Gasps of horror rippled through the tour group.

Looking pleased, the guide turned and held a lantern aloft, then walked down an ominous set of stairs. The group shuffled forward through dim passages. After winding through a warren of turns and twists, the guide stopped. He pressed a finger to his lips, and opened a door. A cloud of sickly-sweet smoke with floral undertones choked the passageway. Some coughed, while others inhaled the thick richness. Isobel wrinkled her nose. Opium.

The tour group pushed forward to gawk at the forbidden pleasure. Chinese men and women were draped on lounges and beds. The partakers stared in a trance, thick pipes pressed to their lips, their bodies sprawled and limp. A woman's leg was bared up to her thigh.

Something was wrong. Isobel narrowed her eyes, and then she saw it. One of the men lay on a book. A dingy laborer had pristine fingernails. The woman's body was angled wrong for the leg that extended from a silk wrap. And a ragged beggar wore silk slippers.

"This is staged," she whispered in Riot's ear.

She felt him chuckle. "Fay Chie makes a fortune from his slum tours."

"By duping gullible tourists of delicate sensibilities."

Riot nodded. "No harm done."

A loud bang echoed in the passageway, and Isobel jumped with the rest of the group. But Riot didn't flinch. Another theatric.

"Hurry!" Fay Chie said. "Police raid. Come, come quick. We go escape route."

The group pushed forward with a wave of alarm. The woman in front of Isobel tried to swoon, but her gentleman shook her arm. "Not *now*, Phyllis." She recovered in remarkable time.

Shouts and banging followed on their heels as the tourists ran through the dimly lit maze. Isobel and Riot strolled after them at a more decorous pace. Fay Chie stopped at an intersection. He held up his lantern and peered down the passage, listening, but the sounds were dim and faraway.

"We are safe. We are many stories under city. *Six* stories.

Some go much deeper. Careful. *Boo how doy* down here. Hatchet man."

The air was wretched and cold, the darkness complete save for a single lantern on a hook. Phyllis swooned. From the way the woman fell forward, Isobel knew it was a true faint. Her gentleman failed to catch her. Another woman cushioned her fall, and the two went down in a tangle of finery.

Rather than jump to their rescue, Riot squeezed Isobel's arm. She followed the slight motion of his chin. A single ribbon hung from a peg at the edge of light. Isobel wagered it was blue.

When the women were untangled and revived, the group shuffled forward. Riot and Isobel edged back into the shadows, waiting for their footsteps to fade.

"I could swear we're only two stories underground."

"One, actually."

Isobel glanced at him in surprise.

Fresh air caressed her cheek. Without warning, Riot stepped in front of her, and drew his revolver. She squinted into deep darkness. A section of wall was missing. Feeling utterly vulnerable with her twisted ankle, Isobel gripped her walking stick, preparing for a fight.

A faint scuffing came from the passage, and a light drifted from the dark. A bent old man hobbled forward at an agonizing pace. The lantern wobbled in his hand. Isobel glanced over the old man's shoulder, expecting someone else, while Riot looked to both sides.

The old man beckoned with a crooked hand. Hardly threatening. Riot consulted her silently, and she lifted a shoulder. He uncocked his revolver and it disappeared as quickly as it had appeared.

As soon as they stepped into the secret passageway, a panel slid closed. The old man didn't slow, or speed up. He hobbled at a snail's pace.

"I'll die of boredom at this rate," she murmured.

"Better this than a gunfight."

Biting her tongue, she counted the twists and turns, and kept glancing over her shoulder to check their back trail. As usual, Riot was relaxed, his left hand dangling casually at his side. But she knew better. He was as alert for an ambush as she was.

One crate looked much the same as the next, and scents wafted on mysterious currents, bringing smells of incense, gunpowder, fish, flowers, and roasting pork. The press of Chinatown seeped into the tunnels.

The bent old man stopped at a dead end. Clawed fingers bumped over the brick wall, and a moment later, the wall swung inward. Isobel gaped. It seemed a portal to another world, decorated with rich carpets, tapestries, silks, delicate mahogany furniture, and warm light. And a beaming girl in loose tunic and trousers.

"Sarah," Riot breathed. Heedless of any ambush, he rushed inside, and she threw her arms around him. Isobel followed at a more cautious pace. No waiting guns, no hatchets or hot pokers.

Sarah said something, but her words were muffled by his waistcoat. Riot gave Sarah a final squeeze, then knelt, gripping her shoulders so he could search her eyes. "Are you hurt?"

"I'm all right."

"Has anyone harmed you? In *any* way?"

"Only scared me to death. I swear I'm fine, Mr. Riot. I knew you'd worry, but Mr. Sin said it wasn't safe to leave."

Isobel turned back to the old man. In front of her eyes, he transformed, straightening and growing until he brushed six feet. Isobel took a step back on her bad foot, and nearly fell when her ankle twinged.

"Careful, Mrs. Kingston." And then he pulled off his face.

———

A SERENE MAN STOOD IN FRONT OF THEM. HE PEELED AWAY gray whiskers and the lines around his face, and even the queue that hung down his back. With shaved head and flaw-less skin, she estimated that Mr. Sin was somewhere between Riot's age and her own.

"Silence was necessary, I'm afraid. For Miss Byrne's safety. I am Sin Chi-Man." His words were heavily accented, and he pronounced his name as See-in Chee-mahn.

"It's you," Riot said.

"It is I." Sin gave a tight smile.

"Who is he?" she asked.

"He answered the door at Lee Walker's when I first met Sarah. I thought he was the butler." Riot kept a protective arm around Sarah's shoulders.

"I was not amused by the mess your short friend made."

"But Uncle Lee doesn't have a butler." Sarah looked from one wary man to the other. Sensing tension in the air, she blurted out, "Mr. Sin rescued me. He caught me and pulled me out through the skylight just when I was about to fall. The man banging on my door would have gotten me, otherwise."

Whomever Mr. Sin was—for better or worse—there was that. But that didn't mean Isobel and Riot entirely trusted Sin Chi-Man.

"Is Uncle Lee all right?"

Sin busied himself with his coat of rags. So he hadn't told Sarah about her uncle's death. Riot drew Sarah off to the side, and Isobel joined them. As he spoke soft words, the girl's lips trembled, and tears rolled down her cheeks.

"It was those men!" she burst out. "The men from that building by the beach."

"Did they harm you?" Riot asked again.

"They tried to." As Sarah told them what happened, Isobel wondered why she had ever felt a twinge of sympathy for William Punt.

The telling opened a dam that had been building for days. As Riot comforted the girl, Mr. Sin disappeared into the interior of his home.

Isobel studied the false door, until she spotted its mechanism. Satisfied they could escape if need be, she limped over to an archway. Harmonious. That was the word that came to mind as she looked into the adjoining room. Simple, uncluttered, with every piece of furniture at a precise angle, each complementing the next. She was drawn to an ornate chessboard. The armies were jade, the details exquisite. A game was in play, and before she could help herself she nudged the black Queen into a better position.

Ever curious, she walked across the plush carpet, and pulled a curtain aside. A small room dominated by a dressing table. And clothes, racks of them. Wigs, makeup, and false faces atop wooden heads. She had only ever seen the like in a theatre. Lotario would be in heaven.

A soft rustle of cloth alerted her. Isobel turned to find Mr. Sin standing behind her. He had exchanged his disguise for a simple gray robe, the type that officials wore. But she wondered if it was simply another disguise. What face did Sin Chi-Man really wear?

"Tea, Mrs. Kingston?" he asked.

Isobel made an impatient sound. "Don't call me by that name. Miss Bel will do. One *E* and one *L*. I want answers. Who are you? Why were you at Lee Walker's home?"

"I find tea relaxes the mind." He glanced towards the other room, where Sarah was busily blowing her nose on Riot's handkerchief. "We have much to discuss."

When Isobel stood her ground, he extended an arm towards a nook of chairs. There was nothing for it; she was hardly in a position to interrogate him. She relented, and sat.

Soon after Riot and Sarah joined her. The girl was subdued, puffy-eyed and red-nosed. She went straight for Isobel, wrapping her arms around her shoulders. Isobel stiffened in surprise. It made the girl squeeze even harder.

Sarah pulled away, concern in her bright eyes. "Did you hurt your foot looking for me?"

"It's only a sprain. I'm relieved you're safe." The words felt inadequate. And she silently chided herself—Isobel's mother had been as distant with her as she was behaving now. Determined to be as unlike her mother as she possibly could, Isobel patted Sarah's arm with what she hoped was affection. It seemed enough.

Sarah retreated, sitting beside Riot on a settee. She seemed on the verge of another breakdown, as she twisted the handkerchief in her hands. Riot placed a hand over hers, soothing her agitation with a touch. She leaned into him. A child without kin. Adrift, but not quite alone.

Sin reappeared with a tray in hand. As he poured four cups of green tea, Isobel found herself mesmerized by his movements. Fluid and precise, a sort of dance. When each of them held a cup in hand, Sin sat down across from them, cradling his teacup. Long fingers caressed the porcelain. Was he nervous? Isobel wondered how often he entertained guests.

In a rare occurrence, Riot broke the silence. "Thank you for saving Sarah. I'm in your debt."

Sin inclined his head. "Miss Byrne," he said. "Perhaps now would be a favorable time to practice your calligraphy."

"I'd rather not." It wasn't defiance, it was fear. Sarah felt safe where she was.

Riot squeezed her hands. "It'll be all right, Sarah."

"Do you swear?" There was more to that question than calligraphy.

"On my word."

Reassured, Sarah walked over to a desk, and sat. A part of Isobel wished she could believe that everything would be all right, but even as a child she had been suspicious of those words. Most especially now. She felt like a rogue queen surrounded by two armies.

"Who are you?" Isobel asked again.

"Sin Chi-Man," he repeated. "I offer you my real name. What you really ask is *what* I am. And *why* I am."

Both Isobel and Riot waited.

"Spy. Informant. Detective. Savior. Robin Hood. Or, if you prefer, *Consulting Detective*." He said the title with a flourish.

"Like Sherlock Holmes?" Irony dripped from her voice.

"Only *Chinese*." He offered her a tight smile. "But I am not so foolish as to bandy my name about in a city of enemies. Only two people know of my existence. One of those is dead."

"The second being Sarah?" There was a warning in her voice. This man was as dangerous as a person came. Isobel didn't trust him.

Sin crossed his long legs, and took a sip of his tea. "My secret is safe with the girl. Adults never listen to children."

Isobel swirled her tea in its cup. "*We* do."

"You are rarities."

"Who now know of your existence," she pointed out.

Sin nodded. "A gesture of goodwill on my part."

"Do you really expect a child to keep a secret?" Isobel asked. She wanted to push this man, to spark a reaction that would shatter his mask.

"What will Miss Byrne say? That a Chinese man pulled her through a skylight, flew with her over rooftops, and burrowed through the city sewers to a silken lair where he taught her the Oriental secrets of calligraphy?"

Sin had a point. People would imagine Tobias was influencing her. Last week, the boy had claimed it was Spring-heeled Jack who'd stolen his mother's pie off the windowsill.

"What were you doing at Lee Walker's home?" Riot asked.

"Investigating *Sing Ping King Sur*," Sin said. "It is an old case. A tedious one. The same case I was working on with Zephaniah Ravenwood."

Isobel's teacup chattered against its saucer. She quickly set it on the table, marveling at Riot's calm. Not even a flutter of lash.

"*You* were Ravenwood's informant—the one who visited him in the conservatory."

"*Sing Ping King Sur* was a whisper at the time. As it is today. Four years ago, I first heard its name on the lips of a dying hatchet man. And when no other whispers reached my ears, I started to wonder if it was a tong at all. Then came the Broken Blossom Murders, and you. And then Ravenwood."

Sin frowned into his teacup, turning it gently in his hands. The tea swirled with barely a ripple. "There have always been white men profiting from tongs, but I wondered, what if they had stepped even further into our world? Ravenwood realized this, too. The list you seized from Mr. Jones Jr. was proof."

"Jones' account book?" Riot asked. The one they'd found at the bottom of the fishing basket that was being used to transport mutilated girls.

"Yes." Sin held out his hand. "May I see his walking stick?"

Isobel glanced at Riot. He nodded. Sin took it from her hand as if it were a revered relic. He balanced it with care, studying its length. "While you were raiding tong headquarters and taking your rage out on furniture—"

Isobel stiffened with anger, but Riot gave a slight shake of his head. He might not take offense, but she could damn well be angry for him.

"Ravenwood, against my advice, took this proof to the police." Sin's long fingers caressed the silver knob. He thumbed a bit of filigree, twisted the shaft once, tapped the side, and unscrewed the knob.

Riot sat up straight, more surprised than Isobel. Twenty years with Ravenwood, and he hadn't learned all his partner's secrets. Sin dipped his finger inside and slipped out a rolled-up bit of paper. He handed it to Riot. "This is why your partner was killed."

Isobel moved to the settee to read it. "Lumber shipments?" she asked.

"I never gave this list another thought," Riot admitted. "I theorized the lumber yard was being used to legitimize profits from illegal activities. But that seemed trivial compared to catching a butcher of children."

Isobel studied the numbers. "This hardly seems like an obscene amount of money."

"Unless you move the decimal point to the right. Twice," Sin said. "The documents that Mr. Riot recovered from various tongs were maps. This is the key. Those names are beneficiaries of slavery, opium, and gambling. The lumber yard was a front, and the white men on that list were profiting from a ghastly trade."

There were powerful names on the list. Small wonder Ravenwood was killed.

"San Francisco is China's gateway to America. A direct link from Hong Kong to New York. All goods travel through here. Flesh, opium, silks, gold, gunpowder—all highly profitable."

"What did the police say?" Riot asked.

"That they would investigate the matter."

Riot gave a shake of his head. "Ravenwood knew the police were corrupt. Why would he go to them?"

"What else could he do?"

Sin's question lingered. Isobel and Riot were in that same position. How do you fight against corruption that taints the highest corners of government?

"Perhaps Ravenwood was looking for a reaction," Isobel said.

"If that was the case, he was successful. A price was put on both your heads."

"We already had a price on our heads."

"This was different," Sin said. "This reached the Barbary Coast." Guns for hire. Cutthroats. Every gunslinger in San Francisco would have been aiming for Ravenwood and Riot. "When I informed Ravenwood of this new development, he went to speak with Pak Siu Lui."

"Why?" A vein on Riot's temple stood stark against his flesh.

"I'm surprised you even need to ask."

"I'm asking it all the same."

"Siu Lui smuggles girls through customs and delivers them to the Queen's Room. She is a broker of flesh, and she knew who was killing those girls. It was a small leap of logic to conclude that she knew who was behind *Sing Ping King Sur*."

"Even if Siu Lui knew, she wouldn't have told Ravenwood. She walks a fine line between life and death."

"Ravenwood did not approach her for information." Sin took a sip of his tea. "He went to barter for your safety. To protect you."

I have made a deal with the devil.

"Ravenwood suspected the two of you had a history— that she cared for you, so he approached her as a mediator. That's why he told you nothing of this."

Riot stood and turned away, his gaze on Sarah.

Sin tilted his head slightly. "What is Siu Lui to you? I can think of no woman more dangerous in this city."

Silence answered. And then a soft, "It doesn't matter."

"It may," Sin said.

Riot ignored the observation. "What were the terms of the agreement?"

"That Ravenwood would hand over the names in exchange for your safety."

"But he kept the original," Isobel pointed out.

"He knew a skilled forger."

"Why didn't he barter for his *own* safety?" she asked.

"That was not possible. He knew too much, so he took his chances."

"I dragged him into it," Riot whispered.

"One might say he dragged *you* into this business."

Riot smoothed his beard. "I don't believe it."

"That he would use Siu Lui as a mediator?"

"That he would be so…" Riot trailed off. Emotional. That was the word Isobel filled in silently.

"It makes sense," Isobel said.

Riot glanced at her in surprise.

"I'd do the same thing if I were in his place. To protect you. I tried that a few weeks ago." It hadn't gone well. "I doubt he went there to offer himself up as a sacrifice. He probably wanted to make it clear you had no knowledge of those names." *I sign my death warrant.* She wondered what the contract had looked like.

"There is honor among thieves. Both Chinese and white," Sin agreed.

"*Honor?*" Riot bit out. "They hired a brute to slaughter him and kill an old woman."

"I did not say those thieves had honor."

"What was his plan?" Isobel asked.

Sin shook his head. "I do not know. I was his informant —his eyes in Chinatown, not his confidant."

"No one was." Riot gestured towards the walking stick. "Whatever his plan, they killed him, and then used me as a weapon."

Sin ran his fingers over the intricate silver knob. "A cunning stroke that rid *Sing Ping King Sur* of *Hip Yee*, who was in the process of unifying the tongs. You interrupted that meeting when you tossed dynamite onto their table. And then you shattered any hope of unity when you attacked the *Hip Yee* leaders."

"It wasn't an attack. It was vengeance." Riot stood apart from both Sin and Isobel. Alone. That haunted look was back in his eyes. It tore at her heart.

"I wondered if I could trust you," Sin admitted. "But I realized afterwards that you were not a man on a rampage. Not one out for blood. You sought justice that night."

"I walked in shooting."

"You did not shoot a poor old beggar in an alleyway."

"How did you…" He trailed off, and touched his temple. Pale as death, and just as rigid, she knew that look in his eyes —a memory, a ghost, someone from his haunted past. "That was *you*."

"The night you attacked *Hip Yee*, the night Ravenwood was killed, I was doing what I do best—listening and watching."

The pieces clicked. "Disguised as a beggar," Isobel said. Sin was the beggar who'd saved Riot's life and carried him to an undertaker.

"A killer would have shot that beggar to hide his deeds, but you stayed your hand. You were not a man seeking vengeance, but justice."

Riot swallowed. He had no words.

Isobel narrowed her eyes. "And recently, you were investigating Parker Gray and William Punt. That was you, too. The vagrant in the alleyway outside *The Drifter*."

"Yes."

"You left me to the dogs," Isobel growled.

"You ruined my surveillance. And spooked Punt," snapped Sin.

"You knew about it and did nothing?"

"I was gathering information."

"Were you going to *watch* for another three years?"

"*The green reed which bends in the wind is stronger than the mighty oak which breaks in a storm*," Sin quoted Confucius.

Isobel tightened her fists. "Tell that to the men Andrew Ross injected with bubonic plague!"

Sin pressed his lips together. He took a breath, nostrils flaring, one inhale, and a long exhale. When he looked at her again, the serene mask was back in place. But she had needled under his skin—it was still a victory. "*You* spooked them, Miss Bel. Not I. I did not know what they were doing. My...skills are limited outside of Chinatown." He gestured towards his eyes. They were widely spaced, and narrow with a pronounced epicanthic fold. "No amount of makeup can hide these."

"You've known about *Sing Ping King Sur* for *three* years. So you sat and *watched* this organization dig itself in after you dumped Riot at an undertaker's to die. All of the names on this list are men who have gained influential positions in the past three years."

"I did what I could." Sin screwed the knob back onto the walking stick.

Isobel shot to her feet. "*What* precisely did you do? You hid in shadows just like the rest of the cowards."

"Bel," Riot warned.

Sin stood, meeting her eye. He towered over her, but she paid it no mind. "Even if I had found the ear of an honest inspector—do you think a jury would believe a word I said? Or even the Consul General's testimony? There is a better chance of a jury taking the word of a white prostitute. Judges are bought, police profit, and politicians gain influence from *Sing Ping King Sur's* activities."

Isobel opened her mouth, but words were lost. Sin was right. For decades, Chinese immigrants could not testify against white citizens. A white man could shoot a Chinese man in cold blood, and as long as there were no white witnesses, a hundred Chinese couldn't testify against the murderer. The law had been recently overturned, but law didn't change hearts.

"You could have tried," she said stubbornly.

"I did not have proof."

Isobel glared. "You dumped the *proof* in an undertaker's to die."

"And my most recent proof was dumped down the sewers because a hot-headed, bumbling woman meddled with my investigation!"

Isobel bristled.

"Mr. Sin. *Miss* Bel." Riot put an arm between them, more to keep Isobel back than to shield her. He glanced towards Sarah, who had turned at the raised voices. "Please," he implored.

Isobel uncurled her fists. Angry, trapped, and helpless, she hobbled over to the chessboard and glared at the armies.

Sin held the walking stick out to Riot. Slowly, he accepted it, his fingers tracing the silver filigree. "The proof fled," Riot whispered. "I took the walking stick with me."

"It doesn't matter. They are only words on paper."

Isobel cocked her head. *The pen is mightier than the sword.* Moves, strategy, and outcomes raced ahead to a conclusion. There was no saving the Queen, but the *game* might still be won.

"Dare I ask?" a voice interrupted. Rare of him. Indicative of his worry.

"It's nothing."

He touched her arm. "Bel?"

"I'm tired and frustrated." And afraid. She turned away from him. With those knowing eyes—he'd unravel her thoughts if she gave him a chance. "I'd like to offer an apology, Mr. Sin. You are right. I did blunder things. A great many things."

Sin looked down his nose at her. "Perhaps I would do things differently as well, but the past cannot be changed. I

propose a new future. One of cooperation. I suggest we pool
our knowledge."

Isobel glanced at Riot. He was as wary as she. They had
no reason to trust this man. But what choice did they have?

"It seems we know more than you," Isobel pointed out.

Sin arched a brow. "I believe I know why Parker Gray
targeted Vincent Claiborne."

36

SACRIFICE

"I DISLIKE LEAVING HER THERE," RIOT SAID. HE STOOD ON A cable car runner, while Isobel sat on a bench. She was eye level with his waistcoat, and he had leaned in to speak in her ear.

"I know." Her words were nearly lost in the rattle of wheels. "We don't have a choice."

His knuckles whitened on the pole. They had been backed into a corner; Isobel saw only one way out, but Riot wouldn't like it. *She* didn't like it.

They did not speak the rest of the clanking trip. At the top of Nob Hill, they disembarked, Riot helping her navigate the runner.

Skies were blue, the air crisp, and the sun bright. She inhaled fresh air, and savored the hint of sea that was always carried on an easterly breeze. Isobel turned to look down at Chinatown. Wind had dispersed some of the haze that hung over the Quarter, but not all of it. She had stumbled into a conspiracy, and in an effort to destroy evidence, William Punt had released cages of infected rats. How many more lives would be lost?

Turning her back on the Quarter, she focused on the moment. It was a pleasant walk, a slow amble on Riot's arm that was uncomplicated by speech. Isobel closed her eyes. She wanted to remember everything about this moment— the feel of his arm under her hand, the cry of gulls overhead, and the easy pace he assumed for her hobbling gait.

Isobel had never wanted a quiet life, but now she ached for it with all her heart. One more walk; one more morning together; one more storm to holler at. But it couldn't be.

The sun was setting over the Golden Gate when they returned to Ravenwood Manor. Mr. Meekins lounged on a rocking chair on the porch, a book in his dark hands and a shotgun across his knees. When he caught sight of them, he made to rise, but Riot shooed him back down.

"All quiet?"

The big man patted his gut. "Quiet as a stuffed mouse. It don't even feel like work, Mr. Riot, not with the meals being served."

"The gas and water?" Isobel asked.

Mr. Meekins shook his head. "Sorry, no. Mr. Tim paid the bill again, but then the company turned it back off."

There was a well, an old outhouse, and chamber pots from decades past, but with so many borders, it would be far from convenient.

Riot opened the front door for Isobel, and they were greeted by two expectant faces. Jin and Tobias were sitting on the stairs, waiting. Jin took one look at them and shot to her feet. "What happened?" she demanded.

Riot gestured for her to keep her voice down. The children leaned in close. "Sarah is safe, but not a word. She's still in danger."

Isobel answered Tobias' question before he could blurt it

out. "She witnessed a crime. Make sure you both keep looking forlorn and worried. Understood?"

Two heads bobbed as one.

Isobel hobbled over to the hallway telephone, and picked it up.

"The telephone's been turned off, too," Tobias said.

"I don't need to make a call."

An operator's voice came on the line. "I need to speak with Mrs. Wright. Tell her it's Miss Bonnie."

"Absolutely not, Bel."

"I'm not asking you."

"Then why tell me?"

"Because we're partners, Riot."

"And yet I have no say in your plan."

The two stood apart, and their words lingered in the room. Riot was as rattled as she had ever seen him. She was rattled, too. Isobel hadn't wanted to tell him of her plan, but if she waited another day, she'd turn coward and run.

The fire popped and wood shifted, sending sparks spiraling up the flue.

Isobel took a breath. "I won't put this on your shoulders. This is my choice to make. You beat yourself up every day because you feel like you dragged Ravenwood to his death. But he made his own choice."

"You *cannot* do this to yourself."

"I'm done for already. You know that."

"You're looking at two years, minimum." It was close to a growl. "You barely tolerated a *single* night in jail."

Isobel swallowed. "I'll manage."

"Don't do this. You could be sentenced to the jute mill instead of the women's ward in San Quentin. You could get six or more—" Riot couldn't finish.

She tilted her chin. "I'm young and strong."

"*Think* this through."

"I have—that's the problem." The mist in his eyes clutched her throat. She limped to the window and threw it open to breathe in the crisp night.

Riot stepped closer. She could feel the intensity of the man standing at her shoulder. "I can't let you do this."

Isobel narrowed her eyes in thought. Truly curious, she turned. "How are you going to stop me?"

Riot opened his mouth, then clicked it shut. He rubbed his beard, and looked around the room as if the answer were there. "Bel…"

"I'm already ruined, but the game isn't lost."

"It's not a game!" After his sharp outburst, Riot turned. His shoulders shook, and his hand strayed to his temple. Isobel let her forehead fall against his back. She felt him relax and lean into her, one equally supporting the other. She slid her arms around his waist, and he covered her hands with his own.

"I apologize."

"Don't apologize for caring about me," she said softly.

"We'll find another way."

"How?"

Riot didn't answer, but she knew what he was thinking.

"By delivering a quieting dose of lead to my husband?" she pressed.

Her question was met with silence.

Isobel took a step away, and Riot turned to meet her eye. "If anyone is going to shoot Alex, it'll be me—not you. Take your heart out of this, Riot."

His fists curled. "How can you ask that of me?"

"Just for *one* moment," she pleaded. "Is it a good plan?"

"It's a gamble."

"Would you wager on it?" she asked.

"The stakes are too high." His gaze settled on her. Tender, warm, and afraid.

It was hard to find her voice. She swallowed down a lump in her throat. "Alex issued his threat two days ago. And yet there isn't a single mention of me in any of the newspapers. He's not planning on making this public," she reasoned. "Instead, he'll pull strings to manipulate us from his office. It's already begun. God knows what he's done to my parents in these past days. I've asked Lotario to check in with my brother Emmett, but even if he hasn't started in on them, Alex will hound me and anyone near me until we are crushed. And he'll try to have you killed. That doesn't even address our issues with *Sing Ping King Sur*. As a witness to Parker Gray's conversation, Sarah is in danger. As long as we remain silent, we remain powerless."

Riot took her hands, and pressed them to his heart. "We'll leave San Francisco. Together. We'll make a home in Europe. London, if you wish."

She shook her head. "There are others like us, Riot. Others who have been blackmailed, manipulated, and ruined. Can we really step aside and allow innocent people to be crushed underfoot?"

Riot held onto her hands as if they were a lifeline, and she held his just as tightly. "We cannot," he whispered.

Isobel's eyes flashed with steel. "*Sing Ping King Sur* thrive in shadow. This will shine a light so bright on their organization that it will send them back into their holes."

"It *might*."

Isobel looked to the chess board. "As slim as our chances

may be, I'll take it. If I'm to be ruined, it will be on *my* terms. This city loves a good fight, Riot, and I intend to start one."

37

THE GATES OF HELL

Tuesday, March 27, 1900

ISOBEL KINGSTON STOOD AT THE GATES OF HELL——A wrought-iron fence spaced with pillars and topped with stone lions. Why Lions? Cats were horrid guards.

Two months.

Her throat was dry. How had she managed to live in this house?

You deceived yourself.

Her facade of cool logic had dictated that the mind was stronger than the body. But Isobel had learned something from her ordeal: she was only human.

Squaring her shoulders, she pushed the gate open, and limped up the driveway. She swept the windows with her eyes, pausing on Alex's bedroom window. The suitcase she carried was heavy, and her hand hurt. Swallowing, she forced her fingers to relax.

The engraved walking stick in her right hand had a reassuring weight to it. She thought of the man who had once carried it. The secrets he had uncovered, and the final sacrifice he made.

How had it come to this?

A pair of men waited on the front steps. Watchdogs. Isobel recognized one as a man who had shadowed her while she was living at the residence. Hired detectives. Alex had watched her every move. But her brother Curtis had known her. He'd known three months ago that she'd shake those watchdogs.

Alex and Curtis had both played the game with their eyes wide open, but Isobel and Riot had only just realized a game was being played at all—a game in which they were pieces rather than players. That was about to change.

The second watchdog was new. She guessed he was the clean-shaven fool who had tried to follow Riot. Detectives shadowing detectives. She should have had Smith tail one of them just for the irony of it.

"Mrs. Kingston." Bailey gave her a smug look—one she wanted to bash in with a crowbar. He swept off his bowler, showing the bald patch he tried hard to conceal. "Welcome home."

She ignored Bailey and watchdog number two. Without pausing, she walked up the steps. The door opened.

"Mrs. Kingston," March said. Stone-faced and bald, the butler spoke without inflection. It was somehow worse than a sneer. "You are expected."

Mabel appeared to take her coat. The girl gave a tight smile and a quick bob. But when she reached for the suitcase, Isobel kept a firm hold on it.

"Is Alex home?"

"Mr. Kingston is in his study."

Isobel tightened her grip on the walking stick, and marched past the butler.

"If you'll wait, I'll announce your arrival." March was at her side. She tucked her stick under an arm, and swept off her hat, slapping it against his chest. Her butchered black hair made his feet trip.

With a tilt of her lips, she shoved the office door open.

Alex Kingston sat behind his desk. He glanced up at her, and leaned back, a satisfied look on his bullish features.

"I tire of your petty manipulations, Alex."

"You are four days late. If you think that won't cost you...it will. You'll have groveling to do, wife. And it'll be on your knees."

Isobel slapped a red token on his desk. "You'll be the one groveling. However, I find the prospect of you dropping to your knees repulsive."

His face reddened, and he surged to his feet, planting both hands on his desk.

Before he could rage, she cut off his tirade. "Your client is about to be framed."

"Shut your mouth."

"Vincent Claiborne."

"For what?"

"A conspiracy to bring bubonic plague to San Francisco for his own profit."

"You're a lunatic."

"You married me."

"For the sport. Now you're just irritating."

"My brother Curtis said the same thing just before he attempted to murder me. But as you see, I'm still alive."

"You think I still believe that story Atticus Riot fed the newspapers?"

"I don't care what you believe. But you've stepped into a heap of trouble, and you don't even realize it yet."

Alex huffed like a bull dismissing a yapping dog.

"You don't believe me?" she asked. "Then I'm sure you won't mind if I call the health board to inspect Vincent Claiborne's properties. Because that's precisely what would have happened if Lee Walker's trial had proceeded as planned."

"I don't give a damn." He moved around the desk, and she backed up.

"If you lay a hand on me, a marksman will peg you in the head with a bullet."

Alex froze. He glanced at his open window.

"Don't even think about it. Close that curtain and you will have a group of dangerous men at your doorstep."

"You can't threaten me."

"Do you know what that token represents?"

He glanced at it, anger clouding his eyes.

She sighed. "I know you blackmail, manipulate, and bully anyone who gets in the way of the Southern Pacific Railway. You're their trained dog, Alex. That token represents the Pacific-Union Club's enemies. Do you think the men who pay you will react well when they hear you passed up a chance to deliver a blow to *Sing Ping King Sur*?"

His eye twitched.

"So you've heard of them?"

"How do you know…" He looked at her with a new light in his eyes.

"You think me some mindless society woman who happened to notice a connection between you and my father's misfortune? I am much more. I'm a snake, Alex. And you invited me into your bed."

"That will make breaking you all the more satisfying."

Isobel clucked her tongue. He was so predictable. "I once knew a little boy like you. His parents spoiled him. They handed him everything he wanted, and more. He destroyed every single gift. And yet he would look longingly at the fishing pole I'd fashioned from a stick and a string. You're nothing but a boy; you'll never be satisfied."

"For an instant, I will be. Then I'll toss you in the gutter after I'm through with you."

She glanced at her nails. "That is until your client is framed for murder."

Alex scowled down at her. He didn't like being the one in the dark. "Have you come to bargain?"

"In exchange for a divorce and your word that you will never meddle, manipulate, or interfere in my affairs again. That protection extends to my family and associates— including Ravenwood Manor."

Alex crossed his arms. "I have my own detectives."

"Like the fellow out there who tailed Atticus Riot, then tried to hide from him in a barber's chair?"

His jaw worked.

"I'm sure you've heard that Lee Walker is dead."

"It was a fire."

"You think that was an accident?"

"He settled out of court with my client."

"No one knows that but you, Vincent Claiborne, and Lee Walker."

She brandished the token in front of his face. "The 'accident' was staged, Alex. Your client is being set up. Would you like to know why?"

He grunted.

"Your word."

"You have it." Isobel met his eyes. Did she trust him? No. Did she have a choice. Always. But there was nothing for it now.

"Parker Gray and Andrew Ross set Lee Walker up to

lose at the racetracks. He couldn't pay, so they forced him to stage that accident."

"For a settlement?"

"No." Sin Chi-Man had filled in the missing pieces. Details that would have taken them weeks to uncover. "Vincent Claiborne has a number of properties adjacent to Chinatown. It's no secret that property developers like him have their eyes on the Quarter. It's prime real estate. Last year, as you well know, Claiborne expressed interest in buying the properties next to his own. But the sellers wouldn't budge. So he turned to you. You began your bullying tactics—cutting off gas service, water, sabotaging sewer lines."

"You have no proof."

She ignored him. "Petty but effective. You made a grave error, however. You targeted a cigar factory and a lumber yard. Their contracts mysteriously began to dry up, the same way they did for my father. Supplies weren't delivered, and that created issues. What you didn't realize was that you were poking at a bigger dog: *Sing Ping King Sur*.

"I'll wager someone approached you, but you didn't listen. You gloated the same as you are now."

His silence confirmed everything she'd guessed.

"Under your pressure, a few property owners were forced to sell, but the lumber yard and factory were stubborn. Uncommonly so. You intensified the pressure. You went so far as to bribe city officials to declare the building a hazard and hand out a number of citations. Production came to a standstill. A win. But in the process you made a very vindictive and calculating enemy."

He glared. "An enemy who is doing what?"

"Slowly closing you in a meticulous and careful trap. At

trial, Claiborne's account books will be thrown open for the public. His finances will be scrutinized. And I'm sure they will find a number of suspicious transactions—or perhaps that he has little money left. Investors won't give him a second look. But most of all, his properties will be inspected by city health officials, and they will discover the remnants of a laboratory in a basement of a building with his name on it. Since he's made no secret of coveting Chinatown for himself, he'll be charged with conspiracy to spread the plague."

"There won't be a trial. I took care of that."

"Yes, you took care of it. That's precisely what people will think when they discover Lee Walker was murdered in a fire."

"This is insane."

"No, *this* is genius. Utterly untraceable. You wouldn't have known until your client was behind bars. *This* is strategy. *This* is skill. Not your blundering, Alex."

He lifted his shoulders. "I'm a brute. I've never imagined myself any different, nor do I want to be. It has served me well these years." He looked around his well-appointed office.

"Do you really think a mind like this will abandon a plan? The plague still lingers. The Pacific-Union Club will have you to blame."

"Who will they believe? *You?*"

"They know what you are. Your reputation will be proof enough, and *Sing Ping King Sur* will conjure whatever they wish. You interfered with their gold mine of illegal imports. They are not happy, and they will not forget."

"This 'manufactured plague' will close the ports you claim they use."

"Do you think these people only operate in San Francisco? There's always Los Angeles. Your clients, however, will feel it right in their pocketbooks."

Alex leaned forward. "There is nothing here I haven't handled before—not rival businessman, not tongs, and not willful young women." She took a step back. "You cannot threaten me."

"I'm not threatening you. I'm here to help."

"I don't want your help." He grabbed her arm. "I want my wife."

Isobel tried to twist away, but his grip was solid. "I warn you, Alex. I will show you no mercy."

He yanked her hard against his body. She could smell his breath, feel his body, the contours of the man.

"I suggest you let me go," she said through her teeth.

"There is no waiting gunmen," he growled. "There is no rifle aimed at my back. I hope your lover comes for you. When he trespasses on my property, my men will gun him down like a dog."

She struggled against his hold.

"Let. Me. Go."

Alex bent his head to hers, and forced his tongue past her lips. Isobel clicked the catch on her suitcase, and dumped it towards his trousers. The stench was revolting; the slush that fell onto his clothes and carpet was sickening.

"Shit!"

She backed up with a wild grin. "You shut off Ravenwood Manor's water. Here is proof of your efforts—the tenants' chamber pots. I can play just as dirty as you, dear husband." Isobel tossed down her suitcase, and left the ruined office.

ISOBEL SMILED AT THE MAN WAITING OUTSIDE THE GATES. HE offered his arm, and she slipped her hand through, taking in a deep breath of air. She felt free.

"No suitcase," Riot noted.

"No suitcase," she confirmed.

Alex hadn't accepted her truce. Their course was set.

He pressed her arm to his side.

"Sapphire House?" he asked.

Isobel thought about his question. "I think I should like a very large meal."

Riot didn't respond. He couldn't. He found a cafe in a park, under the sun, and they sat and ate and talked.

When the first newsboy appeared with the evening edition, Riot folded his napkin, and rose to buy a newspaper. Isobel recalled her conversation with Cara Sharpe the day before.

The woman had looked up from the stack of papers Isobel had handed her. "Are you sure about this, Charlie? Or should I say, *Mrs. Kingston*."

"I'm closer to Charlie than the other. And yes, I'm positive. Will you help me?"

Cara tossed the typed papers onto a table. "Why?"

"By helping me, you'll be helping yourself. This is an exclusive story."

Cara reached for her cigarette case. "Why rat yourself out, Charlie? This is a man's world. You'll end up in prison."

"I have my reasons," Isobel said. "I need this published."

Cara took a long draught of her cigarette, and blew out a slow breath. "After you were fired, I cornered Jo. She recognized you from society functions. After some investigating, she discovered the truth, and wrote an article exposing you—only the editor refused to publish it."

"Are you surprised?"

"It's not a well kept secret that most newspapers are on the payroll of the Southern Pacific for 'friendliness'. But I was surprised this article was blocked." There was a question in her voice.

"Alex wants to control me. He's humiliated, and he doesn't want this made public. Not on my terms, at any rate."

Cara tapped her cigarette over an ashtray. "*The Examiner* might publish this. Hearst recently broke ranks with the other newspapers. Although his motives are selfish—it's another opportunity to boost his paper—he's lending credibility to the Health Department's claims."

"Do you know him?"

Cara smiled like a cat. "I know everyone in this business."

"Will you help me?"

"I like your brass, Charlie. And it'll make one hell of a story."

Just then Riot slid a newspaper under her nose. Front page of the *Examiner*: **Isobel Kingston Lives!**

Cara had kept her word. Not a letter was changed from the article Isobel had written. She looked across the table at Riot, but the small victory was bittersweet. This would very likely be their last meal together for a good long while.

38

THE STORM

THE COURT ROOM ROARED WITH LAUGHTER. "ORDER! Order!" Judge Adams banged his gavel, but the laughter was drowning out his demands. Alex Kingston fumed, and Isobel looked over at him and smiled. His fists curled.

Mr. Hill shouted an objection, but his voice was lost in the tumult. A bark cut through the laughter. Smoke twined around the revolver in Judge Adams' hand, and a fresh bullet hole had been added to the wooden beam over the bench.

The crowd quieted instantly. Judge Adams set his revolver down, keeping it within easy reach. He scowled at the court room for a long minute.

"Your honor," Mr. Hill said.

"Yes?" Adams barked.

"Mr. Riot was not present during this alleged conversation with my client."

Judge Adams glared at the attorney. "You objected already."

"A mere reminder, your honor."

Judge Adams looked to Riot. "Are you saying Mrs. Kingston wrote the newspaper article that led to her arrest?"

"Yes."

Adams glanced at the defendant. "*Why?*"

"We needed an audience. The entirety of San Francisco to be exact."

"Is my court room a theatre?"

"Far from it," Riot said. "Your court, I trust, is an administration of justice. But the city is not, your honor. My partner was murdered in his attempt to expose the men behind this organization. If Mrs. Kingston and I had taken this information to the police—the investigation would have been blocked at every turn. And I have no doubt we would have shared the fate of Zephaniah Ravenwood.

"However, reporters are relentless detectives." Riot paused to look at the murder of reporters in the back of the room. The scratch of pens stopped, and each looked up in turn. Riot saw determination in their eyes. "Mrs. Kingston and myself have just set a multitude of detectives loose on the city. Every judge, policeman, attorney, and newspaper that attempts to obstruct the investigation will draw attention to itself. It will be plain as day that they were actively working to close San Francisco's ports. I have no doubt that the pen will prove mightier than any gun."

His gaze settled on Isobel. She graced him with a small smile—one he had glimpsed in breathless firelight, tangled limbs, and the softest of whispers.

"Do you have proof?" Judge Adams asked.

"We do." Riot dipped his fingers into his breast pocket, and the doors flew open. Parker Gray entered with a cigar between his lips and a Colt Lightning in each hand.

Gunshots filled the court room.

When the smoke cleared, Atticus Riot stood in the witness stand with the judge's revolver in hand, a bullet hole in the wall behind him, and a tear in his coat. Screams and shouts echoed in the packed court room. Riot looked to Isobel. She was pale as death, a tear through a puffed sleeve. Blood covered her dress, but it wasn't her own. It was the man in her arms. Lotario Amsel was slumped over the barrier.

39

A VISITOR

Wednesday, April 18, 1900

ISOBEL PACED LIKE A TIGRESS IN A CAGE. BACK AND FORTH, pressing her hands against her stomach. This was torture, this was pain—the unknown fate of her twin.

The door at the end of the hallway opened with its usual scream. She rushed to the bars, pressing her face against the metal. A large policeman filled the hallway.

"Have you any news?" she asked.

The policeman stepped aside, revealing another visitor —a much smaller man. Isobel sucked in a breath.

"You have ten minutes." The guard turned, and exited.

Isobel reached through the bars, and Riot took her hand. "Tell me."

"He's out of surgery, but not danger."

Isobel shuddered. Her knees gave out, and she slumped against the bars, sliding down to the floor. Riot went right down with her, and leaned in close. His hands were warm, his eyes as deep as any ocean. She pressed her forehead to the metal, and he brushed his lips against her skin.

"Your family is with him, Bel."

"*I* should be there." Tears streamed down her cheeks. She didn't notice. "Why did he do that?"

"You know the answer."

"He should have gotten down, not stood in front of a damn bullet meant for me."

"It's not in his nature."

"He's a fool."

Riot worked his arm through the bars, and buried his fingers in her hair. It was the best embrace he could manage. "Knowing his sister as I do, I've come to expect foolishness. Some might even call it sacrifice."

"I feel like I'm stuck in a bad dream," she whispered. "But when I fall asleep in *this* dream, Lotario is safe. And I'm with you." She moved her head, brushing her forehead against his soft beard.

Riot took a shaky breath. "I half expected the judge to throw the case."

"But he hasn't?"

"No."

"I heard about Judge Adams when I was in law school."

"All two months of it?"

At another time, she might have laughed, but not today. "He has the highest conviction rate in San Francisco. And that's saying something."

"I doubt it's a coincidence that he was handed your case."

"If only Parker Gray had shot my husband." She scrubbed at her cheeks.

"Don't give up yet," he whispered against her skin.

Isobel gathered the tatters of her control. "Is Gray dead?"

"Yes."

"I hope you weren't charged with murder."

"I was not."

"That's a relief."

"I handed over the list of names from the lumber yard, and Consul General Ho Yow provided the old records we confiscated during the tong raids. Every newspaper in California and beyond ran an extra, names and all. Your plan worked." And yet Isobel was still in a cell. But then she had never believed things would work out differently.

"You were masterful on the witness stand."

"I was lucky."

"Don't gamblers make their own luck?"

"I'll be sure to this evening."

Isobel paled. "Be careful."

"With a surname like mine?" Riot gave her a lopsided smile, flashing a chipped incisor. He reached into his coat pocket, and handed her a small bundle.

"It's too round for lock picks," she said, testing its weight. Without ceremony, she unwrapped the gift, revealing two muffins.

"Miss Lily sends you her love. She's concerned you're not eating."

"But not you?"

"Of course not."

"You're a terrible liar."

"Only with you."

She took a bite. Cranberries, lemon, and sweetness burst on her tongue. For a moment, she felt alive again.

"Considering your usual meals, I wouldn't have thought the poor quality of prison food would have had any affect on your appetite."

"I don't notice much of anything here."

Riot reached in his pocket again. This time he brought

out a tattered bracelet strung with beads. "This is from Jin. On loan. She said you have to give it back to her when you're released or she will never forgive you."

The little bracelet blurred. Isobel gently took the bracelet. It was old and dirty, and she feared it might fall apart in her fingers. Through her tears, she worked loose a little knot, and widened it enough to slip it over her wrist. She turned the filthy thing around her wrist once. The thought of the scarred little girl gave her strength. What were a few years in prison compared to the life that Jin had endured?

Isobel shook herself, shedding despair, and savored a muffin, tucking one away for later. When she had licked her fingers clean, a smile played at the corner of her lips. "I wanted to ask you. During the trial you said love came later. How much later?"

"When you held that knife to my ribs."

"That's what I thought."

40

THE ENGINEER

Curiosity had always been one of Atticus Riot's failings. That, and a hot head. The latter had been tempered by time (or so he liked to believe), but his curiosity had only grown. After Isobel's nightmare and Jin's revelation about *The Master*, the pieces had clicked. The mastermind behind *Sing Ping King Sur* came into the light. But they had kept that card close, waiting to spring their trap. Only the mastermind hadn't been swept up in the resulting arrests. He and Isobel had expected as much.

Riot stepped into an elevator. The operator—a young boy in a red coat and polished buttons—asked him his floor.

"The very top please."

The boy snapped to his duties, and the elevator groaned upwards. When the lift stopped, the boy pulled back the doors. Riot flipped him a five cent piece, and walked out onto the polished marble, his shoes clicking with each step.

He stopped at a window to peer down at Market. The building lay in the shadow of two rivals: the *Call* and *Chronicle*. A fitting place for a mastermind to hide. Riot had walked this corridor four months before, on his way to the offices of Curtis Amsel. Only this time, when he handed his card to the desk clerk, he asked for a Mr. Jonathan Thorton —Curtis Amsel's senior associate.

Leather chairs, polished oak, and sweeping views. The office screamed successful, but practical—no different than most in the city. When Riot entered, the older gentleman behind the desk stood. "Mr. Riot, I expected you sooner." He offered an amiable smile. "May I return your courtesy and be the one to pour you a whiskey this time?" Mr. Thorton spoke with a slow drawl, his lips barely moving, his waistcoat straining to contain his girth. Riot had first glimpsed him sleeping in a chair in the brick building on Ocean Beach.

Riot glanced at the other man in the room. Bland eyes, brown hair, and whiskers that a thousand other men in the city sported. Unremarkable in every way. Nearly. The man was as calm and confident as a lion, and that pricked the instincts, stirring up a primal fear in most. Riot had also spoken to this man before.

"I'm glad to see you've found somewhere else to lurk other than my lamppost," Riot said.

Mr. Thorton chuckled. "Oh, don't mind Mr. Wolf." He rubbed his hands over his waistcoat, still chuckling. "Though I do feel that I'm standing between two predators. I assure you, Mr. Riot, we're civil. And I trust you will be as well, or I would have asked you to hand over your guns."

Mr. Thorton walked over to a decanter, and plucked the crystal top from its hole. He poured two glasses. "Won't you sit?" he asked, holding the glass out.

Wolf put his fingers on his coat, and slowly lifted it away from his chest. He showed Riot a gold cigarette case in his breast pocket, and slowly removed it. When he stuck a cigarette between his lips, Riot accepted the glass and sat.

Thorton settled in his own chair, and took an appreciative sip of whiskey. "You see, Mr. Riot, I'm a businessman, not a common thug."

"But you profit from thugs."

"I profit from human nature. If not me, someone else will. And I assure you that person would be less discerning than myself."

"Men like Parker Gray and William Punt?"

Thorton scowled, his bushy brows drawing together. "They were a disappointment. Damn sloppy. You know, I admire you and Mr. Wolf. There's an art to your..." He nodded to Riot's holster. "...craft. I had hopes for Gray, but he turned out to be a bully."

"So you sent him to silence Isobel and me?"

"I did not. They lost control of the game, and instead of rethinking their strategy, they reacted. But the damage was already done. Parker Gray acted alone yesterday. I thank you for disposing of him—you saved Mr. Wolf the trouble."

Riot waited, and Wolf smoked in that unhurried way of his.

Thorton folded his hands over his stomach and glanced out the window, letting silence build as he contemplated the view. "You have caused me a great deal of trouble, Mr. Riot."

"I only cause trouble for troublemakers."

Thorton chuckled. "I should think you're one of those troublemakers." He glanced at Riot. "The Southern Pacific Railway runs America. They own both the Democratic and Republican parties, but they haven't been able to completely control California. Why do you think that is?"

"I'll wager you're about to tell me."

"Because we keep the Southern Pacific machine in check."

"*Sing Ping King Sur?*"

Thorton bobbed his head in confirmation. "*Society of Peace and Prosperity.* That is precisely what we do—we keep the peace. Men adore their secret societies, their little rituals and mysteries, playing at godhood. It makes them feel special. And it serves my purposes—it keeps them in the dark. *Sing Ping King Sur* is like the fog that permeates the coast. There's no substance; it's only a veil that romanticizes our city."

"Your meddling kills."

Thorton clucked his tongue. "So nearsighted." And then he looked to Riot's spectacles and chuckled. "But then you are in life, aren't you? Considering your... assassination of *Hip Yee*, I don't think you have room to judge me."

Riot took a sip of whiskey.

"By killing a few, you saved more." The leather creaked as Thorton shifted his bulk. "*Hip Yee* was poised to unite the tongs. A unified criminal organization would have dominated Chinatown and seeped into the city. Together, you and I threw the tongs into a chaos from which they have not yet recovered. It's no different than what I have been doing for years with the Southern Pacific—until now. You broke my chessboard, Mr. Riot."

"You had Ravenwood murdered."

"I'm afraid he knew too much. He threatened to expose me. As with *Hip Yee*, if *Sing Ping King Sur* wasn't here to keep the balance, the Southern Pacific would dominate San Francisco, and men like Alex Kingston would be able to do anything they pleased."

"Do you think that changes anything?"

"I am an honorable man, Mr. Riot. Your partner recognized that, and brokered a deal with me for your safety. But not for his own. He put himself at risk."

"Honor? Safety? You manipulated me into killing *Hip Yee*."

"Manipulated?" Thorton wheezed. "Is that how you comfort yourself? I did nothing of the sort. I simply used human nature to my advantage. Don't think yourself so far above the rest of us. I have honored that arrangement longer than I was required to. I have even extended it to your Miss Bel. Who did you think was keeping her safe in jail during the trial?"

Riot set down his whiskey. "Your men nearly killed us."

"And they paid for their lapses in judgment."

"Did Jones Jr. pay for his lapse as well?"

"He took the honorable way out."

Riot stood.

"I admire what you did with the court case. It was a bold move, but it entailed great risk and a heavy sacrifice. I can ensure that the verdict is favorable for your Miss Bel."

The offer was tempting. "In exchange for what?"

"That you stay out of my affairs."

"Your affairs are everywhere."

"I think you give me too much credit."

"It wasn't a compliment."

Thorton chuckled, and took a sip of his whiskey. "It's not an offer of friendship, only a truce. Why not shake on it." He extended his hand.

Riot stared at the offer. Isobel could go free. But the longer he considered accepting the offer the sicker he felt. "I don't like your methods," Riot finally said.

Thorton smiled. "What will you do now? Do you think anything will come of your stunt? Do you imagine I'll be imprisoned?"

"I could shoot you."

Riot glanced at Wolf when he said the word. The man

didn't even flinch, only took a drag of his cigarette, and let the ash fall onto the carpet.

Thorton leaned back and spread his arms in surrender. "One human isn't behind corruption. It's money, Mr. Riot. Forces aren't changed by the killing of one man, or by putting another behind bars. San Francisco will only spew out another man like me, or worse."

"Death is too kind for you. I'll see you in a cold cell one day." Riot tipped his hat, turned his back, and started walking for the door.

"I could have her killed tonight."

Riot stopped in his tracks, and cocked his head. Why was the man goading him? He turned slowly. The way Mr. Wolf stood behind Thorton pricked his instincts. Not so much bodyguard as guard.

Riot looked from the gunfighter to Thorton. "But you won't."

"Why is that Mr. Riot?"

"Because you were outmaneuvered."

JONATHAN THORTON GRUNTED WHEN THE DOOR CLOSED. "Well, Mr. Wolf. I did try." Resigned, he loosened his tie and collar. "Who do you think would be left standing in a duel?"

Mr. Wolf smashed his cigarette into a crystal ashtray. "Gunfighters kill, Mr. Thorton. It's not a pissing contest."

"But aren't you curious?"

"Curiosity isn't the reason I'm still alive."

Thorton sighed. "No imagination. I used to like a good duel, back in the day. Damn laws make business so damn complicated nowadays."

Mr. Wolf inclined his head in agreement, but Thorton

didn't notice. His gaze was on the city below. "So few men have vision anymore. I had expected better of Mr. Riot."

"You thought he'd join us?"

"Hoped." Thorton turned in his chair to smile. "He keeps his emotions close. I appreciate that. Hard to find anymore. Curtis went after that sister of his because he was paranoid. Jones failed to notice a murderer under his nose. Parker thought too much with what was between his legs. And William Punt." Thorton slapped his hand on the desk. "Panicked! But Mr. Riot and Mrs. Kingston would have gone far."

"And you?"

"I put my faith in the wrong men."

Wolf reached into his breast pocket. "That you did, Mr. Thorton." He placed a token on the desk.

Thorton tugged his waistcoat taut. "May I finish my whiskey, Mr. Wolf?"

Wolf nodded, and walked out of the office.

41

A FINAL CARD

Tuesday, May 1, 1900

AFTER A STRING OF WITNESSES, CROSS-EXAMINATIONS, accusations, and droning testimony, Isobel Kingston had one final card up her sleeve. That card sat on the witness stand.

Mrs. Alice Wright was a woman of a certain age. Tall and robust, with a gold-plated pince-nez perched on her prominent nose. Wisps of red hair curled out from under a flowery pink hat, adding a good six inches to her six feet.

"Where are you employed, Mrs. Wright?" Farnon asked.

"The Pacific Telephone and Telegraph Company, on Montgomery." She was taciturn and direct. Judge Adams grunted with approval.

"What are your responsibilities?"

"I supervise the switchboards."

"How long have you worked as a supervisor?"

"Six years. Pacific Telephone acquired my husband's telephone company. I was in the habit of running things, so naturally I kept at it."

"Would you relate to the court the events you witnessed

pertaining to this trial?"

Mrs. Wright gathered herself up, an imposing presence
in a witness stand that suddenly seemed too small. "On the
twenty-third of March, the offices of Alex Kingston were
connected to the San Francisco Gas and Electric Company.
The conversation lasted thirty seconds. Five minutes later, a
connection was made between the offices of Alex Kingston
and Spring Valley Water Company. Again the conversation
lasted approximately thirty seconds.

"On the twenty-fourth of March, the offices of Alex
Kingston were connected to Pacific Telephone's billing
department. After some questioning of my personnel, I
learned that a gruff man had ordered the line at Ravenwood Manor to be disconnected. When I checked the
records, I confirmed that Ravenwood Manor had settled
their bill. In fact, they had always been prompt in paying it.
I reconnected the line.

"The following day, on the twenty-seventh of March,
another call was made from the offices of Alex Kingston to
the San Francisco Gas and Electric. I overheard a brief
exchange while I was helping an operator with a static issue.
A man ordered the gas to be turned off at Ravenwood
Manor."

"Can you identify that voice, Mrs. Wright?"

"I can."

"Can you name the speaker?"

"It was Alex Kingston. He was quite upset."

"And how do you remember the exact time and dates,
Mrs. Wright?"

"I have an excellent memory," she replied briskly. "But
operators also keep records for purposes of billing."

Farnon smiled, and picked up a stack of neat papers.
"I'd like to submit the billing reports for the offices of Alex

Kingston, as evidence of his tampering. Thank you, Mrs. Wright. I have no further questions."

"Does the prosecution have any questions?"

"I do, your honor," Hill said. He stood, and placed his hands on the table. "Mrs. Wright, you do know that eavesdropping is a criminal offense?"

"Yes."

"Do you often eavesdrop on telephone conversations?"

"I *often* fix connection issues, Mr. Hill. Telephone clarity is a matter of pride at The Pacific Telephone and Telegraph Company."

"I see. That's commendable. As someone who has experienced such issues, I know how difficult it is to make out a voice on the end of a line. Why, I wouldn't know the voice of my own mother with such distortion."

"I know your mother, Mr. Hill. You haven't spoken with her for two years."

The court room snickered. And Judge Adams gave a warning growl.

Mr. Hill smiled. "I'll be sure to ring her after this trial, and convey your regards. But that doesn't change the fact that there was a connection issue." Hill looked to the jury. "I'm sure any number of these fine gentlemen have experienced crackling on a line, and know how difficult it is to make out what the other is saying, let alone identify the caller."

Mrs. Wright looked down on Hill with abject disapproval. "I know what I heard."

"Did the caller identify himself?"

"No."

"So it may have been any gentleman employed at the Law *Offices* of Alex Kingston. Thank you, Mrs. Wright. I have no further questions."

42

THE VERDICT

A MOB OF MEN AND WOMEN CROWDED THE STEPS OF THE courthouse, trying to shove their way inside. Questions battered Riot as he pushed through the jam. He found no relief inside. Isobel Kingston's resurrection, and subsequent court hearing had whipped San Francisco into a frenzy.

"One word would ignite that mob like a wildfire," Tim said.

"At least it's not a lynching." The two men shared a look —both had lived through San Francisco's vigilante days. Those days weren't that far behind.

"Miss Bel definitely has public support."

"Will that matter?" a girl asked. Riot looked down, wondering how Jin had got there. She stared up, her dark eyes calculating. Hadn't he left her at home?

Instead of chastising the girl, he placed a hand on her shoulder. "It might. Stay close. You shouldn't be running around alone."

She scoffed, but didn't argue.

"I'll hang back," Tim said.

Riot and Jin bullied their way into the court room. The press coverage was worse than usual. Isobel Kingston would take the stand today.

Marcus Amsel, tall and bent, stood and gestured them forward. "Mr. Riot," he greeted. The old man's hands encompassed his own, warm and forgiving, and ever hopeful.

Riot returned the gesture, and inclined his head to a scowling Mrs. Amsel, who sat beside her youngest son. Lotario was as pale as death. He sat hunched forward, lines of pain marring his face. His left arm was in a heavy sling that immobilized his shoulder.

"Isobel is going to kill you when she sees you here," Riot murmured as he sat beside her twin.

"Dead is the only way I'd miss this." Lotario's voice was faint.

Jin leaned forward to glare at him across Riot. "Don't worry, we will carry you to *sau pan po* after you die in court."

Lotario stuck his tongue out at the girl. The gesture heartened Riot, until Jin replied with a crude gesture.

Riot pushed her hand back down. "Behave," he said under his breath.

"I don't think that's possible for a *Wu Lei Ching.*"

"*Fahn Quai,*" Jin hissed at Lotario. Isobel's mother looked her way, and Jin quickly sat back to hide behind Riot. Those steely eyes could wilt anyone.

Conversation dropped as a side door opened, and the bailiff escorted Isobel into the court room. Wisps of hair stuck out from under her simple hat. Over the past month, her hair had begun to lighten and lengthen. The blue of her coat softened her eyes, and the ruffled blouse at her throat gave her an aura of polite society.

As she took her seat at the defendant's table, she caught his eye, and then her gaze slid sideways. A number of emotions passed over her: relief, joy, and finally anger. Lotario waved. Isobel set her jaw, sat down, and leaned in to speak with her attorney.

The chamber door opened, and Judge Adams marched in looking disgruntled and harried in black robes. This trial had lasted far longer than his others, where defendants had the good sense to plead guilty. The judge was notorious for dolling out maximum sentences to anyone who dared to plea 'not guilty'. In Isobel's case that maximum was six years.

"All rise," the bailiff announced. The audience rose, and Riot helped Lotario to his feet. The young man trembled from the exertion. "Court is now in session, Judge Adams presiding. Please be seated."

"The prosecution has the floor."

"The prosecution calls Isobel Kingston to the stand."

Isobel walked across the well with purposeful steps. After being duly sworn in, she sat, and Mr. Hill stood at his desk.

"Mrs. Kingston, the defense has done an excellent job of painting you as a victim of circumstance. And yet I have a statement from a man named Frederick Ashworth that paints you in a less than favorable light. Do you know Mr. Ashworth?"

"I spent an afternoon with him."

"In his statement, he claims you abducted, restrained, and interrogated him. Is this true?"

"No," Isobel said.

"You didn't abduct him?"

"Fredrick Ashworth was under the impression that I was a woman of the underworld. He invited me into his rooms, leaned in close, and whispered his pleasure. Mr. Ashworth requested a rather boorish service. I proposed another. He agreed to be tied up and throttled, only I didn't charge him for my services."

Laughter erupted in the court, along with a number of outraged cries of protest.

The prosecutor cleared his throat. "That was hardly what Mr. Ashworth was expecting."

"What do you imagine he was expecting?" she asked innocently.

"Mrs. Kingston, kindly stick to the point. And refrain from vulgar comments."

"That will limit my answers, your honor."

The judge shot her a baleful warning that she returned with a smile. The knot between Riot's shoulders tightened, but her answers only became more spirited. She was going to get herself hanged at this rate.

For the next three days, Isobel was stripped of reputation and dragged through the mud. And yet she came alive on the stand, answering every question as unapologetically as she had lived her life. San Francisco fell in love with the spirited young woman.

Finally, at the beginning of day four, Judge Adams addressed the jurors. "The jurors will put circumstances aside. Your responsibility is to decide whether Mrs. Kingston is guilty of fraud beyond a reasonable doubt. In plain words, did Mrs. Kingston fake her own death?"

The law was harsh.

"Are you ready with your final arguments?" Judge Adams asked.

"Yes, your honor," answered the defense and prosecution.

Closing arguments droned on, but Riot barely heard the impassioned words. The prosecution painted Alex Kingston as a love-struck man, greatly grieved and wounded by his adulterating wife. And the defense reminded the jurors of the extenuating circumstances that had driven Isobel Kingston to take action. But Riot knew it was hopeless—the jurors had already made up their minds.

The jurors were sent out to deliberate, and court was dismissed. As the conversation around him rose to a fevered pitch, Riot sat quietly, an empty shell, wishing he had accepted Mr. Thorton's offer.

TWELVE JURORS FILED INTO THE COURT ROOM. ATTICUS Riot checked his watch. They had deliberated for a scarce hour.

Judge Adams eyed the jurors. "Will the jury foreperson please stand?"

A middle-aged man with a squint stood. He folded his hands meekly in front of him.

"Has the jury reached a verdict?"

"We have, your honor."

Judge Adams nodded for the juror to proceed.

"Although circumstances were extraordinary, we find the defendant, Isobel Saavedra Amsel Kingston, guilty as charged."

The world dropped from under Riot's feet. Murmurs from the gallery turned to angry shouts. Lotario sat stunned, and Jin shot to her feet, shaking her fist and shouting with the rest of the audience.

Time slowed to a crawl. The next six years stretched before Riot—the woman he loved would spend two thousand one hundred and ninety lonely days and nights in a cold cell. Riot couldn't breathe. Numb, he stared at the woman in front, focusing on the minuscule—the shape of her ears, the elegance of her neck.

Isobel's shoulders straightened, she planted her hands on the table, and surged to her feet. And with a voice that cut through storms, she shouted, "I want to divorce this blackguard!"

The audience fell silent.

"This is not the place for a divorce," Judge Adams growled.

"You're a judge," she shot back. "Divorce us now, or we'll be forced to have the same trial over again."

"You'll be in prison either way," Alex snapped.

She ignored him and the judge's gavel. "I want half his money!"

Alex fumed. "You're a lunatic!"

"And yet you married me."

"I'll commit you to an asylum!"

"Will you do that from your prison cell? Your honor, I say again, divorce us now and we won't clutter your court. But I demand compensation."

"You're in no position to demand a settlement!"

"You purposefully ruined my father's business."

"Lies!" Alex bit out. "It's that same drivel you approached me with in the summer."

"And you *blackmailed* me! I want a divorce."

"This is a fraud trial not a divorce court," Judge Adams stated.

"Same thing," she retorted. "Fraud. I had no idea Alex would be such an ape-like lover in the bedroom, only minus the physique."

The audience roared with amusement. And Alex Kingston turned red.

"I should have known by the size of your hands," she added, cheekily.

"I demand a divorce, too," Alex growled. "The verdict is guilty. She won't get a penny of mine. And your father *will* be ruined."

Voices raised to a deafening pitch as a shouting match between husband and wife filled the court room. Both ignored the hammering gavel. Judge Adams appeared on the verge of an apoplectic fit.

"Order!" he roared. "Divorce granted! Get out of my court room—*both* of you. Court is adjourned!" He slammed his gavel on the bench.

Isobel turned to Riot—triumph shining from her eyes. He couldn't account for it, then the penny dropped.

As soon as the stenographer had finished his notes, Farnon shot to his feet. "You closed the case before sentencing her!"

"Oh, but he did," Isobel said. "He granted me a divorce."

43

THE WIDOW

Friday, May 11, 1900

THE SUN SHONE DOWN ON RIOT AS HE STROLLED THROUGH Golden Gate Park. All of San Francisco seemed to be enjoying the day. Couples strolled arm in arm, and children played, while a steady stream of landaus and carriages bounced over miles of pathways.

It didn't take long for a carriage to slow at his side. A woman sat alone, veiled in red with dainty gold flowers. Deep pools of black stared at him from behind the veil.

"Mr. Riot."

"Jesse."

She lifted her veil. Her skin was ivory, and her hair black as ink. She arched a perfectly penciled brow. "It's a beautiful day, A.J."

"It is," he said.

"And yet you are alone."

Riot spread his hands.

"Will you join me?" she asked.

Riot glanced at the driver, a man in a skullcap and a long queue. "I'd rather walk."

Pak Siu Lui stirred from her seat. Riot opened the door, and offered his hand. "Wait here, Jon," she said, accepting his offer.

Two white horses stamped impatiently. With Mr. Jon's gaze boring into his back, Riot strolled arm in arm with the most dangerous woman in San Francisco. Pak Siu Lui led him towards a secluded pathway under an arch of branches. A breeze rustled through leaves, and he felt her relax into his arm.

"How is Miss Amsel finding prison?"

"I'll find out in a few days." To avoid a retrial, Isobel had compromised, accepting a reduced sentence: six months in an asylum, forty-six days of which she had already served during the trial. She was set to be released in September.

"When I heard you'd returned, I was hoping to visit you, but you threw yourself in front of another damsel in distress. You were never one to waste time."

"Isobel is hardly a damsel."

Pak Siu Lui smiled. "She's certainly spirited, if reckless. I've seen young women like her before. They burn brightly and briefly, until the world uses them up and tosses them to the gutter. She won't last."

Riot stopped under a broad oak, and turned to face her. He snapped his fingers and a white token appeared.

Siu Lui laughed, her eyes dancing. "You always delighted me with your tricks when we were children. I suppose some things don't change."

"I'm afraid they have changed. I think this belongs to you, Jesse."

"Is that because it has a white blossom on it? Where did you find it?"

"You know where I found it."

"Do I?" She clucked her tongue. "Coincidence is a curious thing—the mind grasps for connections to make sense of chaos."

"We used to use that to our advantage when we swindled the gentry."

"I miss our games."

"I don't think you ever stopped playing."

"Do you think I'm the criminal mastermind behind *Sing Ping King Sur*?"

Riot didn't answer.

Siu Lui touched the wing of white at his temple, brushing fingers through his hair. "You have that look about you—the patient stare of a boy content to wait for days beside a hole. Do you really want to see the animal hiding in the shadows?"

"I'm looking at her. You had Ravenwood murdered."

Her hand dropped. "It was business. Like most men, he couldn't conceive that I was the mind behind *Sing Ping King Sur*. I was touched when he bargained for your life. I offered him a deal to simply walk away. He refused my offer."

"You used me."

"I had forgotten what a fragile heart you have." She rested her hand on his chest. "I could have had you killed a hundred times over." Her whisper chilled his blood. "Consider preserving your life as part of my debt to you."

"I never asked for repayment."

"And so I can never repay you. Years ago, you risked your life and your freedom for my own. You're the only person who has truly loved me."

Riot took her hand in her own. "Why?" he rasped.

"*Be extremely subtle even to the point of formlessness. Be extremely mysterious even to the point of soundlessness. Thereby you can be the director of the opponent's fate,*" she quoted. "It amuses me to pull the strings of men."

Siu Lui inclined her head towards the road, to the passing carriages and gentlemen on horseback and bicycles. "These men playing at gods—call it revenge for all I have endured at their hands." She brushed his knuckles with her lips. "Save for yours."

A muscle in his jaw twitched.

Siu Lui looked up at him through long lashes. "What now, A.J.? Have you come to kill me?"

"You know I can't."

"Then we're at a draw."

"It appears that way."

"I sometimes wonder how our lives might have been…" She trailed off, eyes clouding with grief.

Riot cleared a lump from his throat. "If you weren't my sister?"

"*Half*-sister. Or so our mothers claimed." Siu Lui slipped her arm through his own, and they continued their stroll under the trees. "It won't make a difference, I know, but I do regret that I could not come to amicable terms with your partner."

"He wasn't that sort of man."

"Neither are you." Siu Lui seemed to float on his arm, never quite touching the ground. "Will you marry?"

The question caught him off guard. "That's entirely up to the lady in question."

She hugged his arm. "She'd be a fool not to marry you. And I don't think she is. So as my wedding gift to you, I'll yield victory and withdraw from San Francisco."

Riot drew her to a halt, searching her face for deception.

"You don't believe me."

"Do you blame me?"

She smiled. "I drove you out of San Francisco for three years. I'll leave the city for the same period of time."

"A timely offer considering your men unleashed plague-infested rats under your home."

"There is that." She stood on tiptoes to place a kiss on his cheek. "Goodbye, brother."

Riot didn't relax until she was ten feet away. Just when he did, she stopped, and cocked her head without turning. "And A.J.? Consider our slate clean. Meddle in my affairs again, and I'll meddle in yours. I do look forward to meeting your wife one day."

44

AFTER THE STORM

Monday, May 14, 1900

SAO JIN FOLDED HER ARMS OVER HER CHEST. "*THIS* IS A prison?"

Atticus Riot turned to look at the girl. Jin glared at a trickling fountain in front of a stucco building surrounded by palms and oak. Flowers burst with color at its edges, and music drifted on the breeze.

"Maybe it's worse inside?" Sarah suggested.

"Horror can be found in the quaintest of settings," Riot said.

Reassured, Jin adjusted her oversized cap and kept walking. The girl had refused a dress, and since her wide-sleeved tunic and loose trousers would attract attention, she was wearing one of Tobias' new suits.

Completely opposite of reassured, Sarah stared at the building with open dread. Riot stuck his elbow out, and Sarah slipped her hand through his arm.

"The word 'quaint' is enough to spark horror in some," he said for her ears alone.

"Like for Jin and Mr. Mor—" Sarah sighed. "What on earth should I call her?"

"You can always ask."

"I hope she hasn't suffered too much." But any worry Sarah might have had was quickly dispelled by a cheerful woman sitting on the fountain's brim in front of *Bright Waters Asylum*. She had a pet rabbit on a leash.

"Hello, Miss Meredith. And Mr. Darcy."

Curly red hair poked from under the woman's straw hat. She peered at Riot through a pair of thick spectacles. "Oh, it's Mr. Riot. Mr. Darcy told me we would see you again."

"It appears he was correct."

Jin and Sarah began looking for this mysterious man.

"Is Mr. Darcy ever wrong?" Riot asked.

Miss Meredith leaned in closer, and put her hand up to shield giant rabbit ears from the truth. "On occasion."

"It happens to the best of us."

"It does," Miss Meredith sighed. "I suppose you're here to visit Miss Amsel?"

"We are."

"She's been such a delight to have. So pleasant and amiable. It's a shame about her shoulder though. I dare say she shouldn't be taking part in the music sessions."

"The music sessions?" Riot asked.

"Why, yes, she's such a delightful dancer."

"I see."

Miss Meredith leaned closer to the leashed rabbit. "Mr. Darcy says I shouldn't take up any more of your time. He's sure you're eager to see Miss Amsel. She's around back, under the oak."

Riot tipped his hat in gratitude.

As they walked around the building, Jin and Sarah kept

casting backward glances at the woman. "Where was Mr. Darcy?" Sarah finally asked.

Jin tripped over her feet, but caught herself. "Pleasant, and *dancing*? What have they done to Captain Morgan?"

Riot had his suspicions.

The music was coming from a phonograph. A ring of women with flowing hair and loose white gowns moved in a circle on a stretch of green grass. A woman in a blue dress and white apron led the afternoon exercises. She stopped, and stretched her fingers towards the sun, and ten women followed suit.

Jin's feet stuttered. The girl looked horrified.

"How lovely!" Sarah exclaimed.

"Lovely? This place is full of *wun dan*."

"What did you think an asylum was?" Sarah asked.

Riot smiled to himself as he stooped to pick a bouquet of flowers from the garden. Leaving the children to their arguing, he walked across the green towards a sprawling oak tree. A woman in a flowing tea dress reclined on a wicker divan. Her hair had softened, the edges growing out and the black dye fading. The sun caught a tendril of gold in the black.

The woman opened her eyes. "Hello, Riot."

He sat on the edge of the wicker divan, and took her hand. "How did you hurt your shoulder?" Her left arm was in a sling.

"Getting out of a bath. Are those flowers for me?"

Riot plucked a single daisy from the mix. "This one is for you."

"Not even a kiss?" she asked.

Riot brushed his lips against the back of her hand, then folded her fingers around the daisy.

"Oh, I've missed you." She glanced over his shoulder. "And you girls, too—*both* of you." She beckoned the children closer, greeting Sarah with a hug.

"What do I call you?" Sarah whispered.

"*Mr.* Amsel," Jin growled.

Sarah gasped.

Lotario huffed. "*How* did you know?"

Jin thrust a finger at his wrist. "*That* is not my bracelet. It is a fake."

Lotario glanced at the frayed imitation, and sighed. "We couldn't quite capture the decrepit state of decay that lends your bracelet its beauty." His voice dripped with sarcasm. "Did I fool you, Atticus?"

Riot shook his head. "I'm afraid not."

Lotario put his nose to the flower. "You mean you gave me a flower and kissed my hand knowing it was me?"

"Of course," Riot said. "Bel is alive thanks to you."

Lotario sat up a little straighter, but then winced. He fell back on the divan, looking drained from the excitement.

"How is your shoulder?" Riot asked.

"It hurts. Ordinarily, I would numb it with copious amounts of alcohol, but Bel won't let me. Dr. Bright has me on a regimen of healthy eating, hydrotherapy, and manual manipulation, which isn't as exciting as it sounds."

Riot cleared his throat, and inclined his head slightly towards the two girls.

"Well, it's *not*," Lotario said. Gray eyes flickered to Sarah. "Oh, dear. Come here before you fall over."

Riot hopped to his feet, and quickly steered Sarah to the divan. The girl looked like her world had just been tipped upside down. "You cut your hair," she said faintly.

Lotario patted her hand. "Dr. Bright, the alienist, calls it 'mirroring'. I never feel right unless I look like my twin. It makes me feel...detached. It's also amusing. The staff is utterly confused. I sat in for Bel during her talking cure session with Dr. Bright yesterday. He had *no* idea." His eyes flashed. "By the end of the session he was reaching for every monograph Sigmund Freud ever wrote."

Riot shot him a warning glance. He did not feel up to explaining Freudian theories to two young girls. Lotario caught his hint, and quickly changed the subject. "Bel is off somewhere..." He fluttered his fingers towards the trees. "Walking, or climbing some god-awful cliff."

"I'll find her."

"It's only been a week and she's already restless." Lotario seemed about to say more, but then looked to the girls. "Why don't you both go climb a tree for a moment."

"Why would we climb a tree?" Jin asked.

Lotario's eyes widened. "My dear child, do you mean to say you've *never* climbed a tree?"

Jin looked up at the oak's branches, and Sarah grabbed her hand. "Come on, I'll show you. I'm terrible at it, but I'm sure you'll take to it like a duck to water."

After the girls left to examine the trunk, Lotario motioned Riot closer. "Since I'm here willingly, I'm in one of the bungalows. I don't mind sleeping in Bel's ward room though."

With those suggestive words, Riot touched the brim of his hat, and left the children with Lotario and their tree climbing. He picked up Isobel's trail twenty feet from the green, and followed it to the same stream where the two of them had spent the night after Virgil Cunningham blew himself up with a stick of dynamite.

Isobel reclined against a tree trunk. Leaves rustled overhead, and the stream trickled at her feet. From her damp hair and glowing skin, he surmised she had taken a dip. She was sleeping, a book lay open over her stomach. Riot stopped to appreciate the scene. Under the sky and leaves, she was free of stone and bars. His heart swelled.

Riot snapped a twig in two on purpose. Isobel opened her eyes, her hand reaching for her pocket. But then she saw him, and stopped. A smile danced in her eyes.

"How's prison?" he asked, removing his hat.

"Tolerable."

Riot offered a hand, and she accepted, letting him pull her to her feet. The book dropped to the ground, forgotten, as she wrapped her arms around his neck. After a number of breathless minutes, Riot surfaced. Isobel pulled away to meet his eyes. She ran her fingers through his beard.

"I think I'm dreaming," she whispered.

"It's the best kind of dream."

"Let's not do that again."

"Kiss?"

"Spend a single night apart."

Riot rested his forehead against her own. "That's a fine idea, Miss Amsel."

"I'm so relieved to have my name back."

Those few words said everything—months of strain, of blackmail and abuse, all the gut-wrenching days of her trial were over. He stared into her eyes, and she held his gaze for a long minute. "We managed."

Isobel grinned. "It was close."

Riot grunted. "I thought we'd lost, but you pulled a card out of your sleeve. That was brilliant."

"What precisely did you think I was doing for two months while I studied law at Berkeley?"

Riot cocked his head.

"While everyone else was staggering over trivial assignments, I researched every legal loophole in existence. I'm not the only one with an ace up her sleeve, Riot."

"I never cheat."

"And you *never* lie."

He crossed his heart, and she snorted.

"You look well," he said.

"It's good to be free. Or nearly. It helps that Lotario checked himself in for recuperation. He needs it. And if I were honest... I need it, too." Isobel glanced up at the swaying branches, closed her eyes, and took a deep breath of fresh air. "We were lucky, Riot."

"You made your own luck."

"By the skin of my teeth."

Riot tightened his hold on her, and her eyes slid to the side. "Did you bring me flowers?"

He started in surprise. Flowers littered the ground. He had forgotten all about them the moment he laid eyes on her. "I did."

"It's fortunate I'm not the flower type."

Riot took a step back, and reached into his coat pocket. "I had planned on hiding these in the bouquet. I'm afraid I botched that plan." He handed over a set of lock picks and wrench. "You'll finally have time to practice."

Isobel laughed, and kissed him again. She bent to tuck the lock picks inside her coat. "If I can't open a lock after six months, I'm going to give up the detecting business for good." She glanced his way. "I expected you sooner. Did you throw yourself into another case without me?"

Riot shed his coat, loosened tie and collar, and sat. He leaned against the tree trunk, stretching his legs towards the stream. "I was wrapping up loose ends."

She arched a brow.

"Jonathan Thorton was found dead in his office. Self-inflicted gunshot wound. This was curled in his fingers. Inspector Coleman showed it to me." Riot flicked a white token to her.

Isobel frowned at the blossom imprinted on the surface. "This is different than the one I found next to William Punt."

He nodded, and told her of his conversation with Siu Lui.

Isobel sat down beside him. "Your *sister*?" she said faintly.

He could only nod.

"I'm sorry, Riot."

"And you were worried about what I thought of Lotario."

"I won't be near as accepting."

"I'd worry if you were."

She turned the token over in her fingers. Riot could feel the gears of her mind turning. "Siu Lui wanted you to make a connection. There was no other reason to leave such a clear marker."

He inclined his head. "I thought as much."

"How cruel," she whispered.

Riot could only swallow the lump from his throat. "I don't know what to do."

Gray eyes sharpened, and then softened. "For now..." She flicked the token into the stream. It landed with a faint splash. "We take our winnings and thank the stars for our victory."

"I'd be more apt to thank *you*, Bel."

"Only if you do it properly."

"I plan on it."

The edge of her lip quirked, and he drew her into his

arms. She turned and settled against him. They sat in comfortable silence, listening to birds and the sway of trees.

After a time, Isobel stirred in his arms. He suspected she had fallen asleep. "What now?" she asked.

"Marry me."

"I've only been divorced a week."

"It will cause a scandal," he murmured against her ear.

Isobel laughed. "You know me so well."

"People will be *shocked*."

"I doubt that."

"Society ladies everywhere will faint."

"I think they'll be more apt to jealously."

"Your Mystery Detective articles may not be as exciting."

"Women *love* a married man."

"Do they?"

"Hmm."

Isobel sat up, and turned to look at him. "I will marry you on one condition, Atticus James Riot."

"I'll get down on one knee—two, if it pleases."

"Considering you're sitting, don't you have to stand first?"

Riot flashed a grin. Those teeth. He made to rise, but she pulled him back down, and found his lips again. When she pulled away, all the whimsy had vanished. "My condition," she reminded.

Riot braced himself.

Isobel touched the tattered bracelet on her wrist. "That we adopt Jin and Sarah as soon as we're married."

Riot stared, speechless. Then his face softened, his eyes warming until she thought she'd melt. "And they say you don't have a heart," he whispered.

Isobel cleared her throat. "I need a capable crew. Adopting them serves my purposes."

"Of course it does, Bel."

The edge of her lip twitched. "Don't tell anyone."

"It will be our secret."

"I hope to have many more with you."

CONNECT WITH AUTHOR

.

If you enjoyed Conspiracy of Silence, and would like to see more of Bel and Riot, please consider leaving a review. Reviews help authors keep writing.

Keep up to date with the latest news, releases, and giveaways.
It's quick and easy and spam free.
Sign up at www.sabrinaflynn.com/news

Now available:
Book 5 of Ravenwood Mysteries
The Devil's Teeth

HISTORICAL AFTERWORD

I love weaving fiction into the gaps of history. Truth and lies blur, to create an intricate tapestry. San Francisco had such a wild reputation that the rest of the world doubted the stories coming from the city, even when they were reported by such reputable newspapers as *The London Times*.

So what, you might be wondering, is fact?

The bubonic plague in San Francisco was real. It is believed to have come over on the SS *Australia* on January 2 1900, the very steamer Riot traveled on from Honolulu. Honolulu had a plague outbreak that resulted in Chinatown being burned to the ground. In San Francisco, despite health officers' inspections, the plague skipped six blocks to kill Wong King Chut, a lumber yard salesman who resided in the Globe Hotel.

Chinatown was quarantined. Twice. But the barbed wire fences conveniently skipped by white-owned businesses. There was a ransom note sent to Consul General Ho Yow asking for ten thousand dollars to remove the quarantine on Chinatown. However, the consul's detectives were unable to trace the source of the demand.

Merchants, politicians, and newspapers decried the plague as a 'yellow disease' and generally attempted to discredit Dr. Kinyoun, mocking him at every turn. Seeing the plague as a news opportunity, Randolph Hearst broke ranks with the other San Francisco papers and started taking the plague seriously. One of his reporters, J.A. Boyle even went so far as to volunteer for the Haffkine vaccine, in order to report on its effects in an article.

Mandatory vaccination of Chinese residents was real too. Including the poor girl who tried to climb out of the third story of the 920 Sacramento mission home, and broke both her ankles.

Merchants and politicians did such a good job of discrediting health officials that the bubonic plague was able to gain a foothold in San Francisco. Eventually it spread to the East Bay, where it infected American wildlife, which is why there's still pockets of bubonic plague in wildlife today.

Developers and politicians did have their eyes on the prime real estate of Chinatown, which many of the elite considered a 'festering sore' at the foot of Nob Hill. Through the years, there were numerous attempts to drive the Chinese out of Chinatown.

The mayor at that time, James Duval Phelan, was anti-Chinese. He would later run for U.S. Senate under the slogan, 'Keep California White'. Phelan pushed a Chief of Police into office who the *Morning Call* printed this blurb about: '*We predict that the man elected will be Lawrence's Esola— and then may the Lord have mercy on everybody in that great city who is innocent.*'

Phelan was part of the Bohemian Club—a secretive organization of powerful men still alive and thriving today. Recently, the *Washington Post* ran an article: "Bohemian Grove: Where the rich and powerful go to misbehave." It's said that the planning of the Manhattan Project took place in the Grove, leading to the creation of the atomic bomb.

Alex Kingston is based on a real attorney: Abe Ruef. The rich and powerful kept the attorney on retainer for his services, including bribing and manipulation for his clients' benefit. In 1902, Ruef founded the Union Labor Party, which he used to set up a puppet mayor under his control.

A zealous newspaper editor, Fremont Older, was determined to expose Ruef. It took years of tireless work and a whole chain of wild events: detectives shadowing other detectives, abductions, spying, the dynamiting of a witnesses's home, hired gunfighters, bribed jurors, and even a court room shooting, where an attorney was shot in the back of the head just before a court session began. The attorney survived. In the end, Fremont Older realized that Ruef was only a small cog in the graft machine.

Sing Ping King Sur is based on unconfirmed fact, or a whisper of it. I came across a single line in Richard H. Dillon's *The Hatchet Men*. The organization was so secretive that its existence was never confirmed or denied. Sin Chi-Man is also based on a vague reference to a super secret Chinese detective in Victorian Chinatown.

What about Isobel's final court room stunt? That too is based on truth. A cat burglar by the name of Mack was caught red-handed as they say. After pleading guilty, Mack's attorney declared that since it was a daylight burglary, he should only get five years instead of the fifteen for a night burglary. The judge argued that he was caught after sundown, and the attorney argued that he had been arrested five minutes after the sun had set, so the burglary was done in daylight. An argument ensued. It flustered the judge so much that he forgot to arraign Mack, and closed the case.

Mack was released after a year. He went on to become a respected doctor.

And that brings me to another fact of San Francisco: reputation. San Franciscans loved a good fire, and they loved a good fight. They tended to side with the person who started the fight. They also loved spirited women of questionable reputations, who smoked and gambled, and shamelessly dressed in male clothing. Big Alma, Lillie Hitchcock Coit, and Aimee Crocker, to name a few.

I've only shared the tip of the iceberg of my research. San Francisco has a wild past: gun-dueling newspaper editors, feuds, vigilante justice, mobs, shoot-outs, and more larger-than-life people than I can remember.

I think Joshua Norton sums up the city. In 1859, he proclaimed himself Norton I, Emperor of the United States. He had no formal political power, but he was treated deferentially, citizens sometimes bowing in the streets as he passed. Currency was issued in his name, and honored. San Franciscans celebrated his presence with a city-wide wink. And he's honored every year, even down to this day.

That same spirit endures. In 2013, residents came together to turn San Francisco into Gotham City for a five year-old cancer survivor who wanted to be Bat-Kid for a day. It's safe to say that when it comes to San Francisco, the more outlandish the story, the more grounded in truth it's likely to be.

ACKNOWLEDGMENTS

No book is written alone. I'd like to thank my editors: Annelie Wendeberg, Merrily Taylor, and Tom Welch. My beta-readers: Alice Wright, Erin Bright, Rich Lovin, Lyn Brinkley-Adams, An-Sofie, and Chaparrel Hilliard. My daughter, who I use as a sounding board to work through complicated plots. For a thirteen year-old she is *extremely* helpful.

My husband, for putting up with me. Whenever I start writing a new book, my family rolls their eyes in dread, because I turn into a pacing, fidgeting, 'head-banging-against-wall' writer. I find myself hard to live with while writing; I can only imagine what my family must think.

Do people actually read the acknowledgements? I'd like to thank my dog, Kelly. My chair. My computer. I mean, really, what could I do without my computer? Can you imagine having to write and revise each page by hand? The delete key is close to my heart. And spellcheck. Thank you, spellcheck, for passing those occasional odd spellings that reflect the usage of 1900 America (my editor, Tom, added that last bit about era appropriate spelling).

Finally, to my readers. Thank you! And even more so if you've left a review. Reviews keep writers writing.

ABOUT THE AUTHOR

Sabrina Flynn is the author of the **Ravenwood Mysteries** set in Victorian San Francisco. When she's not exploring the seedy alleyways of the Barbary Coast, she dabbles in fantasy and steampunk, and has a habit of throwing herself into wild oceans and gator-infested lakes.

Although she's currently lost in South Carolina, she's lived the majority of her life in perpetual fog and sunshine with a rock troll and two crazy imps. She spent her youth trailing after insanity, jumping off bridges, climbing towers, and riding down waterfalls in barrels. After spending fifteen years wrestling giant hounds and battling pint-sized tigers, she now travels everywhere via watery portals leading to anywhere.

You can connect with her at any of the social media platforms below or at www.sabrinaflynn.com

GLOSSARY

Bai! - a Cantonese expression for when something bad happens (close to the English expression, 'shit')

Banker - a horse racing bet where the bettor believes their selection is certain to win

Bong 幫 - help

Boo how doy - hatchet man - a hired tong soldier or assassin

Capper - a person who is on the look out for possible clients for attorneys

Chi Gum Shing - 紫禁城 - Forbidden Palace

Chinese Six Companies - Benevolent organizations formed to help the Chinese travel to and from China, to take care of the sick and the starving, and to return corpses to China for burial.

Chun Hung - a poster that puts a price on someone's head

Dang dang - wait

Digging into your Levis - searching for cash

Din Gau - 癲狗 - Rabid Dog

Dressed for death - dressed in one's best

Faan tung - 飯桶 - rice bucket - worthless

Fahn Quai - White Devil

Fan Kwei - Foreign Devil

Graft - practices, especially bribery, used to secure illicit gains in politics or business; corruption.

Hei Lok Lau - House of Joy - traditional name for brothels in old days

Hei san la nei, chap chung! - 起身呀你個雜種！- Wake up, you bastard!

Highbinders - general term for criminals

Kedging - to warp or pull (a ship) along by hauling on the cable of an anchor that has been carried out a ways from the ship, and dropped.

King chak - the police

Lo Mo - foster mother

Mien tzu - a severe loss of face

Mui Tsai - little Chinese girls who were sold into domestic households. They were often burdened with heavy labor and endured severe physical punishments.

Nei tai - you, look

Ngor bon nei - I help you

No sabe - Spanish for 'doesn't know' or 'I don't understand'. I came across a historical reference to a Chinese man using this phrase in a newspaper article. I don't know if it was common, but it is a simple, easy to say phrase that English speakers understand.

Pak Siu Lui - White Little Bud

Sau pan po - 'long-life boards' Coffin Shop

Si Fu - the Master

Siu wai daan - 小壞蛋 - Little Rotten Eggs - An insult that implies one was hatched rather than born, and therefore has no mother. The inclusion of 'little' in the insult softens it slightly.

Slungshot - A maritime tool consisting of a weight, or "shot," affixed to the end of a long cord often by being wound into the center of a knot called a "monkey's fist." It is used to cast line from one location to another, often mooring line. This was also a popular makeshift (and deadly) weapon in the Barbary Coast.

Sock Nika Tow - Chop your head off - Very bad insult

Wai Daan - 壞蛋 - Rotten Egg

Wai Yan - 壞男人 - Bad Men

Wu Lei Ching - 狐狸精 - Fox Spirit

Wun Dan - Cracked Egg

Wun... ah Mei - Find Mei

Yiu! - 妖! - a *slightly* less offensive version of the English 'F-word'.

Made in the USA
Middletown, DE
24 January 2023